BREAKING FREE

Breaking Free

Disclaimer

This is a work of fiction, a product of the author's imagination. Any resemblance or similarity to any actual events or persons, living or dead, is purely coincidental.

* * * * *

Cover Photo Courtesy of Shutterstock

Formatting and Cover Design by Debora Lewis arenapublishing.org

ISBN-13: 978-1530729906
ISBN-10: 1530729904

BREAKING FREE

Pearl Gladwyn Burk

*To my husband, Bill, who continues to encourage me
and give me the confidence to reach my goals.*

Acknowledgments

Many thanks to my husband for accompanying me around Massachusetts researching the Underground Railroad as well as Lawrence, Kansas where many of the historical events took place.

Also, many thanks to my photographer doing business as dburk photography,www.dburkphotography.com, http://picasaweb.google.com/dave.burk, 617 962 2536 (cell), 781 272 2722 (home)

CHAPTER 1

APRIL 4, 1855, MALDEN, MASSACHUSETTS

EACH POUNDING FOOTSTEP moved Lee closer to a fate she knew was waiting for her. She had run this path from Mr. Pyne's blacksmith shop to the Hillside Home for Boys for more than six years; however, today, she would give anything to run the other direction. She knew she had broken a rule and that she was going to be severely punished for it. There was no way to get out of it because she had turned in the evidence herself. She could only hope that her secrets would remain hidden.

Her young charges would be waiting for her just around the next curve and she wasn't going to let them know how she felt. She had to set an example of what a young, educated reliable boy should be. It wasn't always easy to fool them. Soon, they appeared sitting in the emerging grass watching for her. She knew that these ten weary six to ten-year-old boys had been hard at work that afternoon digging and planting the new spring vegetable garden and that they would be ravenous.

Slowing down to catch her breath, she prepared to meet the familiar onslaught as the boys ran to meet her. She managed to stuff her dangling shirttail into her waistband and jam her cap into her back pocket before they reached her.

"It's good to see you're all in such high spirits," she said, ruffling the hair of the boy nearest her. "Are the carrots sprouting yet?"

"Ah, come on," they chorused. "En't had time."

She made a quick check of their hands and faces. "Wow! Everybody's so clean you're sparkling. How'd that happen?"

Teasing was good for them and Lee enjoyed their reaction as they punched each other and giggled their way into the dining room.

The late afternoon sun cast its waning light into the large double doorway as Lee and her boys joined the other hungry and fidgety boys trooping into the building. A welcome breeze blew in through the tall open windows but it did little to refresh the exhausted children or to ease the all-too-familiar tension hanging like a shroud over the room as thirty boys took their places behind their chairs.

Lee scrutinized her boys as they impatiently waited for their supper. They were so young and vulnerable but wanting to be tough like the older boys. They had been thrown into a hard life by circumstances beyond their control, just like she and all the boys in that room. She often wished these young ones had a better way of life than she had, but she had survived so far and so would they.

"You're a good-looking bunch o' bucks," Lee whispered from her place at the head of the table. "Now, just keep quiet and you might even put a smile on Mr. C's face when he comes in here."

"Oh, sure," the boys muttered.

"His face'd crack to pieces if he smiled," Toby said under his breath and a wave of stifled giggles ran the length of the table.

Lee glanced at the doorway where Jonas Carver stood scrutinizing them like a vulture on a bare tree branch. A surly arrogant man of fifty-five, he held his six feet straight and tall as a pine tree standing guard over its saplings.

"Sh'up," Lee hissed.

"Mr. Bellamont," Mr. Carver bellowed. "Control your charges if you want any of them to receive their meal."

Deadly silence filled the room. No one was willing to give up a meal for a few seconds of nonsense. Lee had impressed on her boys many times that, as the youngest of the orphans, they ranked at the bottom of the list in the order of things.

"If you do somethin' to make Carver yell at me, you can bet I'll find some way to pass it on down to you."

She had never had to make good on that promise and she was glad because she wasn't sure what she would do. She really liked her charges and they seemed to like her, too.

When she became a monitor, she had explained to them that they were inmates in an asylum and, as its owner, Mr. Carver, was their warden. She added that all the boys hated being there but, since that's where they found themselves, they were coping the best they could by sticking together and helping each other as much as possible.

Satisfied that everything was in order, Carver tapped his cane on the floor and six uniform lines of boys filed toward the kitchen to pick up their filled plates and return to their tables. From across the room, Lee caught a glance from her best friend, Cal. They exchanged looks of shared disgust.

The noisy scraping of chairs on the wooden floor grated against Lee's already chafed nerves as the boys took their seats at the three long tables crowded into the otherwise bare room. Lee knew her boys would sit quietly once they started eating. Too often, they had seen a plate of food whisked away from a boy who dared utter a single word.

As she ate, Lee stared out the window and noticed buds forming on the oak and maple trees, a sure sign that winter had given way to spring. It was much like the day she and her mother, Charlotte, first arrived at the Home. It was spring and Lee would never forget the tightness that wrapped itself around her heart that day. She was only five years old but could still remember the frightening impression left by the entrance gate with the devil's face staring out of the black cast iron. "I am a boy. I am a boy," she whispered to herself as Charlotte pushed their way through the opening. She grasped Lee's hand as though to draw courage from her, but Lee was too young and too frightened to have any courage to share.

Now, Lee glanced around the room and realized how deeply ingrained her life had become in the overall life of this group. There had been a day when successfully fooling them had been challenging. In time, she found that she no longer played at being a boy. It felt so natural. She no longer felt different. This was truly her world.

Only the scraping of metal spoons against metal plates broke the silence inside the naked walls of the dining room. Mr. Carver moved among the tables in a staccato quick step, occasionally tapping a boy's back to make him sit up straighter. He hesitated behind Lee's chair and said gruffly, "Remember. My office."

Like trained soldiers, the boys concentrated on eating and finishing in the fifteen minutes allowed. Each boy rinsed his dish, spoon and cup in the pan of water at the end of the table and returned them to the kitchen to be ready for breakfast at five o'clock the next morning. Then, following a rigid routine, all the boys less than fifteen years old shuffled to their rooms to study for an hour before dropping on their cots, exhausted. That hour was free for the older boys who worked full days and no longer attended classes. Carver encouraged them to read from his selection of books in the orphanage library but, so far, he hadn't made it a requirement.

Lee liked to read but there was something dearer to her heart for that valuable hour at the end of the day. Every free time they were given during the past eight years, she and Cal had raced each other down a path into the woods behind the orphanage to a specially selected pine tree. It had become their private place where they challenged each other to games of mumblety-peg or marbles and laughed at their own made-up jokes. For the past year, however, they spent that time mostly sharing their thoughts.

Today, Lee would be late. After cleaning up her dishes, she went to the office exhausted and wishing to get this over with as soon as possible. She stood waiting. Her fears were confirmed when Mr. Carver stomped into the room and slammed the door behind him.

"Mr. Bellamont. Look at me when I speak to you," Jonas Carver ordered, his voice filled with controlled fury.

That was impossible for her to do. The prickly end of a wayward strand of hair was burning her eyeball and she was unable to blow it away.

"Look at me!"

She took a deep breath and shifted her gaze to the angry round eyes glaring at her from across the desk. The stubborn hair was causing her eye to water and an unwanted tear ran down her cheek. He would think she was about to cry and she couldn't let that happen. She took a chance and swiped her sleeve across her forehead, pushing her hair out of her eye and drying her cheek at the same time.

"Did I give you permission to move?"

"No, Sir."

The air in the room was stifling, and tension hung like a curtain of dense fog inside its walls. There was a tempest brewing beneath the tightly drawn skin of Carver's face. The set jaw, pinched brow and flaring nostrils indicated there was a switching in his mind for sure.

He continued through pursed lips. "Although you are a heavy burden on me, I have allowed you to live in my orphanage because your mother is our cook. That in no way exempts you from the rules the other boys are required to obey."

How many times had she heard these words over the past ten years? *Many, many!*

Lee stretched her five-feet five-inches as tall as she could and tried to follow Mr. Carver's face as he paced back and forth behind his desk. The threat implied in the constant tapping of the birch switch against his rigid palm sent a shudder down her back. Shifting her feet to steady herself, she felt sure he would strike her to the floor.

"I told you to stand still."

"Yes, Sir."

Lee had been in this spot before and recalled her mother's words following the last switching she had received. "Lee, I have nowhere else to go; nowhere to take you. You must follow his rules, like them or not; otherwise, he will send us back to begging in the streets."

Since then, Lee had obeyed Mr. Carver's every command until this week and that was why she was in his office at this moment. She had grown up believing she had to prove herself by being tougher than the boys and she would be tough now. Knowing how much he would hate it, she stuck out her chin and stared into his eyes.

"You have a bright mind for learning, so I taught you to read and to work with numbers. You are strong, so I found you employment as a blacksmith's apprentice. There are many boys out there eating garbage and sleeping on the streets who would die for a benefactor such as I." The slap of the switch against the desktop bit sharply into the air like a snap of lightning on a dark stormy night.

Mr. Carver stepped around the desk, thrusting his head forward until his face was inches from hers. "I should not have to remind you, young man, that your entire week's wage is to be given to me. I found only one dollar in your envelope this week." He took a deep breath and screeched, "What did you do with the remaining half-dollar? Where is my money?"

Gasping at the foul odor attacking her nostrils, she held her breath. The wide brown stripes on the wallpaper behind his head began to flow in waves before her eyes.

"I lost it," she said, unable to hide her contempt. He wasn't aware of her mother's illness but he wouldn't care anyway. She wasn't about to tell him she used the money to pay a doctor to come treat her mother. In all her years under Carver's reign, she had never seen him show a sign of sympathy for anyone.

Rage rumbled across the room, rebounding from its walls and gathering in the hand grasping the wicker switch.

"You thief," he roared. "Bend over and grab your ankles. That will be ten strikes today."

That was four more strikes than he had ever given Lee, or any of the boys. She braced herself for the inevitable pain. She knew better than to try to escape the blows. The switch had come down on the middle of her back once, and she had vowed never to endure that again. There were no tears and no sound from her throat, which angered him all the more. The slender rod struck ten times.

"Get out," he gasped.

CHAPTER 2

THERE WAS NO way Lee could have raced Cal after that switching. The roughness of her pants shifted across the welts on her buttocks with every step as she eased her way between the giant pines to where he was stretched out waiting for her. It would have helped to go directly to her room and sit in some warm water and Epsom salts, but she wanted to see Cal. This was the best part of every day when she could be alone with him and bask in his nearness. The warmth that surrounded her heart when they were together in this secluded place was getting more intense all the time. At the moment, however, that warmth was desperately competing with the pain in her backside. She dropped to her knees beside him onto a thick soft bed of pine needles and drove her palms into the ground, straining against the painful throbbing. She felt no shame or humiliation because most of the boys had experienced the switch, but there was a hatred that grew deeper every time she or any of the boys were beaten.

"I guess Mr. C really gave it to you, huh?"

"Ten strikes."

"Holy bageebees. That's more than he's ever given. He musta really been mad."

"Oh, yeah. He was. He thinks I stole fifty cents from my pay and I guess I did. I took it to pay Dr. Simon to come see my mother. I told Carver I lost it."

"What's the matter with your mother, if you don't mind my asking?"

"Haven't you noticed how pale 'n thin she's getting?"

Cal shrugged his shoulders and mumbled, "Yeah, but I thought she was just tired from all the work she does."

"She en't been feeling good for a long time, and I finally just told her I was getting the doctor in to see her. She sure put up a fuss about it."

"Why?"

"She's scared that if Mr. C finds out she's sick, he'll kick us out."

"She's probably right. He's mean enough to do that."

"Course he is. He musta been born in a briar patch and he's still feeling all those prickles. My mother thinks something really awful happened to him and now he hates everything and everybody." Lee dropped to her stomach, wondering if she would ever be able to sit down again.

"How're you gonna run the race Sunday? He's hell-bent on 'his boys' winning for him. Don't know how he expects you to run with sores on your butt." Cal irritably scratched behind his ear.

"Oh, he's probably already forgotten about the switching. He'll make me run. They're only welts. I oughta be okay enough by then."

She spoke with more confidence than she felt. She found that when she gave problems a positive twist, she could handle them much better. She had received that bit of wisdom from her mother who had gotten it from the small Bible she kept under her pillow. She read aloud from it to Lee every night before they went to sleep and then she would pray. It helped them both to get through the next day and to keep their secret, which had been very hard to do at times. Sometimes she wanted to share this with Cal but never found the right time.

Cal sat up and locked one leg over the other, angrily flicking an ant off his shoe. "Someday I'm gonna kill that old son-of-a-bitch."

"You wouldn't!" Lee protested.

"Guess not but I'd like to. He thinks he's done so much for us but he's beaten us and starved us into submission and made us feel like we're nothin' more than a blight on the face of the Earth."

"But if he didn't keep us, we'd be living with the rats and filth in the streets."

"He counts on us believing that." Cal hurled a rock at a tree, missing it by inches.

"Well, it's true. My ma and I know what it's like out there. Cal, she grew up in a wealthy English family and had good schooling and learned good manners. When she married my da, her own da disowned her. That's what he did!"

"Why would he do a thing like that?" Cal asked, angrily flicking pine needles with his thumb and middle finger.

"Because he was some kind of a *bigwig* in the Church of England. My da is a Catholic from France. By marrying him and becoming a Catholic herself, Ma disgraced the family name. My grandfather said that was unforgivable."

"Gee! What an awful thing to do."

"He sent them off to America without even knowing Ma was gonna have me. He didn't want them around to embarrass him." Lee's eyes grew distant as though searching for something lost in her mind. "I en't ever seen my da."

Except for the twittering of a pair of birds above them, an unusual silence fell between them.

Breaking the silence, Cal asked, "Why en't you ever told me all this before?"

"Didn't think you needed to know. Don't really know why I'm telling you all this now, but that's the story of my life so far," Lee said quietly into her hands while crunching her knuckles as she often did to relieve her tension.

"Do you know what happened to your da?"

"No. He's out west somewhere. Ma thinks he's dead 'cause he promised to come back and get her, but he never did."

"Then I guess you two really are grateful to Carver."

"Sure, but don't get the idea he's been nice to us. He needed someone to work for him and, believe me, he's been demanding and mean. Ma puts up with it cause she don't have a choice."

Cal studied her face with a puzzled look. "You must look like your da."

"Why do you say that?"

"Because you sure don't look like your ma. I always wondered why but I never thought it was important enough to mention. Since we're talking about all this, I guess I'm curious again," Cal said, nervously rubbing the spot behind his ear.

"Yeah, I know. I've looked in the mirror and wondered why my hair is brown and hers is kinda reddish and wavy. My skin's lighter than hers and I don't have any freckles on my face like she does but, I've always figured I look like my da."

Lost in thought, they looked at each other and smiled, not exactly the kind of smile a buddy gives to a buddy but a smile that spoke of something deeper, something hidden. They each turned away, knowing that something had just happened between them. Cal jumped up and leaned his back against a tree and stared into the darkening woods behind them.

The pounding inside Lee's chest overcame her pain in her buttocks and she turned her head away from him as a flush raced to her face. She buried her head in her bent elbow. What just happened? She had to get hold of herself. She took a deep breath and swallowed hard and looked up at him. He was still looking away, his face flushed. She had to change the subject. She had to get beyond this moment. It couldn't be real.

"You en't gonna tell about that fifty cents, are you?" she asked in a voice that betrayed her in every way.

"Carver won't hear it from me," he said, his voice strained. "I'll tell you one thing, though. He's done that to you for the last time." Saying this, he turned to look at her.

"I don't need protecting, Cal. I've always taken care of myself. Leave it alone," she said with a firmness that surprised Cal.

Her arms were falling asleep so she eased herself onto her back and stared up at the patches of darkening blue peeking through the branches of the tall pines stretching so confidently above her. She brushed the wayward hair from her eyes revealing to Cal their stunning green depth. In an instant, his pleasure turned to shock and a fierce red flush filled his face again.

"Blast it," she said. "Why are you starin' at me that way? Stop it."

"I can't." He searched for words but couldn't find good ones so he stammered, "Lee, what the hell? You... you... you've got b-b-breasts."

A weight hit her chest, crushing the breath from her lungs.

"What the...? Oh, damn."

She looked at herself and saw what he saw. She had been so emotionally involved in their conversation that she hadn't felt her binder shift but there it was, across the top of one breast, just enough to reveal the secret she had kept for ten years. Cal, her best buddy for all those years and the one she had grown to love, now knew what she was. She could see the chaotic state of bewilderment that had overcome him.

She rolled away from him and gingerly got to her feet as the pain in her buttocks intensified. Her face burned with humiliation and the heat of it made her dizzy. She had been blushing a lot when she was around Cal but this was a fire she had to put out soon. She reached under her shirt and pulled the binding back in place, fully aware that he was staring at her.

With the binder in place, she continued facing away from him. She would have to say something soon but her feelings for him were out of control. He would walk away and hate her for her deceit. They would never share their "buddy" thoughts again. How could they? A deep chasm had come between them.

She couldn't remember when she first noticed the depth of his brown eyes, or his perfect mouth that always seemed to be smiling at her and now, what was she going to do? It had taken painful discipline not to show him how much she was attracted to him and the thrill she felt when he smiled at her unexpectedly, and the smile they had just shared before she rolled over. They had been boys together for so long. The two of them had climbed trees, dug for worms, played marbles, raced, been in trouble and, recently, they had talked about girls. Now, she didn't think she could ever talk to him again.

Cal stared thoughtfully at her back. Although he was shaking, he had taken control of his emotions and knew one of them had to break the silence.

"Lee," he said. "Turn around and look at me."

"I can't."

"I know you're embarrassed but so am I. A lot. Shocked, more than anything. I gotta say, I never once dreamed you were a-a-anything but one of the boys."

"You can't even say it, can you? I'm a girl. A girl—not one of the boys. I can hardly say it either. I've been one of the boys too long."

"Okay, I'll say it. You're a g-g-girl. There, I've done it. Now, we've gotta look at each other and we've gotta talk about this."

He touched her arm and she slowly turned toward him.

"So, what do we do now? You gonna turn me in?"

"Never."

"I don't know what to say," Lee said, staring at the ground.

"I don't either but I've had some things on my mind for a long time and I think this is a good time to talk about them." He took a deep breath and the words tumbled from his mouth as though Lee would get away before he could get all of them said.

"We've grown up together since we were little kids and we've been best friends for years. I thought I knew you but I guess I didn't."

His words caught on the lump in his throat when his emotions tried to regain control but he continued.

Lee tried to turn away but Cal took her arm and pulled her back. "Don't. Just listen to me. I need to tell you this."

"But we have to get back before we're missed," Lee argued, revealing the fear that had taken hold of her.

"We still have time."

Lee hesitated and Cal took advantage of it.

"I've been wondering why your voice hasn't changed and why you're not getting that soft fuzz on your face. And it's always seemed like you had to try harder than everybody else, like you had to prove something and," he hesitated, "your face is too pretty for a boy."

Cal caught his breath and shifted his gaze to the ground as though something there could help him choose his next words carefully. He bent down and picked up a handful of pine needles, staring at them as he let them run through his fingers.

"I'm glad you're a girl," he said, barely breathing. "Relieved is the word, actually. I've spent a lot a sleepless nights worrying about why I like you so much more than just a buddy. Sometimes at night, I can't get you out of my mind and it's been getting scary. I was getting very anxious to leave here and stop thinking so much about you."

Lee buried her face in her hands to hide the fresh flush burning there. She shook her head in disbelief. Now it was her turn to tell him about the nights she had lain awake listening to her mother's labored breathing and thinking about him, longing to tell him who she really was. She wanted to tell him how her heart raced when she saw him in the morning, at suppertime and here at their pine tree.

"I've thought about you, too," Lee whispered to the ground beneath her feet. Her charade had gone on so long that it was difficult to unveil her thoughts. She was a boy and she thought like a boy. She raised her head and dared to look at him. Hesitantly, she added, "I thought being best friends would be enough but now I don't think so."

She cupped one hand under the other and crunched her knuckles to keep her hands from shaking. A bird flew noisily from a branch sending a pinecone to the ground nearby while Lee concentrated on the area around her feet. Cal waited. She began to talk again, deciding to look at him.

"I've pretended all these years and I don't know how to unpretend. Lately, I've been wondering who I really am. I don't think I know. How am I gonna fit into the world out there when I leave here? Look at me. I'm wearin' boy pants and shirt and these are sure not girl shoes. I've never worn anything else. Good grief. Can you see me in a dress? I'm sixteen in a few weeks, and then I'm on my own out there in a world I en't seen except as far as the Boston Common. The whole thought of it scares me to death." Lee was shocked at her sudden candor but she was finding it easier to open up.

"Dr. Simon says my mother is dying and can't last much longer, maybe only weeks or days. She don't know I know. And that scares me too. It's just been the two of us and soon there'll just be me." Saying the words aloud put a reality to her mother's dying that hadn't been there before and a deep well of sadness filled her. She moved to a tree and leaned against it to keep herself from falling in a heap. These last few moments with Cal had become desperate. "I don't know what I'll do without her. She's my mother. She's my life." Her eyes moistened but she couldn't cry. She never could cry.

Eyes filled with compassion, Cal reached for her hand. "I'm really sorry, Lee. Truth is, I'm overwhelmed for you. I can't even imagine what you've been through all these years but you've sure done a good job of foolin' us. I wanna help you but I don't know what I can do." Cal hesitated, taking in the sight of her just as he had always seen her. "You're right. I can't see you in a dress but I'd like to," he added and squeezed her hand.

The warmth from his hand flowed into her and filled her. "You can help by keeping my secret and all of what I just told you."

"You can count on me. You know I'm out of here on the sixteenth of this month. My uncle cuts off my trust then and like Carver says, 'no pay, no stay'."

"That don't give us much more time together," Lee said. "Feels weird holding hands. Guess we can't let anyone catch us at it." The thought brought a chuckle to her tight throat.

"That would cause some buzz among the boys," Cal said, his eyes twinkling mischievously. "It sure feels strange but I like it. I could get used to it."

"I don't know how a girl's supposed to act when a boy holds her hand. It's kind of embarrassing even though I like it, too."

"I en't never been around girls either but maybe we can explore this new stuff together. What's your real name?"

"Lisa," she whispered.

"Lisa," he repeated in a voice choked with emotion. He felt her hand tremble along with his own. It was too much to grasp all at once. It would take some time.

"Remember, you can't call me that while we're still at the Home. You might forget and call me Lisa in front of somebody else. Ma always calls me Lee, even when we're alone."

"Okay, but just until we leave here."

"We'd better get back. Let's hope the old man isn't waiting for us."

They said good-bye and Lee headed to the back door leading to her sleeping quarters. She looked back for an instant to wave but Cal was gone. She slipped quietly up the stairs to her room, wondering if this was all a dream. Tomorrow, she would know if it were true.

Breathless from her encounter with Cal and the anxiety that came with it, she leaned against the door and closed her eyes, waiting for her heart to slow down. It only took a few minutes for her to realize that the room was exceptionally quiet. Lee had become so conscious of Charlotte's heavy breathing at night and now that was absent. Startled, she went to her mother's bed. At the sight of her, fear clutched Lee's heart. She went down to her knees and put her cheek next to Charlotte's nose, praying for a breath. She felt the faint warmth of life, shallow as it was, but she was breathing. Lee leaned back on her heels, flooded with relief. *Thank you, God.*

In the moonlight filtering through the windowpane, Charlotte's complexion looked gray. Lee leaned her elbows on the bed and rested her chin in her palms as she studied her mother's face through the wetness gathering in her eyes. Here was the woman that carried her when she was too small to keep up; the woman who had worked so hard under the worst conditions for an evil man just to make sure her daughter had food for her stomach and a pillow for her head. Lee thought back to the beautiful healthy robust woman that brought her to this place. How had she become this thin fragile person lying before her now? This hadn't happened overnight but when had it started? *Where've I been that I didn't notice until lately? How did I miss seeing that I was losing her?* Lee choked on a strangled sob. Tears tried to come but they were locked inside her along with the ability to cry. She was a boy, a calloused boy, when it came to crying. For ten years she'd been told that it was a sissy thing to do.

"Mama, I'm sorry, but for most of those years I wasn't aware of the sacrifices you were makin' for me," she whispered. "Guess I was too busy makin' a place for myself among the boys and keeping it."

She stared at her mother and saw her eye lids flutter. "You're too sick and too exhausted right now to even know I'm here, but maybe you're hearin' me." Charlotte's hand moved. It could have been reflex but Lee hoped it meant she was listening. "Mama, don't go. I need you. I can't hold myself together if you leave me."

Lee buried her face in Charlotte's hand. The seriousness of her mother's illness, the hatefulness of Mr. Carver, and, just now, the unveiling of her secret to Cal had pulled Lee's emotions in too many directions. She shifted her position and tried to get up but the throbbing from the beating intensified. She needed to treat the welts.

"There's something I have to do, Mama, but I'm right here with you, right here in the room."

She reached under her mother's bed and searched their box of supplies for the Epsom salts left over after Lee's last switching. She poured all of it into the washbasin and added water from the pitcher on the table. After removing her pants and placing the basin on the floor, she eased her buttocks into the small space. It was a tight painful fit and she hoped she wouldn't be stuck there for the night. It had been so much easier to slip in and out of the pan when she was younger. She pulled her legs up, rested her head on her knees and longed for her mother to speak.

When her eyelids began to droop, she wriggled out of the basin and eased herself onto her stomach in her bed. Soon she fell into an exhausted sleep in which Cal and her mother walked away from her into dense woods, too far ahead for her to catch up to them no matter how desperately she cried for them to wait. In the morning, she was surprised to find tearstains on her pillow.

CHAPTER 3

SHARP STINGING PAIN assaulted her skin with each running footstep as she made her way to the blacksmith shop the next morning. It had been a long time since she had coped with pain like this but she gritted her teeth and determined to handle it.

She grimaced as she heaved a heavy bucket of water against the edge of the cooling trough that ran the length of the hearth. Resting the weight on her bent knee, she carefully poured the water into the long narrow reservoir while casting a quick glance across the fire to check its status. She moved confidently and quickly from the cooling trough to the fire, removing clinkers, adding coals and pumping the bellows. She could shoe a horse and repair a piece of equipment as quickly and skillfully as her employer. Well, maybe not quite, but she knew she was good at smithing and farriery and she liked what she did. She supposed this occupation was the one positive thing Carver had done for her.

It seemed an eternity ago when she began learning the trade from John Pyne, a skilled and respected blacksmith in Malden. She stared through the open door where he was working on a wagon wheel and thought about the first time she had entered this shop. The memory remained as strikingly clear as though it had happened yesterday.

Mr. Carver had brought her here two weeks before her ninth birthday when a spring storm was gathering. She was just short of four feet tall with legs that barely stretched up to the running board of the buggy where he sat impatiently waiting for her.

"Come on, boy. Climb up here. Mr. Pyne is waiting for you." His words spit from his mouth, smarting against her face and ears like fierce sleet in a winter's storm.

Grabbing hold of the canopy brace, she pulled herself onto the running board just as the whip cracked across the horse's back. With a strength born of terror, Lee hoisted herself up to the seat as the horse lunged forward. Clinging to the brace with both hands, she froze, pinching her eyes closed to shut out the dizzying sight of the ground speeding past beneath them. The pounding of the horse's hooves grew louder and hell drew nearer with each crack of the whip.

"Open your eyes, boy, and see where you're going. This is the only time I will take you down this road. Don't expect me to be there to pick you up when you finish your work today," Mr. Carver shouted above the noise.

Paralyzed with fear as she slid dangerously toward the edge of the seat while speeding round a curve, she forced her eyes open and tried to memorize the landscape flying by: small house with vines growing up the side and across the front door; dead pine tree split by lightening; lane of houses; stone barn; general store; more houses. She just knew she would never make it back to the orphanage that night and she would never see her mother again. Then it struck her. That was exactly how the old man wanted her to feel. He was trying to terrorize her and she wasn't going to let him get by with it. He could get his kicks some other way but not with her. She fought back the angry tears and swallowed the lump in her throat. She would show him. She looked up at him and grinned.

Why was he taking her to train as a blacksmith? Why couldn't she work in the garden or the field with the other kids her age? She felt like she had been singled out for special punishment by being banished to a distant land to work alone under the evil hand of a strange monster for the remainder of her days.

The wheels rumbled noisily, dipping in and out of the wandering dry ruts of the road while Lee's head throbbed, ready to burst with visions of wicked faces, whips and hot irons. It didn't help that the sky had turned dark and lightening cracked in the distance.

So far, Mr. Carver was the only adult male she had ever known and she feared and hated him for his meanness to the boys and, especially, to her mother.

The buggy came to a stop as abruptly as it had taken off, nearly tossing her across the dashboard and out of the buggy. Tossing its head and digging its hooves into the ground, the horse pointed its nose in the direction of the water trough and snorted as sweat rolled off its neck. Mr. Carver didn't seem to notice. The rumbling of the carriage wheels was replaced by a loud, steady, hammering noise accompanied by waves of heat pouring from the forge through the large entrance. A huge tree, whose buds were just beginning to burst, splayed its branches over the building, water trough and hitching posts outside the shop.

"Here we are, boy. Look alert." She could see that Mr. Carver was exhilarated from the ride and his voice was filled with cutting sharpness.

"That was an exciting ride, Mr. Carver," Lee said as bravely as she could through her chattering teeth.

He glared at her and climbed out of the buggy. Lee released her grip and straightened her stiff fingers. She dropped to the ground to follow him as he picked his way around the odds and ends of metal, iron tires and horseshoes scattered about the floor and spilling out the door. Stepping toward the entrance, a rain-coated breeze blew refreshingly across her face, followed immediately by a wave of heat that swallowed her up as she moved inside. The smell of sweat and molten metal assaulted her nostrils. She was sure she had just taken her last breath of fresh air as they stood in the room filled with tools hanging from the walls and leaning against the brick sides of a large open furnace that filled the center of the space. A tall black-haired man, with the same dark hair covering his arms down to his fingertips, stood over the open fire holding a long iron rod that glowed red as burning coal. Lee gasped, already feeling the touch of hot metal on her skin. She stared at her feet, unable to look into the man's face for she was sure it was Satan himself standing before her.

The man nodded his head acknowledging their presence. He continued to strike the blazing rod, spewing blistering rays of sparks with each blow.

"Here's the boy I promised you," Mr. Carver shouted impatiently above the sizzling sound as the man slipped the glowing metal into the water. "He's a bit small but don't let that fool you. He knows how to work and he learns well. Isn't that right, Mr. Bellamont?"

Lee heard the heavy boots turn in the dirt floor.

"Yes, Sir," she answered with all the confidence she could muster.

"Look up when you speak," Mr. Carver ordered.

She gathered her courage and raised her gaze from the floor to the top of the large brown leather boots and slowly forced herself to look up to the thick black leather apron, gasping when she caught sight of the sledgehammer dangling from his hand. She tried to move but fear and the weight of Mr. Carver's hand on her shoulder held her in place. The pressure of his hand forced her to look higher, all the way up to the top of this mountain towering over her.

"Hello dare, young man." There was such softness in the deep rolling voice coming from that immense body that her face was drawn to his. Captured by the kindness in his eyes, she wanted to fling her short arms around his huge belly in gratitude. From that moment on, she learned to love him like a father. From the instant he flashed that first warm smile down into her terrified eyes, she was determined not to let him down. She was sure she would be happy coming here for the remainder of her life.

"I vill expect you every afternoon except on Sunday," Mr. Pyne said. "Dat day is reserved for de Lord."

She felt Mr. Carver stiffen. "When he turns fifteen, he will come all day. He will be finished with his schooling then."

For the next two years, Lee worked hard to learn to do all the maintenance chores required to free Mr. Pyne's time for the real work of a blacksmith. By the end of that period, Lee knew the name of every tool and when it would be needed. Emblazoned on her mind, helped a time or two by experience, were Mr. Pyne's unforgettable words that everything in the blacksmith shop was either hot, sharp or heavy. "So be very careful. Test de metal with a wet finger before picking it up. Always think about what you are doing," he told her that first day.

She found his German accent easy to understand. She was aware that he worked hard at pronouncing his w's and th's and, most of the time, he did very well, but there were always the slips into v's and d's. He teased himself about the slips but Lee never found them humorous. Her respect for him ran deep.

She became skilled at keeping the fire at the correct level and the water at the correct temperature. She returned the tools to their proper places after they had been used and eagerly sought ways to assist her mentor while watching every movement of his skilled hands. She would stay until she had to run hard to arrive in time for her supper. In only six months, she could run the mile and a half in eight minutes.

On her twelfth birthday, Mr. Pyne handed her a ten-inch rod of iron and said, "Here, let's see if you can make a knife blade out of dis."

Trembling with anticipation, she picked up a pair of tongs and clamped it around the rod, burying it in the fire. She had watched Mr. Pyne do it so many times and knew just how much the metal should glow before placing it on the anvil. When she pulled it from the fire, she glimpsed the smile on her teacher's face. He watched her raise the mallet and drop it on the hot iron. She listened for the tone as it struck, knowing how it should sound to get the exact weight to begin fullering the metal. Her first tap was too light so she hit harder the second time.

"You are unusually skilled at dis, Lee," he said when she finished the project. "I truly believe you are ready to learn de craft." Lee loved the way he rolled his r's and, in time, had to keep herself from picking up some of his speech patterns.

"Thank you, Mr. Pyne. I've got an unusually good teacher."

He had not changed during the years she worked for him. He had been patient and she had been true to her word. She had learned well. Often he called her "son" instead of Lee and she wondered if he would be disappointed if he found out she was a girl. He talked to her about the world, his old country of Germany, the things going on in Malden, the president and God. She felt so filled and wished her mother could meet him. Mr. Carver taught her to read but Mr. Pyne taught her to understand.

Now, she cast a glance toward Mr. Pyne and watched him withdraw an iron bar from the fire and lay it across the anvil. His hair had turned the color of salt sprinkled with a dash of pepper but remained thick and curly. His eyes were still filled with kindness.

"Here, son. Hammer out the blade while I go take care of Mr. Stanton."

Lee moved quickly and began flattening the glowing iron. She rarely spoke to customers but listened intently to everyone that came into the blacksmith shop. Mr. Stanton, an employee of the New England Emigrant Aid Company, always spoke of things that set her imagination soaring. How she wished she could ask him questions but she knew better than to interrupt their conversation. Always impressive in his bowler with the narrow turned up brim and his clean white shirt and black suit, Lee thought he must be the richest and most intelligent person in the whole area.

"You know, John, blacksmiths and farriers are needed in the Kansas Territory, what with thousands of people moving into and through that area heading west. You should consider going."

"Not on your life."

"Why?" Gabe asked.

"Indians, Gabe. I'm not ready to dodge de arrows while I do my work. No thank you."

"Haven't you heard? The government is moving the Indian tribes to the Oklahoma Territory so there's no need to worry about them anymore."

"I bet," John said, his words filled with familiar skepticism.

Lee plunged the flattened iron into the water trough. To her dismay, the loud sizzling as she passed the glowing metal into the cold water drowned out the next few words. The small world surrounding Carver's orphanage seemed only an anthill compared to visions of the vast rolling prairie in far-off Kansas Territory and she hungered for more stories of the unknown place.

"But Missouri is right next door to de Kansas Territory and it is a slave state," John said as he pounded the last nail into the shoe on Gabe Stanton's horse.

"Yes, but the Utah and New Mexico territories will be allowed to decide for themselves if they will be slave or free when they petition to become states," Gabe said.

Lee stopped what she was doing and listened. *Slavery! I thought they were talking about Indians.*

Gabe continued. "Like I said before, Squatter Sovereignty. Let the people decide. The Missouri Compromise said slavery is prohibited in the Kansas Territory but there was lots of opposition to that. Last year, Congress took the issue seriously and, being influenced by Senator Douglas, they passed the Kansas-Nebraska Act and gave the settlers in those two territories the choice to be slave or free."

Gabe gathered the reins in his hand and prepared to leave. "Eli Thayer is working on financing anti-slavery people who are willing to settle there. There's going to be a real battle over that land. Lots of people from Massachusetts are eager to go. Think about it, John."

"Don't have to. I don't believe in slavery but I'm not going," he said as Gabe climbed into his buggy and rode away.

Lee laid down her polishing cloth and picked up the bellows. Thoughts of Indians and black slaves tumbled on top of each other in her mind as she pumped air into the coals. She could relate to both of them, particularly the slaves. Her own life had never been free and she had the marks on her backside to prove it. She was aware, however, that she had one big advantage. She had a skill that she could sell and she knew she was good at it. Mr. Pyne had taught her well. Some day she would break free of Mr. Carver and the orphanage and go west, maybe to the Territory of Kansas and work as a blacksmith. She didn't know how or when she would do this but she was sure her time would come.

The deep roll of Mr. Pyne's voice invaded her thoughts. "Very well done, Lee. You will maybe take my place some day."

"I can't see that happenin', Mr. Pyne, but thanks. I'm glad you like my work."

Familiar creases appeared above his dark round eyes as he studied her. "You are very strong and muscular for someone who is slight of build. Your size and, yes, your overall appearance makes you look so w-wul-vulnerable dat I wonder if de older boys try to take advantage of you." He stroked the emerging hair on his chin. "Mm. I bet you could fight them off if you had a mind to."

Her heart skipped a beat. Had he guessed her secret? Involuntarily, she cast a quick glance at her chest, relieved to see that the binding was still in place. "I'm one of the older boys now, Sir. We get along. I beat one of them up when we were little and nobody's messed with me since."

"Very good. I wonder if you know how strong you are. I bet you would be surprised. You have been handling dat heavy mallet for several years now. Here, hold up your arm." Mr. Pyne grabbed Lee's wrist and bent her arm at the elbow. "Now, tighten your muscle."

Lee did as she was told. "See, I knew it. Very hard. You should enter one of de public fights sometime."

That would end my deceit for sure. "No thanks. I don't have the heart for fightin'." As she put the tools in their places, she added, "I'll stick with the runnin'. I hope you can make it to the races on Sunday."

"I plan to be there to see you win," Mr. Pyne said confidently.

CHAPTER 4

LEE DARTED UP the steps to the room she shared with her mother and filled the washbasin with fresh water from the pitcher on the commode. Carver allowed them one bar of lye soap every three months so she and Charlotte used it sparingly; however, today she pulled it from the box and attacked the coal dust and sweat with a vengeance, turning the water and the towel black and her face and arms pink. Humming happily, she worked her brush through her hair until the strands lay neatly across the tops of her ears. She vigorously brushed the dust from her shirt and pushed the shirttail neatly into her waistband. In a few moments, she would see Cal, the thought causing the all-too-familiar thrill to ripple from her head to her toes.

"My, my, Lee. One would get the impression you were getting ready for something special."

Startled, Lee turned to see her mother standing in the doorway. "I thought you were in the kitchen. Please, Ma, don't tease me."

"Someday you'll be able to set aside those terrible trousers and put on a dress and be what you are." Charlotte sat down on the edge of the bed looking pale but courageous. "I just came up to take a little of the laudanum the doctor gave me. Supper is ready and your boys must be waiting for you. Mr. Carver actually gave me Teddy today after I asked for some help. Poor little Teddy. He's only seven years old but he's trying hard to do a good job. He's been a big help."

Lee picked up the bottle and measured out the medicine for Charlotte. "I'd help you if the old man, I mean Mr. Carver, would let me but he always refuses so I quit askin' him."

Charlotte continued to sit on the bed as the medicine took effect. "Now, what's all this fuss you're making?"

"I just feel like cleaning up more than most times."

Lee sat down beside Charlotte and took her hand. "Ma?" Lee hesitated, unsure of how her mother would respond. "Sometime, could I try on one of your dresses? I've tried to imagine what it'd be like to look like a woman."

"My dear child. You are growing up, aren't you? And right before my eyes. You're almost sixteen years old and I'm afraid I've neglected to teach you the things you need to know to get along in the world outside this orphanage."

"I've only been thinking about it lately." Lee frowned at her reflection in the windowpane.

The look of dismay did not escape Charlotte. "What have I done to you, Lisa?" The name startled the warm intimacy of the room, much as a lost wanderer suddenly appearing among familiar friends. "I fear that I see a spark of love in your eyes. That could be dangerous for you."

"Don't worry. I won't get you and me into trouble. I know how hard you've worked to take care of me."

Charlotte smiled and raised her arms inviting Lee into the circle they made. "You know, daughter, we may find ourselves outside this institution soon and you should know how to mingle with people other than these poor waifs. We'll talk more about it at bedtime tonight and if you have something you want to tell me, I'll be here to listen. Right now, we'd both better get downstairs."

While Lee had been preparing herself to meet Cal in the dining room, Cal was outside the livery stable watching the setting sun change the sky from blue to shades of amber. It would soon be dark. Pacing back and forth at the stable door, he waited impatiently for the last horse to be returned.

If he expected to eat that night, he should be on his way back to the orphanage. He could count on Lee to control the boys at his table but that would make Carver insanely angry again. Cal had gone without his evening meal before so that didn't trouble him, but he wanted to see her again before bedtime. Lisa. Lisa. He had practiced saying her name. Lisa. He wanted to get used to thinking of Lee as Lisa but sometimes it stopped him in his tracks as he tried to transform his long time buddy into a girl — a girl he loved — a girl who loved him. In her boy clothes, she still looked like his buddy, she still talked like his buddy but she was somebody else now, somebody he'd been in love with for a long time and hadn't understood why. He was overwhelmed with the strangeness of it all. What if he hadn't seen what he saw? What if he had left the orphanage and never known? He shuddered as darkness grew deeper.

He checked the stalls one more time as he listened for the sound of the last wagon to be returned for the day. With the exception of that one missing horse, he had curried and fed all of the exhausted animals. They would rest a few hours and be taken out on the streets again before the sun came up the next morning, some to pull trolley cars and some to pull the delivery wagons and carriages lined up outside.

For the past seven years, Cal had been working for Dan Todburn who owned one of the horse rental businesses in Malden. Mr. Todburn had offered to keep him on when he left the orphanage and Cal had accepted the offer with gratitude. He had decided long ago that renting out horses was a profitable business but he would never have enough money to start a business of his own. He liked Mr. Todburn and would stay with him as long as possible.

In the distance, Cal heard a horse and wagon approaching but the unevenness of the hooves hitting the ground disturbed him. He ran to the stable door and gasped at the sight of the Farriday Delivery wagon approaching with Mr. Farriday lashing his whip and screeching curses at the struggling horse. Cal took one look at the animal and knew that it had made its last delivery. Pulling the horse to a halt, Mr. Farriday threw the reins at Cal and jumped to the ground.

"That bastard gave up on me today. I had to whip the daylights out of him to keep him moving or I would have been delivering those iron pokers on my back. You tell Mr. Todburn that I want a horse that works tomorrow. Understand?"

"Yes, Sir," Cal answered, keeping his eyes lowered as he listened, sending the fire of his anger toward the ground beneath his feet.

When the sound of the man's footsteps disappeared, Cal looked up and stared across the horse's back. "Damn it," he said aloud into the emptiness left behind.

Quickly, Cal unhitched the horse and pushed the small delivery wagon into its nightly storage space. Cal took the reins and eased the weary animal toward its stall while running his hand affectionately down the long neck. He removed his shirt and dipped it into the water trough, then laid it across the cuts and welts on the horse's back and flanks. A low painful whinny bubbled from deep in the horse's throat as its front legs crumpled beneath him. Cal jumped back, pulling his shirt away as the horse fell to the ground. Dropping to his knees, Cal began running the palms of his hands along the animal's head and neck, speaking softly into his ear.

"You're gonna be all right. You go ahead and die. It'll be better that way. Your heart's going to stop any minute now. Just let go."

The large dark eyes took in Cal's face and opened wide as the last gasp of breath sounded in his throat. Cal picked up the currycomb and brushed the sweaty brown coat of the dead animal. "Everyone should leave this world with some dignity," Cal muttered as he walked away to find Mr. Todburn.

By the time he left his employer, it was too late for his meal but he hoped Lee would be waiting for him. In the waning twilight he caught sight of her sitting on the wall at the entrance to the orphanage grounds. When she saw him, she waved him toward her.

"Come and sit. I brought you something to eat," she said, a shyness creeping into her voice.

"Thanks," he said, scratching behind his right ear and reaching for the wrapped bread and sausage. He too felt shy now that they were together again in their new awareness.

For a time, they sat staring at the ground or into the distance and finally at each other.

"We've never been afraid to talk so what's the matter with us now?" Lee asked. "This is stupid."

"You're right. Maybe we need to talk about what's gonna happen to us after I leave here in a few days."

"I doubt that I could get over to the livery to see you. Maybe you could meet me in our usual place in the woods some time. Course, I'll probably be out of here soon, too. Then what?"

"I guess we'll have to wait and see. I think we can figure out some way to see each other."

"By the way, why is your shirt wet?" she asked, touching his sleeve.

He told her about the horse while he finished eating. He grew quiet as he finished.

"Wow," Cal said, taking a deep breath and looking at her out of the corner of his eye. "That wasn't so hard. Telling you that was almost as easy as it was when we were buddies but it was a lot easier talkin' to you when we were slapping each other on the back and kidding around."

"Maybe we oughta just keep treating each other the way we always have. It'd be easier on both of us. Maybe we shouldn't try to change things too fast."

"But I've got this awful urge to kiss you," Cal said, courageously looking her straight in the eye.

"Whew! Me too."

"Stand up."

Hesitantly, he opened his arms and she slipped into his embrace. He heard a giggling sound that grew louder as he squeezed her to him. Soon they were both tittering into each other's necks relieving the tension. Then, with hesitant deliberation, he took her face in his hands and kissed her on the mouth. She felt a heated flush rise to her face as she responded.

"This is so weird," she whispered when he released her.

"It does feel strange, buddy boy," he said. "But I could get used to this. I'm sure glad you turned out to be a girl."

"I hope I can learn to act like one."

"You're not doin' too bad, so far," Cal teased. "I hope I know how to treat one."

"You're not doin' too bad there, either."

They continued to cling to each other, sharing the beating of their hearts and hoping no one was watching.

"We'll get the hang of it, I'm sure," Cal said. "For now, I guess we'd better go inside before Carver sends someone out to find us."

After cleaning up the kitchen, Charlotte wearily climbed the stairs to the room that had been home to her and Lee for the past ten years. The steps had grown steeper and wider apart over the past year of her illness and she found it necessary to tug on the handrail to pull herself up to the next step. How much longer? How many more times would she be able to lift her legs, one at a time, to get to the top? Not many, she thought.

There were things she needed to tell Lisa—not Lee. A warmth enveloped her with the renewing of Lisa's real name but a dread came with the thought of opening up the door to the past. She should have done it long ago but she had put it off as long as she could. Now she must or there would be no time left to do it. The thought was unbearable but she was afraid of the consequences to her own future with the Lord if she didn't. She must tell Lisa.

Charlotte Bellamont sat on the edge of her bed and held her small silver hand mirror at arms length. She stared at the reflection in it and tried to find the young girl with long flowing auburn hair and hazel eyes that had loved Lisa's father with a hidden passion seventeen long years ago. What she saw was a pale thin replica of a once vibrant and beautiful woman.

Charlotte felt the phlegm collecting in her chest and tried to hold back the cough. Her arm trembled with the weight of the mirror. Exhausted, she lay down on the bed and prayed for strength. It wasn't easy to die. Only last week, Dr. Simon had told her that it was only a matter of a few months, maybe weeks. Although she wished desperately to have it over with, she clung tenaciously to every moment, afraid to let go, afraid to say *good-bye* to Lisa and afraid of what would happen to the young girl after she was gone. Without the laudanum Dr. Simon had given her, she knew she could not bear the pain. She hated that Lisa knew she had resorted to the terrible drug in order to find the strength to do her job.

Lisa was a constant reminder of the days when she, herself, was young, when her life was full and happy, before the terrible things started to happen that changed her life. If only she could have provided Lisa with the friends and good things she herself had known when she was growing up, before the lies. She wished that Lisa could have known the man who fathered her.

Charlotte propped the mirror against her pillow and spoke aloud to her image. "It's not your fault that he doesn't know about his daughter or that you didn't go looking for him to tell him. You had a child to take care of."

Shoving the bottle of laudanum under her pillow, she moved to the small table beside her bed, picked up a pen and began to write on a blank sheet of paper. The words did not come easily.

My dear daughter, she wrote. *There is so much I have to tell you before…*

CHAPTER 5

SUNDAY ARRIVED UNDER a clear blue sky for the opening of the Boston Spring Festival. A pleasantly cool breeze boosted the energy and excitement stirring among the hundreds of people gathered on the Common and the adjacent Gardens. Groundskeepers had removed all signs of winter residue from the walkways and bordered them with an array of flowers in glorious bloom for the festivities. Toe-tapping music poured from the gazebo in the center of the Gardens while actors prepared to perform on a small temporary stage hung with thin black muslin curtains. Floating water lilies drifted on a pond near a miniature theater where marionettes performed their antics before a group of giggling children.

In the southeast corner of the Common, Lee ran in place preparing for her race. She still carried a reminder of Wednesday's switching but she was not going to let that hold her back. The other two racers from the orphanage joined her as Mr. Carver paced back and forth, his eyes daring them to let him down.

Charlotte had bound Lee's breasts as securely as she could without cutting off her air. Blousing her shirt at the waistband helped to hide what the binding could not. Over the past year, Lee had found it more difficult to disguise her maturing figure. She shuddered at the thought of the consequences if her secret were discovered today, of all days. It would cause such a public humiliation for Mr. Carver and, no doubt, would ban him from entering his boys in future contests. She envisioned the dreadful consequences to herself and her mother. She passed her hand under each arm to check the position of the band one more time.

As she did this, she glanced across the track to the people lining up to watch the races. Not only young boys and girls but also men and women of all ages were excitedly working their way to the edge of the track. She was stunned that some were elegantly dressed and smiling at her from under delicately laced umbrellas, many with ringlets and curls circling their faces. There was an air of confidence about them and she found herself smiling back. She could envision her mother among them had her life not taken a bad turn. Lee ran her calloused fingers through her own hair and knew she could never fit into a scene like that.

"Lee," Carver shouted as he paced nervously along the sidelines of the freshly marked track. "Get your mind on what you're doing or you'll go without your supper today."

Such threats meant very little to her and did nothing to persuade her to try harder. She knew what she could do. She also knew she could lose this race and humiliate him if she wanted to. But she wanted to win for herself and the boys at the Home, and that's what she intended to do.

Mr. Carver's face wore the deep furrows of longtime strain and the tension of his current self-imposed demands. He wanted that two-mile trophy. But, more than that, he wanted to win the other two races as well. This year, he wanted it all. He was sure he had the talent among his boys to win. He had entered his best runners: one in the half-mile race; one in the mile race; and one in the two-mile race. Of course, he put his best runner in the longest race and that was Lee. He knew Lee was fast and no doubt would win. He watched Elizabeth Mangrove talking to her runners near the starting line. They were listening intently and nodding their heads, their feet shuffling excitedly in the dirt. Suddenly, they raised their fists in the air and shouted, "Win. Win. Win."

Carver threw his head back and laughed. *What did that accomplish? I threatened my boys with extra chores and no breakfast for a week if they didn't win. I know how to get what I want.*

With fifteen minutes to wait until the start of the races, Lee and the other runners moved about, exercising their muscles to keep them warm and supple. Lee searched the crowd for Cal but he had disappeared. *It would be like Carver to send him on an errand just when the race would start.* It had only been three days since Cal had discovered she was a girl and they had learned of their love for each other. A warm tremble grabbed her heart and spread down toward her toes. *Love? Is that really what it is? How can we ever know, trapped as we are? What could we discover if we could break out of this cocoon we're in and become butterflies—free to be and to do what we want.*

Suddenly, she realized that her daydreaming had caused her to miss the start of the half-miler. Her own race would start soon and she had better be ready for it. Anxiously, she searched the crowd for Cal; needing that burst of energy he gave her just by being nearby.

A track had been leveled around the perimeter of the Common and was considered to be one mile long. The runners in her race would run that distance twice but that didn't seem like much of a challenge to her. Her mother had warned her not to be too confident because another runner could have trained, as well, and could give her some real competition. *Time,* however, had always been her competitor, except for the times she raced Cal into the woods, and *time* would be her competitor today. She could easily run a mile and a half in eight minutes and, today, she felt sure she could run the two miles in less than ten—yet, there was always the possibility that someone else could do better.

Since this was the first year for the two-mile race, a growing wave of spectators was moving into the area surrounded by the track. Excitement grew as children and adults alike cheered their favorite runners while pushing and shoving their way into the best places from which to watch.

Lee watched their movement, hoping Cal would appear among them. Just as she took her starting position with the other three runners, she spotted him with Mr. Pyne in the front row a short distance down the track. They were waving wildly in her direction and when they caught her eye, they cupped their hands around their mouths and shouted, "Go for it, Lee." She knew she couldn't lose now. She had to win for them. Carver would take the glory but she would have the satisfaction of giving the gift of the win to her friends.

Her feet flew in the dust while she filled her lungs and ran. This was no strain as her body had been tried and tested by countless hours of running and her muscles responded with precision. She ended the race a full ten seconds ahead of the second place winner. Cal ran to her side, slapping her on her back in boyish congratulations but wanting to throw his arms around her.

Carver shoved Cal away, nearly pushing Lee aside as she accepted her trophy and the compliments from the officials. She didn't keep it long. He grabbed the trophy from her hands and waved it to the crowd. He was excited. His boys had won the first two races as well. This was his year and he was letting everyone know how he felt about it.

"Looks like we'll eat tonight," Lee whispered to Cal as she moved away from the ceremony.

"Yeah and I'll bet you've had your hands on that trophy for the last time."

"Well, trophy or not, you and Mr. Pyne were here to watch me win. You two gave me that extra energy to do it." Wistfully, she looked at the ground. "I just wish my mother could've been here."

Cal was tempted to put his arm around her shoulder and was glad when Mr. Pyne did that. "Looks like you have some good news to take home to her, eh, son?"

Lee looked into his eyes and smiled. "Yeah. She'll be excited."

"Cal," Carver shouted as he walked toward the trio. "Take the boys home in the wagon. Mrs. Bellamont has a treat waiting for you all. Make sure you keep things under control. I don't want to come home to any problems." He turned and walked away with his arms wrapped around his spoils.

"What a pathetic man," Cal murmured

"Yes," Mr. Pyne added quietly.

Cal pulled the wagon into the shed behind the main building and the three winners jumped to the ground. Shouts and pounding footsteps bounded toward them setting off wild barking from the dog shed.

"Can you try to shut them up?" Cal shouted to one of the younger boys. "Give 'em something to eat."

"Don't know why he ever got them," the boy grumbled. "He never lets 'em out of their pen."

"They're bloodhounds he got from the Army that were used to hunt down slaves and such. Three boys disappeared from here a couple of years ago," Cal explained. "Haven't you ever heard him say he's ready to find us if one of us pulls that stunt on him again?"

"Yeah. Guess so." The boy stumbled off to the shed dragging another boy with him. "Come on. Help me out."

"Slow down," Cal called, waving his arms at the other boys barreling toward him. "You know Carver gets upset when the dogs start barking."

"Did we win?" the boys shouted as they came to a standstill.

"You bet we won," Cal said. "All three races."

"Where's the old man?"

"Out celebrating," Lee answered.

"Yeouee," the boys yelled in one voice as six of the older boys picked up the three winners, pulling off their shoes as they headed for the large pond adjacent to the vegetable garden.

"No," Lee screamed, kicking as she pleaded desperately for Cal to stop them.

Cal recognized the panic in her eyes and knew he had to keep her out of the water. He ran to the front of the excited group, waving his arms and shouting for them to stop but they continued on, knocking him to the ground as they stepped over him.

"Don't do this," he shouted above the sound of the barking dogs. He jumped up and followed them, screaming, "Get back to the house."

But like a freight train out of control, they charged to the edge of the pond and tossed their victims into the water.

Cal dropped his shoulders in defeat. "You shouldn't have done that," he said, shaking his head.

Lee took a deep breath before she hit the water, knowing she could be in deep trouble when she went up for air. Going down, she felt the water's force push the binder up all the way above her breasts and on her way back up, the water sucked her clothes tight against her body.

Good-natured laughter floated from the shore as she broke the surface. The two boys headed for land but she began to swim away from shore.

"Hey, Lee. Where ya goin'?" called Harrison.

"For a swim, now that I'm in here."

"You guys go on up to the house and get your treat. I'll wait for Lee," Cal said as calmly as he could. "Carver could be back any time. He's in a rare good mood. Don't spoil it."

Most of the boys headed for the house but the six carriers sat down to wait for Lee. "Hey, if Carver catches Lee in the lake, we'll be here for him. We'll take the blame," Charles assured them.

Both Lee and Cal could see that they had lost.

"I'll be in more trouble than you know," Lee shouted. She felt the binder riding loosely under her armpits. Efforts to pull it down over her breasts were useless. Cal knew what she was trying to do and when she shrugged her shoulders at him, he knew it wasn't going to happen while she was in the water.

"Before I get out, I wanna know if you guys can keep a really big secret from the old man. It's a matter of life or death for me and my mother."

"That's easy," Charles answered. "I'll keep a secret from that old fool any time, especially a 'really big one.'" He chuckled. "You with me?" he asked the other boys.

"We sure are."

"Then, get ready for a huge shock—and I mean a *huge* shock—a really big one. I'm countin' on you because if I can't, my ma and I are out on the street tonight."

Their faces reflected their bewilderment. "What're you talking about?" They looked at Cal's worried face. "Do you know what Lee's talking about?"

Cal nodded. "Yeah and I seriously doubt you're ready for this. It really is life or death that you guys keep what you are about to see from Carver."

"Well, then, I guess you'd better let us see what's so darned shocking," Charles said, searching Lee's face as she reluctantly paddled toward them.

Lee took a deep breath and walked out of the water, her clothes clinging to her body. The six boys gasped as she turned away from them and struggled without success to put the soaked binder back in place.

"I don't believe it," Harrison whispered hoarsely. "Damn. Can't be. You've been foolin' us all these years?" He rolled back on the grass and beat his fist against his forehead. "Damn. This is too much."

"I don't believe it, either," Charles said, shaking his head. "Why y-you beat the daylights out of me when we were little." He began to laugh. He laughed until his eyes watered and he gasped for air. Harrison joined him.

The other boys sat stunned, grinning sheepishly and keeping their eyes to the ground, not knowing what to say. "Too much," one of them echoed.

"Believe it," Lee said. "And it en't funny. Carver will kick me and my ma out the minute he hears about this. You gotta keep my secret. Please," she pleaded.

"How did you do it? And why?" Harrison asked.

"We were livin' on the street when Ma heard about this cooking job. She left me outside when she talked to Carver. She told him she had a kid and he told her she could only work here if that kid was a boy. So I became a boy and believe me, it wasn't easy at first."

They were full of questions, especially how Cal had found out.

"I've been her best buddy all these years and I never guessed but I sure was wondering about a few things like why she wasn't growin' fuzz on her chin," Cal said, grinning mischievously at Lee as he gave them a brief version of his own shocking discovery.

Lee fidgeted with her arms crossed over her breasts as she stared over their shoulders. "You know Carver could be back any minute and I need to get into some dry clothes."

"She's right. Can she count on you guys?"

"Of course. It's gonna take us a while to swallow this anyway," Harrison said, adding, "So don't you worry. We won't snitch."

"Thanks," Lee answered, praying they meant it. Something like this would be hard to keep to themselves.

All six boys jumped to their feet, not quite recovered, but ready to escort Lee back to the house.

"Wait," Cal demanded. "I want to see you all spit in your hands and swear to keep this secret. You know what'll happen to her if that old devil finds out."

"Right," they said and spit and swore together.

Cal tried to feel sure he could trust them. He had known them since they were little kids and he counted on their mutual hatred of Carver to bond them together. One thing he was sure of, Lee was frantic and worried about her mother and this revelation just added to her concerns.

Lee walked into the parlor in dry clothes just as Mr. Carver appeared bearing the trophies and a pompous self-satisfied smile. The boys were sitting on the floor talking and enjoying their treat of sweet fruit tarts and milk and, as usually happened when Mr. Carver entered the room, the boys grew quiet with apprehension.

"Come on, boys," Carver urged. "Eat up. Enjoy. I've had a big day." He held up the trophies. "Look at what *I* won. These are *my* trophies and they're going right up here on the mantelpiece."

He placed the trophies on the shelf and muttered, "Hee hee. That Miss Mangrove thought she could win with her sweet talk. Hee hee. I showed her."

An angry silence settled on the room like a dense fog.

"Why were you soaking wet this afternoon?" Charlotte asked when she and Lee were finally alone that evening.

"I'm afraid I've got bad news, Mama," Lee's voice showed the strain of the day's events. "The older boys threw the three of us winners in the pond to celebrate. Cal and I couldn't stop 'em."

"So, was that bad?" Charlotte asked with a touch of fear.

"Oh, yes." Lee took a deep hesitant breath. "Seven of the boys now know I'm a girl."

"Oh, dear," Charlotte gasped weakly from her seat on the side of her bed.

"We're in trouble, Lee."

"Maybe not. They all spit in their hands and swore to keep it to themselves. That's a solemn oath among us boys… umm… I mean, among the boys."

Charlotte stretched out on the bed and Lee realized again how thin and pale she had become.

"How did you ever make all those tarts today and the meal this evening?"

"I don't know, dear. I just kept on going on… and going… on."

CHAPTER 6

LEE RINSED HER dish and set it on the shelf at the pass-through to the kitchen. She noticed that the soup pot still simmered on the stove and a head of cheese remained uncovered on the table but her mother was nowhere in sight. It had been a meager meal but it was all her mother was able to put together. Lee had begged her to stay in bed that morning but she would have none of it.

Stepping aside for the other boys to deposit their dishes, Lee called to Cal who was just leaving the room.

"Boy, you look awful. What's the matter?" he asked, rushing toward her.

"I think something's happened to my ma."

"Where is she?"

"I don't know," she said, grabbing his arm and pulling him toward the kitchen, hoping desperately that Carver was not watching. "I need you to come with me."

They rounded the corner into the kitchen but Charlotte was not in the room.

"Oh, no," Lee cried as she rushed to the stairway and found her mother collapsed on the bottom step. Lee fell to her knees and grabbed Charlotte's hands. "Mama? What happened?"

"Stairs are just too much for me today," Charlotte whispered.

"Help me carry her up to her bed," Lee said, reaching for her mother.

Cal waved Lee aside and lifted Charlotte in his arms like a baby and easily carried her up the stairs to her room.

Charlotte moaned and opened her eyes as he gently laid her down. She took several deep breaths before trying to speak. Confusion stirred in her eyes as she stared at the two of them, searching for words to say. Finally, her eyes rested on Lee and she said, "Sorry. Just couldn't... keep on... going on... anymore."

Recognizing the intimacy passing between mother and daughter, Cal knew they needed to be alone. "I'll go put the stuff away in the kitchen for you, Mrs. Bellamont," Cal said, trying to disguise the emotion that overwhelmed him.

"You're a good man, Cal. Will you watch out for my Lisa?"

"Yes, Ma'am," he said, hurrying quietly out of the room.

"Don't tell Carver," Lee mouthed to him as he shut the door.

Charlotte closed her eyes and appeared to lose her strength and her will.

"Mama. What can I do to help you?"

"Nothing, my dear daughter," Charlotte whispered. The room echoed with Charlotte's labored breathing. Opening her eyes, she struggled to speak again. "I need to tell you something... tonight... no matter what...."

Tears threatened beneath Lee's eyelids. "I know, Mama. Dr. Simon talked to me after the last time he came to see you."

"Did he tell you I'm dying?"

"Yes."

"I don't have much time. I don't think I can get up out of this bed ever again."

"I'll run for the doctor," Lee cried, heading for the door in panic. Her mother seemed to sink deeper into the bedding.

"No, my dear," Charlotte whispered. "There is nothing more he can do. He told me I would just have to let it happen. I'm sorry, Lisa." Charlotte spoke her name as softly as love floating in on a cloud. "Lisa, my little girl." Charlotte opened her palm toward Lee, inviting her to come closer. Lee dropped to her knees and took her mother's hand, pressing it to her cheek.

"Cal is a fine boy and I hope you can find a way to be together." Charlotte closed her eyes and seemed to be drifting away. Lee laid her face against her mother's cheek and choked on tears that still couldn't come. Charlotte whispered, "When you leave this horrible place, hold your head up proudly and walk and talk like a lady. You won't need to be a boy anymore. You will have your butterfly wings. You will be free of this place."

Charlotte paused, building up strength to continue. "But you are so unprepared... so young... to go out into the world by yourself."

Unable to respond, Lee waited, feeling Charlotte's warm quick breaths against her cheek.

"I'm so sorry for the life I brought you into," Charlotte whispered. "Living such a lie... didn't expect it... end this way."

Lee leaned back and looked at her mother's face; gray as the pillow on which it lay.

"And don't forget to pray the prayers I taught you."

"Mama," Lee whispered. "Please. Save your strength."

"Hush, Lisa. I'm dying and we both know it. Let me finish, please." She drew another breath and continued, her eyes moist and distant. Her breathing became shallow and then she spoke again but too softly for Lee to hear all the words. It sounded like she said, "Your mother and father loved each other very much." Charlotte appeared agitated and tried to speak again. "I have loved you, my dear child, since you were born."

Charlotte stared beyond Lee's face, lighting up in recognition of someone familiar, as her words became those of a penitent talking to a priest. Lee felt like an intruder, but she stayed to hear.

"I loved... as she did... father wouldn't... didn't... want... so long ago... missed him... have a daughter... not had fair chance." Charlotte's eyes suddenly opened wider and she asked, "What will happen to her?"

In her last effort to speak, she raised her head as her glazed eyes searched the room once more. She fell back on the pillow exhausted.

With renewed effort, Charlotte murmured indistinctly, "Father, forgive me for my sins… terrible thing to do… help her… I'm sorry."

Lee's heart split in two as she listened. "I love you, Mama. I always will," she whispered. "Don't worry 'bout me. You were good to me and I'm truly grateful."

Charlotte's sightless eyes stared at the ceiling. Her spirit had slipped away with her last plea and now she was at peace. Lee closed her mother's eyes and stared at the silent figure on the bed. So desperate just seconds ago and now so quiet. There was a break in Lee's heart that would not mend. She laid her head on the bed and tried to accept the reality. Her heart pleaded for her mother to open her eyes one more time and say one more word; knowing, however, that it wouldn't happen.

It was just after midnight when they said good-bye but Lee stayed by her mother's bedside until a ray of sunshine touched her cheek telling Lee it was time to inform Mr. Carver. Spent and desolate, she quickly packed her own and her mother's meager belongings in the same bag they had brought with them years ago. Carefully, she wrapped her mother's treasured crucifix and the small Bible in the folds of the dress she had just packed, set the bag by the door and stepped into the hall to search for Mr. Carver. It was Wednesday, April 11, 1855. She was fifteen years old, alone and homeless.

She found him yelling at two boys in the kitchen as he angrily scuttled about, slamming the porridge pot on the table and screaming at the boys to get some wood for the fire.

"Get your mother down here right now… or… or… you're both out of here."

"We'll be out of here soon," Lee, said, swallowing the tears that wouldn't flow from her eyes.

"Good lord. What's the matter with you? Just get her down here to make breakfast for the boys and then you can leave."

His face was getting red and bloated. He sucked at the saliva gathering in the corners of his mouth.

"Go! Now!"

"My mother can't come. She's dead."

The two boys stopped what they were doing and stared at Lee and then at Carver whose face seemed about to explode.

"What do you mean 'she's dead'? She made supper last night. You have to be wrong."

Lee backed up toward the door as he approached her with his fist raised. Cal stepped in between them and Carver stopped.

"She's dead, Mr. Carver," Cal said as calmly as he could. "You'll have to make breakfast yourself this morning."

Carver dropped onto a stool as the impact of the news made it into his agitated mind.

"We're leaving together now to go into town and make burial arrangements," Cal said and took Lee by the arm, leading her away.

"Get her body out of this place as soon as you can and… and… keep this to yourselves. We don't need to disturb the day for the boys." He glared at the boys standing behind him. "And that means you, too."

Lee and Cal went in search of Father John Ryan of the Immaculate Conception Church. Recognizing how destitute and alone she was, the priest reached into the church's Poor Box and helped Lee purchase a bare wooden coffin and make arrangements for a place in the small Catholic cemetery. Father Ryan arranged for the church's burial committee to take care of the body and dig the grave. In the late afternoon, Cal and Lee followed the small wagon carrying her mother's body away from the Home. They watched as it was respectfully placed in the basement of the partially completed church to await burial the next morning.

As they left the church, Cal led her to a spot under a tree and handed her a piece of bread with a chunk of cheese, then he took a piece for himself. "I snatched this from the kitchen last night. Didn't figure the old man would let you in for a meal anymore."

She leaned into his shoulder as they ate, letting the quiet time of day soothe their bruised emotions.

"I came back up to your room last night after I cleaned up the kitchen but I didn't want to interrupt you and your ma," Cal said, breaking the silence.

"She died just after midnight."

"I knew she was gone. I came by again in the middle of the night. I shouldn't have but I was so concerned about you." He pulled her closer to him. "He was hard on you this morning. I really hate that man."

"He's going to let me stay in the room tonight if I scrub it down. So that's what I've gotta do when we get back."

"I'll come help."

"That'll make him good and mad and you'll be out of there before your birthday."

"He won't find out."

It was eleven o'clock by the time they finished cleaning and Cal sneaked back to his room promising to be back before sunup.

Lee slept restlessly with her bag beside the bed, longing for her mother and wishing Cal could have stayed the night. She was so grateful for him but what was to happen to them after she was gone? And where would she go? She had decisions to make. She was wide-awake long before she heard Cal's tap on the door.

Lee buried her mother at six o'clock Thursday morning joined only by Cal, Father Ryan and three of his lady parishioners who came along to offer Lee comfort. They huddled together in the early morning chill and listened to Father Ryan pray the Latin prayers after which Lee and Cal found themselves alone. Together they began pushing the dirt onto the wooden box until the burial crew came to take over. Lee picked a small bouquet of pink thistle and placed it on the grave. Kneeling, she said her last good-bye and, as the night turned into day, she knew her own day had turned into night. Cal wrapped his arm around her shoulders and led her away.

CHAPTER 7

JONAS CARVER WAS waiting for her when she returned to the orphanage to pick up her belongings. Lee stood across the desk from him and searched his face for a hint of sympathy. The tightly stretched skin over the high cheekbones added coldness to the indifference in the dark menacing eyes. He ordered her to take her things and get out immediately. Bright shafts of sunlight poured in through the window behind him, making it difficult to see his face clearly. He was an ominous form towering over her and the bag lying on the floor at her feet.

"You and your mother deceived me far too long. This is a home for boys only and your mother knew that. I have been made a fool for ten years and I can tolerate the sight of you no longer." His breath came in short angry gasps.

"How'd you find out?"

"I overheard some of the boys talking about your dunk in the pond."

"You spied on them," she hissed.

"But, of course. That is my privilege."

Anger surged through Lee's body, replacing any fear she might have had for this man.

"Then you knew before my mother died. Why did you wait 'til now to bring it up?" she asked sarcastically.

"I was going to throw you both out yesterday when I found out but your mother decided to die before I could. It was only through my benevolence that I allowed you time to remove her from the premises. Besides, I wanted the room cleaned up."

Lee felt the hot flush of her outrage rising out of control. Her face contorted into angry lines. "You merciless beast."

"Hah! You are right. I have no mercy for dregs like you who live on deceit in order to preserve your trivial little lives."

From the corner of her eye, she saw the birch switch resting at an angle across the corner of the desk. She inched her way closer to it. Mr. Carver turned toward a sound outside the door and, with a single movement, Lee picked up the thin stick and slashed it hard across his face. He grabbed his face as blood spurted through his fingers.

She heard heavy footsteps move toward the door. Heaving her bag across her shoulder, she jumped out of the open window. Once she hit the ground and gained her footing, she sprinted down the path toward the woods. Stumbling on a rock, she fell and rolled down an incline; her bag tumbling on ahead of her. Ignoring the pain, she jumped up, retrieved her bag and ran headlong into the dark shelter of the trees.

She stayed on the well-worn paths knowing she could outrun anyone coming after her even with the added weight of her bag. Experience told her she was running in a southerly direction, which meant that she had at least two miles of woods to battle before she reached the wide clearing at the Mystic River. Knowing that Carver would come after her, no doubt with the dogs, she counted on the heavy plant growth at the water's edge to provide a hiding place and the water to absorb her scent. It was a chance at best but she had to take it.

The morning sun sent filtered rays through the branches of the pine trees providing some light on her dark pathway. She was within sight of the river when she heard the dogs.

Cal was nearing Mr. Carver's office when he caught some of the cold and hurtful words Carver hurled at Lee. Cal ached for her, knowing the pain she felt in the loss of her mother. When he heard the sudden slap of the switch against flesh, he dashed into the room and was shocked to see Carver covered in blood and Lee leaping out the window.

Cal ran to the window and watched her disappear into the woods. Turning to Carver, he was met with the hateful stare of an angry man in pain and humiliation.

"Help me, you idiot."

Cal ran to the kitchen and returned with a wet cloth. Mr. Carver wiped his hands and held the cloth against his face. "Get the dogs," he screamed. "We're going after her."

Dave and Howard, two of the boys involved in Lee's dunking, were repairing the wooden gate to the vegetable garden. Cal motioned for them to follow him. On the way to the dog shed, Cal told them what happened.

"Good for her," Dave said.

"Carver's going after her with the dogs and I'm going with him to make sure he doesn't find her or, if he does, he doesn't hurt her. Do you wanna go with me and help protect her from this maniac?"

"Sure," they both answered at once.

"I wanna stall as long as we can, though," Cal said. "Let's give her time to get away."

When they finally arrived at the door of the house with the dogs, Mr. Carver was furiously pacing back and forth waiting for them.

"Did you lose your way or what?" he barked.

"Sorry. They were restless and hard to leash," Cal said.

Carver looked at the two calm bloodhounds and charged, "That's a lie."

He grabbed their leashes and led them into his office to sniff the floor and the window ledge for Lee's scent. When he thought they had enough, he turned to the boys and said, "Let's go."

"Shouldn't you take care of your face first?" asked Howard.

"There's time for that later. I need to catch that girl," he said, pressing the cloth against the bleeding wound.

"Girl?" Howard whispered to Cal.

"He overheard you guys talking."

By now Carver was well on his way into the woods running along behind the dogs. The same rays that shone through the branches to guide Lee revealed to Carver the broken branches and footprints along her path.

Easing herself into the chilly water, Lee quickly followed the shoreline to an area where the overhanging bushes and plant growth were thick enough to conceal her. She slipped under the welcome coverage and continued moving, grasping muddy roots and rocks to help pull herself along. She heard voices and laughter drawing near. Daring to peek out of her hiding place, she saw a rowboat approaching with two couples that seemed to be enjoying an outing on the river. She hoped its wake would hide the ripples made by her movement as she lengthened the distance from the place she had entered the water. She believed she had gone at least forty feet when the growth began to thin out. Grasping a thick root to stabilize herself, she tucked her bag between her chest and the riverbank and pulled herself in as tightly as she could, closed her eyes and listened for the approaching dogs.

"Ahoy, you in the boat out there," Mr. Carver yelled.

Startled, Lee realized that he was only a few yards away and the dogs were noisily sniffing the ground. She was sure the pounding of her heart was sending out ripples on the water revealing her hiding place. Breathing a desperate prayer, she closed her eyes and waited.

"Hello there," answered a voice from the boat. "It's a beautiful day, eh?"

"Forget the day. Have you seen a young girl in this area?"

"No, but we did see a young boy."

"That's the one we want. She's a girl dressed like a boy."

Lee's heart sank. They were going to turn her in. She was about to go under water and swim away as fast as she could when she heard someone from the boat yell back, "He jumped in the water right about where you're standing and started swimming toward the other shore. That must have been a good ten minutes ago."

"Thanks," Cal shouted.

Cal? When the sound of their footsteps faded away, she dared steal a glance and saw Cal, Dave and Howard following Carver in the distance. *They must have come along to protect me. Thank you, my friends.* She glanced at the boat but the people turned their back on her and continued on their way. *Thanks to you, too.*

When the search party was out of sight, Lee ran deep into the woods again and found a sunny spot off the main path among the trees. She removed her shirt and pants, wrung out the water and scraped off the mud while keeping her eyes and ears tuned to her surroundings. After spreading her clothes on the ground to dry and pouring the water out of her shoes, she checked the contents of her bag and found them mostly dry. Slipping into her mother's dress, she sat down in the warm patch of sunshine against a tree to begin gathering her fractured thoughts.

The silence of the woods wrapped itself around her, drawing her into a sense of her mother's presence through the feel and scent of her dress. So much had happened in the twelve hours since her mother died that she hadn't had time to accept her death. She wanted to cry but the tears didn't come, so she buried her face in the folds of the dress and searched for solace there. Remembering the disconnected thoughts and jumbled words during her mother's last moments, Lee wondered what it all meant. What was her mother trying to tell her? *I may never know, Mama. I can't ask you now.*

She listened to the silence of the woods, broken only by the call of a bird or the scampering feet of a small animal. What would she do now? There had to be someplace she could go, but where? Certainly not to Cal at Todburn's because Carver would look there first. He'd go to Mr. Pyne's shop, too, but maybe he wouldn't go to the Pyne's house behind the shop. A plan began to form in her thoughts. She would go to Mr. Pyne after dark when, hopefully, Carver would already have been at the shop looking for her. Maybe Mr. Pyne would hide her or maybe not. *It's worth a try.*

She was tired and hungry. The bread and cheese from Cal was the only food she had eaten since supper on Tuesday. She reached inside the bag and pulled out the crucifix and her mother's Bible, pleased to find that its pages were dry. She put the book in the bottom of the bag. Taking the crucifix, she pressed it against her breast remembering what her mother had told her. *Your father gave me this crucifix when we first met. I've treasured it all these years. Take it with you wherever you go. Pray as I've taught you to do. Ask the Lord to be with you and help you. He will.*

She leaned the crucifix against the tree and went down on her knees. Even though she had joined her mother all these years, prayer had never meant much to Lee. She had recited the prayers her mother had taught her but most of the time her mind had wandered off. Now, she wanted to pray something meaningful. Her broken heart needed healing and she needed to find a sense of direction.

She closed her eyes and listened to the breeze passing through the trees and a small animal, perhaps a squirrel, darting by. She waited and listened—a minute, two minutes, three minutes passed. Then, a soft blanket of warmth wrapped around her and a wave of calmness flowed into her heart. *Thank you, Lord. I feel you're here with me now. I need to ask you to watch over me and help me find a way out of this. I shouldn't have hit Carver like that but I hope you can understand that I lost control. He's just so mean and he's nearly driven me crazy at times. If it was wrong, I'm sorry but I can't say I wouldn't do it again—under the same circumstances, o'course. Bless my mother. She always said she'd be with you when she died so I guess she's there with you now. I'm so tired and I want to talk to her so bad. Will you tell her I miss her?* Lee paused and leaned back on her heals. *Oh, and thank you for not letting Carver catch me and please keep Cal safe. I'd really like to see him again.* She turned and leaned her back against the tree, falling asleep with the crucifix clutched against her breast.

A cool breeze brushed her face and awakened her. She was startled to find the sun disappearing behind the trees. Her clothes were mostly dry and she felt rested but anxious to be on her way. It was a good distance to Mr. Pyne's house and it would be difficult to find her way through the woods after dark. Quickly, she tucked the crucifix into her bag, changed into her shirt and pants and began to run.

By the time she reached the blacksmith shop, the moon had disappeared behind the clouds, burying the shop and the house in deep shadows. There was no sign of life in either building. Perhaps they had gone to bed early or were not at home.

She decided to check the back of the house. As she rounded the corner, she stopped short and drew back. There was Mr. Pyne holding the back door open for several people slipping quietly from a wagon into the dark house. She counted four of them. As soon as the last one disappeared, the wagon moved on and the back door closed. She waited. The house remained dark and silent. It was as if the entire scene had not happened. Her heart pounded as she realized the people were black: two women and two men. *They must be runaways. Is he hiding runaway slaves?* She began to shake, partly from the cool air but a lot more from nerves. She knew this meant trouble if he was found out. She leaned against the house, giving herself a moment to calm her nerves and decide what to do.

The minutes ticked on and she was at a loss. Suddenly, she saw movement on the road leading to the blacksmith shop and two men came into view, both carrying rifles. They hesitated and pointed to the house. Lee knew who they were and knew what she had to do. She hugged the foundation of the house and crept to the back door. When she was outside their view, she stood up and knocked. The door opened a crack and Mr. Pyne stared down at her.

"Mr. Pyne. It's me. Lee. Let me in—quick."

A hand reached out and pulled her through the door.

"What in de world do you do here at dis time?" Mr. Pyne said, the anger in his voice unleashing his German accent. "Dat man Carver vas here earlier and…"

"We can talk about that later. Right now, there are two men coming toward your house with rifles," Lee warned.

"Oh, God help us."

"Tell them that wagon just dropped me off. I'm your nephew from Boston and…"

The knock on the front door was loud. Lee looked around quickly and saw no sign of the other visitors. They had simply disappeared.

She picked up her bag and followed Mr. Pyne into the parlor where he lit an oil lamp and opened the door.

"Yah?"

"We're deputy marshals tracking down some runaway slaves that we're told came into this area. We'd like to come in and talk to you about that."

Lee held her breath. She was awed by Mr. Pyne's display of quiet confidence. "My wife is now in bed. My nephew just a few minutes ago came and we will soon be in bed, too."

"Your nephew just arrived?"

"Yah. That is right."

"We would like to come inside and say hello to this nephew of yours."

Lee moved well into the parlor dropping her bag beside her in plain view. Her heart hadn't slowed down since she left the orphanage that morning and she feared her tension would throw suspicion on Mr. Pyne.

"Den come in but be quiet and do not my wife wake up."

They stepped inside and looked critically at Lee and then apologized to Mr. Pyne.

"We know you're a good citizen, Mr. Pyne, and that you have run a successful blacksmith business here for many years. We also know those runaways were brought into this neighborhood and we intend to find them."

Both men studied the room carefully, tapping on the floor where they stood.

"You understand that as a good citizen, you're required to report any runaway slaves that you might know about. That's the law."

"I know dat very well. Absolutely."

"If you hear anything, you know what to do. Remember, there's a fine of one thousand dollars and six months in jail for not turning them in."

"I know dat, too. Absolutely."

"We'll be leaving but we'll be checking out the surrounding area. Enjoy your nephew's visit."

When the door was closed and locked, Mr. Pyne sat down at the kitchen table, visibly shaken.

"Dey will be back when dey don't find what dey look for." His accent was unguarded even as his tone became quietly apologetic. "You have walked into something I think you would never have guessed would happen in my house. I'm thankful you came, young man. You are a godsend. Ve are in your debt."

CHAPTER 8

JOHN PYNE DIMMED the lamp and tapped on the bedroom door. "It is all right, Rebecca. They have gone. You can now come out."

Hesitantly, she scanned the parlor as she moved through the doorway when her anxious eyes landed on Lee. John gave her an assuring nod.

Rebecca hurried to the kitchen where she reached into a large box and pulled out four small loaves of corn bread. Lee hardly dared breathe as she watched her place them in the depression made by holding up the corner ends of her apron. Somewhere in this house were four runaway slaves, but there was no sign of them. Shadows cast by the flickering light of the kerosene lamp in the eerie silence sent a chill down Lee's spine. She listened for the sound of breathing but heard nothing. Rebecca Pyne and the loaves disappeared followed by the quiet closing of the bedroom door. It was then that Lee noticed her employer's hands trembling. He gave her a disquieting look as he motioned for her to sit down at the table with him.

"You by now must know that you have come into a very dangerous situation. If you want to leave, you better do dat right now because those men will be back."

Lee collapsed onto the seat across from him. There was no one, not a soul but herself to rely on at the moment or in the foreseeable future, she thought as she stared at her hands squeezed into two balls in her lap. Only a few days ago, she had two lifelines: her mother and Cal. Today, her mother lay in a Malden graveyard and Cal, perhaps, was lost to her forever. She had no home and no relatives and no money. The truth was, she was on her own and penniless.

The orphanage had been a good training ground for solving problems and facing difficult situations but now, the thought of her future, even of the next day, overwhelmed her. The weeks and months ahead looked dark and daunting. Maybe, in time, she'd be able to grasp that special confidence her mother had in God. She admitted to herself that today when she prayed, it felt like God was with her. It had been a comfort.

"You need to make up your mind before they come back."

"Well, Mr. Pyne, I don't have anyplace to go but if it'd be easier on you and Mrs. Pyne, considering what you're doin' here, I'll get out," she said, looking directly into the eyes of the man she had placed her trust in years ago. There was no rejection in his face, only a deep concern. She didn't want him to recognize the feeling of vulnerability that had overcome her. She studied his face and then dared to add, "But, if you don't mind, I'd like to take my chances with you. Tell Mrs. Pyne she can trust me."

"I believe you, Lee, but terrible things soon could happen here. Those men could think you helped us." He hesitated. "I have watched you for many years so I know you have a good mind and a strong will. You can maybe help us." Shrugging his shoulders in resignation, he added, "It was good you were here tonight. If you want to stay, you are welcome."

He walked around the table and placed his arm around her shoulders and said, "Son, you will have to try to be comfortable on de sofa tonight. It is late and Rebecca and I enough have had for today. You look like you feel the same way. Tomorrow you will tell us why you have come to us tonight."

Lee took comfort in the warmth of his arm around her shoulders. The size of the huge man she had first seen at nine years old had diminished during the years that she had grown taller. The kindness he had shown her then, however, had not diminished but had increased. No matter what happened after today, she would forever be grateful to him, and to Mrs. Pyne as well.

Behind the closed door, she heard the faintest sound of a sliding panel and the quick snap of a lock.

"Where are they?" she whispered.

"It is best you do not know."

Lee curled up under the quilt Mrs. Pyne had put out for her on the sofa and was grateful for a warm place to sleep. What she wouldn't have given for one of those little loaves but the Pynes had too much on their minds to think about the possibility that Lee was hungry as well. Her complete exhaustion overcame her curiosity and hunger and she fell into a sound sleep. Somewhere in her dreams, she heard a rap on the door and loud voices. She peered from under heavy eyelids and realized she was not dreaming. An agitated Mr. Pyne stood at the front door in his nightshirt and cap.

"It is de middle of de night," John grumbled.

"We know that," said one of the deputy marshals that had visited them earlier. "But we've been unsuccessful so far. A neighbor said they saw a wagon with five or six people in it and it was heading this way. We'd like to take a look around."

From her place on the sofa, Lee called out, "That would be the wagon that brought me here and there were only two people in it."

"That is what we told you when you were here de last time," John confirmed. "Whoever gave you that false information could be de guilty ones. Maybe they want you to look someplace else than to them."

"We thought of that so we had a look around their place. Didn't find anything."

"You will not find anything here either so please go away and let me and my family sleep," John said firmly.

Lee detected a controlled irritation tinged with fear in Mr. Pyne's voice.

"Not until we take a look around inside."

"If you force your way into my house, I will have to speak to the township council first thing in de morning."

"You will just have to do that because we're going to take a look around. Get your wife out of bed so we can search all the rooms."

"You leave your guns outside. I will not have dem in my house." John warned.

"We don't care what you'll have or not have," the man said, using the barrel of his rifle to push John out of his way.

Lee jumped up but was stopped before she could move aside.

"Young man, you stay right where you are and we won't bother you," one of the deputies said to Lee as he moved further into the room, setting his lantern on the floor.

Lee saw anger rush John's face. His hands folded into fists for an instant and then opened again as he stepped ahead of them and called Rebecca from the bedroom. Resignation and fear mingled in his eyes.

For the next five minutes, the two men tapped on the floors and walls of the small three-room house. They rolled up the carpet in the parlor looking for a trap door to a cellar. Lee detected a growing irritation in them as they moved from room to room without success. Finally, they gave up the search and left saying, "They are hidden somewhere in this neighborhood."

John closed the door and collapsed into the chair next to the sofa, his ashen face sinking into his trembling hands.

"Dat vas a close vun," he gasped.

The dawn came up like a curtain rising on a new play. The drama of yesterday was still keen in Lee's memory as she woke up to the sound of voices behind her. She peered over the top of the sofa but no one was there. Quietly, she stood and walked toward the wall between the parlor and the bedroom. There, she heard unfamiliar voices in subdued conversation with the Pynes.

"Thank you, suh. We understands that."

"I don't know how soon we can get you on your way. You'll have to be as comfortable as you can make yourselves in there until we figure out how to move you on. Those men have complicated things," Rebecca told them.

"We can do it, ma'am. Don't you worry none about us. We hates that we is causing you trouble."

"We'll bring you out into the room for some fresh air soon and give you food and water but, otherwise, you'll have to stay hidden. They almost got all of us last night."

Lee heard the panel slide shut and got back to the sofa just as John came into the parlor. Even though he looked pale, there was a calmness that had replaced the fear of the night before.

"So you are awake," he said.

"Yes, Sir."

"Well, come into the kitchen for something to eat and tell us your story."

She frantically bit into the small loaf of bread placed before her and gulped the cup of milk offered her. She realized Mr. Pyne was staring at her in astonishment.

"How long since you have had something to eat?"

"Two days," she answered with her mouth full of bread.

Rebecca had walked into the kitchen and watched for only a moment before she quickly placed several slices of ham in from of Lee and filled her cup again.

"Take your time and don't eat too fast," Rebecca urged. "Eat this and then let the food settle. We'll give you more in a few hours. Don't want you to make yourself sick."

When Lee finished eating, she leaned on her elbows feeling a bit ashamed of her poor manners. "Sorry 'bout actin' like a pig. I'm sure grateful to you both."

"Now, young man, tell us what to you has happened. Why have you not come to work?" John asked.

The early morning sun sent a single shaft of light across the table through the only window in the kitchen. It was going to be a bright clear day but not in the hearts of the people sitting at the table as Lee unfolded her story beginning with the death of her mother. She hesitated before telling about her encounter with Mr. Carver and then decided it would be best to first tell them about the dunk in the pond and the discovery of her secret by the six boys. The Pynes would be shocked and very disappointed in her for lying to them all these years and she hated that. Mr. Pyne had told her several times that she was the son he never had. Maybe they wouldn't like her as a girl, but she knew it was time to clear things up.

"I didn't wanna come out of the water but I had to. I knew they would see right away that I wasn't one of them." Lee paused and stared at the Pynes, watching her words take on meaning for them.

"Not one of them? What do you mean?" John asked, a perplexed frown appearing above his eyes.

"I mean I'm a girl making believe I'm a boy." Lee wished there was an easier way to say this but she couldn't see how. This was a fact and this was the only way to tell them. Mrs. Pyne gasped and stopped what she was doing. Mr. Pyne started to say something in his astonishment but stopped when Lee began to talk again.

"My mother made me be a boy when I was five years old so she could take the job at the orphanage. Carver let me live with her in the room above the kitchen so that kept me away from the boys' sleeping quarters. I just had to be very careful when I played with them during the day. I'm going on sixteen and it's been getting harder and harder to hide it from them." She knew she was blushing and hated it. "There were six boys that saw me come out of the pond and they all spit in their hands and swore to keep my secret. My best buddy, Cal, already knew. He found out a few days before that after Carver gave me a really bad switching."

To Lee's surprise, John leaned his chair back against the wall and chuckled. "Rebecca and I have been wondering about you for a few years already but you are so strong and you do such good blacksmith work that we thought we might be wrong. I'm glad you tell us this. It is a relief to know." He dropped his chair back on its four legs and leaned toward Lee. "I cannot imagine what your life must have been like to pretend every minute of every day. How in the name of heaven did you do it?"

Mrs. Pyne took a seat at the table with them, shaking her head in amazement. "I can't imagine that awful Mr. Carver not getting an inkling of what you were doing."

"He was too busy keeping us in line to notice. I was most afraid when he switched me. He never made any of us drop our pants." Lee blushed. "He sure would have known then."

There was no way to explain exactly how she did it. "At five years old, I watched the boys closely, especially the way they acted and talked. They called me a sissy when I'd cry and they'd pick on me. That made me mad so I started kicking them and fightin' back. I got real good at fighting as I got older and when I was seven, I whipped the daylights out of another seven-year-old and they all left me alone after that. Most of 'em became good friends, mostly because we all knew we had to stick together to survive that place."

"It will take me some time to fully grasp this, Lee," Mrs. Pyne said. "Is your name really Lee? What shall we call you now that we know?"

"My name's Lisa. I'd like for you to call me that. I'll keep on answering to both names until you get used to it. I'll have to get used to it, too. My ma always called me Lee ever since I can remember. While she was dying, she called me Lisa."

"Oh, my," Rebecca muttered as Lisa told about her last encounter with Mr. Carver and her escape. "You poor thing."

The lines in John's face deepened and his voice rumbled in angry concern. "He is an evil man." He brought his fist down on the table top and continued, "I knew you were in trouble but I have been too busy with my own problem to ask you about it until now. Carver came by yesterday afternoon when he could not find you. He did not say what happened or why he wanted you. He just wanted me to watch for you. So, it was you dat got his face."

Lisa was surprised as the corner of John's mouth curved in a hint of a smile.

"I did it on impulse. When he said those mean and terrible things, I just went crazy. His switch was on the desk right in front of me and I just picked it up and swung. Got him right in the face. I jumped out the window and ran."

John set his coffee cup on the table. "I always suspected that man of mistreating his boys but I did not have proof. You always did your work for me and never complained about him. I did not see him often but when I did, he seemed to have evilness in him."

"He's likely to come by again, don't you think?" asked Rebecca.

"He could. It looks like we have two problems now on our hands. But do not worry, Lee—Lisa. If he comes by, we won't let him find you. In de meantime, we have to figger out what we are going to do with all of you."

"I wanna go out west to the Kansas Territory."

"Kansas!" John said in surprise.

"I heard Mr. Stanton talkin' to you about it. He said they needed good blacksmiths out there."

"Well, I guess he did, didn't he?"

"I just have to figure out how to get there."

Rebecca stoked the fire in her cast iron stove and set a pot of water on top. "I'm going to start some soup. I think you're both hungry and so are our people waiting to get out of here." She was more comfortable talking about the runaways in front of Lisa now, which made Lisa feel like family, knowing the family secret.

"We may have to go with you if we don't get ourselves out of dis trouble we are in," John said.

A sudden banging reverberated across the house and John rushed to the parlor. Before he reached the door, a familiar voice shouted, "Pyne. Open up."

John turned to Rebecca and motioned for her and Lisa to go to the bedroom. Lisa picked up her bag and followed her. Rebecca lightly tapped twice on the wall and a lock clicked on the inside. The wall slid open and she motioned for Lisa to squeeze inside. Lisa pushed her way into the space, drawing in her shoulders to make herself smaller. She found herself scrunched against another person and the wall. Her lungs seemed to collapse even though she felt air coming from somewhere.

As soon as the lock clicked again, John went to the door and faced Jonas Carver who pushed his way around John and stepped into the house, his eyes searching each corner of the room. When he headed for the kitchen, John grabbed his arm and ordered, "Hold it right dare. Dis is my house and you have no right to push your way in here. What do you want?"

"You know what I want. She's got to be here. I've searched everywhere else."

"She? What the… who do you talk about?" John asked.

"I mean Lee. He's a she; a lying wench. She did this to my face and I want her punished."

"Dat boy is not here. He is not a girl so stop calling him dat."

"I don't believe you. She'd have to go to someone she knows."

"Get out!" John shouted, his anger out of control. "Go look someplace else. If Lee is gone, then I am de one who should be angry. He is a good blacksmith and I need him. If he don't come back, it looks like I can blame you for dat—so go—get out of here." John pulled on Carver's arm, dragging him to the door. With one push, he sent Carver flying out the door and onto the ground. "Now, get out of here and don't your face ever show here again."

There had been deadly silence inside the wall during the angry exchange. Even though they all felt the floor shake when the door slammed shut, no one moved until a double knock sounded and a hand from inside reached around Lee to unlock the panel and slide it open.

"Come out. All of you," Rebecca said. "You can spend some time out here in the bedroom and, if necessary, relieve yourselves in that corner." She pointed to a covered slop jar partly hidden by a tri-fold screen. "If you hear us say 'move', then you hurry back into the wall."

Lisa's heart responded to their joy as the four runaways stepped out of their dark confinement and moved hesitantly into the room. For a few moments, she had shared their experience. When she had stepped into the hiding place, she felt helpless and trapped—at the mercy of others. With Carver on her heels, she also knew how it felt to be hunted down like an animal, knowing there would be dreadful consequences if caught.

Rebecca and Lisa joined John in the kitchen where he was sitting at the table sipping his coffee from a saucer.

"How do they rest in that space?" Lisa asked.

"There is space enough for two of them to lie down at one time. So they take turns. The others can sit," Rebecca said. "They tolerate it because they know they will be in Canada soon, if all goes well."

"And I'll be in the Territory of Kansas, if all goes well. We all know I can't stay here." The words were said but there was no way to explain the loneliness and the anxiety that were hidden in them.

"I have been thinking about how we can help you," John said. "I have figgered out how I am going to get those people out of here but I do not know what to do with you, Lisa. Do you have any ideas? You must have had some thoughts on that when you decided to come here."

"I wanted a place to spend the night was all," she said. "I wanna go on into Boston to the New England Emigrant Aid Company office and see if they'll let me go with them. I just wish I knew when the next group leaves."

"Gabe Stanton left a handbill with me de last time he was here. I will get it from de shop."

Soon he returned and handed the leaflet to Lisa. "Looks like one is going out on de seventeenth," he said. "I think you would need a sponsor or some money, no? You have any money?"

Lisa's face fell as she replied, "Not even a penny but I've got a trade and Mr. Stanton said they need blacksmiths and farriers out there."

"That is right," he said, leaning back in his chair studying Lisa. "And you are a good one. Boston is only seven miles down de road. I think we can figger out a way to get you there. Maybe we can ask my friend Gabe for help. He knows you for all de years you have worked for me. I think he will know what you need to do." He swirled the coffee in his saucer as he pondered the problem. "Let me give some thought to dat idea."

CHAPTER 9

THE NEXT MORNING, Lisa watched Mr. Pyne leave for the shop and wished she could go work with him but he said the threat against her was too great. She agreed thinking that another encounter with old man Carver was not something she wanted to cope with this day, or any day. It occurred to her, however, that there was one thing she could do now that her true identity had been exposed. She could remove the binder that had become so much a part of her that she often forgot it was there.

"Mrs. Pyne, when you have a minute today, would you help me take care of something?"

"Of course, Lisa. As soon as I finish with this pie dough."

An apple pie sat ready to go into the oven and a small ball of leftover pastry lay in the middle of the breadboard. With her palms, she flattened the dough into a circle and covered it with layers of soft butter, sugar and cinnamon. Rolling the piece into a long cylinder, she cut it into bite-size pieces, arranged them on a baking sheet and placed it in the oven with the pie.

"We'll snack on these when they are done."

She wiped up her breadboard and hung it up on the wall. "Now, Lisa. What can I do for you?"

Lisa was pleased that both Mr. and Mrs. Pyne were making an effort to use her real name. It had such a pleasing, though unfamiliar, sound to her. Mrs. Pyne found the knots tight and difficult to untie.

"My mother tied those knots the day before she died. It was very hard for her to do. I guess getting 'em wet in the river tightened 'em up."

Lisa's eyes filled but still she couldn't cry. "I haven't been able to cry, but I want to," she confided when she saw the pained look on Mrs. Pyne's face. "The tears start to come but then I get this ball stuck in my throat instead."

"It will come eventually, Lisa. I'm sure of that." Rebecca gave her a warm hug. "Come. I could use your help chopping up some vegetables."

Although Lisa had never worked in the kitchen nor even watched her mother cook, she was glad to help Rebecca prepare food for the fugitives' journey to the next delivery station. It was a good thing to do as it kept her hands busy but her thoughts were not as easy to control. Cal's face appeared in her mind's eye as it had been doing almost constantly since the last time they were together. She wondered if she would ever see him again.

She missed the sound of his voice. She had heard it for the past eleven years during their good and bad times together as best buddies. She wanted to hear the way he talked to her now that he knew she was a girl—his girl. She wanted to feel the warmth of his arms around her. She wanted him to be here with her sharing the friendly warmth of the kitchen filled with the smell of cinnamon and sugar coming from the oven. She searched for something positive to think about but nothing came to mind. Things were just too sad and too uncertain. She sighed openly and wished she could cry away the band around her heart.

"We need to listen well in case Mr. Carver or those other men come to the door again," Rebecca said as she placed a pot of beans on the stove to cook. "I suggest you move your bag into the bedroom, just in case."

When she returned, Lisa leaned against her elbows at the table and asked with some of her old toughness returning, "What can he do to me that he hasn't already done?"

"Turn you in to the authorities for assaulting him, I think. You wouldn't stand a chance against an adult, especially one who fed and clothed you for all those years."

"I'm sure you're right," Lisa groaned. "They en't going to believe any of the stories I could tell."

"He is the one that should be turned in but that's not going to happen."

"What'll happen to you if the slaves are found in your house?"

"You heard the man the other night: a thousand dollar fine and six months in jail. That's what the Fugitive Slave Law states. Some people have had their houses burned down while they were forced to watch."

Lisa cringed. "Why do you do it?"

"Because we believe slavery is wrong and if these people are brave enough to run away, then we feel we should help them get to safety," Rebecca said with conviction. "There were very few people around here when we built our house and shop and they were too busy with their own problems to pay any attention to us, so we got by with putting in the wall and the tunnel completely unnoticed. John's reputation grew and more people came out here with work for him to do, which was a good thing for us financially but it made it more difficult to take in the slaves."

"Tunnel?" Lisa gasped.

"Yes. There's a trap door in the floor of the shop to an underground tunnel that goes to another trap door in the floor of the stable where John keeps the wagon and the carriage. We use either the wall or the tunnel or both."

Completely wrapped up in Rebecca's story, Lisa said, "Then, the whole time I been workin' here, that tunnel's been there and you two have been hiding slaves?" Unbelievable, she thought. "I never noticed a thing."

"That just means we did a good job," Rebecca said, pulling the snacks out of the oven and setting them on the table in front of Lisa. "Help yourself. I will bet you have never had these before. My husband calls them *schnetya*."

"You're right." Lisa carefully picked one off the hot pan and popped it in her mouth. "Umm! Very good," she said as she licked the melted butter mixture running down her fingers.

Rebecca sat down across from Lisa and lowered her voice. "John has decided to move the people out early tomorrow morning before sunup. I don't know how he plans to get them out of the house yet. He will take them north to the next station in Salem and, eventually, they will get to Canada."

"How do you know if they get there safely?"

"We don't. We just do our one little part and hope the rest goes as planned."

Lisa's nerves knotted up at the thought of taking part in their plan. "How can I help?"

"John will let you know if there is anything you can do."

Lisa's curiosity was growing. "How many slaves have you helped?"

"Probably two hundred or so. But I think our time is running out. The rewards for catching runaways, and people like us who help them, can be quite profitable so there are many people drawn into the search. Sometimes they have picked up slaves who have been given their freedom and the courts have allowed these free people to be sold to new masters." She shook her head in defeat. "Last night, John and I decided to give it up. This will be our last delivery."

"That musta been a hard decision to make," Lisa said, cracking her knuckles nervously under the table.

"Yes, it was. We feel like we've been pushed into a change. John thinks he will go to the Kansas Territory after all. Like you said, they need blacksmiths out there and our going would help make Kansas free when it's ready to become a state."

Lisa finished scrubbing a potato and dropped it into the pot where carrots were already cooking. "What'll you do with this stuff when it's all cooked?"

"I'll drain the vegetables and put them in a bag with the bread and the beans and send it along with the fugitives on their journey." Lisa recognized the sadness in Rebecca's voice as she spoke.

"I've been happy in this house and I have some dear friends I will miss." She ran her fingers along the edge of her stove. "I waited a long time for this big cast iron stove and it isn't even a year old."

Lisa understood. She longed for her mother and felt the finality of her death. And she missed Cal. Oh, how she missed Cal. She found herself fighting the depression that niggled around the edges of her courage. She decided that one good thing from all that had happened was that she did not have to return to the orphanage. Also, she had a refuge for the time being. Finally, she had found a couple of positive things to help bring her spirit up.

"After Mr. Pyne leaves, I'll head into Boston. Since I'm a fast runner, it shouldn't take me too long," Lisa said.

"We don't want you to do that. I'm going to take you to the Emigrant Aid Company in our buggy after John is on his way with the fugitives in the morning. But first, we'll stop by Gabe's house to see what he can do for you."

"That's a lot more than I'd expect you to do for me."

"You've been like a son to us for all these years. We can't say daughter because we didn't see you that way then. We're accustomed to seeing you at work everyday which makes you family as far as we're concerned."

"I won't ever be able to pay you back," Lisa said.

"You already have. Now, if you'll get that knife hanging over there, you can cut up some pork for the beans."

Quiet settled in the small kitchen while they worked and pondered their own thoughts. It was getting close to noontime when Lisa broke the silence.

"There's somebody I'd like to see before I take off for Boston. He works about three miles from here. I'd like to head for there when we finish what we're doing."

Startled, Rebecca asked, "How could you possibly go out without being recognized? Carver may have people out looking for you."

"I thought I'd wear my mother's dress and, if you could loan me a head scarf or a bonnet, I think I could walk there on the open road. I'd just be a woman goin' to see a neighbor."

"It sounds too dangerous," Rebecca said.

"I'll wear my pants and shirt under the dress and, if I have to, I can shed the dress and take off runnin'."

"I know. I know." Rebecca shook her head. "It would worry me, though. Must you do this?"

Lisa leaned her palms into the table, her look pleading for Rebecca to understand. "Yes. I may never see him again and I wanna say good-bye."

"You love this man." Rebecca recognized the longing in Lisa's eyes. "May I ask who he is?"

"Calvin Hale. We grew up together at the orphanage. He'll be sixteen on Monday and can't stay at the Home anymore. Cal and I've been friends since we were five years old. He came to the orphanage a few months after I did. He found out I was a girl just last week." Lisa chuckled. "It was a real shock to both of us to find out we'd liked each other more than just a little bit for quite a while. He said he was relieved I was a girl 'cause he was worried about how much he liked me."

Rebecca smiled. "I'll bet he was."

"I know we're young but we've been through a lot together. There en't much we don't know about each other. I think we've grown up faster than some kids with normal lives."

"You are probably right about that." Rebecca stirred the pot of beans. "We're finished here for the time being but don't leave yet. I want to talk to John before you do." She headed for the front door. "If anyone comes to the door, go into the wall."

As Lisa waited, all was quiet except for an early afternoon wind that blew around the corners of the house bringing with it the scents of spring and the rustling of winter's leftover leaves as they swished against the foundation. She sat at the kitchen table and rested her head on her folded arms, her ears alert for any disturbance. The sound of horse's hooves at the back door brought her to her feet. Running into the Pyne's bedroom, she was about to knock on the wall when she heard Rebecca's voice calling her. The open doorway revealed a horse secured to the hitching post and Rebecca scuttling in with a worried smile on her face.

"I brought John's horse, Dusty, for you to ride to see your friend. You have ridden horses before, haven't you?"

"Oh, sure. That's somethin' Carver had us learn to do so we could run errands for him from time to time," Lisa answered, a bit bewildered. "But it don't seem right for me to take Mr. Pyne's horse."

"You must. It is much safer. The chance of your being recognized will be much less."

Rebecca disappeared into the bedroom and returned with one of John's shirts. "Here, put this on. I know it's big but we'll roll up the sleeves and stuff the tail into your pants. He said you should wear his hat as well."

Lisa felt like she was being wrapped in a tent as Rebecca pushed and shoved the shirt into her waistband, rolled up the sleeves to her wrists and secured the buttons. Rebecca gave her a smile and a hug as she inspected what she had done.

"You look like an entirely different person. You should get there and back safely now. You had better get on your way so you can get back before dark."

Reluctantly, but eager to be on her way, Lisa mounted the horse and headed in the direction of Dan Todburn's. She prayed Cal would be there. Her heart beat an unsteady rhythm in contrast to the steady pounding of the horse's hooves.

Cal would be surprised to see her. Her skin tingled and a warmth rose inside her with the thought of seeing him. What if he wouldn't be there? It was April fourteenth, two days before his birthday when he would turn sixteen and have to leave the orphanage. On a normal workday, she knew he would be at the stable at this time of day. *He just has to be there. But what if he isn't? What if he left the Home and changed his mind about working for Mr. Todburn? What if he's out lookin' for me? He doesn't know what happened to me after I jumped out of that window.*

A narrow trail veered off the well-traveled road she was on and she recognized it as a shortcut to Todburn's Livery. Pulling the reins to the right, she guided Dusty into the shaded pathway arched over with the fullness of oak and maple trees and lined with tall sumac shrubs. At times, she had to lower her head to avoid the branches.

Suddenly, her surroundings closed in on her and the silence wrapped itself around her head and chest, growing tighter with each breath. She felt cut off from everything she had ever known. It became difficult for her to breathe around the huge lump in her throat. She pulled hard on the reins and Dusty stopped, impatiently shaking his head and churning up the dirt beneath his hooves. Bracing the palm of her hand on the saddle horn, she leaned forward running her hand down his neck to quiet him. She embraced him and laid her cheek against his neck.

"What 'm I gonna do, Dusty? Can I make something good happen when I don't even know how to be what I am? Will anyone wanna hire me, a young girl who's lived her whole life pretending? Am I really a blacksmith? Can I keep goin' on by myself, without my ma and maybe without Cal?" Dusty whinnied sympathetically.

Closing her eyes, she tried to get hold of herself but she saw her mother's face and the memories they made together consumed her. Her mother was dead. She had no home and she was running from an angry and violent man. In the morning, she would be taken to Boston, most likely to leave for a far off place called Kansas, leaving behind the two people who were the nearest thing to family to her. The man she loved may or may not be down the road and if she found him there, it could be the last time she would see him. She had no money and she owned nothing but what she carried in her bag.

The trees drew her further into their depth, compressing her world to the small circle in which she sat quite still on the horse. There was no way to stop the flood of tears that burst through her resolve. During all the events of her life so far, she had never before felt so alone and destitute.

Dusty stirred beneath her as if he knew her tears had run out and it was time to get on their way. He had patiently waited for new directions while she clung to his neck and sobbed but now those sobs had turned to stuttering gasps for breath and he was restless to move on. Lisa sat up in the saddle and patted his neck. "Thank you Dusty. You're a good animal and a good friend."

She wiped her eyes on the full sleeves of John's shirt and let the breeze blow across her face. There had been a need to release this emotion and now it was done. There was still much to face and her future was questionable but this release gave her a stronger resolve. If Cal wasn't at Todburn's, she would look for him. Suddenly, she realized that she did have family. The Pyne's were her family and Cal was too. And maybe her father was still living and wandering around out west someplace. She would look for him. Maybe Cal would come along. The thought excited her and she clicked her tongue to encourage Dusty to move on down the road.

The end of the shortcut opened onto another sumac-lined road that meandered toward Todburn's. She urged Dusty into a gallop and in minutes they arrived at the entrance to the stables. She jumped down and threw the reins over the hitching post near the huge open doors. Her heartbeat was uncontrollable when she saw Cal cleaning out a stable at the far end. His sleeves were rolled up and she watched his muscles stretch and pull as he pitched out the urine-soaked straw.

He looked up at the sound of pounding footsteps running toward him but he didn't move. He stared at her in bewilderment and she realized he didn't recognize her.

"Cal. It's me. Lisa."

He dropped his pitchfork and ran toward her with open arms. She flew into them as easily as though she had been there many times. He picked her up and kissed her hard on the lips before he set her down.

"I've been worried out of my mind about you. And here you are. How'd you get here? Where've you been? Are you all right?"

"Wait a minute," Lisa said breathlessly, giving him a warm understanding smile. Of course, she thought. All the while she was worrying about him, he was worrying about her, wondering what had happened to her.

"I didn't recognize you in that getup. Where'd you get that shirt and hat?" he continued as he took her hand and led her to a bench in front of one of the stalls. Lisa was still reeling from the kiss and found it difficult to speak. The touch of his palms against hers revived and intensified the warmth she had felt earlier when she thought about him. She leaned toward him and returned his kiss.

"I love you, Lisa," he said and wrapped her in his arms. He let her go but kept her hand in his. "Carver's been on a rampage so I left the Home yesterday. He accused me of hiding you or spiriting you away. He's really nuts now. He's been gone most of the time so the kids are running wild. He got another cook but she doesn't try to keep any kind of order in the place. He's out to find you."

"Where are you living?" Lisa asked.

"Mr. Todburn's lettin' me stay in a room at the back of the stable."

"We're both sort of strays, aren't we?"

He squeezed her hand. "Looks that way."

She told him about her flight and Mr. Carver's rampage into the Pyne's home to look for her. Cal shook his head as she described her hiding place with the runaways and agreed to keep that a secret. He, in turn, told her why he and the other boys were with Carver and the dogs and how they steered him away from the water's edge.

"I knew you were around there some place. I was really scared thinking those dogs would find you."

"Me, too. But, here I am. Now I'm figuring out what I have to do next. Actually, I know what I'm going to do. I just have to make it happen. The Pynes are going to help me."

"What's that?"

"I'm going to go to the Kansas Territory. I can't stay here and they need blacksmiths out there. Mrs. Pyne is taking me to the Emigrant Aid Company in Boston tomorrow."

She saw the deep frown fill his forehead and the bewilderment in his eyes. "But how…?"

"I'm gonna find a way, Cal. I don't know right now but I'm gonna find a way. I have to."

"But you'd be going into something completely unknown," Cal said, his frown deepening. "I'd be worried to death about you. You don't know who or what's out there. That's no man's land."

"Well, I know what's here and I know I have to get away." She studied the concern written on his face. "I've tried to think of a place to go around here but I can't think of any. I can't stay with you or the Pynes. None of you can hide me forever."

"I can see that. But… but… you could be in danger out there, too. People could take advantage of you."

"Come on, Cal. I'm strong and I can run. I think I can take care of myself. I'd probably shock the daylights out of somebody if he tried anything with me. I en't some weak woman. There's still a tough kid inside here." She sounded more confident than she felt but if she had to, she was sure she could do it.

"How would you pay your way?"

"Mr. Pyne thinks I can earn my way and that the Emigrant Aid Company will help. He says I should trust in God so I guess I will. He and his wife are even thinkin' about going, maybe a little later on."

"Where'll you go when you get there?"

"The handbill mentions a place called Lawrence, so I guess I'll go there first. I'll try to find work and save up enough to go on west some day to look for my da. I decided that this morning." Lisa's eyes suddenly sparkled with a new thought. "Why don't you come with us tomorrow? What do you have to keep you here?"

"A job for now. I don't have one in the Kansas Territory." Feeling the palm of her hand on his cheek, his voice became pensive as he continued, "I know you can't stay here 'cause of Carver. He'd track you down for sure. This is a good job, Lisa, and I need to work to support myself. I wanna go where you go but I don't know how we'd live. Maybe I could work and save enough to come out to you with a later group."

"Maybe no one'll help me tomorrow. Then I'll have to think of something else."

"There are a lot of 'maybes' to consider," Cal said, pressing her fingers to his lips.

"I'm so afraid if we don't stay together now, we'll never find each other again," Lisa said, clinging tightly to his hand.

Cal put his arm around her shoulder and drew her to him. "Me, too. I just can't see what else to do."

"I can't either, but we can find a way if we want to bad enough," Lisa said with determination. "Think about going with me. All I'm askin' is that you just think about it. I need to get Dusty back. I've been away too long."

"Maybe I could find somebody that needs a man with a good strong back and knows horses. I guess I could go to that Emigrant Aid

Company and check on that. If they'd help pay my way, I could pay them back in work." He had allowed himself to open up to the thought and then he saw what his words had done to Lisa.

Her eyes lit up and she felt a ray of hope in what he said. "I think that's what they do. They're anxious to get people to the Kansas Territory, especially men who will vote to make it a free state. I have a skill to sell and you know horses. I think they'd be glad to help us get there. We're young and strong. Seems like that's what they'd want."

Caught up in the hopefulness of her words and the excitement in her eyes, Cal said, "I'll do it. I'll go there with you and maybe we can work somethin' out to go together. I've managed to hang on to about twelve dollars in the past ten years which would help buy some food."

"If you get to the Pyne's early enough tomorrow, you could go with us."

He stood and pulled her up by her hands. "I promise I'll do my best to get there soon as possible."

He buried his face in her hair and held her close. In the distance, the sound of a carriage moving toward the stables reached them and they quickly moved to the entrance where Dusty was becoming impatient.

"I love you, Lisa Bellamont. Be safe."

"I love you, too," she replied as she mounted Dusty and headed back down the road. She would leave a part of her heart with Cal every time they said good-bye.

CHAPTER 10

CAL LEANED AGAINST the doorframe as he watched Lisa ride away. They had held each other as long as possible but not long enough. Now she was leaving, perhaps forever. So many things could happen before the next morning. Still feeling the warmth of her cheek and the tenderness in her lips, he was sure he wouldn't survive if she disappeared from his life. They belonged together, of that he was certain but how would they make it happen? The emotion he felt for her had wrapped itself into a slipknot around his chest that pulled tighter with each hoof beat taking her into the distance. Scattered clouds of dust settled on the road as she disappeared.

His heart was pleading with his brain and his brain was losing. "We have to be together, one way or the other," he said aloud as he hurriedly turned to finish his neglected tasks only to stop short at the harsh angry shout from the hated Jonas Carver, a voice he hoped he had heard for the last time. He turned back and faced the yellow weeping wound across Carver's cheek.

"Where is she?" he hissed, clenching a whip in his fist.

Cal jumped back as though the whip were already in the air. "I don't know," he snarled.

"I-I don't believe you." The whip quivered in Carver's hand. "Y-you w-were her buddy," he stammered, sucking at the saliva pooling in his mouth "Y-you have to know where she is."

Cal continued to back away until he reached the entrance to an empty stall, never taking his eyes off the whip. "I told you, I don't know where she is," he shouted. "You chased her away and she's gone."

Carver's eyes flared as he dropped the tail of the whip, lifting the handle, ready to snap it in the air. "You tell me or I'll whip it out of you," he screamed. "Look at my face. I want that girl."

Terrified but defiant, Cal defended Lisa. "She's gone and you deserved what you got." Cal ducked into the empty stall, closing the gate just as the whip snapped like lightning, striking the gate as he dropped to his stomach and rolled against the wall shielding him from Carver.

Carver jumped atop the bench on which Cal and Lisa had so recently been sitting, fiercely cracking the six-foot whip repeatedly in all directions inside the stall, swearing incoherently through the saliva now running down his chin. The whip cracked repeatedly above Cal's head, the tip snapping at the floor sending stinging bits of straw and dust into his face. He turned his face into the wall and cowered there, cringing with every lash of the whip. Two horses that had been returned early reared frantically, their high-pitched neighing adding to the chaos.

"Put down that whip right now," Mr. Todburn commanded, his voice loud, firm and threatening.

Carver turned to face the barrel of Todburn's rifle. He stood frozen on the bench, unable to take his eyes off the man holding the gun.

"Get down and drop your whip." Todburn took a determined step toward Carver and motioned him off the bench with the end of the barrel. "Now!"

Carver's face paled and his body shuddered with the realization that he was no longer in control. He let the whip fall to the floor and stepped down. He moved away from the stall when the gun barrel pointed him toward the door.

"Nobody—and I mean nobody—comes into my place and raises havoc with my horses or my help." He directed his voice toward the stall but kept his eyes on Carver. "Cal, you can come out now. Mr. Carver is heading out and he'd better not show his face around here again. I *know* how to use this gun."

Warily, Cal peered over the top of the wall. Seeing that Carver was under control, he came out of the stall.

Carver reached down to retrieve his whip but pulled back when the gun barrel came between his hand and the floor. "But it's mine," he moaned.

"Get into your gig and I'll toss it to you. You won't use that around here again." Todburn's voice burned the message into Carver's mind as he moved out the door. He caught the whip and hurried away without looking back.

"What was that all about and what happened to his face?" Todburn asked.

"Carver's looking for somebody and thinks I know where she is."

"She?"

"It's a long story," Cal said, still shaking from his recent experience.

"Give me some highlights after we calm down the animals." Mr. Todburn took another look at Cal and added, "Looks like you need to calm down, too. That must have been scary. He didn't get you, did he?"

"No, the whip didn't actually touch me but it sure kicks up a wind, and straw feels like needles when it comes flyin' in your face. Yeah, it was scary." Settling the two horses didn't take long and soon, Cal found himself telling his employer enough for him to understand what had just happened. He included his feelings for Lisa.

"I told her I'd meet her tomorrow at the Emigrant Aid Company to check out joining the next party going to the Kansas Territory. If it's okay with you, I'd like to head into Boston after the horses have been picked up for the day and I've taken care of the stalls."

Todburn studied Cal's face. "You've worked for me for a long time. Are you thinking of leaving?"

"I'm only thinkin' about it."

"I've been thinking about going west myself. My wife doesn't want to go. Too afraid of what's out there," Todburn said remorsefully. "There's such a big movement to go that direction, seems like a good time to get into the horse trade out there." He thought about that a bit and added, "You could do that, Cal. You know all about horses and you're good with them."

"Yeah, but I doubt anybody out there would be rentin' horses. I don't know what I'd do. That's what I want to find out tomorrow."

"You sound like you've pretty much made up your mind about going."

"I want to but I don't know how to go about it. I'm sure Carver'll be after me again." Cal paused. "That's why I'd like to go to that Aid Company and see how it works. Maybe they'll help me." After another pause, he suggested, "Why don't you go with me to their office? See what you can find out for yourself."

"Got my hands full here. Are you saying you're leaving me in the morning?"

"No. I just want to check it out. I'll be back after," Cal assured him.

"By the way," Todburn added. "If Carver shows up again, you head for the house. I'll take care of him."

Sleep evaded Cal that night as his mind and heart battled. He had had no guidance on such matters as love and sense of duty—no father or mother to advise him. He had grown up under the tutelage of Jonas Carver, a man who hated his charges at the orphanage and who thought only of himself; a selfish, nasty, greedy man. Cal wondered why he, himself, hadn't turned out just like him. Perhaps because Carver had been the best example of the kind of human being Cal and the boys did not want to be.

Cal sat up and stared out the small window above his bed. Too restless to stay in bed, he stepped outside to let the crisp cool air clear his head. *If I stay with Todburn, I could probably save enough money to start a business in the Kansas Territory, now that I don't have to give Carver my wages. Then I could take care of Lisa. If I go with her now, I'll spend my time lookin' for another job out there and maybe I'll find one and maybe I won't. But if I stay, I would be in the same kind of danger from Carver as Lisa is. He has murder in his heart.*

By sunrise, Cal knew that if the Emigrant Aid Company would help him, he would go with Lisa.

CHAPTER 11

LISA PUSHED HERSELF to her elbow and listened. The night had been a long and restless one for her and it still had not come to an end. The early morning chill clung to the air and the sun had not yet invaded the night's darkness. Only the moon provided fragments of light through the rippled glass of the two windows in the room. There was movement along with the sound of voices coming from the Pyne's bedroom and Lisa realized that the runaways were out of their confinement.

Rebecca appeared at her side.

"Is it time for them to leave?" Lisa asked, sitting up and pushing her quilt aside.

"Yes," Rebecca replied. "But you and I won't leave until the sun's up. John will be ready for you to help him load the wagon shortly."

Lisa's eyes were slowly adjusting to the semidarkness as she waited for her next instruction. The fugitives had entered the room and seated themselves on the floor against the wall, their elbows resting on their raised knees. The smell of potential danger filled the room and the anxiety that had begun two days ago flared again like new kindling. Lisa wondered how the Pynes had coped with this for so many years.

Horses snorted noisily as they dug their hooves into the ground outside the front door. The sides of the large wagon squeaked as they shifted and rubbed against its deep bed. Lisa's heart nearly stopped at the sound of it. Bringing the wagon to the door was the most dangerous part of the whole procedure, John had told her the night before as he laid out the plan. Sound carried perilously during the silence of the night but it was then that they had to leave and then that the risk was greatest. On all previous movements, things had gone well but with the men hovering around his house this time, he was filled with apprehension.

"They know you are here, Lisa, so there should not be danger to you in helping me the wagon to load. If they are close by, you and I will keep them busy watching what we are doing so they will not see what Rebecca is doing."

Lisa's heart pounded against her ribs as John stepped into the house and whispered his instructions to the runaways.

"I brought my wagon to de front door. While we load it from de other side, you will sneak into the wagon. You do what my wife tells you. She will let you go, one at a time, to the back of de wagon and you slip into de space between the floor and the false bottom. It will be hard to do. You have to crawl on de ground and then slip inside. When one of you is inside, then Mrs. Pyne will let the next one go. You have to lie quiet until we get to de next station." Turning to Rebecca, he asked, "Have they taken care of their personal needs?"

"Yes," she answered. "And they have had water to drink and they each have a bag of food."

They had been whispering in the darkness but now it was time to open the door and begin moving the people out. He motioned for Lisa to follow him, turning back a last time saying, "Let's make dis quick."

Lisa had picked up on John's uneasiness causing her own anxiety to grow to paralyzing proportions as she followed him out the door. Every footstep on the gravel walk seemed to travel through the air to the next town. When she tried to tip toe, John told her to forget it. If anyone was watching, he wanted those people to focus on the two of them going back and forth from the shop to the wagon. If anyone approached them, he would deal with it. He pointed to the rifle leaning against the wheel of the wagon.

It took less than ten minutes to get the four runaways settled inside the narrow confined space. By then, John and Lisa had filled the wagon with several finished pieces of ironwork and much of his movable equipment and tools.

"Can I ask why you're takin' some of your equipment with you?" Lisa whispered.

"Our house and shop could be burned down by the time I get back. I take as much equipment of my trade as I can get in de wagon. If such a thing would happen, we have a plan always to be able to find each other. She will tell you when you go to Boston," he said, heaving the last piece onto the wagon. "Time to go."

Rebecca stood watching and waiting to hand John his bag of ham and bread. Sadness had replaced the look of anxiety in her eyes. When the wagon was full and John was ready to go, Lisa turned her back on them and walked toward the house. She did not want to see or hear their intimate good-bye.

Soon the wagon was in motion, its wheels rumbling across the hard-packed dirt road in rhythm with the steady determined beat of the horses' hooves as John and his cargo followed the night into morning. John had said it would take a good four hours to make the twelve-mile journey and it would be a long ten hours before he returned.

The silence left in the wake of the disappearing wagon put a weight on Rebecca's heart. She searched the house for anything that might be an indication of the events of the past two days. The slop jar—a sure sign to the pursuers. It had to be removed right away. An exhaustive examination of the rooms revealed nothing else. A large clumsy wooden rocker had been squeezed into a narrow space between Rebecca's pump organ and an interior wall of the parlor. It seemed out of place.

"Lisa. Help me carry this rocker into the bedroom. Hurry," she whispered. "We mustn't be here when those men come back."

Before they settled the high-backed rocker against the bedroom wall, Rebecca got on her knees and, with a slender strip of metal, engaged a small lock buried between two floorboards at the base of the wall. She tested the sliding panel and found it stable. Breathing heavily with sweat running profusely down her forehead, she pushed the chair against the wall so that one of the rockers rested over the hidden lock. She then spread a quilt across its back.

"So far, this has been a successful safeguard," she said. "Let's hope it works again." With a far away look that seemed full of memories, she glanced around the room and confided, "In the years we have participated in this so-called Underground Railroad, we have never been under suspicion. I have the dreadful feeling that our day has come."

Satisfied that there was no telltale evidence remaining, she went to the kitchen with Lisa following. Rebecca's next moves were so defined and her concentration so intense that Lisa took a seat at the kitchen table and watched in awe, waiting for a chance to help.

Rebecca slung a cloth bag over a peg at the side of the fireplace and began placing the leftover bread, a slab of bacon, the end piece of a ham, a wedge of cheese and two remaining peppermint pastries in the bag. Hooking the bag to the crook of her arm, she slipped out the back door.

Once outside, Rebecca 's heart raced furiously as she lifted the trap door to the underground cellar. She searched both directions thinking she had heard men's voices gathering like a storm in the far distance. Could just be her imagination, she decided. She knew of the gangs of men who raided houses looking for hiding places for slaves. When they found signs of participation in such activities, they dragged men, women and children out into the open and burned down their houses before their eyes. There was no one in sight and the only sound was that of a breeze whispering through the branches of the maple trees. The morning sun peeked over the treetops providing a meager light down to the foot of the cellar stairs. All seemed peaceful.

She was fifty-three years old and had aided in harboring slaves more than forty times, but she had always stayed at the house to await John's return. This time was different. She knew she had to leave. A shroud of fear enveloped her, becoming a heavy weight on her shoulders. Evil was lurking in the woods and she knew she must hurry with her task.

She added some potatoes, carrots and turnips left over from their winter stores along with several candles and matches. The bag was heavy but she heaved it over her shoulder and climbed back out into the growing sunlight. She was moving fast now and thinking clearly, grateful that she was still thin of build and strong. Placing the door back over the opening in the ground, she kicked dirt and leaves over it as a covering.

Quickly, she returned to the kitchen and motioned for Lisa to follow with her own bag to the shop and into the tunnel that would take them up again and into the carriage shed. At the other end of the tunnel, Rebecca stopped and listened for any sound from above before she pushed up on the trap door.

With her heart pounding in her ears and her nerves taut as a fiddle string, she tossed the bag onto the floor of the buggy and began harnessing the horse. At barely over five feet, it took some stretching to toss the harness over the horse's head and bring it the full length of the body. Lisa went to the other side and helped her. After securing the shafts and the traces she wound the reins around a post.

"You're a good girl, Betsy," Rebecca whispered, patting the horse's neck.

Lisa stood back and watched as Rebecca checked the small trunk strapped to the back of the buggy. A cast-iron skillet, copper saucepan, teakettle, two plates and some cutlery were wrapped in a woolen blanket. The sun was full in the sky when she finished.

"Toss in your bag and let's get going," Rebecca said. "We'll talk on the way."

CHAPTER 12

AN AMBER GLOW filled the eastern horizon as the emerging sun turned the night into a new day. At Todburn's Livery Stable, vendors noisily led horses from their stalls, harnessing them to wagons still partially filled with unsold items in anticipation of another day's struggle for their livelihood on the busy streets of the city. Cal made sure that a full feedbag was placed in each wagon and assisted in getting the mobile merchants on their way. As soon as they were gone, he moved quickly, cleaning the stalls and filling them with fresh hay for their return in case he was late getting back.

By the time he got underway, a thin cloud had moved across the face of the sun without totally blocking out the rays shooting from its edges. Believing that Lisa and Mrs. Pyne would be well on their way by now, he avoided the Pyne's house and headed straight for downtown Boston.

Two hours later, he reached Beacon Street beside the Common, the only part of Boston familiar to him. Hot, exhausted and without a clue as to where to begin looking for the Emigrant Aid Company, he snaked his way eastward through a crowd of rude bustling people, barking dogs and boisterous children playing amid a chaos unlike anything he had ever seen. Heavier horse drawn wagons dominated the street while smaller carriages and carts darted in and out among them.

He found himself distracted by the confusion and unaware that he was being edged into the lane of heavy traffic until he found himself staring at two horses coming directly at him pulling a loaded wagon. Cal leaped out of the way and fell sprawling on his back directly into the path of a horse drawn streetcar loaded with passengers, many of them clinging to its sides. Desperately, he tried to roll away from the hooves of the horses bearing down on him. Two strong hands grabbed him under his shoulders and pulled him out of harm's way but sending both men sprawling on the ground.

Scrambling to his feet, Cal bent over and grabbed his knees taking deep breaths to keep from vomiting while his stomach muscles contracted in spasms of pain and his traumatized nerves burned like needles under his skin.

"You must not be from around here," the older man said after getting to his feet and brushing the dirt off his pants. "This has to be the worst place to try to cross this street."

Still gasping for breath, Cal said, "Wasn't crossing the street. I was pushed."

"I'm not surprised. Are you going to be all right?"

"Yeah," Cal said, still quaking from the shock. On impulse, he reached over and shook the man's hand. "I can't thank you enough for savin' my life."

"Think nothing of it. Just be more cautious from now on," the man said and disappeared into the crowd.

Cal waited until he calmed down and caught his breath before he jogged across the Common to a place where he was able to cross without encountering so much traffic.

He stepped into the first doorway that stood open to the street and found it to be a small newspaper office. Three men were concentrating on a number of sheets of paper spread out across a table. He heard their musings as he leaned against the doorframe catching his breath. "If we run that story, we'll kick up an outburst of …." The man stopped abruptly when he saw Cal watching them.

"Excuse me," Cal said. "I'm lookin' for the New England Emigrant Aid Company office. Can you tell me where it is?"

The men rolled their eyes and chuckled as they examined Cal.

A man whose head was held up by a stiffly starched white collar and whose small oval lenses clung to a short flat nose said, "You look very young to have abolitionist leanings. Are you planning on heading to the Territory of Kansas to help give the slaves a safe haven?" Another chuckle entangled in a snarl, even more insolent than the first.

"Well, ah," Cal stammered, surprised at the tone of the question. "I need to find work and I wanna go west." Cal studied their faces and then boldly added, "If that helps the slaves, I guess that's a good thing."

One "Humph!" followed another as they returned to their study of the papers.

"I guess this means you en't gonna tell me how to get to their office?"

The men looked at each other and one of them shrugged. "What's the difference? He'll find it anyway, right?"

The other nodded.

"It's on Winter Street just a short distance south of here. It's Number Three, I believe." The man shrugged his shoulders again and turned back to the papers.

"Thanks for your courtesy," Cal said, unable to hide his disdain.

Cal stepped away from the door and began to run. He would soon find out if they had lied to him. He turned on Winter Street and saw the sign hanging above a door ahead announcing EMIGRANT AID COMPANY, ONE FLIGHT UP. He bounded up the stairs and found himself facing a large room full of people, some sitting on the floor or leaning against the wall, waiting their turn to speak with a man and a woman seated at a long table filled with fliers, pamphlets and forms. He smiled his relief as he caught his breath.

"Young man, if you want to talk to them, you need to sign the book up on the table," a voice said to his back.

Cal turned and looked into a pair of friendly eyes peering from under heavy eyebrows and a wrinkled forehead.

"Are you talking to me?" Cal asked.

"Yes, I am. I just thought you should know."

"Thanks a lot," Cal said as he hurried forward and placed his name at the bottom of a long list.

It would take awhile for his turn to come up but he didn't mind since Lisa and Mrs. Pyne weren't there yet, unless he had missed them. It didn't seem like there was much he could do except wait.

The room was nearly empty by the time it was his turn to step up to the table. It had taken over an hour and Lisa and Mrs. Pyne had not shown up. Had he missed them or had something happened to them? A desolate feeling crept over him and he wondered if he should go search for them; but where?

A pleasant and welcoming voice brought him out of his abstraction. "Hello. I'm Mrs. Pomeroy and this is Mr. Thompson. Have a seat and tell us how we can help you."

"Oh... Uh... Yeah," he stammered as he sat nervously on the edge of the chair offered him. "Can you tell me if a woman in her mid-fifties and a boy about sixteen have been in to see you? I expected to meet them here."

"No," Mrs. Pomeroy said thoughtfully looking at Mr. Thompson, who shook his head. "We've seen so many people, it's difficult to remember them all. I don't believe, however, that we have seen a pair that fits that description."

"Well, guess I can ask my question anyway. Uh, is there a chance you could help me get to the Kansas Territory? I've only got twelve dollars. That could pay for my food, I think."

"Do you understand what the Emigrant Aid Company is about?" asked Mr. Thompson.

"Well, I think so. I've been told you'd like to help abolitionists go to the Kansas Territory to vote to make it a free state when that time comes up."

"We don't make that a requirement but we're hoping that's what will happen," clarified Mr. Thompson.

"Well, I need work and I wanna go west and I think slavery is a terrible thing. You could count on me." By now, Cal's face was flushed and he was ready to run but his desire to be with Lisa kept him there.

"I'm not sure we can help you without knowing what you have to offer. What kind of work can you do?" Mr. Thompson asked skeptically. "You appear to be quite young to be going off alone. Tell us about yourself."

"I'm sixteen and was raised in an orphanage in Malden but I'm too old to stay there now." Cal told them of his job and Mr. Todburn's recommendation of his work with horses. "I'm a steady and reliable worker. Haven't missed a day of work in six years."

The two listeners seemed impressed but not too hopeful. Mrs. Pomeroy began leafing through a stack of forms and shook her head. "I see several farmers and a couple of traders but I don't see anyone that deals in horses. Perhaps one of the farmers could use you as a hand on his farm. They are supposed to report back here in this office on the sixteenth to pick up their tickets. That's day after tomorrow. If you can be here then, you can present your case directly to them but I wouldn't hold out too much hope. Check in with us again early that morning and we'll see if we have anything else for you if those don't work out."

"Thanks. I really appreciate your help," Cal said, turning away so that they couldn't see his disappointment.

Discouraged, he took the names of the farmers and got up to leave. Heading for the door, he hesitated and turned back. "Mind if I sit on the floor here by the window and wait a while? I'm sure my friends'll be here soon. I'll stay out of your way."

"Fine," the man replied.

Rebecca clicked her tongue against her teeth as she flipped the reins across Betsy's back. "Let's get going, Betsy."

Lisa's admiration for Rebecca had increased as she watched her through the past few days. Her poise and sense of purpose during such a time of tension and fear had an overwhelming effect on Lisa, calming her own troubled mind—a mind full of questions. What would she ask of Gabe Stanton? Help to get her on the train with a recommendation as a blacksmith? Girl or boy blacksmith? She would have to reveal her secret to him and would he want to give her a recommendation as a girl blacksmith? He would surely have some advice for her.

"I'm sure you have more questions," Rebecca said, startling Lisa out of her contemplation.

"I guess so," Lisa said. "Been wonderin' why you have the pots and pans and stuff wrapped up in that blanket."

"When John and I first started out with the underground, we bought a piece of land quite a distance from our home in Malden. We built a little house there and it is our hideaway in case we are ever found out. If we find ourselves separated, we know where to meet as long as we can get there without being followed. So far, we haven't had to use it."

"You must have been afraid a lot."

"Yes, but mostly when the runaways were hidden in our house. We lived simply and kept our things down to a minimum because we never knew when we might have to leave it all very quickly. We have tried to be prepared emotionally for that, as well."

"I think living like that'd be really hard to do."

"That's why we don't have too much of value in the house. Our main investment is in the blacksmith shop and that's why John takes as many things as he can carry on the wagon when he makes a delivery. I just wish he could have taken my new cast iron stove. I waited a long time for that. When we decided to give up our station, we thought we could start getting some things to make our life easier and our house more of a permanent home. It looks like we may have been a bit premature."

"I can't imagine what it'd be like living like that." Lisa took a deep breath and looked at the sky. "Smells like rain."

Gray clouds had sneaked in unnoticed from the western horizon and now threatened to cover the sun. Lisa usually loved the smell of a spring rain but today it dampened her spirit and sent a chill through her body. She had struggled hard to keep up her courage during the few days since her mother died but things were happening so fast.

"Once I get on that train and know where I'm goin', I'll feel better," she mumbled under her breath. The air was taking on a chill. A sense of foreboding laid a weight on her heart. Lisa prayed it would be one of those days that only brought the threat of rain and that soon the sun would be out completely again.

Rebecca was lost in thoughts of her own. "I worry so about John when he is delivering," she whispered.

The two women buried themselves deep in their personal concerns until they reached the other side of Canal Bridge that spanned the Charles River.

Knowing they would soon be at Mr. Stanton's house brought Lisa back from her dark mood and gave her hope. Rebecca led Betsy around Mill Pond to Prince Street where they asked directions. It didn't take long to discover that Gabe Stanton was not at home and would not be back from New York until some time Tuesday.

"Well," Rebecca said. "That's that."

"Now what?" Lisa asked, unable to disguise her disappointment.

"We have to think about our options. We could go back home or we could go to the Emigrant Aid Company and get some information."

"The train's leaving in three days on the seventeenth. If I don't get on it, I don't know where I'll stay until the next one leaves, if there is a next one."

"Lisa, I've lived long enough and seen enough to know that every problem has a solution. Sometimes that solution isn't what we think it should be but things always manage to work themselves out. We'll just take this one step at a time. I think the first step is to go to the Emigrant Aid Company and see what we can find out there." She hesitated and then added, "Do you have your mother's dress in your bag?"

"Yes."

"I think you should put it on. It seems like people would be more willing to take on a girl rather than a boy. Girls can help with the cooking and caring for children."

"But I don't know anything 'bout girl things like that. My mother started teaching me about being a girl but she didn't get very far with that before she died." Lisa looked down at her feet as a flush crept over her face. "The only thing I know is that I began gettin' this sickness every month and that could be embarrassing being a boy."

"Are you sick now?"

"No."

"Then get changed. We'll see what happens next. Remember, one step at a time." Rebecca stepped down into the street to wait.

It took only a few minutes to get into her mother's dress in the privacy of the covered buggy. After jamming her cap, pants and shirt into her bag, she reached for the crucifix and put it in the pocket of her dress, breathing an instant prayer. When she was finished, she held out her hand to Rebecca. "Let's go."

Rebecca clicked her tongue, flipped the reins and they moved on. Twenty minutes later they entered the Emigrant Aid Company office where Cal jumped up to greet them, his eyes riveted on Lisa.

"Lisa. Mrs. Pyne. Uh, I been waiting for you," he stammered.

He had never seen her in a dress. He wanted to take her in his arms but that sort of behavior in public would only get him into trouble. After shaking Mrs. Pyne's hand, he took Lisa's in both of his and shook it, feeling awkward and ridiculous.

"Well, Calvin," Lisa giggled. "I'm so happy to see you made it to Boston."

"I en't seen you in a dress before," he whispered. "You... ah... you're beautiful."

Lisa smiled and laughed for the first time in days. "Never thought I'd hear you say anything like that to me."

It was nearly noon by the time the three of them reached their turn. They stepped up to the table where Lisa and Rebecca were invited to take the only two chairs while Cal stood beside Lisa.

"Mr. Hale," Mr. Thompson said, looking across at Lisa and Rebecca. "I thought you were waiting for a young boy and a woman."

"Well... ah," Cal stammered, unable to come up with a reasonable explanation.

"I'm Mr. Hale's aunt and I asked him to meet me here. I just happened to bring a niece instead of the nephew I told him would be with me," Rebecca said pleasantly. "These young people want to sign on with someone to go to the Kansas Territory. Mr. Gabe Stanton is a friend of mine and my husband's and we were hoping he could help us but he is off on a journey to New York and won't be back until next Tuesday. Do your records list anyone that might take them on to work for their transit?"

While Mrs. Pomeroy leafed through the papers again, Mr. Thompson said, "As we told Mr. Hale, he is welcome to come back early on the sixteenth when the passengers arrive to pick up their tickets. He may find someone then that will take him on."

Mrs. Pomeroy spoke excitedly as she held up two applications. "Here are two widowers and they both want someone to help care for their motherless children. It appears they want someone older than..." she looked at Lisa.

"I'll be sixteen in four weeks."

"Good. Then that should be satisfactory, I would ..."

"But you will have to come early on Monday as well, for we have no way to contact them before that," Mr. Thompson interjected. "In fact, I remember they were going to look for someone in the meantime. There is a good chance they won't be successful, however."

Mrs. Pomeroy continued, "Mr. Ramsey is a farmer and Mr. Tilson is a machinist. Since you two are related, maybe one of them could take both of you."

Cal stole a glance at Lisa and saw that she was as excited about this as he was. Cal found it difficult to keep from grabbing her hand.

"In the event that none of this works out, when does the next group leave?" Rebecca asked.

"On the twenty-fourth," Mr. Thompson said.

"Let's go, children," Rebecca said, guiding them to the door. "Thank you very much for your help. They will be here on the sixteenth."

She ignored the perplexed looks on the faces of the two workers as they watched the trio leave.

"Well, what will we do now?" Rebecca puzzled aloud as the three of them squeezed into her small buggy.

Lisa and Cal stared at each other not knowing what to say.

"I know that Lisa and I could be homeless," Rebecca said. "Should we go find out?"

Betsy took it upon herself to answer that question as she began trotting toward Malden on a road so familiar to her that she needed no encouragement. She was taking them home.

Lisa took a quick glance at the sky and was glad to see that the clouds had disappeared. *It's all going to work out just fine.*

CHAPTER 13

THE SPIRAL OF black smoke coiled upward. Rebecca brought Betsy to a stop on the top of a knoll where she fearfully studied the dark rising column.

"Oh, no," she muttered. Leaning forward in her seat, she squinted in the direction of her house. "Is it my house? It looks like it's my house. It has to be my house." Her breathing came in short desperate gasps as she crumpled backward into the seat.

Lisa grabbed Rebecca's limp arm to keep her inside the buggy. "Mrs. Pyne. Hold on," she urged as Cal jumped from the buggy and raced around to Rebecca's side.

Rebecca, her eyes closed, began breathing slowly and deeply while Lisa and Cal waited anxiously. They watched as her body began to calm down and gain strength. Several minutes passed before she took one last deep breath and opened her eyes. "There now," she said, perceiving their concern. "I'll be fine. I just needed to get hold of myself. All these years, I have prepared for this day not realizing how really devastating it would be. My house is burning and maybe the shop too. Poor John will come home to this. Looks like we have a problem that needs some handling."

"What'll we do?" Lisa asked.

"That's what we will have to decide right here and now," Rebecca said, dabbing at her eyes.

Now that she seemed to have herself under control, Cal turned toward the smoke and wondered how he could help. His eyes lit up as he turned back to her. "I could go down there and see what I can find out. Maybe it isn't your house after all."

"But wouldn't that be dangerous?" Lisa asked, her nerves biting at each word.

"Nobody knows me around there. I'll just be walking by on my way to work. That shouldn't be a problem."

"If you would do that, Cal, I would be most grateful," Rebecca said with a deep sigh. "Please be very careful. We don't know what else those men are capable of doing."

"You need to pull off this road into those trees. Stay there 'til I get back. It could take me a while so don't you go and leave. I wouldn't know where to find you. Okay?" he asked, looking from Rebecca to Lisa.

They nodded and he took off running down the road. When he was within sight of the house, he slowed to a walk. He was stunned at the sight. The shop and the house were smoldering ruins and he could see that there had been no attempt to put out the fire.

He strolled up to a man standing on the property who appeared to have a purpose there. "What happened?" Cal asked.

"Who are you?" the man asked suspiciously.

"Name's Cal. I'm on my way to work."

"Where's that?"

"Todburn's Livery, but what's that matter to you?"

"We just don't want any snoops around here." The man studied Cal and changed his tone. " *Whoever* burned down this house did it because these people were caught sneaking runaway slaves into Canada."

"Wow! I heard about people like that. You catch 'em in the act?"

"Not me. But there's been talk around here for a while about these people." The man's voice became edgy and he began to walk away.

"Can't you tell me what happened?" Cal persisted.

"Well, I guess I can tell you what I know, since I happened to come by just as it was going on. The people wouldn't answer their door so we, I mean, *the men* broke in and found a sliding wall and a tunnel for hiding runaways. Well, there was no question after that."

"So, they'll come home and find this? What a shock. There's a big fine for hiding slaves, isn't there?"

"You bet. And jail time, too."

"So did you catch 'em? The owners of the house, I mean?"

"Not yet. But they'll get caught."

"Don't hardly seem worth doin', does it? Such a waste to destroy a perfectly good house on purpose. Is this what you usually do—burn down their houses?"

"Seems to be the best way to set an example. Say, kid, you're asking too many nosy questions. You'd best get moving or I'll turn you in for being a snoop, or maybe an accomplice."

"Okay, okay," Cal said, shrugging his shoulders. "Just curious is all."

He could feel the man's eyes following him as he walked away, so he headed in the direction of the livery. He would find another way to get back to Lisa and Mrs. Pyne. Depression became a meaningful word to him as he thought about the man's animosity toward the Pynes or anyone helping the runaway slaves. By the time he reached the buggy, he was determined more than ever to go to the Kansas Territory to help bring it into the union as a free state.

His return route brought him up behind the buggy. It had been over an hour since he left them and he was relieved to see that they were still safely tucked away among the trees. Mrs. Pyne was slumped in the seat, her head resting against the side of the buggy. She appeared to be asleep, but he doubted it. The seat beside her was empty. Startled, he scanned the area and saw Lisa leaning against a tree a short distance away. He opened his arms as she ran toward him. "Lisa. My heart stopped for a minute there. I thought somethin' had happened to you."

"I couldn't watch the road very well sittin' inside that thing," she said, pointing to the buggy.

Cal realized that he hadn't talked to Lisa and Rebecca about a way to defend themselves while he was gone. He had figured that if they were out of sight, they were safe. Apparently, Lisa had been fearful.

"What did you plan to do if somebody showed up?" Cal asked, more than a bit concerned.

Lisa brought her mother's crucifix from behind her back "I was gonna hold this up to stop them."

"Hold it up to them?"

Lisa caught the doubtful humor in his eyes. "Well... um... hit 'em with it if I had to. Couldn't think of anything else to do. I guess I could have fought them off barehanded," she said with a chuckle, flexing the muscles in her arms. "I sure couldn't run and leave Mrs. Pyne sitting there all by herself."

"It looks to me like it was a good thing for them that they didn't come," Cal teased.

"Okay. Have your fun, but it was scary."

"I know. I'm glad you're okay."

"What did you find out?" Rebecca had come up beside them.

He reported the things he had seen and heard.

"Did you see my new cast-iron stove sticking up out of the ashes?" she asked sadly.

"No, I didn't. They must have moved that out before they started the fire." Rebecca appeared to be unable to speak as she stared into the distance, grief settling deeply into the lines of her face. "I hope they haven't picked up John. I pray he's safe."

Lisa took Rebecca's hand and added her own prayer for John's safety. "I guess we oughta pray for our own safety, too, don't you think?"

Rebecca nodded and patted Lisa's hand. "I wonder what they did with Dusty. I should have tied him to the buggy when we left but that would have been too obvious."

"The man didn't say anything about a horse, Mrs. Pyne. Wouldn't you suppose they'd let a horse go before they set fire to a place? Maybe they took him."

"They are evil men, but I don't think they would purposely destroy a horse." She paused and studied the ground. "Our next step has been decided for us," Rebecca said, finally. "We will head for the cabin in the woods."

Cal was thoughtful and unsure what to do. "I'm thinkin' I'd best get back to work. The horses will be coming in soon. I told Mr. Todburn I'd be back to help."

"You can ride with us for a way if you like."

Cal followed Lisa into the buggy and Rebecca guided Betsy back onto the road.

"Do you want to meet us somewhere Monday morning?"

"I don't know. It's all kind of up in the air for me," Cal mused. "If I can't find someone to sponsor me, then I'll need a job here. It can't be with Todburn because old man Carver is ready to whip the daylights out of me if he catches me off-guard." Cal stared at his hands briefly, then asked, "Would you wanna tell me how to get to your hiding place when I get this all figured out? I'll be careful not to be followed."

Rebecca told him several ways to get there and described it in detail. She had not seen it for years but there was no doubt in her mind that it would still be there. She headed Betsy back down the road the way they had come.

"You'll have to walk a mile or so to get to the livery," she said. "I don't dare go too close to town. Those men are on the lookout for me, I'm sure."

When she went as far as she dared, Cal reluctantly climbed out of the buggy. He thanked Rebecca and reached up to kiss Lisa on the cheek. He did not say good-bye. His eye caught a glimmer of the shiny crucifix hidden in the folds of her skirt and he smiled.

It was an hour later when Rebecca turned the buggy into the long narrow path leading to the cabin. There were no wagon tracks to follow but the trees on each side of the lane formed an arch over their heads leading their way. Lisa could hear animals scurrying about in the woods. They hadn't had intruders for a long time.

Lisa braced her feet against the floorboard when Rebecca unexpectedly brought the buggy to a halt. "We need to go back and cover our tracks before we go on."

They worked quickly using their feet and small tree branches to spread the dirt and leaves across the betraying evidence of their entry. "That will do," Rebecca said as they climbed back in the buggy. She guided Betsy the remaining distance to the front of a small house, partially hidden by overgrown grasses, sumac and ivy. It sat quietly and serenely in the middle of the woods, unaffected by the turmoil in the minds of its visitors. Lisa was reminded of the woods behind the orphanage but there was a difference in the character of the two. There was a peacefulness here that touched her spirit upon entering this sanctuary. She touched the crucifix in her pocket and prayed, *Thanks for gettin' us here safe.*

Rebecca immediately grabbed the large butcher knife from the box in the buggy and began hacking through the growth to clear a way to the front door. Lisa pitched in to help by pulling the weeds out by hand. Twenty minutes later, they pushed the door open and stepped inside. Except for a thick layer of dust, the little one-room house was very inviting. Everything was in its place and undisturbed. Overcome by the strain, Rebecca sat down at the table and wept into her folded arms. It appeared to be her turn for a good cry.

Lisa quietly closed the door and returned to the buggy to deal with her own problems. She propped her feet on the dashboard and leaned back, getting consolation from the silence of the surrounding trees. The cry she had on the way to the livery was the first and last time she had wept since she was six years old. The boys at the orphanage had given her a good grounding in the "boys don't cry" principle. Shaming and teasing had been their method and she never forgot it. To be a boy, she was not allowed to cry.

She missed her mother desperately—the sound of her voice, the touch of her hand, her comforting smile. Her mother's death left an emptiness in Lisa's heart that would never be filled. There was so much that still needed to be shared. *I haven't even had my sixteenth birthday. How am I goin' to make it the rest of my life without you, Mama?*

A fawn poked its head out of the woods, its eyes searching the area. Weaving a bit on legs that were not yet strong enough for running, it started toward Lisa but stopped, its ears perked up, listening hopefully. Lisa listened, too, but heard nothing. She slipped out of the buggy and stood still, watching to see what the fawn would do.

"Where's your mama?" Lisa asked softly.

The fawn closed the gap between them and nuzzled the back of Lisa's hand. Cautiously, Lisa turned her hand over and gently rubbed the fawn's face with her fingertips. "Are you alone, baby? If you are, we're two of kind, aren't we?"

Suddenly aware of Betsy moving about near the house, the fawn turned and hurried fearfully back into the woods. "Hope you find your Mama," Lisa called after her. *At least I have Mr. and Mrs. Pyne for now; but for how long?* Returning to her refuge in the buggy, she began to worry about Cal finding them in this hiding place so set apart from the world. The crucifix, which she had returned to her pocket, felt warm in her hands and she prayed for guidance and safety for herself, Cal and the Pynes.

When Rebecca opened the door, Lisa hurried back to the cabin. "This is some kinda place, I mean, it's nice," Lisa said, clumsily. She wished she could say things like a lady would say them but the boy in her kept coming out of her mouth no matter how hard she tried.

"Yes, it is. It has been waiting here for eight years, just for us to use under these circumstances. Now we're here. If all goes well, John will join us tonight and perhaps Cal will find his way here, too. By the way, he is a very nice young man. I like him very much."

Lisa's heart swelled. Mrs. Pyne's approval was like getting it directly from her own mother. She eagerly helped carry the things from the buggy into the cabin. Together, they swept the years of accumulated dirt and grime out the door and wiped off the furniture. Outdoors, Rebecca primed the pump and found the water very drinkable, which was not a surprise to her as John had dug the well deep with little chance for it to become contaminated by the natural elements surrounding it.

Betsy eagerly drank from the trough John had built alongside the pump and Rebecca and Lisa filled their cups repeatedly as they quenched a thirst that had built up over the hours. Neither of them, however, had taken the time to think about the trip to Boston Monday and the danger that might lie in wait for them along the way.

Rebecca went back inside and Lisa squatted on the ground near the door to watch for Mr. Pyne or Cal to come down the path. The grandeur of the lofty pine trees, crowned in a golden glow from the disappearing sun, fed her weakened spirit. Numerous times, she had seen her mother bravely face what appeared to be insurmountable problems and saw her become stronger because of them. *Mother set an example for me lots of times. I just need to always remember them. I guess she's still teachin' me even though she's....*

Maples, oak, birch and pine trees shared the woods, their branches interlocking to form arched entrances to its secrets. She could hear birds flitting among the new leaves that filled the recently bare branches of winter dormancy. A gray squirrel sprinted across the path in front of her and stopped, sat up and stared at her, then disappeared into the darkness. Lisa chuckled at the animal's curiosity. She felt like she had entered another world and its inhabitants were inspecting her, a stranger in their midst.

Not ready to live in a dress, she had changed into her familiar pants and shirt. They had eaten a bit of the ham and bread even though neither of them had been hungry. Rebecca's worries about John kept a lump in her throat that made it hard to swallow. Lisa's thoughts were on Cal and their Monday morning attempt to get passage on the train.

Lisa quietly cracked the door and peered inside finding that Rebecca had rocked herself to sleep, her hands folded across her lap. Gently closing the door again, Lisa returned to her vigil outside, this time sitting on the narrow step and leaning against the door. There was no way she could fall asleep. It would be a long chilly night. April nights could still be cold and damp. They couldn't build a fire or light a candle so she hoped the moon would be bright; otherwise, she wondered how Cal and Mr. Pyne would find their way into this obscure refuge.

She heard her mother's words as though they were being breathed into her ear. "Whenever you are afraid or don't know what to do, kneel before the crucifix and pray for help. He is always with you." She had kept the crucifix in her hand or in her pocket since the morning and now, as she had done when escaping the orphanage, she knelt before it. The shadowy silence wrapped her in its blanket and she was comforted. "Thank you, Mama. Thank you, God." She had never learned to trust God as her mother had trusted Him but she had never faced the problems her mother had faced. *This seems to be my time to learn.*

The distant sound of heavy hooves and rolling wagon wheels cut into the night and into her dreams. She stirred and found that she had fallen asleep stretched out across the step, her crucifix still leaning against the foundation beside her. Betsy, who had been freed of her braces and left to roam the small area, whinnied excitedly and moved toward the sound. As the wagon drew nearer, Lisa jumped up calling for Mrs. Pyne.

Just as the horses appeared in the clearing, the cabin door flew open and Rebecca rushed out to meet her husband. He brought the horses to a standstill and hurried toward her with outstretched arms. They clung to each other as their private world of sorrow surrounded them. Lisa, unable to share their loss with them, hurried down the lane to cover the wagon tracks as best she could in the darkness. She was sure it was long after midnight.

Relief had replaced the deep concern on Rebecca's face when Lisa rejoined her in the cabin.

"I'm happy for you that Mr. Pyne made it here safe," Lisa said.

"He had to go a very long way around to get here and was stopped twice by some renegades roaming around outside of Malden. He's hungry and tired."

"Wow. How'd he get away from them?"

Rebecca reached for the ham and bread and laid them on the table along with the pot of cold cooked vegetables. "He showed them the barrel of his gun and they ran." She was slicing the ham when John came in.

"Well, Lisa," he said. " *Now* what do you think of dis muddle you walked into?"

"It's a lot like my own life lately, 'specially since my ma died. I made my own muddle worse when I slashed Carver." She placed a filled plate on the table in front of John.

John took a spoonful of vegetables and held it, taking time to explain, "I am going to eat and den sleep. When de sun comes up, we plan."

CHAPTER 14

WHEN CAL ARRIVED at the livery, he found Mr. Todburn busy unhitching horses from their wagons and contending with exhausted vendors who were irritable and quarrelsome after their long day on the streets.

"Glad to see you, Cal," Todburn shouted over the noise as he worked on removing the harness from the first of two large Percherons hitched to an oversized wagon.

Cal hurried into the commotion and began working on the gear of the other draft horse. Together they cleared both horses of their traces and led them toward adjoining stalls, making their way through the straw and dust stirred up by the horses hooves and blown about by a strong wind rushing through the stable. Cal's mind was clouded with thoughts of the burned house and grave concerns about Lisa and Mrs. Pyne on their way to the hideaway. He worked more from force of habit than from conscious thought about his task.

"You must have something stressful on your mind, Cal," Todburn said when they found themselves working back to back.

"I guess it shows, huh?" Cal nervously scratched behind his ear.

"Sure does."

"Will you have time to talk after we finish?" Cal asked

"Of course."

Two hours later, they sat across from each other in Cal's sleeping quarters. Cal's elbows rested on his knees and his chin on his fists. "Don't exactly know where to start," he said.

"How about starting with this morning when you left here."

"Guess that'd be the easiest," Cal said beginning with his encounter with the two men in the print shop. Todburn chuckled when Cal described their appearance and their "humphing" at him about going to the Kansas Territory. When he finished that part of his story, he said, "The people in the Emigrant Aid Office suggested I come back early Monday morning to talk to a couple of farmers who've signed on. Might be they would sponsor me and let me work off my fare when we get to the Kansas Territory."

"Sounds reasonable. I'd hate to lose you, Cal. You've been a good employee."

"I've liked my job here, Mr. Todburn. I wish you'd go too and I could work for you out there." He hesitated as he straightened up and looked Todburn in the eye. "I don't want to leave but old man Carver is out to get me and he will, sooner or later, if I stick around here."

"I've seen the bloke lurking around outside. I had to point my shotgun at him again to get him to go so, I have to agree with you about him."

"There's more. Guess I can tell you all of it. The word's probably already been spread around."

Todburn's eyes burned with anger as he listened to the story of the smoldering ruins of the house and the escape to the hideaway. "Those two women must have been frantic. I'd be frantic," he emphasized, "if my wife were alone and running from those contemptible people. What a vile thing to do."

"You'd better not let anyone around here know you're an abolitionist or you may lose your business, too. You're not hiding slaves, are you?"

Todburn thought a long time before he answered. "Have. In the past. Quit about two years ago. Made my wife too nervous."

"You're probably safe then. By the way, the Pynes had a horse. We don't know if they let it burn or if they took it. Can't believe they'd let a horse die for what its owner did."

A light came on in Todburn's eyes. "That's odd. Sam Johnson came by around noon today with an older horse and wondered if I had a use for it. He said he'd found it wandering around loose down the road here and he didn't have a place to keep it where he lives. I've known him for years but he lives on the other side of Malden and rarely shows up around this area. The whole thing was strange... him being in this neighborhood... then to find a horse... humm... just didn't seem to jibe with what I know about him."

"Where's the horse now?"

"Wonder if he took part in the burning. Hard to imagine...."

"Mr. Todburn?" Cal asked again. "Where is it?"

"Oh, yes. Hitched to the post outside my house. I didn't have a place for him in the stable. Would you know the horse?"

"Sure would. His name's Dusty. Lisa rode him over here yesterday."

They both jumped up and rushed out.

"That's him all right." Cal cautiously approached the horse making sure Dusty saw him coming. "Dusty. Remember me?" he said gently as he slowly laid his palm on Dusty's neck.

Dusty neighed and prodded Cal's neck with his nose. "Good boy," Cal said. "The Pynes are really gonna be glad to see you." Then he turned to Todburn. "Or do you want to keep him?"

"No way do I want to keep him. He's the Pynes horse and he belongs with them. I just can't imagine Sam involved in something like that. Sure goes to show you, you don't always know your friends."

"Guess I'd best finish with my story, huh?" Cal asked. When Todburn nodded, Cal continued. "I'd like to go talk to those men Monday, if it's good with you."

"Of course, but I doubt I'll see you back here. I'd be sorry about that but I understand your thinking. It'll be hard to replace you." He chuckled with a glint in his eyes, "Maybe Carver will have another boy to send me."

"Hey, that'd be fine for you. There are lots of good kids livin' there. I'm sure there are some who'd be glad to work for you."

"I was kidding but, if there are more like you, I'll be glad to take one of them. I have an idea Carver won't be making an offer, though, since I've had the gun on him twice."

"He's a greedy man. That always comes first. Show him the money and he'll forget about the gun."

"Since tomorrow's Sunday, and there won't be anyone comin' in for their horses, do you suppose I could leave tonight?"

"Don't know why not," Todburn said sadly. "Can you find your way to their hideout at night?"

"If there's a good moon, I can. Probably better to go at night, anyway."

"Guess you'll have to ride Dusty bare back... although, come to think about it, I've got an old saddle I haven't used for years. The leather's split in a couple of places. I always meant to get rid of it but I guess there was a reason I didn't. Won't be too comfortable but better than nothing, I suppose. I got an old blanket to put between Dusty and the saddle so his back doesn't get sore."

"That's more than I could expect of you, Mr. Todburn. But, I'll take it," Cal added quickly. "I've got a few dollars saved up. Do you suppose I could buy some food from your wife to take with me?"

"I'm sure but I doubt she'll take your money. Call it a farewell gift; that is, in case you don't get back."

Cal returned to his room and stuffed his belongings into his bag along with the cheese, bacon, baked beans and a large apple dumpling from Mrs. Todburn and the week's pay from Mr. Todburn. As he closed the door to his room for what would be the last time, he found Mr. Todburn waiting for him with a cup of apple brandy.

"It just occurred to me that you have a birthday Monday. Actually, my wife reminded me of it. So we'll drink to your birthday and your new life. This should help keep you awake and alert until you get there, too."

Cal had never had brandy before and it sent a warm feeling through his body, filling him with courage. "Thanks. That should do it all right."

Impulsively, he threw his arms around Mr. Todburn. "Thanks for everything."

Their conversation and his preparations had delayed his departure until well into the evening. He mounted Dusty and headed down the dangerous and unknown road he had chosen to take. He had forgotten all about his birthday. On Monday, he would be sixteen; a man on his own with only one person who cared for him. He knew in his heart that he and Lisa were meant for each other and that he had made the right decision to join her. He would soon be with her, perhaps for the remainder of their lives.

He turned down an unfamiliar road and painstakingly reviewed the directions he'd been given earlier that day. The moon cast a chalky glow, slightly illuminating the way before him and creating ghostly images among the trees that often overhung the path. He set his eyes straight ahead and spoke soothingly to Dusty—and to himself—while watching for unexpected movements and listening for unusual sounds.

CHAPTER 15

A TRANQUIL SILENCE filled the little house and stretched its breath across the clearing in which it stood. Even the animals of the woods seemed to be at rest beneath a moon that cast a milky glow through a thin layer of clouds. Betsy and the draft horses had succumbed to the restful peace enveloping the sanctuary and slept at their tethers.

Dusty and Cal merged into this scene, tired but relieved to have made the journey without incident. At the familiar sight of the other horses, Dusty shook his head and nickered excitedly.

"Shhh! Quiet boy. Don't wanna wake anybody up," Cal whispered in his ear while rubbing his palm along Dusty's neck. "Shhh!"

Dusty settled down at Cal's touch. Cal lapped the reins around the tether post and removed the saddle. "You don't need to wear this thing all night," he whispered and Dusty thanked him with a warm nuzzle. Cal placed the bag of food on the step and the bag with his belongings under his head as he dropped onto the grass next to Dusty. "We'll just rest here until someone wakes up," he said as sleep overtook him.

Rebecca stepped out the door into the early morning sunlight and nearly fell over the bag of food on her way to the outhouse.

"Cal!" she shrieked. "And Dusty!"

Her cry brought Lisa and John to the open doorway.

Lisa dashed to Cal's side as he sat up, rubbing his eyes. He squinted at her, trying to wake up and remember where he was. Lisa fell to her knees beside him and threw her arms around him. "You got here. You made it. I was so worried and here you are." She squeezed his neck and kissed his cheeks. "Oh, my," she said, glancing up at the Pynes. "Sorry. Guess we shouldn't… well… you know… this…."

"Oh, for goodness sakes," John said. "We know you are glad to see each other just like Rebecca and I were last night."

Rebecca excused herself while John ushered Cal toward the door. "Just a minute," Cal said, as he retrieved the bag of food.

"When did you get here?" Lisa asked.

"I've been here a couple of hours, I guess. It's hard for me to tell. I fell asleep right away."

"You must be tired and hungry," John said.

"Yes, to both. I brought some food to share. Mrs. Todburn sent me off with a good-sized bundle."

While they shared their rations, Cal told them about Dusty and about what he planned to do.

"Rebecca and I plan to sign up with the Emigrant Aid Office on Monday so neither of you need to worry about your fares. What we do need to worry about is how to get a wagonload of smithing equipment, a buggy, and four horses into Boston and on dat train without being seen by those scoundrels who are after us."

Cal's eyes were heavy. "Would any of you mind if I curled up someplace and get some more sleep? I've only had that short time out there on the ground since before sunrise yesterday."

"Young man, you go right over there on that bed and close your eyes," Rebecca ordered. "I doubt we'll bother you much with our conversation."

"Thanks," Cal said, looking at Lisa for her approval.

"Get goin'," she urged and waved her hand toward the bed, watching him stretch across it and pass out immediately.

"Don't think we'll hear from him for a few hours," John said. "Wish we had some coffee but, since we don't, we will have to think sharp without it. We have the whole day to come up with a plan so I think I will start by finding me a tree to lean against and put my brain to work."

"Me, too," Lisa said. "We've got things to get done and just so many ways of doin' them. I guess we can put 'em all in a row and then pick and choose later."

"I'll do my thinking in here in my rocking chair," Rebecca said. "It just seems like there's not enough time to get everything going by the time the train leaves on Tuesday." She shook her head and sat down to begin rocking. "We don't have enough food to last until the next train on the twenty-fourth so we have to go Tuesday. Somehow, we're going to have to get our money out of the Malden Bank Monday. Can't leave that here. There are the horses, the buggy and…" She leaned her head back, closed her eyes and began rocking.

"Well, Rebecca, you certainly have given us more than a plateful to think about," John said and stepped outside to find a tree. Lisa followed him.

The sun was about to reach its high point of the day when John stood up, stretched and climbed into the wagon. Soon he was stooping and lifting and shifting things around. Lisa heard the shuffling and walked up the wagon's tongue to see what was going on inside.

"I doubt I can take these heavy iron pieces on the train so I'm sorting my farrier tools from the forge tools. They are mostly too big and heavy but I think I can manage some of the smaller ones like these pincers, a couple of rasps and even this paring knife. Oh, and this." He held up a long thin handle of metal with a long tassel of horsehair attached at one end. "I'm sure there are flies out there so I better take this fly switch." He smiled, mischievously.

"I don't see why you can't take it all," Lisa said. "Seems like you could do this sortin' after you find out how much weight you can take. All this stuff will be in the wagon anyway when it goes into the boxcar. Won't take up any more space than the wagon."

"You're making a lot of sense, Lisa. I'd hate to have to buy all new equipment when I get there."

"Hope I'll be workin' for you," Lisa said, squinting up at him.

"Of course you will, Lisa. Of course you will."

"Can I help?" Cal had come up unnoticed. "I'm ready to pitch in."

John jumped over the side of the wagon to the ground. "What I would like to do is change the appearance of the wagon. It's probably one of the most recognized wagons around the Malden area, since I've made shop deliveries in it for years."

The three of them moved back away from it and studied its features.

"I see one thing that would change it drastically," Lisa said. "Remove the false bottom. With that wood, we could build another seat behind the driver's seat and it would look like a wagon for a farm family."

"That is a very bright idea," John said, studying the sides of the wagon. Climbing back inside, he rummaged around his equipment and handed down a crowbar and two hammers, one of them with a claw. "These tools should help us get that job done without too much trouble."

With John and Cal on opposite sides of the wagon prying out the nails and Lisa under the wagon pulling down the boards as they were loosened, the false bottom was removed in less than an hour.

"Well, dat went well," John said, brushing the dirt from his shirt as Lisa crawled out from under the wagon sputtering and covered with dirt and dried disintegrated refuse from the years of hauling people in the tight enclosure. She ran toward the pump with Cal at her heels. Cal began pumping and Lisa put her head under the running water, using her hands to splash her face and wash out her hair.

"That was disgusting," she muttered to Cal as she opened her mouth and took in a huge draft of fresh air.

The false bottom lay in strips on the ground at their feet. Rebecca found them pondering how to cut the wood to fit across the wagon for a seat.

"We can measure it with my traveller but then how do we cut it?"

"Well," Rebecca said, "if it doesn't have to look smooth and perfect, you could try my kitchen bone saw. I wondered why I threw that in at the last minute. This must be why." She looked at John for approval and when he nodded, she went to get it.

"I guess you can use your files or rasps or whatever else you have there to work on the edges. Of course, I know they are for use on your metal but you can give them a try. After all, we're kind of primitive right now," Rebecca added with a chuckle.

"We appreciate dis, Rebecca," John said. "Probably won't be any good for cutting up meat bones after we finish."

"I don't care. Just get this done."

After some bruises and cuts and a lot of hard work, they finally wedged the seat into the sides of the wagon and stood back to survey their work.

"Jump up there, Cal, and see if de seat will hold your weight."

"This is great," he called from his perch behind the driver's seat.

"It doesn't even look like the old wagon," Rebecca said. "Now all we have to do is figure out how we can get ourselves safely to Boston. Come inside and we'll have a bite to eat and talk about it."

CHAPTER 16

A LAYER OF gray clouds hid the morning sun as John and Cal hitched the draft horses to the wagon. Betsy shifted restlessly in her traces nearby, responding to Rebecca's sad words and gentle stroking. Dusty tugged anxiously at the rope securing him to the back of the buggy. They had worked well into the night completing their plans and now they were ready to carry them out.

John took a deep breath of the fresh morning air in an attempt to control the anxiety swelling up inside of him. So much responsibility rested on his shoulders. So many "ifs" were involved in what they were embarking on. Lives were actually at stake in their venture into the unknown. He was very aware that the others looked to him for strength and guidance. Could he live up to their expectations?

"Smells like a spring rain is coming but de clouds don't look very threatening. It would be more encouraging if we had some sunshine." Trying to relieve the tension, he turned toward his wife and asked, "So, Mrs. Pyne, how do I look? Do I look like a young man again?"

"Well now, Mr. Pyne. You do look younger," she said, tilting her head to the side and giving him a flirtatious grin. "With your hair trimmed and thinned out, Cal's cap almost fits your head." She reached up and pulled it down a bit more on his forehead.

"I feel rrridiculous. But if you think dis will work, then I feel sure dat it will," John said, nervously slipping in and out of his German accent.

Lisa chuckled. She had always loved the way he rolled his r's. She had tried it from time to time but couldn't get her tongue to vibrate against the back of her teeth the way his did. Maybe you have to be born German to make it work, she mused.

"Check to see if anyone you know is in the bank before you go in, especially that Sam Johnson," Rebecca instructed. "But he's probably too busy chasing after people like us and burning down their homes to be out on the street at this hour."

Lisa was sure they could hear the unsteady beating inside her chest as she twirled to show her costume for approval. "With your long shawl covering my mother's dress, nobody will know me either, 'specially since you pinned my hair back like a lady's and loaned me your bonnet," she said, pulling the shawl more securely around her shoulders. "Course, old man Carver's the only one looking for me and he won't recognize me in this getup." Lisa looked at John and chuckled, "I feel r-r-ridiculous, too."

"Well, you don't look ridiculous," Cal said coming around the side of the wagon. "You look very pretty to me."

Lisa felt a blush spring to her face. "Come on, Cal. It's me, remember?"

He slipped his arms around her and pulled her to him. "My best buddy is now my sweetheart. Can you believe that?" he asked, looking at the Pynes.

"Unbelievable, but it's time to get on our way," John said sorrowfully, hugging Rebecca and climbing into the buggy. Lisa climbed in beside him and they disappeared down the dark pathway to the main road. Their plans were to pick up their savings money at the bank in Malden and, with luck, sell the buggy and Betsy to John's friend, Cyrus Matson, a carriage dealer. They would then head for Boston on Dusty and meet Rebecca and Cal at the Emigrant Aid office.

Cal and Rebecca boarded the wagon with Cal taking the reins. He had made friends with the horses and they responded willingly to him. John's tools and the bags with their personal belongings, along with the remaining food, were riding in the bed of the wagon.

"This en't gonna be too comfortable for you, Mrs. Pyne," Cal said.

"If my husband can ride this thing for hours on end, I can certainly take it as far as Boston," she said, straightening out her full skirt beneath her and propping her feet up on the footboard. "Let's get moving."

"Right," Cal said as he clicked his tongue and turned the horses toward the path to the road.

"It's too bad that your husband's hat is too big for me so I'm the only one that hasn't been made over. Carver's the only one looking for me so that's a chance we'll take. He wouldn't expect me to be ridin' a wagon like this with a woman like you." He looked at Rebecca out of the corner of his eye and said, "No offence, Mrs. Pyne, but he wouldn't be expecting you and me to be together. By the way, you don't look so different to me."

"Let's hope none of those horrible men who burned my house down recognize me." She reached up and straightened the glasses perched on the end of her nose. "I don't need these specs except for my knitting and reading but I thought I'd wear them as a distraction. I can hardly see a thing five feet away from me with them on. I thought braiding my hair and turning it into a bun might change me a bit, too."

"I guess so. If I wasn't so close to you, I probably wouldn't recognize you."

They had come out to the road at the end of the narrow path. A glance in each direction revealed a quiet emptiness giving them the courage to proceed. There was no sign of John and Lisa.

"Things are going to work out fine in the long run, Cal. I just feel it in my heart."

"What do you suppose is gonna happen to your little house?" Cal asked.

"I don't know. Maybe someone will discover it some day and wonder who lived there. They'll find a bed, a table and a rocking chair. I imagine they will spend some time spinning tales about the unknown people who left them there. I'd love to hear their stories."

"Might be, if you ever come back to Malden, it'll still be here waitin' for you."

"I can't see that happening," she said with a sigh. The depth of her heartache filled her eyes and Cal turned away, not knowing what to say to ease her pain.

They rode along in silence, each with their own thoughts but on the alert for any unusual movement on the road or in the woods. They would head south as far as possible before turning east, keeping a good distance from Malden.

Cal felt like an anvil was riding on his heart. There were so many negatives in what Mr. Pyne and Lisa were attempting to do in Malden and no assurances that they would make it to Boston. It had been Mrs. Pyne who insisted that Lisa should be the one to go with her husband rather than herself. She was sure that she and John would be recognized if they were together. It had been hard for Cal to separate himself from Lisa in this dangerous situation, but he reminded himself that the Pynes had already lost so much and still faced the chance of losing each other.

Mrs. Pyne's voice startled him. She had removed her glasses and was staring down the road. "Those two horses coming toward us just came out of that path in the woods up ahead. The riders look very young from here. We'll just nod a 'good-morning' and keep on going. Just stay calm."

"I will," Cal said as he raised his fingers to his forehead and nodded saying, "Mornin'."

Mrs. Pyne smiled at them even though a slipknot was tightening around her throat as she studied their expressions.

One of the young men turned and rode along side Cal while the other inspected the wagon.

"Where ya heading?"

"Into Boston. Where you headin'?" Cal asked.

"None a your business."

"Right. Just tryin' to be neighborly, same as you."

"What's in the bundles?" asked the man inspecting the wagon.

"That," Cal said, "is none of *your* business."

"Stop the horses," ordered the youth at Cal's side reaching across to grab the reins. Cal tightened his hold on the reins and slammed his elbow into the boy's arm causing the horses to rear back and dig into the road. The boys moved back while Cal calmed them down.

Rebecca's hand slipped inside the folds of her skirt.

The two boys moved in again, one of them grabbing the reins and sending Cal backwards into the wagon.

Rebecca jumped up. "Drop those reins and don't either of you touch those horses or one of you is going to carry the other one home," she shouted. "This gun is loaded and I'm not afraid to use it."

Startled, the boys raised their hands, recognizing the anger in her eyes and the steadiness of her hand as she pointed the barrel at the boy nearest to her.

"We was just funnin' with you. We don't have any guns."

"Well, I do and you are looking into the barrel. Which one of you wants to take the other one home?"

"Don't shoot. We're leavin'." They kicked their heels into their horses' sides and sped back the way they had come, never turning back to see what was happening behind them.

"See that you don't come back," Rebecca shouted after them, keeping the gun on them until they were out of sight.

Cal picked himself up and slid back onto the seat. "He took me by surprise. Lost my balance," Cal said trying to hide his embarrassment.

"Are you all right?"

"Hurt my dignity some is all. Makes me mad I didn't see it comin'. It won't happen again." Cal looked at Rebecca in awe. "You were ready for them, though. You were so... so..."

"I wasn't so anything, except scared," Rebecca said, settling back on the seat and laying the gun down beside her. "Just a couple of kids looking for a thrill; renegades in the making." She made a fist of both

139

hands and took several deep breaths. "Never know what people like that are willing to do."

"Yes, Ma'am," Cal said with deepened respect for her. He cleared his throat and asked, "Would you really have shot one of them?"

"My husband taught me to use this gun for a reason. I've never had to use it but if they had tried to take our horses or hurt us, yes, Cal, I would have shot one of them and I meant for them to know it. The one that pushed you over—I pointed the gun right at his forehead. He moved fast."

"You really set my heart to racin' when you pulled it out. I didn't have any idea you had it."

"There was no need for you to know about it. John decided I should carry it. He took the rifle. We intend to get on that train tomorrow," she said with renewed determination.

Cal's heart was slowing down and for a short while he had forgotten about the weight on his heart. The horses were calm and plodding along steadily and evenly again. "Let's hope they don't go get help. We're still a long ways from the Emigrant Aid Office," he said with a deep sigh.

"Let's hope John and Lisa get there to meet us."

John and Lisa sat quietly in their buggy outside the bank waiting for someone to unlock the door and open it for business. A scattering of people was appearing in the area and John imagined they were employees of the businesses along Pleasant Street. He leaned back as far as he could into the buggy seat and pulled his hat down over his eyes leaving just enough visibility to see who came near the bank.

"I'll watch de people and you watch that door," John said, pointing to the front of the bank building.

Lisa saw someone move past one of the windows inside the bank and watched anxiously, hoping that person was on the way to open the door. Her nerves were as tight as a kite string in a high wind and growing tighter with each minute of waiting. She felt like she had lived another entire lifetime since her mother died. At the orphanage, time had passed quickly, especially on the days she worked for Mr. Pyne, but now, as she anxiously waited for this danger to pass, time seemed to stand still and that tragic Wednesday seemed an eternity ago.

At last, someone opened the door, stepped outside and looked around. "Mr. Pyne. It looks like the bank is open now."

The bank employee stepped back inside and John sat up, pushing his hat back up on his forehead. He studied the street in both directions and found it satisfactory. "I will be back as soon as I can. Remember, if anyone comes to you, it is best if you act like you can't speak. If something goes bad, you come into de bank."

"I'll be fine," she said, wrapping her hand more tightly around the crucifix inside the folds of her skirt. "Besides, remember I'm tough. You haven't forgotten the muscle I built up over the years working for you, have you?"

"But now you wear a dress."

"Yeah. Wouldn't it shock somebody if a woman knocked him out?" Lisa couldn't hold back a chuckle. "Besides, I got my pants and shirt on underneath for riding behind you on Dusty after we sell Betsy and the buggy."

"Looks like you thought of everything." John grinned and headed into the bank. He removed Cal's cap when he passed through the doorway.

Lisa watched him until he disappeared and then vigilantly observed the comings and goings of the people on the street. She felt like she was walking a tightrope without a balancing pole.

"Mrs. Pyne?" Lisa felt his warm breath behind her ear and lurched toward the sound with her crucifix raised, ready to strike. He had come from behind the buggy without warning and nearly stopped her heart.

"Hold on there, miss," he said, grabbing her wrist. "I didn't mean to startle you. I thought you were someone else."

She jerked her arm from his grasp.

He stepped back and surveyed the horse and buggy, leaving her space to jump to the ground. She gripped her crucifix threateningly but didn't speak. She gasped for air, thumping her chest with her palm as she imagined a frightened speechless person would react. She wasn't much of an actress but she was sure her face and eyes had shown surprise and fear, because that was real.

"You can settle down now. You didn't get hurt," he said sardonically. "I had every reason to believe this rig and that animal tied behind it belonged to John Pyne, the blacksmith. Does this belong to him?" His question had a definite threat in it.

A few guttural sounds convinced him that she was unable to speak.

"You can put that cross down now. You wouldn't want to hit anyone with that anyway, would you?" He tried to grab it from her and it dropped to the ground.

Lisa shook her head vehemently, pushing on his chest to get him away from her. A gathering of people began moving in on him.

"What do you think you're doing, Sam?" a man in the group asked.

"Just trying to talk to her. She's crazy as a loon. She tried to kill me."

"Sure she did, Sam," another man spoke up. His sarcasm was supported by chuckles from the other witnesses to the incident.

"Think what you want," Sam said and walked away in frustration.

"Are you all right, young lady?" asked a man in a black bowler hat and a black woolen business suit.

She nodded and mouthed a "thank you."

He helped her back into the buggy and handed the crucifix to her. He headed for the bank door while the gathered people disappeared in several directions.

Shortly, John came out of the bank, hopped into the buggy and clicked his tongue at Betsy. "That was Sam Johnson."

"I figured it was. For a while there, I wasn't sure I'd get out of that predicament without giving him a serious sock in the jaw. The man in the bowler hat helped."

"That was de bank president. When he came inside, I could see he was disturbed by what happened. He was still talking about it when I walked out."

"I guess you got your business done in there."

"Yes, I did. Now we need to get rid of this buggy and Betsy," he added sadly. "Sure do hate to leave her. Rebecca loves her horse. She's still got a lot of life in her. Someone else will get to enjoy her now."

"That man really made me jump. He sneaked up on me from the back of the buggy. I thought my heart would stop."

"I saw it all through the window, Lisa, but I couldn't come help. You handled it very well. I'm proud of you. I truly think you're strong enough to have knocked him out if you had tried."

"I almost did when I heard 'Mrs. Pyne' and felt his hot breath behind my ear."

"I think we are lucky you didn't. That might have brought more attention on us than we want. It's over so now we will move on to de next phase and hope we meet up with Rebecca and Cal later today."

Lisa leaned back in the seat, remaining vigilant. She tightened her hold on the crucifix hidden in her skirt intending to pray but she noticed that the front had

pivoted slightly away from the back. She squeezed but the pieces refused to go back together. Not wanting to answer any questions at the moment, she kept it in the fold of her skirt and ran her fingers along the edges and felt something protruding from the beam. It felt like the edge of a piece of paper. *This is strange. Who could have put something inside? It could be a letter but from whom?* She was told that her father had given the crucifix to her mother before he left for the West. She would have to wait until later to see what it was but the mystery was distracting her from her current concern. Using her fingernail, she pushed the edge of the paper back inside and found that the parts moved smoothly back together with a click. She was not ready to share this discovery with Mr. Pyne.

She closed her eyes and prayed for a miracle.

CHAPTER 17

AFTER SOME GOOD-NATURED haggling, John and Cyrus came to an agreement on a price for Betsy and the buggy.

"She has a few years on her but she's a good horse, Cy. Rebecca is very fond of her and it broke her heart to say good-bye."

"Tell Rebecca that I'll either keep her or make sure she goes to a good home."

"She'll be glad to know that."

"I can't believe you're leaving us, John, but under the circumstances, I can understand." He lowered his voice and added, "Who knows. I may be next."

"We had already decided to stop. This was going to be our last delivery but it turned out to be one too many," John whispered. "If you ever get out to de Kansas Territory, look for us in Lawrence. That is where we will be, if we make it safe out of this town." He leaned closer to Cyrus' ear. "Watch out for Sam Johnson. He's de one who took my horse to Todburn's livery. He said he found it roaming around. Sure! He took it there after burning down my house."

John swung himself onto Dusty's back. "We need to go. Rebecca and Cal will be waiting for us in Boston."

"Safe journey to you, John; to you and yours." He raised two fingers to his forehead in a farewell salute. "God go with you."

John returned his farewell and Lisa nodded as John pulled her up behind him. She straddled the horse with some difficulty until she pulled the long skirt up to her waist and tucked it in under her thighs. Her pants and shirt had come in handy more than once since she left the orphanage, but so had her mother's dress. *It will sure be a relief to be one or the other. Am I a boy or a girl? Mostly a boy, I think. I'll need a lot of help to make me a girl.* She closed her eyes and leaned her forehead into John's back.

It was well into the morning and the day had turned bright after all with only spotted clouds remaining. A robust breeze brought them the richly laden salty air from the Atlantic Ocean causing Lisa to wonder what Kansas dirt smelled like. They crossed into Boston on the Charles River Bridge and found themselves on Prince Street. The street was bustling with carriage and delivery wagon traffic. Dusty reared his head and shied as John sought a way through the flow.

John leaned down and stroked Dusty's long neck. "You're not used to so much traffic, are you my boy," John said gently while guiding the animal to Winter Street in search of the Emigrant Aid office. "That must be it up ahead," he said as they turned and saw horses and wagons lining the street, apparently belonging to the people gathered in front of one of the buildings.

"That's it. That's where we were Saturday."

The congestion made it difficult for moving traffic to wend its way through. As John and Lisa approached, they felt the restlessness in the air.

"Do you suppose all those people are waitin' to pick up their tickets for the train tomorrow?" Lisa wondered aloud.

"I don't know. Um... de wagon... I don't see our wagon, do you?"

Riding high on Dusty's back, they had a good view over the heads of the crowd, but the wagon didn't appear to be there.

"I thought they would be here already," John said, his forehead turning into the worried frown he'd been wearing a lot lately. "Let's get down and see what is going on."

Lisa jumped off the horse, pushed her skirt down to cover her trousers and tucked the wayward strands of hair under her bonnet. She caught her reflection in the watering trough that had taken

Dusty's interest. She was startled to see a young woman looking back at her. Was that who she was or was becoming? This was the first time she had seen herself dressed as a girl, but it was only the clothing that made her that. Who was she really? The tough boy Lee or the blossoming soon to be sixteen-year-old girl Lisa? The girl part of her had begun to reveal itself, but would she ever truly become one? She heard John call her name and hurried to catch up with him.

As they neared the Emigrant Aid Office, they saw that the crowd wasn't as large as it first appeared to be. John suggested that Lisa stand at the end of the line while he went in search of Rebecca and Cal. Lisa recognized the fear in his eyes and felt it herself. Cal and Rebecca should be here. Even though the sun's mid-afternoon rays were bright and warming, Lisa felt a chill. Was someone watching her? She pulled her bonnet further down on her face and crossed her arms as though that might provide some protection. Again, she was grateful for the deep full pocket her mother had sewn onto the outside of the dress for carrying things around the kitchen as she cooked. Her crucifix lay there providing some encouragement as it rested against her thigh.

She could feel the presence of people lining up behind her but she hesitated to turn around and look. John had disappeared from her view so she kept her head down and trusted that he would return soon. A scuffle broke out at the doorway and a man shouted, "Hey, you. You can't break into the line. We're all waiting."

John's voice came loud and clear so all could hear. "I am not trying to get ahead of you. I'm looking for my wife and nephew. They should already be here in line."

"Well, go take a look and then make sure you go back to the end of the line if you don't find them," the man warned. "We'll be watching you."

"Fine. Good. You do dat," John retorted as he stepped through the doorway.

The line moved forward as a number of people came out of the building. John was not far behind them. Worry about Cal tugged at her heart and her pain was mirrored in the deep furrows across John's forehead as he approached her.

"They are not in there. De people in charge tell me they have not been here yet."

"Then something must have happened to them," Lisa said anxiously.

They kept their place in line as the crowd dwindled and the afternoon began fading away.

John's frown deepened. "I do not know what is best to do. Wait longer or go search. But where?" John's voice broke as he spoke.

Lisa took his arm reassuringly. "Maybe they had trouble with the wagon," she said without feeling the reassurance she tried to convey to him. "They know we're here so, no matter what happened, this is where they'll come. I think we oughta wait here."

They were moving into the room with only five people ahead of them when John mused, "Maybe I should go ahead and get our tickets and a place in de freight car for de wagon and horses. Then we have until morning to find them." John studied her face. "What do you think?"

"Ask if you can get your money back if you don't make it on the train."

"Good idea." At his turn, he stepped up to the table and asked the question.

"Yes, but you can also exchange them for tickets on the train leaving next week," Mr. Thompson said.

"I don't have a choice," Lisa reminded him quietly. "I can try to get a place with that couple the lady told me about that want someone to help with their children."

"We have just as much need to get away as you do," he whispered.

The decision was made and the tickets were purchased. They were told that there was very little room left in the freight cars but that their wagon and three horses would probably still fit.

"The passengers are all responsible for feeding their own stock. Have you made arrangements for that?" Mrs. Pomeroy asked.

"No, Ma'am. Is there a place to buy feed for them along de way?"

"If you get to the train early tomorrow, like around four in the morning, there will be someone there to sell feed, but it will go fast."

"We will be there," John said and added under his breath, "if we can find de rest of our family."

Outside, they found a place to lean against the building and wait. Lisa thought of Cal as she watched a rag wagon fight its way through the flow of vehicles and people. The ragman called out his wares. " Rags, here. Get your rags here. Rags for everything. Every purpose. Here. Here." His voice traveled above the pounding hooves and rolling wagon wheels. Ignored by the crowd, he continued to hawk his wares. Could be that Cal had taken care of the ragman's horse at Todburn's. The thought caused a swelling in her heart. She closed her eyes to keep unfamiliar tears from seeping out.

"Lisa. Mr. Pyne. Lisa." Her eyes sprung open and she searched in the direction of the familiar voice. Jumping off the rag wagon was Cal—alone.

"Where is my Rebecca?" John asked, his frightened eyes following the ragman's cart.

Lisa recognized the frustration and worry pouring from Cal's eyes. Then she saw the blood glaring at her from the front of his shirt. "Oh, magod. What happened?" There was no question Cal was exhausted to the point of collapse.

"Mr. Pyne," she said. "Look."

John saw the blood and paled, grabbing the post tethering Dusty. "Where is Rebecca?"

"She is all right, mostly."

John grabbed Cal's arm. "What do you mean by mostly?"

"Mrs. Pyne is still on the other side of the Charles. We were attacked by six renegades." He stopped to catch his breath. "You'll have to excuse me. I ran all the way across the bridge and into Boston until I saw Mac and he gave me a ride this direction." He patted Dusty and leaned against him for support.

"Rebecca is alive?" John's voice broke.

"Yes, Mr. Pyne. I think she has a broken leg and I couldn't get her here by myself." Pausing again, he seemed to be getting his breath back. "We were going to hide her in the woods to wait while I came to get you, but then she remembered the Harver's that you did some work for. We were 'bout a mile from their house. It took me a while, but I got her there. She was in a lot a pain when I carried her so I found a stick she could use as a cane and she hopped on one leg with her arm around my neck." He laid his arms across Dusty and pressed his forehead against the horse's side. He took several deep, steadying breaths while John tried to be patient.

"Were de Harver's home?"

"She and her son were. The boy went for the doc and I took off for Boston to find you."

"Tell us what happened."

"They took the wagon and everything in it. They surprised us from behind. They were on foot and jumped into the wagon before we knew what was happening. They were rough. They pulled us over the side of the wagon to the ground. She didn't have a chance to use her gun. They took that away from her, too."

Lisa dared to speak up now. She couldn't hide her concern any longer. "What's the blood on your shirt? Do you need a doc?"

"Naw. I scraped my chest on the side of the wagon when I went down. Mrs. Harver cleaned it up with some kerosene. It didn't bleed much."

"Do you know who they were?" John asked.

"Not by name, but we ran into two of 'em earlier and Mrs. Pyne scared 'em away with her gun. I guess they went for help."

The street was quieter now as many people had moved on and shops were closing. Lisa clutched Cal's hand. There wasn't anything she could say.

"We need to find a place to stay tonight. Before all this happened, I thought we would spend de night at a place called de Lowrey about a fifteen minute walk from here." John paused and tapped a fist against his thigh. "Things have changed now. I have to find a way to get Rebecca here tonight. We have train tickets for tomorrow."

"What about your friend Gabe Stanton?" Lisa asked. "Maybe he's back from New York. He told you he'd help you if you ever decided to go to the Kansas Territory, didn't he?"

"You must have been listening while you were working," John mused aloud.

"Well... yeah. The things he told you made me wanna go out there long before I ever had to escape this place."

"He lives several miles from here, but Dusty could get me there fast. I am sure he would loan me a cart or buggy to get her back here." John stroked Dusty's side thoughtfully. "We can't all ride Dusty... so...." John looked at them for help.

"Cal and I can walk to Stanton's or we can wait for you around here someplace. Whadya think, Cal?"

"Waitin' is fine with me." He wrapped his arm around Lisa's waist and added, "Yeah. We'll be just fine."

John was deep in thought. "It will be dark soon and I need to be on my way. I have a lot to do and what I have ahead of me could take most of de night." He pulled out his money pouch and pulled out three dollars, handing them to Lisa. "It would be best if you two go to de Lowrey and rent a room. We will get there some time before morning, if all goes well." He shook his head. "I have to believe it is all going to work out for us." He looked at Lisa. "Take out your crucifix and say a prayer. We are in hard times right now with Rebecca's injury added to our worries about Sam Johnson and Jonas Carver."

Lisa touched her crucifix and nodded. "I started prayin' before Cal showed up and I'll keep on 'til the four of us are safely on the train out of here."

"That will do for now but you may have to keep it up after we are on our way to dat Kansas country."

"You all could join me, you know," Lisa invited, looking from one to the other. "I wouldn't have made it to your house, Mr. Pyne, without His help."

"I am surely aware of dat," John admitted. "If for some reason we don't get back here tonight, we will meet you at de train between four and five in de morning. I have a feeling Mrs. Stanton will insist I bring Rebecca back to their house for de night. I'll have to return de rig anyway." He shook his head again as though to shake away his doubts. "Don't know how I will get her to de train but I'll get her there." Then he studied their faces. "If not, you two go ahead. Here are your tickets and some extra money for food."

He hugged them both, mounted Dusty and rode out of sight.

CHAPTER 18

LISA'S HEART LOST its hold as she watched John ride out of sight. He had been her lifeline since she first found her way to his house in her desperate attempt to get away from Jonas Carver. Her hands shook as she put the money and the tickets into her pocket and grasped her crucifix. Then she remembered Cal. How could she forget Cal standing beside her, patiently watching her and waiting for her to speak. She slipped her free hand into his. He took it warmly and laced his fingers through hers.

"I have this dreadful feeling we're on our own," she confessed.

Cal squeezed her hand. "We'll take care of each other no matter what happens."

"Here, take your ticket—just in case."

"In case of what?" Cal asked, startled.

"In case somethin' happens to me or we get separated."

"That en't gonna happen."

"It could, if Carver gets a notion to come check the trains."

"In that case, we'll hide together," Cal said. "Remember, he's after me too."

"Take the blasted ticket anyway," she said, thrusting it into his hand. "All four of us are targets. Any one of us could find ourselves alone. We'd have to go ahead on our own no matter what." She paused to take a breath and a look behind them. "I feel like a hunted animal, always checking 'round to see if those wicked eyes are searching for me."

By now, the sun with its afterglow had disappeared below the horizon and a thin layer of clouds had moved in to blanket the moon. Cal tugged at her hand and pulled her in the direction of the Lowrey. "Let's get going. I en't got any hope of gettin' a room in that place but we can try." He cast a glance behind them assuring himself that no one was following. "I have this feeling in my gut that someone's back there stalking us."

As they walked, they began to see small clusters of families in the empty spaces between buildings and others sitting alone in the shelter of doorways. Lisa stopped and stared at several large crates scattered here and there against the buildings and a sense of fear returned as though she were four years old again and walking the street with her mother.

"There'll be a street kid or two in each of those," she warned. "The families are okay. They probably don't have the money for a room so they're waiting out here 'til time to get on the train. At least they got blankets and food. They'd best be careful cause that food will disappear if they go to sleep, maybe even if they don't."

"I guess I'm just feeling those people starin' at us," Cal said with a sense of relief. "But I guess we oughta keep a lookout anyway."

As they hurried past the last family and into a cluster of small mercantile offices, the street narrowed and the sound of their steps on the dark cobblestones echoed against the dark buildings. Lisa and Cal saw them at the same time; two figures walking toward them, one taller than the other.

"Street boys," Lisa said. "They don't fight clean. Wish I'd taken off this dress."

"We can handle 'em," Cal whispered as the boys drew nearer. "Remember the fight you had with Matt Stoner?"

"I was still a kid then." She tensed. "Get ready. They're spittin' distance."

The street boys stopped directly in their path. "Got any money?" The tough confident voice came from the taller boy. The boys took a step closer. "I said, do ya got any money?"

Lisa and Cal took a step toward the boys and kept their eyes sharp for any sudden movement. The tall boy's arm shot out and grabbed Cal's upper arm while Lisa threw up her bent arm and fended off a jab from the other boy. Lisa threw her fist against the boy's face sending him to the ground. She kicked him hard and held him down with her foot, ready to kick him again if he dared to get up. He didn't move.

The other boy was retching from a punch Cal had landed in his stomach.

"Is that your little brother?" Cal asked.

The boy nodded as he gasped for breath.

"Then take care of him. My *lady* friend hurt him bad."

Lisa gave the boy one last thrust to his chest before removing her foot. The boy groaned and rolled over reaching for his brother's hand. The brothers helped each other stumble away as they retreated into the dark shadows, their curses reaching Lisa's and Cal's ears until the boys were out of sight.

"That was easier than I thought," Lisa said as they moved on. "Mr. Pyne was right. I'm stronger than I think I am."

"Did you see the surprise on their faces when we stepped *into* them instead of backin' off?" Cal asked with self-satisfaction. "Bet they're more careful who they take on next time."

"Yeah, I'll bet, too. Those kids might have the meanness to kick up a fight but we're in a lot better shape than they are."

Clinging to Cal's hand, she stared at the cobblestones beneath her feet as though each carried one of her problems. Her hand was throbbing from the blow she had given the boy.

"This is some kinda life," she said quietly as depression crept up on her and she slowed her pace without realizing it. Using Mrs. Pyne as a model, she had tried to talk and walk more like a woman but all that had been cast aside tonight. She had reverted completely to her boy's ways, but she had to do it to save herself and Cal. A tear at the bottom of her dress revealed a portion of her boy's pant leg. The bonnet she had started out with had disappeared. She was overcome with a sense of loss, bringing pain to the place where her heart was still hanging limply from seeing John ride away. Cal was still with her, but her mother and John were gone, along with the only life she had known since she was five years old. So much had happened since running from the orphanage. She had been on the run for only five days, but it seemed like a lifetime and the weight of it was heavy on her wounded heart.

"What's the matter, Lee?"

It was good to hear Cal refer to her by her old name, the name he had called her by for nearly eleven years.

"All of sudden I feel like I'm wanderin' around in a desert without a bearing to count on. It's like I'm not sure which way to go and I'm not sure who I am. I fight like a boy and walk like a boy in a girl's dress. I've got muscles hard as a rock and I'm tough inside. I think I love you like a girl would but you're my buddy and that en't gonna change." She let go of his hand and pounded a fist into her palm. Cal noticed the blood.

"Let's get a room and we'll take care of that hand. Then we can talk." He recognized the distress on her face and wondered what he could say to help.

Neither spoke the remainder of the way. Lisa clung to her crucifix even though she knew she didn't need it to get an answer to prayer, but it was a symbol of her faith and gave her a physical reminder of her hope.

"Did you pray us through that?" Cal asked with a twinkle in his eyes when they arrived at the Lowrey. It was an attempt to bring her out of her dejection.

"You bet, smarty. You'll catch on sometime," she said, showing a small sign of recovery.

An elderly man was asleep with his head down on a small desk in the hotel lobby, his green eyeshade askew and pushing into the back of his neck.

Cal knocked loudly on the counter top where the registry book lay open. He glanced at the page and saw that there were two room numbers without names behind them. It took another knock for the man to open an eye and peer at them sleepily.

"Yeah?"

"We're lookin' for a room," Cal said.

"Do you have money?"

"A little. How much do you want for one room?"

"One dollar."

"One dollar?" Cal shouted. "We only want it for one night."

"You married?"

"No, we're brother and sister," Cal lied. "We're traveling with our aunt and uncle tomorrow and they en't gotten here yet. They'll be here in a couple of hours."

"One dollar," the man slurred.

"That it?" asked Cal

"That's it."

"Let's go, Lisa. That's robbery."

It was dark outside when they walked through the door. They hadn't gone ten steps when they heard the door open behind them. "How much can you pay?"

"Twenty-five cents," Cal answered.

"Come on in," the man said reluctantly. "Don't really want the rooms to be empty all night." He took their money and pointed toward the back. "Up a flight of stairs at the end of the hall. It's a good room even if it's in the attic."

"Where's this other empty room?" Lisa asked. "Our aunt's got a broken leg and she can't go up stairs."

"You're only paying for two. They'll have to pay when they get here."

"They will. You can count on that."

The man scratched his head and looked as though he had never encountered two such determined young people before. "Well," he said. "I can't expect any more guests to come tonight. Might as well let you have the one down here. I'm too tired to squabble with you."

Lisa and Cal followed him to the room. It was small and had one window that was open. There were two beds each of which could barely accommodate two average size people, two chairs and a small table holding a pitcher and washbasin. They both noticed that one of the chairs had a lid that covered a chamber pot beneath. They both chuckled. They had been boys together for too many years to be embarrassed by its presence.

As soon as they locked the door and heard the man walk a way, Cal took her arm and led her to the nearest bed.

"Sit," he ordered. "Let me see that hand."

"It's nothin'," she said. "Skin must have broke when it grazed that kid's hand after I hit his jaw. He must have been holding somethin' hard and jagged to hit me with."

"Looks like it didn't bleed much," Cal said, wetting the tail of John's big shirt with the water in the pitcher and wiping her hand clean. "There, that'll do. It won't be a problem if you're careful to let it scab over. 'Course, you know all that," he added with a teasing grin.

His attempt to take care of her warmed her insides and her limp heart began to take hold again. She wondered why she had let herself get so down. She was with the man she loved and she knew he loved her. He was there for her. That should be enough to take her over the next obstacle in her life, but she knew she still had to rely on herself — her own strength, her own faith and her own good sense. She was growing up fast.

"Thanks," she said, lying back on the bed feeling a bit of hysteria coming on. At first, it was a chuckle that soon evolved into uncontrollable laughter. Tears ran down her cheeks. "You should have seen the look on that kid's face when I put my boot on him. Like he couldn't believe a girl got him down."

Cal was laughing by now. "I wonder if they'll ever have the nerve to tell their buddies about this and if… if…" Cal choked, "if any of 'em were watching, those kids will never live it down."

They were both lying back on the bed exhausted and gasping for air.

"What a day," Lisa panted.

"Things can only get better."

"Oh, yeah?" Lisa rolled her eyes at him. "Don't be too sure."

"Well, for now, we're safe in this room. I think." He rolled toward her and put his arm across her. "Can I kiss you, Miss Bellamont?"

"I don't know, Mr. Hale. Will you be kissing your buddy, Lee, or the new girl, Lisa?"

"Well, I hope to heck it's Lisa. The other sounds scary."

"We're all alone. Can you be trusted? This is Lisa askin'," Lisa said, eyeing him suspiciously while remembering some of the talks they had had about girls before he knew she was one.

Apparently, he was thinking about those talks, too, and sat up. "Come on, Lisa. What did you think I was gonna do? I wouldn't do anything even if I wanted to deep down. You mean too much to me and besides, I'm still getting used to you as a girl." He sat down on the other bed visibly offended.

"I'm sorry, Cal. I was just funnin'." She twitched her nose at him and started to laugh. "Come on. No harm done. We need to get some sleep. Four o'clock is just around the corner."

"Stand up, please," Cal said and reached out his hand to help her. "We're gonna be okay. We make a good team, like we found out tonight." He invited her inside a circle made with his arms and she fell inside, laying her head against his chest.

"I want that kiss now if you still have one for me," she said.

"I do," he told her, drawing her close. "It will be my birthday present."

"Oh, drats! I've been so blasted concerned about everything today, I forgot all about it bein' your birthday. Happy birthday, Cal," she said, kissing his lips as she returned his warm and emotional hug.

"Whew! Guess we'd best break this up and get to bed. Morning's not far away," Lisa whispered.

Reluctantly, they moved apart and surveyed the room again. "Okay if I take this bed by the window? Mrs. Pyne can join me when she comes and you and Mr. Pyne can share that bed."

"You know, Lisa, he's a big man. He'll push me right out a bed on the first roll over."

"Then you'll have to sleep on the floor," she teased as she threw herself on her bed.

They pulled up their blankets and settled in. "How are we gonna know when it's four o'clock?" Lisa asked.

"The man said there were other people here who were going on the train so we'll hear them movin' around. Hope so anyway. Goodnight, Lisa."

"I love you," she whispered.

"Love you too," he whispered back.

CHAPTER 19

LISA FELT LIKE she had barely fallen asleep when she was awakened by loud voices streaming in through their open window. Curled up in a tight ball under the thin blanket provided by the hotel, she shivered as a moist chilled breeze blew across her. Stretching out and rolling over to look at Cal, she saw that he was still sound asleep and didn't appear to be suffering from the chill at all. Apparently, he didn't even hear the footsteps pounding in the hallway outside their door.

She put her bare feet on the cold floor and scurried over to him, cuffing him on the shoulder.

"How can you sleep with all that noise goin' on outside? It's time we got to moving along, too."

"Sorry. I guess I was tired. It's still dark."

"Seems like a lot of people know it's time to get to the train so don't you think we oughta get there, too?"

Cal jumped up and slipped into his shoes. "Sure do. This is it, Lisa," he added, suddenly wide-awake. "This is it. We're actually going to get away from this place."

Impatient voices surged into the room through the window as men, burdened with bundles of belongings, yelled at their families to move on. The anxious excitement filling the air had its effect on Cal and Lisa as they jumped from their beds and ran to the window. Directly beneath them, a large woman with a porridge face was noisily lining up her six children, handing each of them a slice of bread from a bundle slung over one shoulder. "Take your sister's hand and let's git," she said, grabbing the hand of the first in line and walking ahead with determined steps.

"They're all girls," Lisa whispered. "Like stair steps: littlest to biggest."

"We'd better 'git' too, don't you think?" Cal asked.

It was then that they both realized they were alone.

"The Pynes didn't make it," Lisa gasped.

Cal straightened up and looked around as though he might find them sleeping on the floor or hiding in a corner. "Might be they only had time to get to the train this morning."

"Let's get outta here," Lisa said, hurrying into the hall and toward the front entrance where a small crowd had gathered waiting their turn to get through the door with their belongings.

"Hold it," Cal said, grabbing her wrist. "Those two street bums could be waiting for us out front. I'll go up and have a look."

Cal sidled his way through the cluster of anxious people moving into the open air, trying not to trip over their children and their possessions.

"Excuse me. Excuse me. Just want to have a look. Not trying to get ahead of you."

Peering over the shoulder of a man near his own height, Cal took a quick look around. The boys from the previous night's encounter stood out like red danger signals. A quick count told Cal that they had gathered at least six other punks to join them. Even though they were trying to blend in with the morning street activities, Cal realized that one of them was keeping an eye on the people moving through the door.

Cal slipped back to where Lisa waited.

"We're in for it if we go out this way. I don't think the two of us can take on eight of them."

"Drats! They must have followed us. Looks like we'd better find another way outta here," Lisa said, turning to look for the clerk from the night before.

The registration book was closed and the clerk was gone.

"Looks like we're on our own. Probably just as well," Cal whispered. "Might be a back door. Let's sneak back there and hope nobody sees us in case those boys ask someone about us."

"These people are all too busy with their own problems to pay any attention to us," Lisa said. "Let's go."

Finding no door at the back of the building, they returned to their room and checked out the window. They saw that several of the boys had moved to that side of the building and were attempting to peer into the hotel windows. Lisa and Cal dropped to the floor.

"We've got to find a way outta this building," Lisa said. "Wonder what happened to the clerk?"

"He's probably hiding from this mess. Let's go see if there's a cellar. Maybe it's got a window," Cal suggested, crawling toward the door.

"So, it's come to this. Forced to crawl on our bellies."

"So what," Cal interrupted. "If it gets us outta here without another fight, it's okay with me."

Once they were outside the room, Lisa and Cal stood up and dashed toward what appeared to be the doorway to a cellar. They impatiently stood aside to make way for an elderly couple slowly climbing the stairs with their baggage. Lisa tugged on Cal's arm and pushed past them. "One of those kids just came in the front door."

Once clear of the couple, they flew down the stairs and into a cellar guest room, grateful to see a small narrow window near the ceiling. Pulling a table beneath the window, Lisa jumped up first. "It en't gonna make any difference now. We've gotta go for it," she said, panting as she pushed herself through the narrow opening, tearing her skirt as she tugged it away from a large splinter on the window ledge. "Oh, drats," she swore. Cal followed and, without looking either direction, they headed toward a shadowed alleyway straight ahead.

Their years of racing each other quickly brought them to the end of the passage that opened onto a narrow street lined with small buildings bearing shingles identifying the crafts offered within. Men were stepping out to get a breath of the morning air before starting the day's business, greeting each other and stepping back in surprise as Lisa and Cal sped past them. Soon they were a long way from the inn and the boys waiting for them.

Hearing hoof beats coming up on them from behind, they quickly slipped into a narrow opening between two buildings, as though they were fugitives from the law. Pausing to look around and catch their breath, they took stock of their situation. They were alone and a long way from the inn and the street punks. They began to relax.

"By the way," Cal gasped. "You're slowin' down. I got ahead of you for the first time ever."

"It's the dress. I en't ever raced in a dress before."

"Maybe you oughta get rid of it."

"Nah. That woman wrote our names on the back of the ticket so they'll be expecting a girl to use it. Besides, I need the pocket and," she paused and lowered her eyelids with a grin, "we may get treated with more respect if one of us is a girl."

"Wow! Now you're thinkin' like a girl," he teased. "So, Lady Lisa, let's see if there's anybody around who can tell us how to get to the train."

"Don't you start anything," she threatened, unsuccessfully attempting to trip him as they headed down the narrow passageway.

They hurried along trying not to slip on the slime created by rotting garbage and jumped aside as a large rat darted across their path and onto a mound of trash. Cal grabbed Lisa's hand and ran. Soon they found themselves in the open air and sunshine where a warm sea-coated breeze greeted them, quieting their racing hearts and lifting their spirits. In the distance, they saw two men coaxing a team of horses to pull a wide wooden grader across a plot of ground. Lisa and Cal approached the men and asked for directions.

"The Western Railroad depot? Well," one of the men said, "you're a good distance from it but it's easy to get there. Just go straight ahead north on this street here and go to the very end. Then turn left and you'll run into it. Can't miss it." The man speaking lifted his cap and scratched his head. "What in tarnation are you two youngsters doing wandering around this area by yourselves?"

"Oh, we en't alone," Lisa said quickly. "We're meeting our aunt and uncle at the train, but we got lost."

"Thanks for your help," Cal added, grabbing Lisa's arm and hurrying away.

Behind them, they heard one of the men say, "Don't know that I believe a word of it."

Cal and Lisa took off at a run until they saw the railroad tracks and people milling about in the distance. Slowing down to a walk, they began looking for familiar faces, both dangerous and friendly, as they joined the stirring movement of people heading for a new and unknown destination.

Lisa and Cal felt the excitement that, for the two of them, was mixed with grave apprehension and concern. The sun was well above the horizon sending a welcome warmth to the people who had slept outside during the night. A cloudless sky looked down on the turmoil taking place beside the five train cars awaiting their passengers.

Lisa and Cal moved toward the edge of the disturbing scene, being especially watchful for Carver who might have gotten the idea they would try to leave Boston. With the train departure schedules conspicuously posted in the depot and on flyers distributed around the city, he would have no trouble finding them. Then there were the street boys to watch for; however, armed deputies could be seen amid the crowd giving Lisa and Cal a small sense of security. Lisa wished she still had Mrs. Pyne's bonnet. Even though her hair had grown, it was still cut like a boy's and made her look like a boy in a dress. She shrugged her shoulders and frowned.

"What's the matter?" asked Cal.

"I feel like a boy in a dress," she muttered.

"You look like a boy in a dress," Cal chuckled.

"Oh, thanks a lot. That helps," she said, smacking him on the arm. "You could suggest somethin' to help me."

"I did. Take off the dress."

"But they may not let me on the train."

"I doubt they'll even look at the name on the ticket. They got their money so what do they care?" Cal said. "By the way, did you look at the ticket to see if your name is really on it?" He pulled his from his pocket and studied it. "I don't see my name on my ticket."

Lisa reached deep into her pocket and withdrew her ticket recalling the note inside the crucifix as her hand passed over it. "Those people asked us for our names and it looked like they wrote them on the back of the tickets."

"You've forgotten somethin'."

"What's that?"

"Mr. Pyne didn't look for names when he handed you our tickets."

"You're right," Lisa said. "He didn't. Don't know what I was thinkin'. Guess I can take off the dress. It oughta help since those street kids are lookin' for a girl. Won't make any difference to Carver whether I'm dressed as a girl or a boy. *He'll* know me."

Lisa looked around and saw that people were wrapped up in their own concerns so she slipped out of the dress and rolled it up under her arm.

"Now, I guess I don't stand out in the crowd anymore. I feel better except I'm really gettin' hungry," she said, noticing that some people carried bags of bread and ham and baskets of boiled eggs. When she saw one woman selling her wares to the passengers, she grabbed Cal's arm and pulled him in her direction. What the woman had left would last them two or three days and she willingly sold it all to them, along with her large cloth bag. They sat cross-legged facing each other between two loaded wagons that were waiting to be moved onto the train. For the moment, the area was quiet but they kept a constant watch for danger. Like two starving children, they dug in and ate.

"There you are. I've been looking all over for you."

Cal recognized the voice immediately and jumped up to greet Mathias Todburn as he came down from his horse.

"Did you decide to go to the Kansas Territory with us?" Cal asked.

"I have, but not today. That's not why I'm here," Todburn said with deep lines forming between his eyes. "Carver came by this morning looking for both of you. He was especially threatening and that cheek of his is festering something terrible. Don't think he's taken time to care for it. He's a sick, angry man."

"Is he comin' here?" Lisa asked.

"I think so. He may be right behind me. I rode here as fast as I could to let you know but it took me a while to find you buried back here among the wagons. Apparently he's never stopped looking for you. This could be his last resort."

"We've been watching for him. He en't our only problem. We fought off a couple of street kids last night and they've got their gang after us this morning. We've been trying to stay out of sight," Cal said.

"It might be best if you got on the train now."

"They're not letting anyone on yet," Lisa said, stuffing her dress along with the crucifix inside the bundle with the remaining food.

Mr. Todburn looked around. "Maybe if I cause a distraction, you can sneak on board." He paused as he pondered what he might do. "Oh, here," he said as he reached into his pocket. He placed a small wrapped package in Cal's hand. "You were a good employee and my wife and I want you to have this. It's not much but maybe it will help you buy some food along the way."

"You've been very kind," Cal said looking at his former employer with affection. "If you get to the Kansas Territory, I'll pay you back."

"No need," Todburn said, waving away Cal's remark. "Make a good life for yourself. I'll look you up when I get there myself. But, now, we've got to get you on the train."

Todburn looked around and saw one of the conductors standing by the last passenger car.

"You two walk on the other side of my horse and as soon as I distract that man's attention, you sneak on board. Got your tickets?"

"Yes," they said, nodding.

Todburn pulled on the reins and walked up to the conductor in a way that put the man's back to the door of the train.

"How much longer until we move out?" Todburn asked

"Should be boarding soon. It's hard to get a crowd like this orderly enough to leave." He pointed toward the gathering. "You can see the deputies are beginning to line them up to board."

Satisfied that Lisa and Cal had sneaked on board safely, Todburn thanked the man, climbed onto his horse and casually rode away.

Lisa crawled down the aisle to the middle of the car and scooted between the seats keeping her head below the window. Cal took the area between the seats behind her and they sat on the floor, leaning against the side of the car.

Cal reached for her hand under the seat and stroked her fingers. "Wonder how we're gonna give 'em our tickets."

"I guess we'll find a way later. Hope so. I en't going out there again."

"Wonder if we'll ever have time to just sit and talk like we used to at the Home," Cal mused.

"All the way to K. T., I guess," Lisa said with a grin.

"K. T.? Oh, yeah—Kansas Territory. You're right. I'll be glad when this train gets to movin'."

"Me, too," Lisa said. "I just wish the Pynes would get here. What if they don't make it? We may never know what happened to them."

"I'm sure they'll look for us when they get to Lawrence."

Suddenly, the noise increased and the passengers began to board. Lisa and Cal jumped from their hiding places and grabbed a seat together. There was no other option but to sit by a window where they were in full view. Lisa turned her back to the window and watched the noisy excited passengers pour into the car.

Cal, sitting at the aisle, dared to peak around Lisa to glimpse outside into the crush of people pressing against each other to claim a place on the train. A commotion was taking place at the edge of the throng where a man was violently pushing people out of his way to get through the crowd. Two deputies were attempting to pull the crazed man back without success. He was screaming something and pointing directly at Cal.

"Oh, magod, Lisa. It's Carver. Don't turn around. The deputies are trying to get hold of him. He's gettin' away. He's knocked someone down. He's lookin' right at me. Tuck your head down, Lisa." Cal continued to watch, horrified, as Carver moved toward the door of the car. "He's almost here, Lisa. We're in big trouble."

Women moved out of Carver's way, cursing him as he passed. Just as he reached the step to the car, two large male passengers stepped in front of him making it possible for the deputies to grab Carver's arms and pull him to the ground. By then, Cal could hear what Carver was screaming. "They're on the train. There—by the window. Get them. They're running away."

While the men and one deputy held him down, the other deputy tied his hands and feet together and moved him writhing and cursing out of the way. Cal saw the conductor squat down and talk to Carver. Soon, he got up and came on board walking directly to Cal and Lisa.

"I'm George Hunt, the railroad conductor in charge of this train," he said officiously but with concern. "That man accuses you of being runaways from his orphanage. Is that true? Do you each have a ticket for this train?" he asked.

They reached for their tickets and showed them to Mr. Hunt.

"He kicked us both out. He keeps kids until they're sixteen and my sixteenth birthday was yesterday. He's been chasin' us for the past few days. He came after me with a whip at the livery where I was working. He must think we took something when we left. Here," Cal said reaching for their bag under the seat. "Check this out if you want. We don't have anything but some food and…." He started to say "her dress" but changed his mind.

"That won't be necessary," Mr. Hunt said and left the car.

Heaving a big sigh of relief, Lisa joined Cal at the window and together they watched as the conductor talk to the deputies while Carver squirmed violently, screaming at the faces in the window.

Lisa paled. "Can you understand what Carver's yelling?"

"Can't hear it but I'm sure it's not good? I bet they put him away in the Boston Lunatic Asylum. I heard Carver describe the place a long time ago but I don't think he ever thought he'd go there."

Visibly shaken, Lisa wondered aloud, "I've never seen anyone go crazy before. If they don't put him in there, what do you suppose he'll do? He doesn't look like he could go back and run the orphanage. I pity those boys if he tries."

"He's out of it. Somebody will just have to go in and take over the Home until he's better, if that ever happens."

Lisa shrugged her shoulders. "Hope you're right."

After Mr. Carver was taken away, they felt safe enough to continue watching the activities outside until the last wagon was loaded onto a boxcar and the boarding area stood silent and empty. Lisa kept her nose pressed to the window as the emptiness overwhelmed her with a sharp suddenness and the void left by the Pyne's absence engulfed her.

An open hand passed in front of her face and broke her stare. "What's the matter, Lisa? You look awful."

"Oh, thanks a lot." She tried to focus on Cal but had to shake her head to get her thinking started again. "Guess I went off a bit thinking about the Pynes."

"Maybe they're in a different car. Right now we oughta feel lucky that we're rid of the old man."

"You're right," Lisa said, giving Cal a half-smile. "I'll be okay. Knowin' we're on our way without them just hit me all of a sudden."

"At least we're together," Cal said and took her hand.

A cloud of steam swept past their window alerting the passengers to be ready to move. The car jerked forward as the coupling connecting them to the car ahead shifted into position. Lisa leaned into the curved back of the wooden seat and braced her knees against the seat in front of her. A long blast from the steam whistle warned people and animals to move off the tracks ahead. Metal wheels ground against metal tracks as more billows of steam filled the air. She dared to breathe a sigh of relief. They were on their way.

CHAPTER 20

"DON'T CALL ME Lisa and stop reachin' for my hand." Lisa pushed Cal's hand away, trying to overshadow a grin with a forced frown deep on her forehead. "Remember where we are. You wanna get us thrown off the train after all the trouble we went through to get on it?"

The bedlam of the platform continued inside the car as people vied for seats to keep their families together. After settling into a seat, many passengers simply leaned back and closed their eyes in an attempt to calm shattered nerves.

Lisa and Cal leaned into the seat ahead of them and put their heads together. They had much to resolve—and soon. They were alone, something they had not anticipated. Lisa was thinking they should say they were older than they were. She wondered if she should change to her dress quickly before it became established that she was a boy. As a boy, she could be Cal's younger brother. Cal could be eighteen and she could be sixteen. On the other hand, as a girl, she could be his sister or his cousin or his sweetheart, which is what she really was. They could say they were going to get married when they reached Lawrence, which was a decision they had already made.

She leaned toward Cal, whispering, "We need to decide whether I'm going to be a girl or a boy."

"What do you wanna be?"

"A girl."

"So, be a girl."

"But then… well… they'd treat me like a girl and what if I'd have to defend myself. Course, I would. Besides, I'm not too good at bein' a girl yet. Look at the way I'm sitting. I don't see any of the ladies sitting all straddle-legged like this." She pulled her knees in and pressed them together. "This don't feel right."

"It don't look right, either. Not now, anyway, while you're in boy clothes."

Lisa leaned back in her seat to think but found herself studying Cal's face. She had taken that face to bed with her for so long that she knew the line of his jaw, the indents made by his nostrils, the dark thick eyebrows, the half-smile on his lips when he talked to her and the way he scratched behind his ear when he was thinking. She had felt much more comfortable with her love for him when they were at the Home. It had even been more comfortable when the Pynes were their companions, but now they had been abruptly cast together on their own with no one to act as a buffer. Neither of them knew much about the world beyond Malden and they had no concept of the distance or what to expect as they headed to the country's vast interior. They would have to work out their future together, and that future had a lot of unknowns. Suddenly, she wanted to be in his arms, but that was impossible. They couldn't even hold hands without creating a situation. Even if they claimed to be brothers, they couldn't hold hands in front of the other passengers.

Cal was deep in similar thoughts when Lisa pulled the bundle out from under the seat and took out the dress. She motioned for him to let her in his place by the window. Cal slipped across the seat into the aisle where he leaned over her, shielding her as she kneeled on the floor and slipped the dress over her head.

"What happened?" he asked when she was finished stretching and tugging the dress over her shirt and pants so that it would hang properly.

"I decided I needed to be a girl. Your girl. I need you to hold my hand without people starin'. I want to feel your arms around me again," she whispered and stood up. "What do you think?"

"Well, now that you've done it, I think it's great. I kinda hoped you'd decide that."

"I'm still tough and I can still run fast and I'm still a blacksmith. That don't change but we're on this train for a long time and I'd rather be what I am, and that's your girl."

The confusion in the car had lessened but conversations were constant and loud enough to obscure their words. She moved so Cal could get back to the window seat. Cal reached for her face and planted a kiss on her lips. "Welcome back, Lisa." Her heart ballooned as it had when they first discovered each other.

He leaned back into the seat, content for the moment. Lisa smiled at him and followed his example. They had a long way to go, but they were together and her troublesome concerns moved out of the way for the moment, allowing her to enjoy the peace and contentment of being at one with Cal. They were going to be all right.

The sun was directly overhead when the train finally began to roll noisily down the tracks. It had taken more than four hours to get the passengers and their belongings on board the Boston and Worcester train for the first leg of the trip west. It was not long until the people surrendered to their weariness and began falling asleep to the monotonous, rhythmic clacking of the metal wheels against the tracks, seemingly undisturbed by the train's whistle signaling a town or a water stop ahead. With Cal's arm wrapped around her shoulder, Lisa's head fell against him as she, too, was lulled into sleep.

Cal watched the landscape pass by and marveled as the hillsides overflowed with trees bursting with new green leaves; their branches sheltering sprouting sumac and colorful layers of ground cover that spoke to him of newness: new sights, new opportunities, new people, new home and new life with Lisa. He wanted to awaken her but decided against it. She would see plenty before they reached their destination but, for now, she had given in to her exhaustion.

Cal was nearly gone himself when he saw the conductor enter the car with a pad in his hand. Seeing that many people were asleep, he spoke up loudly before beginning his walk down the aisle. "Get your tickets ready. I'm here to check them."

There was a stirring among the seats as the passengers became aware of the conductor moving through the car. Cal opened his eyes and pulled his ticket from his pocket, then carefully retrieved Lisa's ticket from her dress pocket, handing them both to the conductor, Mr. Hunt.

Mr. Hunt leaned down toward them and spoke guardedly, "You might want to wake her up. I have something to tell you both."

Lisa stirred. "I'm awake," she said, interlocking her fingers and stretching her arms up behind her head as the boys did at the Home. "What's up?"

A quizzical grin spread over the conductor's face. "I thought you were here with another boy," he said to Cal.

"Yeah, well, I was, but he magically turned into a girl."

"I *am* a girl," Lisa said convincingly, but a bit too loudly. Lowering her voice, she said, "My name is Lisa."

"I was sure I recognized you before as the boy who won this year's two-mile race on the Common."

Fear clutched at Lisa's heart as she prepared to lie to the man. "You're thinkin' of someone else. It wasn't me," she said.

He squatted down and motioned for them to bring their heads down toward his. "Look, kids, I'm not here to judge you. You have tickets and you are on this train legitimately, so don't worry. I have some news for you."

Mr. Hunt looked around. Satisfied that the people were distracted, he quietly continued speaking. "We're stopping at Fitchburg to pick up some people you know. Now, you may not recognize them because they are boarding under assumed names and disguised as best they could. I know you understand the reason for that. Mr. Stanton sent a servant to tell me they couldn't make the train in Boston, but he would have them in Fitchburg by the time the train arrived there. They'll be seated in another car."

Cal had removed his arm from around Lisa when the man came to their seat. Now, he took her hand as relief flooded their faces.

"That's the best news we could have, Mr. Hunt. We've been very worried about them," Lisa said.

"What name are they going by?" Cal asked as he moved his head in closer.

"If the time comes for you to know, we'll tell you."

"Who do you mean by 'we'?" Lisa asked, suspiciously.

"There is a group of men on board who will take care of any problems that might arise. You two will be safe," he assured them.

By now, their heads were nearly touching but Mr. Hunt lowered his voice even more. "We need to keep this between ourselves. Don't go looking for them. You might give them away. We're sure there are men on board looking for people like your friends, but we're not sure who they are or where they are sitting, so be careful of what you say."

"I thought all the people on this train were abolitionists going to the Kansas Territory," Cal said.

"You'd think so but they're not. Some people are going to Chicago or Kansas City or continuing on west, and some could be informants looking for people like your friends." Mr. Hunt paused and glanced around. No one seemed to be paying attention to him, so he continued. "I doubt they'll be in danger after we leave Massachusetts, but we should be careful all the way."

Suddenly, they realized that the car had become very quiet. Were the people settling down or were they simply curious about the whispered conversation between the three of them? Fearful that they may have raised suspicion, Mr. Hunt raised his voice a bit and said, "Well, young lady you do look like that boy that won the race last year. You could be brother and sister." As he spoke, he slipped an envelope in Lisa's hand. "Guard this with your life," he whispered.

Lisa barely heard him but caught the message of his eyes. She put the paper in her pocket to read later on. Doing this, she felt her crucifix and remembered the note tucked inside it. Now she had two things to read secretly. With the long trip ahead of her, she was sure she would find the time to do that.

Mr. Hunt moved on to the next person and reached for the man's ticket. "I have a teenage daughter that I haven't seen in quite some time. Talking to this young lady made me realize how much I miss her. It's a nice age, don't you think?"

"I have no idea," the man said. "I don't have children."

Lisa and Cal were wide-awake as they pulled into the Fitchburg depot, hoping to catch a glimpse of the Pynes boarding the train. Disappointed, they were only able to see Mr. Stanton leaving in his carriage as the train trundled on its way again.

"I suppose Mr. Hunt told them where we are," Lisa whispered. "Guess we won't get to talk to them until we all get off this train. Now that we know they're safe on board, my appetite is back. Are you hungry?"

"I am. Let's have some more of what we bought today," Cal said and pulled the bag up to his lap.

"Good. After that, I'm going to take off the shirt and pants in the toilet at the end of the car. If I'm gonna be a girl, I want to be one all the way down to my skin. I sure will be more comfortable."

She leaned toward Cal and whispered, "You know? I used to look at the women walking around the Common with their parasols and ribboned hats and thought I might want to be like them some day. Now, I don't know why. I doubt I'd want to get all powdered up and act sweet and *charming*. They're so fake."

"You, powdered, hatted and ribboned? Now, that's funny."

They put their heads in their laps and convulsed with laughter. It felt wonderful.

CHAPTER 21

LISA'S KNEES SLAMMED into the seat in front of her, startling her out of her sleep and sending shooting pains down her legs. They had been on the way for less than four hours and already the train had stopped several times to take on coal or water. She rubbed her knees and rolled her head around to loosen her stiff neck. Cal squinted at her through narrow sleepy eyes and grunted. Groans rolled through the car accompanied by the weeping of a small child. A distant orange sun teased the western horizon as twilight drew the curtain on a formidable day.

"Well, that was a short nap. At least we're safely on our way, finally," Lisa mumbled, stretching her legs. A teasing smile spread across her face. "And here we are—just you and me—together—alone."

"Yeah. Feels good, doesn't it?" Cal returned her smile and squeezed her hand. "Guess we can relax now, for a while anyway."

Cal opened the window and a gust of wind blew smoke and cinders into his face. "Whew," he said, slamming down the window and wiping his eyes with his sleeve.

They pressed their faces against the pane and saw a wagon drawn by two horses coming toward the train. Seated atop the wagon were two men; each with a rifle poised upright beside him.

"That's weird. It looks like we're out in the middle of nowhere," Cal said loud enough to be heard across the aisle. "Wonder where those men came from. Wonder what they want."

He gripped Lisa's hand. Fear struck them as they thought of the Pynes. What if these men were searching for them? Would their disguises be effective? Lisa and Cal didn't have to speak the words to know they were both worrying about the same thing.

"Maybe they're train robbers," Lisa said, hopefully.

A man from the other side of the car squatted down beside them. "What are you talking about? What did you see out there that made you say that?"

"We saw a wagon pull up with two men on it, both of them holding rifles," Cal said. "The men must have boarded the train because they're not on that wagon anymore." Grunts of agreement could be heard from the people seated on the same side of the aisle.

Cal and Lisa moved out of their seat to allow the man to see for himself. An anxious quiet settled on the car as other passengers speculated among themselves about what it could mean.

"There's a wagon, all right. You say they had rifles?"

Cal nodded.

The man stepped back into the aisle and walked past several of the male passengers nearby. He spoke guardedly to each of them. "We could have visitors shortly. Be ready," he said, patting his waistline.

Lisa saw the bulges made by their handguns and her heart began to race out of control. Those men were together with the exception of the man behind her; the one who didn't have any children. She glanced over her shoulder and saw him feel for his gun as he shrank into the corner of his seat. She was too frightened to talk to Cal and hoped he was watching and seeing what she saw.

The man, who seemed more of a leader than the others, spoke out again, directing his words to all the passengers in the car. "We could be getting visitors and we don't know who they are or what they want. I suggest you just sit still in your seats and don't say anything. Mothers, keep your children in your lap or near you. Don't let them run out in the aisle." He settled into his seat to wait.

"Wish we knew what's goin on," Lisa muttered to Cal. "We've been sitting in the middle of nowhere for a while now."

"Yeah," Cal said, frowning as he opened the window again. This time it was safe to stick his head out. "That wagon's just sittin' there, empty."

Suddenly, Lisa jumped up to tell the leader about the man behind her but quickly sat back down when the door between the cars burst open and the two men stepped in with their rifles poised.

Women gasped as they leaned over to protect their children who began to cry. Mothers pulled them tightly into their arms and tried to shush them, shielding their eyes from the scene.

Cal jumped up and pulled Lisa into his seat by the window and sat down in the aisle seat, keeping an eye on the men with the rifles. Her heart pounding rapidly, Lisa peeked over the back of the seat at the mysteriously acting man behind them. A nervous snort erupted from his nose when he caught her glance and he quickly shifted his gray, squinty eyes away. Lisa shuddered.

"We're not here to hurt anyone but we will if we have to. We're marshals of the Commonwealth of Massachusetts and we're looking for two people. Names are Rebecca and John Pyne." They scanned the passengers, their eyes resting on some longer than others. Both pairs of eyes stared at Cal for a disturbing few minutes.

Lisa's heart nearly stopped but she kept her senses and leaned back into the seat, every muscle taut to the breaking point. She brushed Cal's arm and felt the tension there.

"Now, we're just going to take a look around and ask some questions. You all cooperate with us and everything will be fine."

The man behind Lisa motioned for one of the marshals to come to him. The man whispered to him briefly and the marshal nodded, immediately stepping to Cal's side. A threatening silence filled the car as the marshal asked, "What's your name, young man?"

"Edward Hale, Sir."

"And you, young lady?"

Lisa folded her hands in her lap and smiled up at the marshal. "Lizbeth Hale."

"Brother and sister?"

"No, Sir. Lizbeth's my wife," Cal answered firmly.

"You can't mean that," the marshal said. "You're not old enough to be married."

"Oh, but we are," Lisa said. "I'm seventeen and Ed is eighteen."

"Well, I'll be damned. Oh, excuse me for that remark ladies." He turned apologetically to the other women in the car.

"I'll bet your mama doesn't know about this, does she?" he asked Lisa.

"No, she doesn't," Lisa said. "But that shouldn't concern you."

Getting his face down close to them, the marshal asked, "I'm also looking for a boy named Lee Bellamont. Used to work for Mr. Pyne," he said, addressing Cal. "Are you saying that you are not Lee Bellamont?"

Staring directly into his eyes, Cal said, "I certainly am not."

The man behind them jumped up. "I don't believe him, Wallace. These two and that conductor, Mr. Hunt, had a long whispered conversation and it sure seemed like a conspiracy to me. Something was very secretive and I know he sneaked a piece of paper to them and she put it in her pocket."

Marshal Wallace studied Cal and Lisa again and said, "Orville seems to think you have something to hide. I'd like to see that paper."

"That's my personal belonging and you don't have the right to read it," Lisa said hoarsely.

"I may not, but I'm going to. Give it to me," he ordered gruffly.

The men in the car were stirring in their seats, but the other marshal stood at the end of the car with his rifle poised waiting for someone to make a move. Lisa desperately tried to find a way out of this. She did not want anyone hurt. If she gave it to them, it may be the end of the Pynes. If she didn't, there could be an uprising among the men in the car and someone would surely die. She searched Cal's face but he couldn't give her a clue as to what to do.

"Come on, young lady Lizbeth, if that's really your name. Hand it over."

It seemed that everyone in the car stopped breathing as she reached into her pocket. As quickly as she could, she pushed the note from Hunt deeper inside, then shifted the front of the crucifix from its back and pulled at the paper hidden inside.

"What's taking so long? Do you need some help?" Marshal Wallace hissed.

"You can treat her with respect," said the man that had been in the aisle earlier.

"Shut up," shouted the other marshal from the end of the car.

Lisa successfully pulled out the rolled up paper and handed it to Marshal Wallace with trembling hands.

"A little nervous, aren't you?" he asked.

"I never had guns pointed at me like this before. Course I'm nervous."

Lisa had no idea what was on that paper but she knew it had nothing to do with the Pynes. She grasped her crucifix inside her pocket and prayed there was nothing incriminating written on it.

He quickly glanced through the letter, muttering as he read.

"This is written to someone's daughter from her mother, except she says she's not really her mother." He looked at the man behind Lisa. "Does this look like the paper she got?"

"Could be. I just saw a corner of it when he passed it to her."

"Who are Adrian and Pierre?" the man asked Lisa, adding an air of haughtiness to the pronunciation of Pierre.

"Pierre is my father." Lisa was having difficulty finding her voice but she continued to speak directly to the man.

"Says here Adrian is your real mother. I'll bet you haven't had a chance to read this yet, have you?" the man said, his tone void of any sympathy or regret for having spilled this news.

Lisa, pale and stricken, shook her head. "I haven't."

Aware of the effect of the man's disregard, Cal put his arm around Lisa and drew her to him.

"So your grandpa wouldn't let your pa see your ma," mused the marshal, seeming to be enjoying himself. "This is quite a story."

Lisa's head was reeling as though struck by a blow.

"Young lady, is this some kind of code or something?"

"No, no it isn't," Lisa answered frantically. "Mr. Hunt said somebody gave it to him to give to me when he got on the train in Boston. Somebody from the orphanage must have found it in my ma's room after I was... after she died."

"I guess it doesn't matter," the man said to the other marshal. "Doesn't tell us anything helpful."

Lisa trembled and slumped weakly into the crook of Cal's arm. He retrieved the paper from the floor where it had fluttered when the marshal let it drop. He wrapped his arms around her while the marshals pursued their unsuccessful questioning of the other passengers.

As soon as they were gone, six men stood up and grimly moved down the aisle to where the informer sat hunched in the corner of his seat and visibly quaking with fear. The train whistle blew and steam billowed and hissed past the windows as it began to move. Darkness had moved in and the moon cast an eerie light through a thin layer of clouds.

"Orville, we think you need to get off this train right now," the assumed leader said firmly.

"But the train has started to move... and... and... we're out in the middle of nowhere. What do you expect me to do, jump?" he quavered.

"That's the idea, so we guess you'd better do it now. You're not staying here. Maybe you can still catch up with your cronies."

The man grabbed his bag and headed for the door with two of the men prodding him on with their gun barrels. They watched him jump and roll, then returned to where Cal and Lisa were seated.

"Now, if a couple of you men will light the lanterns hanging from the ceiling, we'll see what we can do for this young lady."

"She's had a shock. I think she's fainted. Maybe we oughta lay her down on the floor until she comes out of it," Cal said, his words catching in his throat. Mumbling, he added, "She didn't know her ma wasn't her real ma."

Cal was on his knees beside Lisa massaging her hands and gently saying her name until her eyes fluttered open and she looked up at the faces bent over her.

"I'll be fine," she muttered, struggling to get to her feet. After helping her into her seat, she gratefully accepted the cup of water offered to her. "I guess things have just kind of caught up with me. Thank you all." Turning to Cal, she said, "I need to read that letter."

CHAPTER 22

LISA HELD THE letter in her unsteady hands. The aisle cleared as the men drifted quietly back to their seats, respecting Lisa's need to learn the troubling details in the words so rudely uttered by the marshal. An unusual silence settled in the car.

The words were swimming on the page as she began reading through watery eyes.

My dear daughter,

I want to tell you about your father and your mother before this illness takes over. I should have told you from the beginning, but I loved you so much I couldn't do it. You have become my life, my own daughter even though you are not my child by birth. You have been with me since the very moment you were born and I feel in my heart as though you are my own flesh and blood.

At fifteen years old, I was the personal maid and companion to Adrian Kennicot, also fifteen, in London, England, the daughter of a wealthy industrialist. When he came to Boston for a time in 1838, I was brought with them. Adrian met your father and loved him the moment she saw him, but Mr. Kennicot forbade her to see him when their circumstance was discovered.

Adrian was a beautiful and willful girl. She found many ways to see him secretly and I helped her. Your father was a good, sweet man and wanted to marry her, but that was a hopeless wish. He was a Frenchman and a Catholic. Her father held a high position in the Church of England and to marry a French Catholic would be unforgivable. I cried with her, sharing her despair. She did not have the courage to break her ties with her family and run off with him. That is what I would have done.

So, their desperation drew them close and the inevitable happened. Adrian became pregnant. It was then her father locked us both in the house. The world was not to know that their unmarried daughter was with child, especially your father. I tried unsuccessfully to sneak out of the house to tell Pierre what was happening. Adrian and I heard him come to the door many times but he was sent away being told finally that she had been sent back to England. She screamed to see him but her father held her down with his hand over her mouth. She grew to hate her parents and the servants helping to make her a prisoner. When she finally realized that Pierre was gone to her forever, she gave up and became very depressed. She bore their child on May 13, 1839 and named her Elizabeth Marie. That, of course, was you.

Your grandfather had a servant put you in my arms immediately and instructed the household staff to call me your mama. I loved you from the moment I saw you. You were allowed to nurse at your mother's breast as I had no milk; otherwise, you were kept from her. Your grandfather never looked at you and your grandmother was not allowed to. It broke your mother's heart and she withdrew, staying alone in her room. I couldn't help her.

As soon as you were weaned, Mr. Kennicot found me a job in the household of a wealthy American family in Boston, and the Kennicots returned to England. I wanted you to have your father's name so I also took his name to avoid any problems later on.

I thought long and hard about telling you this last thing but I think I must because you are now a grown woman and you must lay to rest the past and make a new future for yourself. Your mother lost the only two loves of her life, Pierre and you. I am so sorry, Lisa, but your mother died the day the family was to board the ship for England. The news was passed among the wealthy families of Boston, friends of the Kennicots. No one knew how she died, at least no one was willing to tell me. I do know that she did not want to live.

While Adrian was still alive, this crucifix was delivered to the door and a sympathetic maid sneaked it to me. I hid it from your grandfather by wrapping it in your blanket. When I accidently discovered the cavity in it, I saw a paper rolled up inside. It may be a note from your father to your mother. I couldn't make myself read it as it was meant only for your mother's eyes. When you were four, I was dismissed from my position and you and I were on our own; thus, the orphanage.

You had two mothers who loved you, and both of us loved your father although he never knew about my love. May God go with you throughout your life. I have written this over a period of time and now I must go to bed as I am so very tired. I love you, Lisa, so very much. I am sorry to leave you.
Mother

Lisa's head was spinning, her surroundings shifting and waving before her eyes. She buried her face in her lap and cupped her hands over her ears. Her entire lifetime fell with a thud at her feet.

Wrapping his arm around her shoulders, Cal laid his cheek against her hair and felt her body quiver. A low guttural moan rolled out from the folds of her dress. "Lisa, what can I do?" Cal whispered in her ear.

Slowly and awkwardly, her elbow pushed at the crumpled piece of paper in her lap until it hit the floor. She began to rock back and forth, dry sobs becoming part of the drone.

Cal flattened the paper on his knee with his left hand, keeping a comforting arm around Lisa. "Oh, my gosh," he said aloud as he read Charlotte's words.

"My name is Fred Williams. We're all concerned about this young lady and want to know if we can help in any way." The man had squatted beside Cal. "It seems she's suffered a trauma. My wife has a wet cloth to put to her head, if that would help."

He grabbed the back of Cal's seat as the train lurched violently and then settled down to a steady grating of wheels against rails. They were suddenly aware that Lisa was deathly still.

"Lisa," Cal shrieked, pulling her up by the shoulders so he could see her face. She was deadly pale and her eyes were dull but she was breathing small shallow breaths.

"Lisa," he gasped as her limp body slid into his arms.

"Here, take this," Fred said.

Gratefully, Cal took the cool wet cloth and placed it on Lisa's forehead. Her eyes rolled toward Cal's face and he knew she saw him. Her fingers crept toward his hand and a collective sigh of relief came at once from those who stood nearby to help.

"I'm very tired," she said. Cal moved out of the way and let her curl up on the seat where she fell into a sound sleep.

"Sometimes, sleep is the best temporary escape from a problem," Fred said. "Apparently, she's had a devastating emotional blow but it appears she'll be all right. She seems to have a strong constitution."

"She sure does. I've watched her take one blow after another in the past few weeks and she's 'toughed' her way through each one. Her ma's death was the worst."

He pulled the letter from his pocket where he had put it when he tended to Lisa.

"This letter was hidden inside her crucifix and it's the one she handed to the marshal to read. He could have whacked her a good one and it wouldn't have hurt as much as it did when he told her what was in it."

"That was a cruel thing to do," Clarissa Williams said with a sympathetic shake of her head. "Worse yet, he seemed to enjoy it."

"Lisa just now read the whole thing for the first time and it had some really shocking news for her, some of it you heard from the marshal. I'll let her tell you about it if she wants to. It's not up to me."

Cal rolled the letter back up and squatted on the floor beside Lisa, studying the face he loved so much. How would he ever be able to help her through this?

He carefully pulled the crucifix from her pocket and returned the tightly rolled scroll to its hiding place. As he moved the pieces back together, he saw the tip of the note mentioned in Charlotte's letter. He was sure it was a love note, now nearly seventeen years old. Perhaps it contained a clue as to Pierre's whereabouts. But, by now, he may be dead as well. Cal hoped Lisa would wait a while to read the note. After the shock of Charlotte's letter, maybe it would be best if she didn't read it at all.

Without realizing it, he continued to grasp the crucifix as he dropped to the floor and leaned his back against the seat, allowing himself to be soothed by the rhythmic swaying of the car as it rolled down the track. He nodded and fell asleep.

CHAPTER 23

IT WAS AFTER midnight when they arrived at Albany where they would change trains. Cal was grateful to discover that the people they had been traveling with would remain together. They were good people who had already been through quite a bit as a group and had begun to create an emotional bond. When it was time to transfer, Lisa stumbled alongside Cal, clinging to his arm. As soon as they settled into their place on the new train, Lisa curled up on the seat and fell back into a troubled sleep.

Cal saw that some passengers were being taken into Albany to spend the night but the people in their car were spending the night in their seats while children slept in the aisle. The next day, they would cross into Canada at Niagara Falls and then head down to Detroit. There was a new world to be seen out there and he wished Lisa would wake up to share the experience with him.

Still holding the crucifix, Cal returned to his place on the floor beside Lisa. Not being familiar with praying, he hugged the crucifix to his chest and closed his eyes whispering, "Just please take care of Lisa and make her better and take care of the Pynes and me, too." He thought he felt a wave of comfort but he wasn't sure. He had given it a try.

In the dim light of the overhead lanterns, he glanced around the car, studying his fellow passengers as they shifted about trying to get comfortable for the night. Anxiety etched itself into most of the faces, especially the women with children. Seated beside them in the aisle seats, the men sat protectively with their hands at their sides where

Cal knew their guns rested in readiness. He had noticed that there was always one man sitting upright and awake whenever the others slept. It was not always the same man, as though a sentinel schedule had been prearranged.

Cal knew which ones were heading for the Kansas Territory and he marveled at their courage. They weren't running away as he and Lisa were. They had packed up wives and children, leaving all that was familiar to go west for a cause they truly believed in. An unwritten alliance was forming in the hearts of these people and he and Lisa were a part of it. He felt safe and comforted. His gaze landed on the Howell's infant, snuggled quietly in her mother's arms. The child would grow up in the wilderness. Would he be the same person he would have been had they stayed in the East? Cal thought not. He, himself, was changing and he wondered what he would become.

Scooting around to see Lisa, he studied her face, realizing that he loved her more deeply every day. He wanted to take away the pain, but there was nothing he could do. She would have to come to terms with this new problem just as she had done with all the others she had faced over the years. But he would be there for her, ready to comfort her when she needed it. Their lives had become entwined many years ago and he couldn't imagine life without her. With these thoughts, he drifted into sleep.

He awoke with the sun streaming onto his face and a pair of brown eyes peering down on him. A wan smile accompanied the pale face. Beneath them, the train rolled steadily along the tracks having left Albany at sunrise.

"Hi," Lisa said, stroking his forehead with her fingertips. "Kinda left you for a while. Sorry about that."

Cal jumped up excitedly and scooted into the seat beside her, handing her the crucifix. "You've been asleep for more than twelve hours and I've been worried to death about you," he choked. "How are you feeling?"

She shrugged. "Hungry, but I'll be okay. Been sitting here thinking while I watched you sleep. Do you know you sleep with your mouth open and make funny little snorty sounds?" she teased.

"Only when I'm sittin' up," he answered, wrinkling his nose at her.

She drew up her knees and placed her feet against the back of the seat in front of her, tucking her dress around her legs.

"Now, that's real ladylike."

"Forgot," she grunted, returning her feet to the floor.

"You sure you're gonna be okay?" Cal asked.

"Told you. I'm gonna be okay."

She put her head down and motioned for him to hunch down with her. "I wanna talk." Cal joined her and waited patiently for her to begin. The words didn't come easily but he could see that she was intent on getting something off her mind.

"When I went to sleep yesterday, I never wanted to wake up. I hurt so bad. All these years, the only steady thing in my life was my ma—Charlotte." She squeezed his hand. "Course you were there, but you were a friend and, well, you know, you could've gone out of my life at any time. But my ma? I never questioned that she would leave me. I was her daughter."

"But it's different now," Cal whispered.

"Anyway," she continued as though she hadn't heard him. "I tried to picture Adrian and her parents and everything that went on during that time. I wanted to go find my grandparents and see what they looked like and, you know, let them see me. Maybe my grandda would love me now that I'm grown. Maybe he'd come to the door and be surprised and happy to see me and then throw his arms around me and say he was sorry. Maybe, since he's rich, he might have a painting of my... ah... of Adrian on the wall." Lisa stopped to take a deep breath and rest her head against the back of the seat in front of her.

She fell silent and just when Cal thought she was finished, she began again.

"When I woke up a while ago, I thought different. Just can't imagine a grandda not wanting his granddaughter. Can't imagine him treating his own daughter the way he did. What a mean, horrible person," she said with conviction. "Why would I wanna see him? Look what he did to my life and Charlotte's and his daughter's and my da's."

She paused to stare out the window, her eyes seeing something in the distance that was not revealed to Cal.

Turning to face Cal, she continued. "I decided my present life en't changed all that much. Yeah, it was a shock to hear about this person, Adrian. When I finally woke up from my sleep, I woke up to something else, too. Even if I was hurt bad, I didn't feel sorry for myself anymore. I got to feelin' sorry for Adrian. She's not really my mother. Charlotte is, or was. Charlotte led a tough life for me and I appreciate it. She didn't have to but she fought for me. Adrian didn't. Adrian's just a name but Charlotte gave me life. She loved me and I know it. And I love her back. I couldn't ask for better. She's my real ma and always will be. Besides, I may still have a da someplace. Who knows?"

Cal was speechless.

"I see Lizbeth is awake," Fred Williams said, standing in the aisle beside them.

Lisa smiled up at him. "I'm awake and I'm gonna be okay. Facts sometimes seem like make-believe when you compare them to reality. My ma always said we had to live with reality. That's what I've decided to do. Can't go through life grieving over what en't been."

"You're a very adult thinking young woman. We're all relieved that you're awake and feeling better." Agreement to his words echoed throughout the car. "We've all noticed that you haven't eaten anything for a while so we put this together for you." He handed Cal two slices of bread covered with sausage and slices of onion. "You may not care for the onion but it's a healthy thing to eat so give it a try."

"We've got a little money. We can pay you for this," Cal said, reaching into his pocket.

"We don't want your money. Consider this a gift."

At the sight of food, Lisa realized that she was famished. "This isn't gonna short anybody, is it?"

"Not at all. In case you hadn't noticed, this train has a water barrel at the back of the car. There's a dipper hanging on the side. I'm suggesting you use it soon since you've gone a long time without water."

She didn't waste any time biting into the bread. As Mr. Williams turned away, she grabbed his arm and held him as she quickly chewed and swallowed. She stood up so everyone could hear her. "I wanna thank you for all you did for me yesterday and for this food just now. And please call me Lisa. Lizbeth's a made-up name."

"I thought so. We're all impressed at how you handled yourself against those marshals."

Cal and Lisa watched him return to his seat, both of them knowing full well that he knew there was more to their story. Somehow they knew he wouldn't ask them, either.

Lisa finished her food and went to the barrel for a drink. When she returned to the seat, she had the envelope from Mr. Hunt in her hand.

"Thought we oughta take a look at this," she whispered, holding it in her lap. She pulled at the flap and brought out the note along with twelve dollars in drafts on a bank in Boston. Lisa quickly stuffed the money in her pocket. The note was brief.

We are at the Stanton's. One of their servants is to deliver this to Mr. Hunt before the train leaves Boston. We hope he gets it there. We will get on the train somehow and, in the meantime, use this money for food and any extra expenses you might have before we see you in St. Louis. Have a safe journey. Hoping to see you in St. Louis.

Rebecca and John

"Look at us," Lisa whispered. "We're rich. You've still got some money left of yours and what Mr. Todburn gave you. We must have more than fifteen dollars."

"Yeah. I hope somebody's selling food at the next stop."

"Think I should read the other letter?" she asked, mulling the thought over in her mind. "Seems like it might be a good time. I can probably handle another shock. Can't be any worse than that first one."

A quivery sensation started in her mid-section and traveled down the length of her arms to her finger tips as she pivoted the top piece from the back of the crucifix and pulled the note from its seventeen-year hiding place. She clasped her arms across her middle and bent her head over her lap, clutching the tightly rolled paper in her fist.

Cal touched her arm and she straightened up.

"I'm f-f-fine. I'm just excited. This paper I'm holding is from my da," she stated in awe. "I've thought about him so much and now, I'm gonna see his writing and read his very own words."

Cal put his arm around her shoulders and whispered, "You want me to read it to you?"

Lisa raised her head. "No. But I want you to read it with me." She unrolled the note and with some effort laid the paper flat across her knee, pressing out the aged creases with her hand. Neither realized that a spellbound silence filled the car.

My lovely Adrian,

You are the flower of my heart, my very heartbeat that keeps me alive. You do not come to meet me anymore and when I seek access to you at your home, I am denied that privilege with such rigid finality that I have come to believe I am cut off from you forever. I am heartbroken.

I have asked a friend to deliver this crucifix to your door and to ask that it be given directly to you. It is hand-carved olive wood and belonged to my mother. I have treasured it as I treasure you. The cavity held her rosary but I have replaced that with this note to you in the hope that you alone will read it. I pray you will find it.

I am heading west with my "funny little furniture models" as you call them. My company believes there is a market for the foldup furniture there. If you ever decide to break from your family, please try to follow me on a path to Kansas City, Missouri. That is where I had hoped to take you as my bride.

I love you with all my heart. I shall miss your sweet kisses and the touch of your skin against mine. I pray for you and for God's blessing on you always.

Yours forever,

Pierre

Darling, I have tucked a miniature painting of me in the crossbeam of the crucifix. I wish I had one of you; however, I know your face will always be in my memory. P

Lisa stared at the note in awe. "I en't never *ever* heard anyone talk like that—never ever."

"Me either," Cal said. "Wish I could find words like that to tell you how I feel about you."

"Oh, come on, Cal," Lisa interrupted. "You say those things to me and I'd probably laugh in your face. I know how you feel about me." She poked her elbow in his ribs and realized that he was blushing. "Oh, drats. You were serious. I'm sor…"

"Oh, shut up," Cal said, trying to cover his embarrassment. "At least you know where your da went all those years ago. If he's still alive, he's probably set up in a business and you'll be able to find him." He paused and stared at her. "En't you gonna get his painting?"

Lisa had been working on pivoting the crucifix farther apart but it seemed the tiny canvas was keeping that from happening.

"It just won't open up. It's stuck," she groaned. "He really pushed that in there."

"Here, let me give it a try." He wasn't any more successful than she was. "If we had a knife or somethin' to reach in there and flatten it down a little so the top could slide over it."

"That sounds scary. I don't want to tear it or break the crucifix." She groaned again and added, "Oh, my gosh, I'm gonna see my da's face."

"Only if we get it out of here and if the paint's lasted all these years."

They had not realized that their voices were carrying into the stillness of the car. Mrs. Winslow came to stand over them, shyly watching their efforts. "Excuse me," she said, clearing her throat. "I have this little tool that can just reach in there and grab a corner and I think you can pull it out then." Clearing her throat again, she said, "I hope you don't mind my interfering."

"You en't interfering," Lisa said. Taking the tool, she grabbed a corner of the canvas and eased it out of its hiding place. Her hands shook so that she thought she might drop the tool as she handed it back to Mrs. Winslow. "Thanks a lot. That did it."

Handing the inch-and-a-half long roll to Cal, she said, "Here. You unroll it. My hands are too shaky."

The train pitched suddenly on the uneven track and the tiny portrait fell to the floor and rolled away. Cal lunged for it and grasped the roll just as it headed under a seat. Breathless and trembling, he returned to his seat and began to unroll the canvas.

"I en't never seen my da," she said to the people sitting anxiously on the edges of their seats to grasp what was happening. "I'm gonna see his face for the first time ever, I hope."

The portrait was tiny but perfect. Lisa was too stunned to speak. There she saw her light brown hair and brown eyes. The similarities she never saw in Charlotte, she now saw in the face on the canvas. Unsteadily, she got to her feet and stepped around Cal into the aisle.

"I want you all to see my da. I never knew him and it's a long story how I got here, but this is the first time I've ever seen his face. I look like h-h-him," she stammered. "If he's still alive, I'm gonna find him."

Lisa held the tiny portrait for each person to see. Each agreed that she did indeed look like him and they were sure she would find him. After all, he was still very young. She returned to her seat and laid her head on Cal's shoulder to let the breathtaking discovery fill her heart and soul. Her life had direction and purpose. For safekeeping, she returned the letters and portrait to their hiding place and held the crucifix to her breast.

"You'll help me, won't you?" she asked Cal.

"That's my plan."

CHAPTER 24

SEVERAL DAYS SLIPPED by in which Cal and Lisa were able to purchase food from vendors at the station stops along the way while Lisa regained her strength. Her revived spirit helped speed up the process. By now, the travelers knew each other by their first names and the women offered their laps to the two infants and three toddlers. Lisa burst out in goose bumps when she was handed little six-month-old Avery.

"Can you imagine Lee doin' this a year ago?" she asked Cal.

"It's kinda weird seeing you do it now," he answered with a mischievous grin. The little boy reached up and caught his finger in Cal's lip. "Wow," Cal said and gently removed the tiny hand. Avery giggled and patted Cal's cheek with his wet fingers.

"Some day," Cal said, searching Lisa's eyes.

"Hope so."

Mostly, the people dozed or simply sat back and watched the unfolding scenery as the train chugged its way westward. Sometimes the changes in the landscape caught their interest but for the most part, time stretched endlessly before them as their bodies synchronized with the random rhythm of the wheels. They had shared their thoughts and their personal adventures until conversation was drained of anything meaningful. On a cloudy and dreary afternoon, one of the men began singing, quietly at first and then robustly as people joined in for the second round.

"The Star of Empire" poets say,
    Ho! Westward Ho!

"Forever takes its onward way!"
Ho! Westward Ho!

Ho! Westward!
Soon the world shall know
That all is grand in the western land;
Ho! Westward Ho

Our Pilgrim Fathers sang the song,
Ho! Westward Ho!
Hear Right should triumph over Wrong?
Ho! Westward Ho!
Still westward many thousands flock,
Ho! Westward Ho!
And sing the shout from Plymouth Rock
Ho! Westward Ho!

Ho! Westward!
Soon the world shall know
That all is grand in the western land;
Ho! Westward Ho!

Lisa didn't know the words but she found herself clapping excitedly to the tune and listening closely as the people sang. By the third time around, she was singing along and Cal was smiling, relieved to see her joining in.

Before they could begin a fourth round, twelve-year-old Eli Holt jumped up waving his harmonica and when the noise subsided, he began playing. First, a slow plaintive "Amazing Grace" while the people hummed along. Then, as though someone flipped a page, he became lively, skipping in the aisle, clinging to a seat when the car jerked and swayed. Everyone sang and clapped their hands to Turkey in the Straw and Buffalo Gals and the sound of it soared out the open windows, across the meadows and through the canyons.

As tired as they were, the spirit in the car was given new birth. Soon others offered their talents to the group. Mrs. Winslow was finally encouraged to perform her bird whistles for them, which were hard to hear because of the noisy clacking of the wheels. They gave her an energetic ovation as she grinned shyly and bowed her way into her seat. Thirteen-year-old Rowena had studied the art of recitation for nearly three years and recited several of the stories and poems from her large repertoire. Her dramatic presentations had the people spellbound. She told them of her problem with stuttering. The recitation lessons had given her confidence and she no longer had the affliction.

Lisa leaned over and whispered to Cal. "Maybe I oughta take some of those recitation lessons so I could sound more like a lady."

"Don't you dare. I like you just the way you are. I like *us* just the way we are."

"Me too. After all, it's going to be just you and me livin' together the rest of our lives."

"Wow!" Cal said running his finger behind his right ear. "That sent a thrill down my spine."

"If the words did that to you, what are you gonna do when it really happens?"

"I'll probably die."

"Oh, no you won't. I won't let you."

He wrapped her hand in his as they leaned back together feeling happy and content.

Time passed more easily as the friendships deepened. The day before they were to reach Chicago, Lisa was stopped on her way back from the water barrel.

"Hey, Lisa. We haven't heard anything from you yet. What can you do to entertain us?" Eli asked with a twinkle in his eyes.

Lisa stopped abruptly; then thought about it and returned his grin. "I can run but there en't no way I can do that here on the train."

"Come on," he dared. "There has to be something else you can do."

Lisa's eyes lit up. "I'll challenge anyone in this car to an arm wrestling contest."

"Oh, really," one of the men said, and they all chuckled.

"Yeah, really," she said, defiantly.

Eli was excited. "I'll be the first and I'll beat you so fast you won't know what happened."

"We'll have to set a box or a trunk in the aisle so we can do it," Lisa said, but two men were already scrambling for a small trunk stored on an empty seat at the back of the car.

It didn't take long and Eli and Lisa were on their knees on opposite sides of the trunk with their hands clasped. Fred Williams said, "Go," and Eli found his arm flattened to the top of the trunk, his face flushed and embarrassed.

"Wow! You're strong—and fast."

Lisa stayed where she was and looked around for another challenger. The men picked Fred to take her on next. He lowered his five-foot-eleven, one hundred seventy-pound frame to the floor and looked Lisa in the eye. "Are you sure you want to do this?" he asked.

"Sure," she said. "All you can do to me is beat me."

They clasped hands and Eli said, "Go." Lisa strained and Fred strained. They held on in spite of the periodic jolting of the train. Lisa's arm began to move his arm downward. She squeezed his hand harder and let out a loud grunt, slamming Fred's arm down to the top of the trunk.

"Now, that's embarrassing," Fred said.

"You let her win, didn't you?" Eli accused.

"No, I certainly did not." He studied Lisa and asked, "How old did you say you are?"

"I told the man I was seventeen but I'm just turnin' sixteen next month... and," she looked at Cal and he nodded. "And we're not married, but we're gonna be as soon as we can."

"How did you get so strong?"

She looked at Cal. "I guess I can tell them a little. Okay?"

Cal nodded.

"I've been a blacksmith's assistant since I was nine years old. I learned the trade and my muscles just got strong from all the lifting and pounding." She pulled up her sleeve and flexed her arm muscle causing some "ah's" and "oh my's." With an approval from Cal, she told them briefly about the orphanage, Mr. Carver and her mother's death. She left out the part about slashing Carver's face.

"So," Arthur Weatherby mused, stroking the graying hair on his chin. "You grew up as a boy. Interesting. That explains a lot."

"What d'ya mean by...?" Lisa stopped. She didn't have to ask as she pulled her knees together and sat up straighter. "Never mind. Guess you all can tell that I have a lot to learn about bein' a girl."

"It's hard to see how you pulled it off," said Fred. Thoughtfully, he continued. "Your mama's dead and you don't know if your father is living or not. So essentially, you're an orphan."

"I guess but Cal and I are together. We were best buddies and now we're... well, you know," she blushed. "He's good with horses and I'm a blacksmith and a farrier. We're hoping to find work in Lawrence. If not there, maybe one of the other towns in the Kansas Territory."

"We're all looking to get established somewhere in Kansas," Fred said. "I'm a carpenter and hope to get in on the building of new towns. Hope you two attain your goals and, young lady, I wish you God's guidance in successfully finding your father. Looks like we're pulling into the Chicago station," he observed.

The conductor came into the car and announced that there would be a long delay in Chicago, allowing them time to get off the train, stretch their legs and have a meal in a restaurant if they wanted to.

Grateful for the chance, the passengers moved off quickly, some groaning as they painfully straightened their knees and put weight on their legs and hips.

"Woweee!" Eli whooped when he stepped down to the ground and into the fresh air. He immediately squatted and began doing deep knee bends.

"Good idea," Lisa said and she and Cal joined him.

"Wow! This isn't easy," Eli said, huffing his way up and down.

"No it's not—not like it used to be," Lisa said, laughing as she tumbled backwards, taking Cal with her.

"We've gathered an audience," Cal said.

"Oh, drats," Lisa gasped from within the billows of her skirt, her bare legs splayed out in front of her. "I forgot."

Frantically pushing her dress down, she jumped up feeling a warm rush to her face. Her eyes sparkled with enjoyment. "Oh, well. That was fun," she mumbled, chuckling as she pulled Cal through the crowd toward the vendors on the station platform. "Let's buy some things before everything's sold out."

They hurried to the bread vendor and found that he also sold hard-boiled eggs and several kinds of cheese. Having bought what they thought would take them all the way to St. Louis, they headed back to their train car to store the food in their bag when someone touched Lisa's arm.

"No hugs," Rebecca warned quietly. "We're just a couple that want to buy you a meal. We're the Weavers, Alice and Ted."

Lisa recognized them immediately in spite of John's powdered gray hair, heavy eyeglasses and farmer's overalls. Rebecca was buried under a peasant's bonnet and a knitted shawl that covered her shoulders and hung to her knees. Lisa pulled back her hug and responded, whimsically, "So nice to meet you. We'd like very much to go eat with you, wouldn't we Cal?"

"You bet. I'll take this stuff and stash it in our bag," Cal offered. "You stay right here and wait for me. I'll be right back."

"The train won't leave without us if we go off to a restaurant, will it?" Lisa asked.

"No, it won't. It won't leave for de next six hours so if we get there and back in that period of time, we will be fine."

Cal trotted back to them while tucking in his shirttail and settling his cap on his head. Lisa finger-combed her hair and wiped her face with her sleeve thinking how refreshing it would be to wash the dress and, maybe, even get a new one someday. A bath, that's what she really wanted, or a dip in a lake would do fine. She was sure everyone on the train was wishing for the same thing. For now, being off the train and in the fresh air was welcome.

"Do you think we still need to worry about the marshals?" Lisa asked.

"Maybe not but Rebecca and I are going to be careful still, until we get to de Kansas Territory," John said.

"We are, too, but I en't gonna worry about that or Carver or anything else right now. I'm so happy to see you two in person and to know for sure that you're okay," Lisa said.

Forty-five minutes later, the four of them were seated at a small round table at the back of a noisy crowded restaurant several blocks from the station, their plates filled with roast beef, boiled potatoes, gravy, green beans and corn bread. This was accompanied by a large glass of ginger beer. Neither Cal nor Lisa could believe the feast that was laid out in front of them. They dug in with gusto and saw that the Pynes did the same.

Taking a breath in between mouthfuls, Lisa asked, "You're walkin' really good on that broken leg. Doesn't it hurt?"

Rebecca smiled a broad relieved smile. "It appears that I only sprained my ankle. Didn't break it as we thought. What a blessing that turned out to be; although, I have to say it was extremely painful when it happened."

"We heard through de grapevine that de marshals were very offensive in their treatment of you, Lisa," John said.

"I would say they were," Cal said. "I'd call one of them downright cruel." He gave them a brief description of the scene in their car during the marshal's visit.

"It's all okay, now," Lisa interjected before he finished. "It took me a while but, after reading the letter myself, I realized Charlotte was my real ma. It gave me a lot more hope of finding my da."

"We're glad to hear that. We were worried about you when we heard the story. I just have one more question. Did they really kick that man off the train while it was moving?"

"They did," Lisa and Cal said together.

"He was sneaky. He had wicked looking eyes. When I turned around and looked at him, he looked like he was up to something. It didn't bother me one bit when the men made him jump. We could see he was scared to death."

John and Rebecca in turn told them that they had no problems with the marshals. They weren't recognized and, the one person in their car that knew who they were, kept quiet. It had been tense, but nothing like what Cal and Lisa had encountered.

When they had finished and laid their forks and knives across their empty plates, John leaned back in his chair and announced, "I saw a pecan pie on the shelf when we came in and I am going to have a piece of it. Anyone going to join me?"

Their stomachs hadn't been this full for days but Lisa and Cal both held up their hands.

When they were halfway through their pie, the door opened and two uniformed soldiers stepped in and looked around. Lisa's muscles tightened around the food settling in her stomach. Cal squeezed her hand under the table.

"Just act normal," John whispered. "They don't know who we are and the two of you have already been cleared." The lines across his forehead deepened.

"Any of you traveling on the train to St. Louis?" asked the taller of the two officers.

Most of the people in the restaurant raised their hands.

"We're here to escort you back to the train. Finish up quickly and we'll head out."

"Is there a problem?" asked a man sitting near the soldiers.

"Yes, there is. The German saloonkeepers here in Chicago are rioting. They've already wounded one of our men and one of their own has been killed. One group of protestors is heading this direction so we came to make sure you got back to the train safely."

The faces at the back table relaxed and Lisa's muscles released their hold on her food.

"What are they rioting about?" another voice called out.

"The law says they can't be open for business and sell whiskey on Sundays so they have been shut down. They don't like it."

As they stepped out into the street, a sound like a freight train bearing down on them came from the north caused by hundreds of feet steadily pounding toward them. Angry voices could be heard above the din. The train passengers found themselves surrounded by ten uniformed men who encouraged them to walk quickly. They did.

Once on the train, Lisa and Cal stared horrified as terrified baggage handlers, vendors and other unprotected individuals darted inside the depot or took refuge behind boxes and wagons scattered about the platform. The soldiers lined up along the station platform and pointed their bayoneted rifles toward the angry mob. Lisa and Cal ducked beneath the window when the first bullet was fired above the heads of the oncoming mob. A mass shifting of bodies sounded in the car as everyone slipped down into the aisle or between the seats, keeping their heads below window level. Another single shot was fired in the air, but the mob kept coming. Suddenly, ten guns fired in rapid succession and all was quiet. Cal peeked out of the corner of the window with one eye, fearful of what he might see. The mob had stopped and no one was on the ground, wounded or dead.

"The soldiers musta fired at their feet or over their heads," Cal said so everyone in the car could hear. "The mob's stopped in their tracks and the soldiers en't moving. They're just pointing their rifles at the marchers, ready to fire again. Looks like the protestors are seriously wondering if it's worth it."

Like the tide heading back to sea, the mob turned and headed in the other direction.

"They've turned and are goin' away," Cal said.

Sounds of relief echoed throughout the car.

"The soldiers are standin' stock-still. I'll bet if one of that crowd turns around, he'll get it." Cal watched until the mob was nearly out of sight and the soldiers lowered their rifles. "Okay. You can get back in your seats now."

Timid Mrs. Winslow, her eyes wide with nervous excitement, exclaimed, "W-w-well, that's an experience w-w-we won't soon forget."

"You can say that again," Eli said, his eyes as excited as hers.

Lisa bent her knees and put her feet on the back of the seat in front of her. "I'm full up. We've got food in our bag and I'm ready to take a nap. We're supposed to be in St. Louis on Tuesday, just seven days from when we left Boston." She looked at Cal. "Can't be much more can happen between here and the Kansas Territory."

His smile said he wasn't so sure about that.

Two hours later, the train screeched to a halt in the middle of a vast nothingness.

"Now what?" asked Linette Winslow nervously staring out the window.

Eli opened his window and stuck his head out in an attempt to see if something was blocking the tracks. "Can't see a thing," he said, pulling his head back inside.

Some of the men rested their hands on their gun handles as they watched for intruders. "Heard some stories about the restlessness along the Missouri-Kansas border caused by our coming to vote for a free state," Fred mused aloud. "Missourians are slave owners and, as you all know, they want to make Kansas a slave state, too. They don't like us being here."

Just then, the conductor entered the car and announced that the delay was caused by the need to repair some track up ahead. "Seems a freight train departed from the track earlier today and it has taken a while to get the track fixed. We'll be ready to start again in less than an hour. Sorry, folks. These things happen."

The passengers were relieved; however, they were not fully convinced the danger was gone. They continued to warily watch the surrounding landscape as they waited.

CHAPTER 25

IT WAS TUESDAY morning and Lisa was perched on a stack of hay bales on the wharf in St. Louis enjoying the feel of a warm wind blowing against her face and ruffling her hair. The sun was reaching mid-sky and they had already waited several hours to board the steamboat resting at the wharf where she sat. For the moment, she was alone and time was passing slowly. They were nearing the end of their journey and she was feeling a bit unsteady inside. Dreams of the Kansas Territory had dominated her thinking for years and now, she was about to have her wishes fulfilled.

The side-wheeler, Kate Swinney, sat light in the water waiting to take on its cargo that Lisa had been told included one hundred ninety-two passengers and their belongings. Only twenty-four of the original group in the New England Emigrant Aid party that left Boston together would be boarding. Some had dropped off along the way and others were heading south to make their homes in Osawatomie in the Kansas Territory. She had been pleased to learn that all of the people in their train car would be joining them on the Kate Swinney.

The wind was picking up and filling the air with the powerful scent of the Mississippi River mud that had been churned up by the side-wheeler as it pulled in early that morning. Lisa breathed it deeply into her lungs. Sure smells a lot different than the Atlantic Ocean, she thought as she studied the monstrosity with considerable skepticism. She brought her knees up to her chin and wrapped her dress around her legs in an effort at modesty and listened to the chafing of the wrist-size lines against the pilings holding the restless boat in place.

Behind a circular slatted covering, she could see the huge side wheel, partially buried in the water and standing to a height several feet above the top of the boat. From the forward section, two enormous pipes stood side-by-side reaching for the sky and belching occasional gray puffs of steam. Two men leaned against the pilot's tower atop the upper deck and observed the loading of boxes, machinery and wagons. Of the boat's two decks above the water line, Lisa guessed the upper one was where the passengers would sleep and eat and while away their time on the 480-mile trip to Westport Landing just beyond Kansas City. The forward section of the lower deck seemed to be divided into stalls for hauling livestock.

She had heard the horror stories of steamers being gouged by hidden tree trunks deep in the water and sinking to the bottom of the river, all lives lost. She thought the "all lives lost" was an exaggeration because some people should be able to swim to shore. She did, however, believe the stories about the snags and sandbars and the problems caused by the low water level of the river. She had heard for a fact that a terrible drought had persisted throughout the past winter and still continued into the spring. At some point along their journey to Westport, they would split from the Mississippi River and steam up the Missouri River where the riverboats had encountered most of their problems, according to the boat captains returning from Kansas City. One captain reported that his passengers had to spend two days on a sand bar before the boat could be dislodged from the mud and started on its way again.

Pawing the ground just beyond the wharf were at least twenty restless horses being restrained by a dozen soldiers. Lisa estimated there were two hundred people milling around behind her as restless as the horses but with no one to control their impatience.

The food vendors swarming the wharf were busy weighing and measuring food to fill the bags and baskets of the passengers for the four-day trip to Kansas City. Tempers were running short, especially among the vendors who had stood for hours in the sun coping with picky irate Easterners who had just heard that the trip may take longer than four days and the food supply could get low. Cal, Lisa and the Pynes had eaten a hardy breakfast early that morning at one of the eateries nearby and purchased a supply of food as well.

As the last of the wagons disappeared on board, Lisa took another look at her ticket.

THE KATE SWINNEY
328 Ton Side-wheeler
Owner: Captain Pierre M. Chouteau
Ticket Price: $15.00 to Kansas City

The price had been written in by hand which told her that the owner could change it at will. Their tickets from Boston included the cost of the river trip to Kansas City but because of possible problems caused by the low water level, the boat owners were tacking on an extra charge of five dollars. She couldn't figure what extra costs the boat owner would have for this trip that he didn't have before. It simply looked like a scheme for making some extra money at the expense of a lot of exhausted people who couldn't get to Kansas City any other way.

And now, they waited. It was April twenty-fourth and the Missouri sun was high in the sky and pouring its heat down on their heads while the wind whipped up a gale, spinning dust into the people's eyes, wrapping skirts around ladies' legs and sneaking under the brims of hats, causing both men and women to chase frantically after them.

John guided Rebecca to a box where she was able to sit and rest her leg. She looked pale, but so did everyone else. Within a month, Lisa expected that everyone from the East would be a healthy tan color after constant exposure to the prairie sun. She could feel it getting a good start on her face right now.

Lisa jumped from the hay bales when men came to haul them aboard. Impatiently cracking her knuckles as she found a post to lean against, she felt very much the boy she once was. Did she dare find a private place and change into her boy clothes? *Naw! Better not. Guess I'll have to put up with this dratted dress 'til I get used to it. How do women put up with it in a wind like this? How do they get anything done while fighting this blasted thing all the time?*

Squinting into the wind, she waved away the gnats and hay bale dust from her eyes. The long wait in the sun was making her lazy or she might have been out looking for something to do. Her mind drifted off to all the happenings since she ran out of the orphanage. It seemed to her like she had lived a lifetime in only fifteen years. Almost sixteen, she reminded herself. She would have a birthday shortly after they arrived in Lawrence.

Her mind wandered off to the Pynes and the older people on the train. How had they managed everything that had happened to them in all of their years and now they were embarking on something brand new without knowing what was ahead of them? Her mother had bravely endured all those years at the orphanage and many of them while she was sick. She thought of the Pynes and their unwavering strength through their terrifying experiences while they were doing something good. She certainly had excellent examples to follow.

Looking around for Cal, she saw him exactly where she thought he would be. As soon as he laid eyes on the horses, he had hurried over to take a look. She watched him talking to one of the soldiers and soon he was running his hand down the long neck of the nearest one. He looked into the horse's eyes and spoke gently to it. The horse nuzzled Cal's neck, causing him to chuckle. The soldier spoke to Cal and it appeared that he was trying to convince Cal of something. Cal was shaking his head. He shook the soldier's hand and hurried back to Lisa.

"You'll never guess what that Cavalry Sergeant wanted me to do," Cal said mischievously.

"Join the Army and take care of horses," Lisa guessed.

"Yeah. That's what he wanted all right," Cal said, squinting at her unbelievingly. "How'd you guess?"

"You had that yearning look in your eyes when that horse nuzzled your neck."

"Boy, that felt good. I've missed the horses and I'm anxious to get back to working with them. I've been thinkin' about it more n' more, the closer we get to Lawrence."

"You wouldn't go and join up, would you?"

"Don't know, Lisa," he said thoughtfully. "Never thought about it before. Look at those beautiful animals. He said the Army needed more men who know how to handle them. I'd be a cavalryman, probably in the Second United States Regiment of Dragoons."

A dragoon! Lisa was thunderstruck. She had been confident throughout this journey that she and Cal would set up a home together in Lawrence and that he would help her look for her father.

"If you join the army, I'm gonna join," she blurted.

"You can't. You're a girl."

"So what! I'm a farrier and a good one. I can shoe a horse as well as the next man. Maybe even better," she said irritably. "Besides, I don't know how much longer I can handle this 'being a girl' thing." Cracking her knuckles irritably, she added, "I fooled you and everybody else for ten years."

Cal studied her face and knew she meant every word. "You can't do that anymore. Your body's changed and your face is a girl's face. You're too pretty, Lisa. The soldier's would catch on real fast."

Lisa turned her head and pouted, then realized that was what a girl would do. Was this "girl thing" catching up with her after all?

Cal touched her face and turned it toward him. He was inches from her lips. "How am I ever gonna show you how much I love you if you en't gonna be a girl?" He brushed her lips with his and she threw her arms around his neck, kissing him hard just as John and Rebecca walked up behind them. Lisa and Cal were flushed and they knew it showed. Pushing herself away from Cal, Lisa nervously straightened her dress knowing that such a public show of affection was looked down on.

John smiled and winked at them. "Don't be embarrassed. It's been a long trip. I just came to let you know that de passengers are beginning to board. I overheard some of what you said just before... well... just before, you know," he said, chuckling at his loss for words. "Lisa, what would I do without you in my shop? I need you to work with me." Then he hesitated and glanced at her from head to toe. "Cal's right. You would never fool de army."

"I en't said I was gonna do it, Lisa," Cal said, kicking at a knot in the wood at his feet. "If I did, it wouldn't mean I was giving up on us. You know how I feel about you." He put his arm around her shoulder and gently pulled her to him. "You and me are meant to be together and that's the way it's gonna be."

John grinned. "I have to agree with that. But now, it is time for us to board," he told them and took Rebecca's arm.

They picked up their few personal belongings and climbed to the upper deck finding it to be a huge dormitory with many small rooms. One room was allotted per family, no matter its size, creating a real problem for the families with more than two children.

"We signed you on board as our niece and nephew so you will share our room," John said in answer to the questioning look from both Lisa and Jack. "Can you handle dat?"

"Sure," Lisa said, grinning at Cal as she remembered the times they had slept outside under the stars together in the hot summer nights at the orphanage. He must have thought about those nights too as he teased her with his eyes. "If I'd known then what I know now...." He felt an elbow in his ribs as they looked into the little room where they saw four canvas cots with a blanket rolled up at the foot of each. The cots looked wonderful and inviting.

"And, by de way, it's time you call us Rebecca and John, don't you think?"

Lisa hesitated to answer. Through all the years, he had been Mr. Pyne. Could she suddenly become so informal with him?

"I guess it'll be like you havin' to learn to call me Lisa after calling me Lee all those years. I guess I can make the change, if that's what you want. How about you, Cal?"

"Sure."

"Good. Rebecca and I are comfortable with that."

Parents noisily herding their crying children onto the boat, anxious people pushing and shoving their way in their search for a room while trying to keep families together created a din that moved Lisa, Cal and the Pynes into their room for sanctuary. Rebecca immediately stretched out on her cot and sighed; the others followed her example.

Lisa decided she could tolerate another four days of travel, floating peacefully along the Mississippi and the Missouri Rivers. She closed her eyes and became conscious of the rocking motion of the boat and the slosh of water against the sides. It was comforting and, for the time being, she could forget the thought that Carver may have followed her and that the marshals may have sent word ahead. She let her mind drift toward thoughts of her father who could be somewhere nearby. She would ask about him and show his portrait to anyone that would listen. In just four days, they would reach Westport Landing and from there, they had only fifty miles to Lawrence. She glanced at Cal stretched out on the cot beside her and prayed they could stay together. She drifted off to sleep, unaware that the boat had begun its journey.

In spite of the sluggishness of the boat's movement in the shallow water and the dangers of bogging down around the sand bars, the passengers were more relaxed and in better moods than on the train. Being in the middle of the Mississippi River was like being on a separate planet, gliding through the atmosphere, safe from intrusion by the many problems they left behind or that lay ahead of them. They entertained each other with their talents and Lisa and Cal never left each other's sides, even when Cal went below to visit the horses.

On a warm afternoon, with the sun relentlessly pouring its rays down on them, Cal and Lisa joined others on the outside deck to watch a dozen men with long poles attempting to push the huge boat through the sludge around a sandbar. They were seven days into what should have been a four-day trip.

Cal put his hand on Lisa's arm and said, "Would you just stop it?"

"Stop what?"

"I've been noticing you imitating the older women and I just would like you to stop."

"How am I gonna ever learn to be a lady if I don't learn from other women?"

"Lisa, I love you the way you are. I like the way you walk and the way you talk. That's how I've known you for all these years." He paused and studied her face looking for her reaction. He saw a sparkle light up her eyes. "You don't need to be all ladylike. Kinda makes me uncomfortable."

"That's a relief," she said and elbowed his ribs. They convulsed into laughter.

"Are you two married?" A pleasantly teasing voice spoke behind them.

They turned to see a rather plain looking woman in her thirties with eyes that sparkled in amusement under the wide brim of the bonnet tied under her chin. Twin three-year-old girls chased each other nearby.

"Well... no," Cal answered, his fingers tightly laced through Lisa's. Responding to the friendliness in the woman's eyes, he said, "We will be, eventually. At least, that's the plan." He cast a teasing glance at Lisa and she felt an annoying blush rushing to her face. "We're still getting used to each oth... I mean, to the idea."

"So you haven't known each other very long?"

"Well, yes—I mean, no. We grew up together. We've known each other nearly all our lives," Lisa said, squeezing Cal's hand and smiling. "But this is different than climbin' trees and racing each other."

"Or trying to stay out of the old man's way," Cal added, allowing the dreadful thought of those memories to show on his face.

For a moment, the woman looked uncomfortable and then she said, "You look like you're sixteen or seventeen. Am I right?"

Lisa and Cal nodded. "Why are you asking us all these questions?"

"Oh, dear. You think I'm just nosy, but that's not entirely true. You've caught my interest. I suppose because you remind me of my husband and me fifteen years ago. He was eighteen and I was sixteen when we got married and we were so happy."

"Were?" Lisa asked.

"Oh, we still are. He's a pastor and we're going to a start a new parish in Lawrence. We have six children. All girls. Those two are our youngest so far." She patted her middle and nodded. "Yes, it seems like the Lord wants me to populate the earth. But I'm happy." And she looked like she meant it.

She picked up one of her daughters and grabbed the other's hand. "I have to be careful they don't slip through the gaps in this railing around the deck."

Lisa looked around curiously. "Where are your other four children?"

"Oh, they're in the arena or in our room. I certainly hope their father is looking out for them," she said, as though there was some doubt in her mind.

Suddenly, the boat began to move smoothly into deeper water and away from the sandbar. The men pulled in their poles and tied them up against the railing on the deck below. A long sigh of relief passed among the people watching. The captain had announced that they could still be two days away from Westport Landing; only one day, if they didn't have to fight more sand bars. He hadn't sounded happy.

"My name is Abigail Mason and my husband is Jed. He'd be glad to marry you whenever you decide you're ready. He could do it right here on the boat."

"Tha... thanks," Cal and Lisa stammered together.

Cal pulled Lisa toward the door to the arena. "We've gotta check on our aunt and uncle. See you later."

"I'm sorry if what I said ran you off," she called after them.

"Oh, no," Lisa called back. "Not at all."

As Lisa lay on her cot that night, she thought about what Abigail had offered. She and Cal had talked about getting married but had not made any definite plans. Now, on this boat, was not the right time. She was sure they would both know when the time was right.

CHAPTER 26

"FINALLY," JOHN HUFFED as he reached his wife who was pressed tight against the upper deck railing by the throng of passengers anxiously waiting to disembark. "Where are de young ones?"

"They're at the tail end of this horde. They said they weren't in a hurry and didn't want to get crushed in the mad rush to reach the gangplank."

"I can't blame dem," John said, placing their bags on the deck and guarding them with his feet. "We are here, my Rebecca. We have reached Westport Landing in Missouri. We are almost at our new home." Lifting his face into the breeze, he inhaled deeply. "De air has a different smell to it. It smells like dust and animals. De clean air of de ocean is now only a dream. But," he continued, "our old problems now are only a dream, too. We will begin again in de new town of Lawrence. I think we can say we don't anymore need to worry."

Rebecca leaned her head into his chest and tried to embrace his confidence, but she wondered.

Bathed in sunshine, Lisa and Cal thrilled at what they saw and the feeling of freedom it brought. From their lofty position on the upper deck, they had an excellent overall view of the Landing and the commercial trade that was taking place.

"It doesn't look like there'll be room down there for all of us on this boat. There are an awful lot of people already down there." Lisa's eyes narrowed as she studied the landscape below. "We'll get lost in the muddle."

"Yeah, but what a great muddle it is. It's a long way from Malden and Carver and it's all new to us." He wrapped an arm around her waist and drew her closer to his side. "I think it's really exciting."

"Me, too," Lisa said, her eyes sparkling as she watched people waiting to leave the boat. "Look. There's the preacher and his wife and all their kids. Hope they don't lose any them in that mess down there."

"I guess I don't have to ask if you're hungry," Cal said.

"Starving is a better word for it. That's the only part of the trip I don't wanna remember," Lisa said as they both thought about the reason why they were famished.

The Kate Swinney had taken nine days to make the four-day trip from St. Louis. To some, the boat had become a prison; to Lisa and Cal, it was quite an adventure and an exciting story to tell their children. The boat's food supply had run out on the evening of the seventh day creating a disgruntled and irritable group of passengers.

Those passengers who had food remaining from their purchases in St. Louis offered to share what they had with those who had none by pooling their supplies and having the captain ration them out to all the passengers. That had disappeared by the end of the eighth day leaving some very hungry passengers and crew to converge on the venders waiting on the Landing.

Leaning against the rail, Lisa clung to Cal's hand, forgetting her pangs of hunger while taking in the sounds carried across to them from the shore. She could not control the pounding in her chest as she truly began to realize that her ties to the past were severed. No more orphanage. No more Carver. No more marshals searching for them. No more Lee—only Lisa. She wasn't sure of that fact but she was going to work toward that end. There was so much to think about and nothing more to fear.

The Kate Swinney blasted its whistle to signal its arrival and came to a stop, ending its overdue journey. The crew lowered the gangplank and the passengers descended like cattle pushing their way to the open fields through a small gate in the corral. Mothers carried their babies while their frightened children clung to their skirts and stalwart fathers attempted to keep their families from being trampled.

"People get really weird sometimes," Cal said as he and Lisa stayed at the rail watching. Their bundle lay on the deck beside them ready to be picked up as soon as all the passengers had disembarked. Lisa took a deep breath of Missouri air and choked. "Whew. I think the wind's blowin' over that stock compound right over to us."

"Guess I won't breathe too deep, then," Cal said, wrinkling his nose.

Westport Landing was noisy and filled with hawkers selling everything the emigrants from the East would need. Lisa and Cal studied the landscape and saw that Westport Landing was confined by bluffs that rose above the small bustling town. They had steamed past the port at Kansas City, so they knew that the city lay above the bluffs and to the east. The Landing was filled with small buildings and lean-to sheds scattered about as though dropped helter-skelter like huge hailstones from the sky. Appearing to have been squeezed out of the way, several small stores sat on higher ground at the end of a wagon path. Lisa hoped one of the places nearby sold food. Her hunger pangs had returned.

Just then, an eager Rebecca and John came up beside them. "I suppose we had best remove ourselves and our things from this floating bucket and find something to eat, first thing. Then, we'll take a look around dis place," John said.

As soon as their feet touched solid ground, they were engulfed by the clamor and commotion created by the steamboat's arrival. There was no need to go looking for help. One of the many young boys moving among the passengers approached John immediately and asked if he could help him find what he needed.

The boy wore a strange cap made of animal fur still bearing its tail. Otherwise, his clothes were much like Cal's except that his pants were being held up by a pair of bright red suspenders and he was barefoot. His shoulder-length hair glowed orange in the sunlight and the ends flipped about in the breeze beneath his cap. From behind his dark brown eyes sneaked a glimmer of enjoyment, or was it a tease?

As though reading from a script, he stated, "My name is Timothy, but I am called Tim. I'm here to be of assistance to you if you need it." Noticing the doubtful look on John's face, his manner relaxed and he added, "There are several of us working for Mr. Bank who knows how confused people can be when they land here. He sends us out to help. He says it helps the newcomers and keeps us out of trouble." His grammar was perfect and his deep brown eyes—yes, they were teasing.

"Well, young man," John said. "If you can tell us where to buy something to eat and a place to sleep, you can tell Mr. Bank dat you have done your job good."

Tim's grin quickly spread from ear to ear as he began walking, motioning for them to follow. Wending his way through the mass of travelers purchasing or still searching for the things they need, his four followers had to step lively to keep up with him.

"Food," Lisa whispered to Cal.

"Yeah, we're headin' for food."

At the large open door to a two-story hotel, Lisa and Cal stopped behind John and listened as he and Tim spoke, both of them shouting to make themselves heard.

"Here's a place to eat and a place to sleep. The restaurant is at the back of the building. It's a good place to eat if you can find an empty table with all these people who just arrived. A lot of people go right over and buy their wagon and a horse or a pair of oxen and take off for the Kansas Territory. They get their supplies and spend their first night out there under the stars. Some of them buy a tent and some of them just sleep under the wagon. I hear the tent comes in handy along the way and, if you're going to Lawrence or some other town not so far away, it's a place to sleep while you're building a house."

"Does Mr. Bank sell tents?" John teased.

Tim's face suddenly matched his hair. "Well, as a matter of fact, h-he does." Tim began to chuckle. "He sells wagons, too."

"All right, young man," John said, placing his arm around Tim's shoulder. "You have done a good job and we thank you kindly." John placed a coin in the boy's outstretched hand.

"Thank you, Sir. If I can be of help again, I'll be around here somewhere. Just look for my red suspenders." With that, he turned around quickly and bumped head-on into Cal.

Tim took one look at Cal and backed away, shaking his head in confusion. "What the…? Aren't you supposed to be working?"

"What are you talkin' about?" Cal asked, squeezing Lisa's hand.

"Who's this girl and why did you change your clothes? What's going on, Con?" His bewilderment was edging him closer to Cal, his eyes staring at Cal's face.

Cal pulled away from Tim, holding out his hand to keep a distance between them. "My name's Cal, not Con. I'm Calvin Hale and I just got off the Kate Swinney so you've got me mixed up with somebody else." Cal pulled Lisa's arm intending to follow John and Rebecca into the hotel.

Tim grabbed Cal's arm. "Have you got a brother?"

"No," Cal said, yanking his arm away.

"Well, you sure look…," Tim began but found himself talking to Cal's back. "You sure look like my friend Con," he declared, breaking into a run the other direction.

Tim's eyes flashed with excitement. There was no mistaking it. That boy was the spitting image of his best friend Conrad. He and Conrad had bonded when they first met a year ago. Both had run away from well-to-do but oppressive homes. Both were blessed with first-rate educations and both were searching for a way to make a living. At times, they talked about going west into gold country and at other times they talked about starting up a business, but they didn't know what that would be and they needed money to do either of them. They were biding their time working for Mr. Bank, not earning much but putting away what they could. He was badly shaken by the appearance of an identical twin.

Tim found Mr. Bank instructing a family on the raising of the tent they had just purchased. Tim stood back, shifting from one foot to the other as the seconds stretched out into long minutes.

"Get back to work," Mr. Bank ordered, holding a half-folded flap in his hand as his customers looked on.

"But I..."

"No buts. There are people to be served and not enough of you boys to go around, so get going." A bald man at only five feet six inches tall, Mr. Bank exuded his authority through thick lips set between cheeks puffed like pastry buns and a very large body that complimented them well.

"I can't find Con," Tim chanced before running back into the milling crowd.

"I sent him to Independence with Sheldon a while ago. Now be off with you."

Stunned, Tim hurried to find another bewildered Easterner to help. Con wouldn't be back for a day or two and, by then, this Calvin person would be gone. Disappointment sent his spirit into the ground under his feet like an arrow dropped too soon from the bow.

CHAPTER 27

THEIR HUNGER SATISFIED with generous portions of sausage, onions, hot buns, gherkins and sweet cake, the Pynes, Lisa and Cal ventured out into the stream of people moving about the landing. Lisa and Cal's concern over Tim's remarks disappeared as they found themselves moving along with the crowd. The odor of cooked sausage and onions wafted out of the restaurant's kitchen to mingle with that coming from the livestock enclosures, but most people had too much on their minds to notice the offensive result.

"Where are we heading?" Lisa asked, grabbing Cal's elbow.

"No place special, I guess."

Suddenly Cal stopped in his tracks and longing filled his eyes as he caught sight of the mounted solders leading the horses away from the boat. Some day soon, he hoped, he would find a way to be with those animals again. Their strength and persistence had always inspired him and they always responded to his affection for them.

Lisa squeezed his arm. "You miss your horses, don't you?"

"Yeah, I do, but there'll be a day when I can work with them again. I feel sure of that."

By the display of revived energy, it was apparent that the boat's crew had been fed as they noisily unloaded the steamer. Cal and Lisa and the Pynes found a spot against a building where they could stand and watch as crates, bags, store supplies, horses and wagons—some loaded with furniture—were being lined up along the wharf. Passengers were returning to recover their belongings. A huge pile of lumber caught John's eye.

"Dat looks like good lumber for a new forge. Wonder if there are any firebricks for purchasing?" he thought aloud. "I think I will go take a look. You come too, Rebecca?"

She nodded and followed him into the crowd. "We will see you in a couple of hours, right here in dis same place," he said to Lisa and Cal.

"Fine. If you need us sooner, find the boy with the red suspenders to look for us," Lisa suggested.

Cal's face darkened. "No need for that. We'll be here."

"Dat boy upset you, didn't he?" John observed.

"Aw, it's nothin', really. I've already forgotten it."

Lisa squeezed his hand. "Sorry I mentioned him. He's gotta be mistaken anyway."

"Is this something I should know about?" John asked.

"Naw," Cal said. "He just thinks I look like a friend of his. At first, he thought I was his friend. Weird, huh?"

"Yes, it is. But unless he comes up with this look-alike friend, I wouldn't give it another thought. I'm sure people get mistaken for other people out here all de time. Everybody's looking for someone they might know."

The Pyne's disappeared in the direction of the lumber and Lisa and Cal moved into the crowd again. There was so much to see and much that grabbed their interest. The clothing store particularly caught Lisa's attention. She tugged at Cal's arm. "Let's see how much some new duds would cost."

Lisa stepped across the high threshold into the general store and gasped, "Look at all this stuff."

There were pants, shirts, caps, coats, shoes and boots displayed along the south side of the store. Men's pants were folded in tall piles on shelves behind a counter that ran nearly the length of the store. Shoes and boots filled the space under the counter and caps joined the pants on the shelves.

Lisa spun around and took in the merchandise on the north side, discovering shelves full of yard goods for making dresses and shirts and window coverings. Glass-covered cabinets held yarns and threads, buttons and needles. Cal punched her arm and pointed to the ceiling where lanterns, bags, baskets, saws and carpentry tools hung like icicles ready to fall on their heads.

From their vantage point, it appeared that the back of the store was lined with shelves of pots and pans overshadowing barrels from which a man was scooping beans into a bag, but that scene disappeared quickly as a crush of people moved in to block their view.

"I en't never seen anything like this in all my life," Lisa whispered as she stood rooted to the floor, staring at the menagerie.

"Course not. Old man Carver never let us out of prison except to go to work and the races."

More impatient people shoved their way through the doorway and Lisa and Cal felt themselves being propelled deeper into the store. The back of the store was already so crowded that it gave the appearance of a pen full of gobbling bewildered turkeys unable to move. Lisa pulled Cal toward the clothing counter where only a few customers were waiting.

"Let's see what it'd cost to cover both of us in something new," she said. "You wanna go first or you want I should?"

"You could check on your things and I could do mine," Cal suggested.

"Nah," Lisa chuckled. "Let's do it together."

"It'll be lots easier for you to look at men's stuff than for me to look at girl stuff," Cal pleaded. "After all, you were a—I mean, you wore the boy stuff all your life, 'til now."

"Well, for your information, it en't easy for me to look at dresses either. How am I supposed to decide what I ought to wear? So you've gotta help me. Pleeeze?"

"Oh, drats. Guess I can," he conceded.

It took about twenty minutes for a freckled-faced middle-aged woman with reddish hair drawn into a large bun at the back of her neck to ask, "How can I help you?"

Lisa pointed down at the sad condition of her dress and said, "I think I need a new dress but I need to know how much it would cost."

"It looks like you could both use replacements. Goodness. How long have you worn those things?"

"More than a year, I guess. We just got out of an orphanage and we didn't get many changes of clothing," Lisa explained.

"Hmm...," the woman mused. "You have any money?"

"Not much."

"No, I suppose you don't. As you can see, we don't have any ready-made dresses. I can sell you some of that material over there and you can make your own or have Debra, next door, sew one up for you. She charges as much as two dollars to make a new one." Her eyes filled with compassion at Lisa's crestfallen face. "Tell you what...." She motioned for them to follow her to a door at the back of the store.

"Chrissy, come out here," she called. "My name is Ramona and Chrissy is my daughter," she explained.

Placing an arm across Lisa's shoulders, she whispered, "Lots of people have gone back home after finding they hated life in the West. Some of them bring me the clothes they bought or made out there and just leave them. Seems like they weren't the types of things they'd wear back home and it might be they didn't want a reminder of their experience. Maybe you can find something. Go take a look. Chrissy will show you."

"How much will they cost?" Lisa asked. "Cal needs clothes, too."

"You can give me fifty cents for the lot. That's just to give me a little something for storing them here."

"That's awfully generous," Cal said, surprised at the offer.

"Maybe you can keep that bit of information to yourself. All right?"

"You bet," Cal said.

Lisa could hardly contain her excitement as she rummaged through the dresses and bonnets while Cal tackled the pile of pants and shirts. Chrissy, a ten-year-old with auburn hair pulled back tight behind her head like her mother's, tried to be helpful by searching for dresses she thought would fit Lisa. Chrissy turned away when Lisa began to pull her dress over her head to try on several the girl had laid out for her.

"That's okay, Chrissy. We're both girls and I'm not shy." Lisa heard a chuckle behind her. "You be careful, Mr. Hale. Don't you look this direction until I say you can."

"Yes, Ma'am."

The girl relaxed and helped Lisa get the new dress over her head. It fit fairly well and the blue was to her liking. It had big pockets sewn to the front of the skirt, which would hold the crucifix just fine.

"Look, Cal. What do you think?"

"I like it. Makes you look real ladyish."

"Now, you both turn your back to me 'til I say you can look," Cal said.

While Cal tried on his clothes, Lisa found another dress with deep pockets that fit. It seems the women in the West had a need for carrying things. She kept it on and folded the other to start a pile along with a bonnet that matched the blue.

"Okay, you can look," Cal said.

Lisa chuckled and spun around pulling Chrissy around with her. "This is the most fun I've had in a long time."

Cal had on a new outfit and held another pair of pants and shirt over his arm. "What do you think?" Cal asked.

"Good choices," Lisa said. "I wouldn't recognize you if I didn't know it was you."

Lisa added two pairs of socks and a heavy sweater to her pile. Chrissy wanted her to take two sweaters but Lisa refused thinking someone else would come along and need one, too. Cal found some heavy socks and a homemade jacket.

"One more thing," Lisa said. "Are there any shoes?"

Chrissy pointed to a corner of the room where a dozen or so pairs of heavy shoes and boots were dumped on top of each other. Lisa was breathless as she found a pair of heavy high-top shoes in excellent condition, a bit too big but that was better than a bit too small. Cal found a pair that just fit. Even though their old shoes were mostly worn out, they decided to keep them.

"Do you feel brand-new, like I do?" Lisa asked.

"Yeah. What will we do with our old clothes?"

Chrissy spoke up and said, "Keep them. Wash them when you get to where you're going. Sometime you'll need something to bind up a wound or a cloth for cleaning. Don't throw anything away. You'll find a use for it."

"I guess we have a lot to learn about living out here," Lisa said.

Lisa and Cal gathered up their belongings and looked bewildered at the size of the bundle.

"We can roll them up in my old dress," Lisa said and began to spread it out on the floor.

"You can have my old bag to carry the extras in," Chrissy said. She disappeared for a minute and returned with a well-worn bag that looked about the right size for their needs. "This has been gathering dust since I was about six years old. I don't think I'll ever need it again."

"Thanks. You and your mom have been very generous. We don't know how to thank you."

"You don't need to. There will be a lot more people bringing in things to replace what you've taken. There are always people who come and can't take this kind of life, so they go back. It looks like my mother and I are here to stay."

They rolled their belongings as compactly as possible and tucked them into the two bags. Cal tied the laces of his old shoes together and hung them across his shoulder.

"Good idea," Lisa said as she did the same.

They were set to go. Impulsively, Lisa surprised Chrissy with a hug which she gladly returned, saying, "I wish you God's blessing in your new life."

Heading for the door, Lisa stopped short. "In all this excitement, I forgot to get some pants for me to work in."

"Work?" Chrissy asked. "Can't you work in a dress?"

"Not really. A dress would get in the way or catch fire."

"What on earth do you do?"

"I'm a blacksmith."

"I've never heard of a girl blacksmith before," Chrissy said, skeptically.

"Oh, I am one all right. Since I was nine years old. That was my job at the orphanage."

"You ain't got any folks?"

"Cal here doesn't but I have a da somewhere out here and I'm gonna try to find him," Lisa said.

"Have you ever seen him?" Chrissy asked.

"Nope, but I've got a little likeness of him. Wanna see it?"

"Sure. Maybe I've seen him or maybe my ma has."

Lisa reached in her pocket for her crucifix and dug into it for the portrait. Holding it out for Chrissy to see, Lisa was filled with excitement. *Maybe some of the merchants here at the Landing have seen him.*

Chrissy stared at the portrait a long time and then shook her head. "I don't know. There's something about him. Go show it to my ma. She sees more people than I do."

Cal caught the change in expression on the girl's face as she studied the portrait. Bewilderment, he guessed. He studied her eyes and her fair skin with a few freckles on her nose like her mother's but her hair was more brown than red. Her father's influence, no doubt.

Customers were crowding around Chrissy's mother seeking attention so she gave the portrait a cursory glance and shook her head. As Lisa and Cal were about to work their way out of the door, Chrissy came up behind them, tugging on Lisa's dress.

"Ma says she wants to see the picture again."

Catching her breath, Lisa pushed her way back to the counter and held the tiny portrait out for Ramona to see.

The woman walked to the window for a better light and frowned as she studied the minute features. "He's so young but he looks a bit like a man named Pierre that comes through here about every six months."

Cal grabbed Lisa as she collapsed against him. She was unable to speak.

"That's her da's name. Pierre Bellamont. That painting was done seventeen years ago."

"He'd be forty-one years old now," Lisa added, having recovered her ability to speak. "Do you know how long it's been since he was here?"

"Oh, yes. Three months ago." Ramona's eyes locked onto Lisa's making Lisa uncomfortable until Ramona said, "I bought a desk from him and it's supposed to be here any day now."

"Will he bring it?" Lisa asked hopefully.

Ramona was lost in thought as she stared down at the portrait. Raising her eyes, she studied Lisa as though the two of them were alone in the room. She seemed to want to say something but held it back. "Oh, oh no," she stammered. "It will come from the East by train. He won't be back for another six months if he sticks to his usual schedule. He's a furniture salesman and travels into the states and territories around Missouri."

Lisa stared into the dark eyes across the counter. "How do you know so much about my da?" she asked.

"I know him very well. I've known your father for more than eleven years. Now I have to take care of my customers," she said and turned to a person standing nearby.

Feeling dismissed, Lisa stared at Ramona and then said, "Thanks an awful lot. You've been especially kind."

Lisa and Cal squeezed their way out the door reveling in their good luck. It was more than they had ever expected from strangers in this new land and to hear about her da right off seemed too good to be true. This day was a good start on a long road ahead.

CHAPTER 28

GLITTERING STARS FILLED the cloudless night sky and a warm breeze blew across the small group clustered around a struggling campfire, its orange flames bursting fitfully from the dry clumps of prairie grass and scraps from a Kansas City lumber mill. Having been forewarned about the lack of trees in the Kansas Territory, John had purchased a bundle of kindling from the lumber company just before they began the final phase of their journey west.

Six families were traveling together, each with new wagons loaded with their purchases. Mr. Bank's had warned them that they would be safer if they traveled in numbers. With his help, they had gathered together an amiable group of people who were heading for the same destination. They had no trouble following the path away from Westport Landing as it was well worn from the many folks that had taken that route before them. Sitting together now, they occasionally burst into nervous laughter as they marveled at having successfully crossed into Kansas Territory.

"We are now here in de Kansas Territory. Already we have friends we made on de way from Boston and we are making new ones here around dis campfire," John said, nodding and smiling at his traveling companions.

"We have a ways to go yet, John," said Fred Williams, smiling from across the fire. "We have a whole new life to put together when we get to Lawrence. We older ones have had a good start on life and bring a good deal of experience to our move. But look at Lisa and Cal. They are young and just starting out. What will they do?"

"She will be my assistant in de blacksmith shop and both of them will help me build it. Lisa is an outstanding blacksmith and farrier. She has worked for me since she was nine years old. Of course, den I thought she was a boy," John began to laugh, his round belly bouncing with each burst. "She was an outstanding boy, too."

Those who had heard the story broke out in laughter with him and those who had not, studied him to determine if he was joking with them or telling the truth.

Lisa and Cal were sitting on the ground leaning against the wheel of John's newly purchased wagon, but close enough to the fire to hear the group's conversation. Behind them, John's three horses were tethered to stakes and munching on the prairie grass, occasionally neighing their pleasure at being free of the corral. Other horses tethered nearby joined in.

"Come, Lisa," John said, turning toward the two and motioning with his hand. "Come and tell them your story, and Cal's, too. You can leave out some of de details. You know which ones I mean."

Moving into the light of the fire, Lisa and Cal found a place to sit between John and Fred. Filled with the exciting events of the day and the awe of being so close to their destination, it was difficult for Lisa to pull from her memory the past she was trying to forget. But John, that wonderful man who had brought them this far and saved them many times along the way, wanted her to do this.

Eager, inquiring faces greeted her across the dancing flames. The Mason's six children had stopped chasing each other and were settling in around their parents. Sleep would soon overtake them. A small animal scampered nearby causing the horses to stir, and a coyote howled in the distance. Darkness pushed against their small circle of light in which they felt like they were the only beings on earth. There was a deep sense of dependence on one another.

"This is nice but kinda creepy," Lisa said, seeking Cal's hand. "Well," she said. "Guess I could start with telling you about the orphanage Cal and I grew up in. There were thirty of us from six to sixteen. The place was run by an evil man named Jonas Carver."

For the next twenty minutes, Lisa told her story, sometimes with Cal's help. She decided not to leave anything out. At times, she was interrupted with gasps or laughter until she came to her mother's death. All that could be heard besides her voice was the crackling of the waning fire. She squeezed Cal's hand as she told about Carver's reaction to her mother's death. Caught in the emotion of the memory, she told them of taking the switch to his face and her desperate escape. Cal filled in his part of the search and Carver's attack at Todburn's livery.

"Now you tell them about what he did at de train station."

Both Cal and Lisa understood immediately. John did not want to reveal his status with the marshals nor his activities in the Underground Railroad. There would be time for that later if it became necessary, but for now, he was asking for silence.

It was getting late, but their friends wanted to hear the rest of the story. When she told of their encounter with Carver at the railroad station, Fred gasped.

"I saw that man. He was insane. That's the man who ran the orphanage?"

"He's the owner," Lisa said.

"So, it was you he was pointing at. When they dragged him away, he screamed he was coming after you."

Lisa turned pale, the glow from the now smoldering fire accentuating her pallor.

Cal placed his arm around her shoulders and drew her to him. "Lisa, you saw the condition he was in. He had to be on his way to the asylum. Besides, he'd been coming after both of us before we left and he never got us. I don't think we need to worry."

"I agree with you, Cal," John said. "I don't think he will be able to run de orphanage either. I wonder what will happen to all those boys." He stared into the embers. "I think we should not think about him anymore." He looked up and smiled at Lisa.

"Yeah. He's not worth thinkin' about," Lisa said.

"Well, de fire is almost burned out and a long day it has been getting all our supplies together. I think I go to sleep now. We all go?"

When he rose, he heard horses approaching in the darkness.

"Who is coming?" he called, squinting into the darkness as several mounted and armed men pulled into the faint glow of the dying embers. Startled by their sudden appearance, the other campers started to rise, but one of the men ordered them to stay down.

"Don't get up. We just have a message for you."

"Who are you?" John asked, still standing.

"Right now, that don't matter to you, old man. Just take heed of our warning. If you're some of those abolitionists coming to Kansas to vote it into a free state, you'd better head back to where you came from or you'll see us again and we won't be so considerate."

With that, they spun their horses around and galloped back into the dark night.

John collapsed to the ground. "Well, dat sure isn't a good welcome."

Reverend Mason, who had spoken very little during the evening, said, "It sounds like the stories of the Missouri guerillas are true. But I came here to vote for a free state and save souls. I am not turning back and, God willing, I will start a new church in Lawrence." He hugged the twin daughters sitting in his lap.

Taking a deep breath to control her nerves, Clarissa Hurd agreed. "We're not going back either. We came here to do just what they said and now, more than ever, we intend to do what we came here to do."

Abiden and Jan Burdett sat quietly and nodded their heads. "We're not going back either," he whispered. "But they were a fearful gang."

"I tell you what I do tonight. I sleep under my wagon with my new Sharp's 1852 rifle across my belly."

All but the preacher nodded agreement. Rev. Mason said, "I don't have a gun."

"You do the praying, Reverend, and we'll take care of any intruders," George Hurd assured him.

"I'll do that. Can we pray together before we go to sleep?"

They rose to their feet and held hands in a circle around the embers of the dying fire as Rev. Mason prayed for their well-being through the night and the remainder of their journey. Lisa crossed herself and reached for her crucifix, wrapping her hand around it and uttering an additional prayer for protection. It was at times like these that she missed her mother the most, especially the sound of her voice and the comfort of her prayers.

Lisa, Cal and Rebecca crawled into their tent and John crawled under his wagon holding the rifle across his middle. The other men did the same. There was something about the prairie night that was both quiet and calming but a bit eerie, too. They would need to be cautious.

Two days later, the six wagons rolled onto Massachusetts Street in Lawrence. What they saw took them all by surprise. Only a few buildings had more than one story, and mingled here and there among them were A-frame structures topped in thatch from the upper beam to the ground. Lisa and Cal were on foot, hurrying hand in hand ahead of the wagons to take it all in. The dirt street was dusty, but hard, as though paved with clay. There had been no rain for nearly a year. There were a few trees in the distance, no leaves underfoot; only dust blowing in tiny swirls across the street and around the corners of the buildings. The air smelled dry.

John pulled up in front of what appeared to be a general store. The other wagons pulled to a stop behind him and everyone climbed down to take a look around. It was mid-afternoon on the fourth of May and the sun was still pouring its heat onto the town and the weary travelers.

"This town looks deserted," Lisa said looking up and down the street for signs of life.

"It's so hot, I'll bet everybody's inside staying out of the sun," Cal said, tugging on Lisa's arm. "Come on, Lisa. Let's go reconnoiter."

"Reconnoiter?" Lisa asked, punching him on the shoulder. "Where'd you pick that up?"

"From one of the soldiers in St. Louis. Means to take a look around. Find out something about a place."

"Well then, let's go do that thing," Lisa said with an excited smile that filled her face.

"Better tell John and Rebecca, don't you think?"

They ran back to the wagon where Rebecca stood talking with the other women of the group.

"John and the men have gone into that office to see if they can find anyone to help us. It looks like everything is shut down for the day. But you two go on ahead and see what you can find out."

"We're gonna reconnoiter," Lisa said, dragging out the "oi" and laughing as Cal began chasing her down the street.

"Don't stay away too long," Rebecca called.

The women watched them and shook their heads.

"I'd like to just let go and run with them. Those two have been through so much. They are young and old, all at the same time. It's good to see them go off together that way. The hard times will come again soon enough," said Abigail, the preacher's wife who was trying to keep her six children corralled near their wagon.

Dust swirls became more intense as a late afternoon wind picked up. Turning down a street, Lisa and Cal began to see women sitting in their doorways fanning themselves as they watched their children play. Some had laundry hanging on a line and most had small patches of tilled soil nearby in preparation for a garden. Quite often, they caught sight of a hand waving in their direction so they waved back.

Lisa and Cal slowed to a walk, finding it difficult to take it all in at one time. A tent would be next to a log cabin that was next to a thatch-roofed A-frame. One house was made completely of stone. Even though the houses were a hodgepodge, they saw that the town itself was built on a grid and each dwelling was on what seemed to be a uniform size lot.

"Boy, this en't anything like Malden or Boston where the streets run every which way," Lisa observed.

"You can say that again."

"Boy, this en't anything like Malden…"

"Stop that," Cal growled and tried to trip her. "Bet I can beat you to that tent up at the corner."

"Bet you can, too. It's this dratted dress," she yelled as she picked up the front of her skirt and streaked after him. They reached the corner at the same time falling into each other as they slowed to a stop.

Catching her breath, Lisa looked around and pointed to the north. "Let's go this way—walking."

Lisa took a deep breath. "So this is Kansas prairie air, hot and dusty. Not many trees. I miss the trees already. No shade to get away from the sun. Yeah, I really miss the trees."

"We'll get used to it here. We've gotta. This is gonna be our home." Cal squinted toward the sun framed by a clear blue sky that reached all the way to the surrounding horizon. "I feel like I'm under a huge upside-down blue bowl with a great golden egg yolk painted on the inside."

"I didn't know you could be so poetic," she teased. "That really was good."

"Oh, come on. Let's head down here like you said."

They had barely moved when a woman came out of her tent screaming and carrying her little boy covered in blood.

"Get the doctor," she cried, waving frantically at them. "My boy's bleeding to death."

Lisa and Cal ran to her and saw the blood streaming from the boy's arm down his mother's dress. The boy whimpered, clinging to his mother, his face buried in her neck.

"Remember Johnny?" Lisa asked Cal.

"Yeah."

"Ma'am. Get a strip of cloth or a cord," Cal said as calmly as he could, measuring the length in the air between his palms. "Let Lisa hold your baby. We can take care of this for you but you gotta hurry. There's no time to go for a doctor."

Her frightened eyes studied them and she was unable to move.

"Go," yelled Cal. "We can save your little boy."

Frantically handing her child to Lisa, she ran inside and came back with a long strip of cloth that Cal immediately tied around the arm above the wound.

"Now go back and get a little piece of wood or a spoon or something strong about four inches long."

Seeing the bleeding slow down, the woman ran back and returned with a small wooden spoon which Cal placed above his first knot. He tied it on and twisted it a bit more and wrapped the cloth around the spoon to keep it in place.

"Do you have something we can wrap around the cut?"

The woman disappeared inside her tent again and returned with a little boy's shirt. "Here, use this. It's all I could find."

"This is good," Cal said as he lightly covered the wound. "He's going to be just fine."

The boy's color was returning to his face and he opened his eyes as Lisa returned him to his mother who broke out into fresh tears of relief. She wiped his face with her apron and hugged him.

"Don't squeeze that arm, Ma'am," Lisa warned.

"Now, we'll go find a doctor for you if you'll tell us where to look. We just got into town from Boston, like a half hour ago," Lisa said.

"I'll take him to the doctor, but please go with me. I can't begin to tell you how grateful I am you came along when you did. He's only a year old and gets into everything."

As they headed in the direction of the businesses in town, a number of women came out of their homes as they passed.

"What happened?"

"Everything all right, Martha?"

"It is now. Jonah cut his arm. These two stopped the bleeding and we're heading for the doctor."

"You know the men are meeting in the Pioneer Boarding House today."

"I know," Martha answered breathlessly. "That's where we're headed."

Martha continued to scurry along while the women kept pace with her for a short distance when one of them realized they were slowing things down and motioned for the others to move out of the way.

Martha was slightly built, not more than five feet tall, but her frantic energy gave her the strength to carry Jonah and to move quickly. Cal offered to relieve her but she would have nothing to do with that. It took only five minutes to reach the Pioneer where Martha burst through the door into a room full of concerned-faced men.

A young man jumped up and ran to her. He took one look at his son and yelled into the room, "Dr. Brewer. Come quickly."

Like lightning, the doctor had the boy in his arms, hurrying to his office with Martha and her husband at his heels. Lisa heard someone in the room remark that the meeting was over for the day.

No one noticed when Lisa and Cal slipped away and made their way back to the wagons.

"What an adventure for our first day in Lawrence," Lisa said. "At least, we found out where all the people were."

"Yeah. Those men looked serious back there when we barged in. Wonder what they were meetin' about."

"Something important, I guess," Lisa replied, shrugging her shoulders.

CHAPTER 29

THEIR PARTY WAS huddled in the shade of one of the wagons when Linette Winslow spied Lisa and Cal coming down the street.

"There they are," she piped in her sweet high-pitched voice, pointing toward them.

Lisa and Cal detected some agitation among the members of the group as they approached.

"It's hot standing here in de street and we haven't found anyone doing business today," John said. "We were about to go looking for you. We were getting worried."

"Sorry," Lisa said. "Somethin' happened and we had to help." She told them about their adventure.

"The meeting broke up when we barged in the way we did. You'll probably see the men going back to their businesses soon," Cal added.

Just as he predicted, men began pouring down the street and into the buildings along the way. Two of the men continued on toward the wagons but turned to enter the claims office.

As they reached the doorway, the man with dark heavy eyebrows turned and said, "You men wait for us out here. We'll be back shortly. We have a matter to resolve before we can assist you."

The men fidgeted impatiently as they waited. It wasn't long until the door opened and they were waved inside.

John moved quickly with the other men falling in step behind him. Lisa made a face at Cal as he followed them in. She turned to go in with him but Rebecca laid a gentle hand on her arm. "It's best you wait with us," she said with an understanding smile.

"Boy, have I ever got a lot to learn and sometimes I don't like it," she mumbled under her breath.

"What don't you like?" Abigail asked.

"Bein' a girl," she answered, kicking the dirt with the toe of her shoe. She started to crack her knuckles and stopped. That was one habit she was seriously trying to break.

"I just can't imagine what you're going through. I can see it's hard for you," Abigail whispered. "When we get settled in, maybe I can help you."

"I hope. Otherwise, I'm going back to bein' a boy."

That made Abigail chuckle. She glanced down at Lisa's figure and said, "Uh huh. Sure you will."

Lisa couldn't help but smile. "I know. I know."

The ladies grew quiet as they waited, each wondering where they would cook their next meal and lay their heads that night. It was Rebecca who first saw the three people approaching.

"Someone's coming," she said and motioned in their direction.

Lisa looked up and began running toward them. "How's Jonah?" she asked when they met in the middle of the street. Jonah looked up at her, giving her a weak smile and putting out his arms for her to take him. Surprised, Lisa looked at Martha. "Is it okay?"

"Yes, it is. He's asking for you to take him."

Lisa took the boy into her arms, being careful not to put pressure on his wounded arm.

"This is Dr. Brewer and this is my husband, Aaron," Martha said, first pointing to a tall lanky bearded man in his fifties and then to a much younger chubby bearded man only a bit taller than she. "I apologize but I don't know your name and the man that was with you. I was too busy and too frightened to ask."

"I'm Lisa Bellamont and his name is Calvin Hale." Lisa grinned when she felt the softness of Jonah's skin as he stroked her cheek with his good hand.

"As little as he is, I believe he realized you saved his life," Aaron said. "We're all so grateful to you."

"That was an excellent tourniquet you put on his arm. Where did you learn to do that?" asked Dr. Brewer.

"Actually, I held him and Cal put it on. We had an accident at the orphanage and that's what the doctor did. He had Cal help him so Cal remembered what to do."

"You were angels sent to me at just the right time," Martha said.

Unable to control the flush rising to her face, Lisa muttered, "Well, I don't know 'bout bein' angels. We were just there checking out our new town. We came all the way from Boston and now we need to find a place to settle down. Our menfolk are all in the claims office right now seein' what they can find out."

Aaron and Dr. Brewer looked at each other and Dr. Brewer nodded toward the door of the office. "Let's go see if we can help," he said. They hurried into the building.

"I need to take Jonah home and put him to bed," Martha said, reaching for her son.

"Let me walk with you. I'll be happy to carry him. I really would like to. You've been through a lot and he doesn't mind my holding him."

"I guess that would be all right." Martha sounded grateful for the relief.

Along the way, Martha told Lisa that she and her husband had been in Lawrence since August of 1854, coming with the second Emigrant Aid party. With them had come some musicians who had entertained them along the way and they became so popular that they formed the Lawrence Band.

"You'll hear them play whenever the settlers have a get-together. Of course, we haven't had time for many of those yet. Aaron and I were here when the town was organized and the town constitution and the rules for the choice of claims were written. Those men you saw at the meeting chose the town officers and set up the city government."

She stopped to catch her breath and was about to reach for her son when she saw that he was sound asleep in Lisa's arms.

"Those men brought in the surveyors who established the meridian line and marked off the lots and streets. Actually, my husband was one of the surveyors and that's how I know so much about it. He's not like most of the husbands around here. He tells me most everything that's going on," she said in a matter-of-fact tone. "I appreciate that in him. He's a good man and a carpenter, as well."

Lisa smiled off and on but remained silent so she wouldn't wake the child.

"Oh, yes. They also named the town. At first they were going to call it Wakarusa after the river that runs south of here but I'm glad they didn't. Can you imagine living in Wakarusa? Another name was New Boston, but people didn't like that either so they named it Lawrence for Amos Lawrence who gave a lot of money to help the people get here and to get the town started. Most people were satisfied with that. But, I have to tell you, unlike Leavenworth, this is an abolitionist town and we're having a lot of problems with the people from Missouri who want to make this a slave state. That's what the meeting was about today."

They found themselves in front of her tent so Lisa carefully handed Jonah back to his mother. "Thank you for lettin' me carry him. He's a cute kid; ah, I mean little boy. And thanks for telling me all this. Everyone in our group is an abolitionist. We all want to see Kansas become a free state. Some armed men rode up to our campsite last night and warned us to go back East if we were abolitionists, but we all decided to come anyway."

Martha took Lisa's hand. "There is more, much more; but we don't have time now. You have to get back and I have to put Jonah to

bed. Please come by when you find out where you 'll be settling."
Studying Lisa's face, she said, "We're both young, you and I. I'm
seventeen. How old are you?"

"I'll be sixteen in nine days. I have a lot to tell you, too, so I'll
come by to see you later. I'm happy we could help you and thanks for
the information."

Lisa walked away feeling like she had made her first friend in her
new life, and this friend was a girl. Her heart was soaring as she
hurried back. When Lisa arrived at the wagons, she discovered that
the men were back and John was talking animatedly to the group. Lisa
slipped in quietly and listened.

"There is a piece of land north of town where we can put our
wagons and spend de night. De man said it might take as long as two
weeks to get de paperwork done legally but we paid our money and
signed de papers so he thinks we should go ahead and move onto our
claims tomorrow. We just can't build anything on them until we get
de final okay. I don't know about you people, but I am pleased with
what I got."

"Those two men in that office seemed very tired and were putting
us off until tomorrow, but when the doctor and his friend came in,
things sure did change," Jed said. "When they were told that Lisa and
Cal saved that little boy's life, those two claim processors took on new
energy. Praise the Lord. We all have claims to check out tomorrow
and we have the two of you to thank. They told me it would be okay
for me to hold church services in my home, once I get set up."

"He told you there are already Congregational, Unitarian,
Methodist and Baptist churches here so how's that gonna affect you?"
Cal asked.

"That's all right. It's a good thing I'm nondenominational. I just
preach the gospel as I hear it from the Lord. As soon as I get a place to
start, I'm going to have a revival meeting, probably Lawrence's first."

Jed moved on toward his wagon and helped his family climb up.
The others climbed aboard their wagons as well and, to the sound of

horses' hooves digging into the hard packed ground and the shifting of leather against leather, the teams moved north following John. A feeling of contentment and goodwill surrounded them as they passed the businesses and the people now walking and riding along Massachusetts Avenue. This would be their home and they were happy.

Later that evening, Lisa passed on to the group all the information she had been given by Martha. "She says there's lots more she wants to tell me. She says the men were meeting today to decide on how to defend the town if it's attacked. Guess they think it might be."

Benjamin frowned as he listened. "That one man in the claim office said we should probably start attending the town meetings right away if we intend to stay here."

Ab Burdett nodded. "He did but the other man said not to start our life here worrying. He said they all live their lives doing what they need to do like building their houses, taking care of their families, running their businesses and all that. Nevertheless, the men are being cautious, just in case."

"Well," John said with determination. "I am going to build my forge and start my blacksmith business on my claim and nothing will stop me from doing that. Of course, I will go to de meetings and help where I can. De man said I should guard my Sharp's rifle with my life. I do that anyway. Now I am going to sleep. Tonight I will sleep in de tent with my wife and de young ones. Goodnight."

Lisa and Cal walked arm in arm outside the campsite, listening to the crickets and cicadas and watching warily for snakes. The dry grass crackled under their feet as he told her about the claim procedure and wondered if he and Lisa would ever have their own property. At the moment, they were just happy to be together. They held each other briefly and returned to the tent. Her heart was singing so contentedly that she did not detect the distant look in Cal's eyes.

Morning dawned clear and bright with the sun's first rays streaming warmth that told the campers it would be another dusty, windy, hot day. The women bustled about checking the bacon and corn bread and pouring coffee for the menfolk. This would be the last morning they would all share a meal around a campfire. They knew they had made valued friendships that would last a lifetime, but today they would move to their own claimed property, giving the campsite an air of excitement.

Lisa was learning her place in the social order and now she smirked at Cal as she poured his coffee.

He mimicked her smirk and chuckled. "This en't gonna last, is it?"

"Not likely." She kicked his toe as she turned back to the fire and raised an eyebrow at him. "But then, you never know."

He choked and spit a mouthful of coffee onto the ground. "Oh yeah?"

By the time the full sun was above the horizon, the tents were down and loaded onto the wagons along with pots and pans used for cooking and eating. Even though they knew they would be seeing each other again, their good-byes were warm. They had journeyed together and now their travel had come to an end and a new chapter was beginning. They wished each other good fortune.

Before pulling away, a young boy came running into the camp with a message. "The town officers are holding a meeting this afternoon in the boarding hall at the Pioneer Boarding House especially for you. There's things you need to know right away so you men get there at two o'clock. What should I tell them?"

"Tell them we'll be there."

CHAPTER 30

A FEW MINUTES before two o'clock that afternoon, John, Cal and the other men from their party walked along Massachusetts Avenue toward the Pioneer Boarding House. The gusting prairie wind blew skittering dust devils at their feet, occasionally swirling them upward into their eyes and nostrils.

The boarding hall was at the rear of the thatch and mud-covered building. Entering through the back door, they detected the faint odor of burnt thatch and wood. One small window allowed enough light for them to see the five men seated in a circle beneath it waiting for them. Aaron immediately jumped up to greet them and directed them to the empty chairs in their midst.

"You already met me and Dr. Brewer. This is Dr. Charles Robinson. He's been one of our most influential men in Lawrence so you'll get to know more about him, in time." Aaron pointed to the other two men. "This is Martin Conway. He was elected to the legislature but resigned. We'll explain that later. And this is Mr. Boyd."

John, Cal, Fred, Rev. Mason, Ab Burdett, George and Henry Hurd and Benjamin Hold shook hands as they were introduced and took their seats.

"I have a question," Cal said. "What's that burnt smell?"

"This building caught fire in January. The part that burned has been rebuilt but the odor hasn't gone away," Aaron explained. "It used to be a lot worse or maybe we're just getting used to it."

"Sorry for the interruption," Cal said. "I was just curious." He sat back feeling foolish for starting the meeting off with a ridiculous question when these men seemed to have more important things on their minds.

"I guess you're wondering why we brought you here. We'll explain everything, but first we need to know if you are here because you are abolitionists and want to vote this territory in as a free state. What are your leanings?"

"Well, I will tell you why *I* am here," John said, and told them about the events leading up to his escape from Malden and the pursuit by the marshals on the train. "I plan to build me a forge and tend to my business but I will definitely do what I can to make this a place to live without slaves. At least those marshals can't do anything to me here."

"Don't be too sure, John" Mr. Bond said. "We have our own things to tell you today that may change that thought."

Each of the other men gave their story until it was Cal's turn and they all looked to him.

"And you, young man," said Dr. Robinson. "It will be interesting to hear your story. How old are you? Do you have a trade? What brings you here?"

Whew! One question at a time. Cal wasn't sure where to begin but he had to tell them something.

Before he could say anything, however, John interrupted, "Cal came with me and my Rebecca; the same with Lisa. She was my assistant in my blacksmith shop for almost seven years. I thought she was a boy all that time until just before we got caught transporting de runaway slaves." He turned to Cal. "Now, Cal, you tell them your story; and Lisa's too. They go together."

"First, I'd like to say that I like workin' with horses and I'm told that I'm good with them. I worked for a man who rented out horses to vendors in Boston but," Cal grinned and looked around. "I can see that there en't gonna be a need for that here for a long time. I don't

260

know what I can do here in Lawrence. I'll just have to wait and see. To begin with, I can help Mr. Pyne build his house and his forge. I've been getting interested in the cavalry but we just got here yesterday so I haven't had a lot of time to think on that."

"Oh, my," John said. "That would make Lisa very unhappy, I think."

"It's just a thought; anyway, when I turned sixteen, I couldn't stay at the orphanage anymore so I moved into the back room of the livery stable where I worked."

Cal told his story, as well as Lisa's, with a bit of help from John. The men listened intently, at times frowning as though believing, yet not believing.

Dr. Robinson began to speak then with a voice that rang of intelligence and authority. "We all came to Lawrence with the hope of starting new lives and helping to make this a free state. Not many of us realized the problems we would face in setting up a brand new town where nothing had been before. We knew there would be opposition to our abolitionist movement but not to the extent that we have encountered so far. We have formed a town and set its government to satisfy the majority of people here. We don't care who comes to settle here but we're trying to get the idlers, parasites and the weak-hearted to move on or go home. It takes courage to face the future in this territory and we're going to need a lot of it, I'm afraid."

Dr. Robinson got to his feet and paced the floor as he fell deep into thought. "As to why we asked you to come here today, we do this with all the new people if they are willing to listen. You see, we want you to know what you'll be facing in case you want to turn around and head back home."

John shook his head vehemently, as did the others. "No, no."

"Many people have returned to their homes in the East when they smelled the danger surrounding this town. And some of them just didn't have the pioneering spirit when they saw the deprivations they faced like hauling water from the springs and living in tents or other kinds of makeshift dwellings until the mill is set up. It's not an easy life, let alone the worry about the Missourians."

"We came today to learn. Tell us everything. It won't make a difference as to whether or not we stay but we need to know. We've heard stories. Tell us if they're true," Fred said. "We've come a long way."

Dr. Robinson continued to pace, studying the air around him as he pulled his thoughts together. "Governor Reeder called an election on March 30 last to elect a legislature. That was a fiasco—a total fiasco. There were some two thousand legal voters registered in the Kansas Territory but there were more than six thousand votes cast. Here in our district alone, there were eight hundred votes cast by non-residents. I can see you are looking perplexed and wondering how they did it. Well, I'll tell you."

Fire lit his eyes like canon bursts and he stopped pacing. "A thousand men from Missouri camped outside Lawrence the night before the election, armed with all types of guns and knives and a couple of pieces of artillery. They were ready for a fight. On Election Day, they swarmed the polls, refusing to swear they were residents of the territory and, at gunpoint, cast ballots. They pushed the good residents of this district out of their way and refused to let some of them vote, like Mr. Boyd here. When they chased him away, they fired at him and he escaped by jumping into the river."

Dr. Robinson sat down on the edge of his seat and rested his elbows on his knees. Reliving that day had exhausted him and cast a silence on the room. It was several moments before Benjamin Hold, a man who rarely spoke, broke the silence.

"So, you're saying that this Kansas Territory has a legislature of pro-slavery Missourians?"

Dr. Robinson's face lit up. "You understand that perfectly."

"So... so... what happened then? Couldn't the territorial governor dismiss the election and say it was a fraud?" Benjamin asked.

Dr. Brewer now spoke up giving Dr. Robinson a chance to catch his breath. "He was too scared to do anything about it so here we sit, stuck with them for the next two years. We were told to leave or get used to living in a slave state, but we've all invested too much of our time, money and emotion into this territory and we're not leaving. That legislature hasn't met yet but we know they will come up with pro-slavery rules to try to put us down. We're not going." Dr. Brewer pounded a fist against a palm and shifted angrily in his seat. "Dr. Robinson has proposed a resolution for the anti-slavery people of the territory which he will present when we call a convention. He suggests *repudiation*."

Cal's stomach had drawn tight as a kite string around a wrist in a gale. "What does that mean? I mean, I know what the word means but how can people repudiate something that's already set up, even if it's wrong?"

"Good question," Dr. Robinson said, ready to continue. "First, Martin here was elected to the legislature but he resigned and in his resignation speech, he announced that he repudiated the bogus legislature and would not be a part of it. What we can do in the way of repudiating it is to state as a group that, as free men, we will not subject ourselves to the rules of a legislature that was elected by force by men of another state. Then, we'll take care of our domestic disputes ourselves as though the present governance does not exist. We'll announce that we won't meddle in another state's business and claim the right to take care of our own."

"They won't like being ignored but that's what we propose to do," said Martin Conway. "So, what are you thinking now?" he asked, sweeping his eyes across the faces of the newcomers.

"Well, I for one en't afraid. If I could live under the evil eye of old man Carver for twelve years, I sure can handle somethin' like this," Cal said.

Aaron, who was not much older than Cal, spoke up. "You have to be a bit afraid in order to protect yourself. We have to be ready for anything. We may even have to be ready to kill to protect our families and that's why we have a load of Sharp's rifles ordered. We can't let that word out, though, because the Missourian's will stop our shipment and take the guns for themselves."

Dr. Robinson frowned at Aaron. "These folks seem like good people but you probably shouldn't have told them that yet." He turned to the eight new men and said, "For the sake and safety of this town, you need to keep that information under your hat."

"I'm a preacher," Jed Mason said. "I don't know about the killing but I will keep that information to myself and I know these other men, they truly are good men and will not reveal your secret, which is now our secret. I'm sure you have reason to say what you said."

"You bet we have," said Mr. Boyd. "We call them 'gorillas' and they've sneaked across the border from Missouri and killed innocent abolitionist families in their homes right where they sat, unprotected by a town or neighbors. They've butchered them, shot them and strung them up. It's a terrible thing to see. Even you, preacher, would protect your family from the likes of them if you had the means to do it."

The Reverend Jed Mason gasped and fell into the back of his chair. "What have I brought my family to?"

"Well, Reverend, here you're in a town with people who are banding together to protect each other. We're working on a plan and keeping our eyes and ears open. You can help by reporting to us anything you might hear or see," said Dr. Robinson. "You can certainly help build fortifications if need be."

Jed nodded. "It will take a while for us to set up on our claim but you must let me know when I can help. The Lord gave me a good strong body and good working hands as well a mind and heart for Him so, please send out a call when you need me."

"Yesterday, I heard you say you had a Sharp's rifle, John," said Dr. Brewer. "I see you've left it at your campsite today. I'd suggest you hide it when you're not carrying it. Those Missourians come into town quite often and if they were to see that gun, they would steal it from you and you'd never see it again."

"I will do that as soon as I get back to de camp. We are moving onto our claim today. They had some lumber at Westport and I bought a wagonload to start a house. I ordered what I need for de forge and it should be here in two weeks. I should be in business in about a month. Then I can make all de different kinds of knives you and de men in town might want to carry to defend yourselves." John hung his head sheepishly as he realized he was coming on too strong by pushing his business on the good men in the room. "Dat is, if you don't already have them and if you would want me to make them."

"You are a good man, John," Martin Conway said. "I'm sure there will be a need for you in this town. Thank you all for coming. If you have any questions, ever, get in touch with us. Dr. Robinson and Dr. Brewer have offices on Massachusetts Street. The rest of us are on New Hampshire Street, the next street over. You'll soon know where everything and everyone are. There aren't many of us yet."

CHAPTER 31

THE MORNING SUN was teasing the eastern horizon when Lisa was awakened by the sound of pounding hooves and grinding wagon wheels on the morning of July fourth.

Stretching her arms and legs, she tried to wake up her tired muscles. She and Cal had spent the evening and part of the night working with the townspeople preparing for Lawrence's first big Independence Day celebration.

She lay on her back and inhaled the pleasant scent of new wood as she stared at the ceiling of her bedroom, built especially for her directly above the kitchen of the Pyne's brand new house. She was filled with a sense of satisfaction in having helped build this frame house, which she could now call "home." The few hours she had spent in the Pyne's home in Malden had not given her a sense of warmth but had only been a shelter during a crisis. Here, in such a brief time, she felt wrapped in the warmth and love of the people who had become her family and who made these bare wooden walls a home. Below her were the kitchen, the Pyne's bedroom and the parlor which, for the time being, served as Cal's bedroom.

The blacksmith shop was nearby and was now in full operation. What an exciting day that had been when she and John lit the fire for the first time, filled the water trough, and tested the bellows. Everything was perfect. Cal and Rebecca had joined them in their celebration with a bottle of wine John had purchased for the occasion on a trip to Westport.

The house and shop sat in the southwest corner of John's one and one-half acre claim at the northeastern edge of Lawrence where western bound adventurers passed by on the Oregon Trail. He hoped to draw business from them and from the people in the town. Lisa's first job had been to shape a knife blade for none other than Dr. Robinson, himself. She was pleased that the time away from blacksmithing had not weakened her arm muscles. She did discover, however, that Cal could beat her in a race, even when she wore her boy pants. Cal accused her of letting him win. Life was turning out well, so very well.

Lisa pulled her legs out from under the covers and moved over to the single window in her room where she looked down the road that passed near the house. She saw wagons approaching filled with colorfully attired Delaware and Shawnee Indians on their way into town. Hundreds of people were expected from the surrounding counties, invited by the people of Lawrence. There was a fusion taking place among these heroic people who shared a conviction and a purpose and Lisa's heart swelled to bursting when she thought of being a part of this daunting and courageous effort. What had she thought before she came? Escape and not much more. Now that she was free from the oppression of the orphanage and the cruelty of Jonas Carver, she was picking up on the spirit of those who had come to establish a new town and a new state. Being part of that challenge was exhilarating. She lifted up a prayer of thanks as she touched the crucifix that now had a permanent place on the wall next to the window.

She took a deep breath of fresh air and turned away from the window to decide what to wear for the exciting day ahead. The shirt and pants she had worn during the preparations the previous night didn't seem right for her this morning. She had taken some teasing about her femininity and her strength as she worked alongside the men while the other women remained in their homes cooking for the big event. She was probably the only female in town with blisters on her hands.

Well, she would show them another Lisa today. She would show them that she had a feminine side. Selecting the blue dress she had purchased at Westport on the day of their arrival, she pulled it down over her head and straightened out the sleeves and the skirt. She combed her shoulder-length hair and let it hang freely down her neck. From the time she decided to be a girl, she had impatiently waited for her hair to grow into long beautiful waves like she had seen on other women but now that her hair hit her shoulders, she missed the cool breeze around her neck and the casual feel of her boy's cut. *Will I ever be completely satisfied? Probably not.* Splashing water on her face from the basin on her table helped awaken her and added a blush to her cheeks. Gathering a deep energizing breath of fresh air at the window, she bounded down the steps colliding with Cal as he stepped into her path at the foot of the stairs. Laughing, he gathered her in his arms where they lay sprawled on the floor.

"That's one way to greet me in the morning," he said. "I like it."

Rebecca called from the kitchen. "If anyone wants breakfast, they had better get in here while it's still hot."

Cal and Lisa rushed to the table where John was already seated and sipping a hot cup of coffee, something he had been missing since they left Malden. On his last trip to Westport, he bought a tin of coffee at a price twice as high as that in the East, but he couldn't resist the temptation and this morning, he was savoring every sip. Knowing how precious the liquid was to him, Cal and Lisa refused his offer of a cup. They didn't really like coffee that much anyway. The wine, they agreed, had been very tasty.

Rebecca disappeared into her bedroom and reappeared shortly with a ribbon that matched Lisa's dress. Lisa was surprised when Rebecca stepped behind her chair and began combing her hair back from her face and tying it up with a large bow.

"Wow," Cal gasped. "That looks great."

269

John smiled and agreed. "Just think, I used to call you 'son' but I can't do that anymore, for sure. You are a lovely young lady."

"Come on, you guys. You're embarrassin' me."

"Good," Cal said, grinning at her as he finished his biscuit and sausage.

Thirty minutes later, Cal and Lisa stopped by the Pierce's home and, together, the two couples headed toward Massachusetts Street. Lisa carried Jonah who had already begun to pick up on the excitement. They found a good vantage point from which they watched men and women on horseback pour onto Massachusetts Street from the north and the south. White plumes sprouted from saddle horns and the riders wore red, white and blue scarves and handkerchiefs. Covered wagons rolled in with stars and stripes attached to their canvases and teams of oxen pulled wagons full of people displaying the red, white and blue. It was an impromptu parade and the growing mass of people loved it. They were shouting or screaming greetings at everyone above the sound of the wagon wheels, the neighing horses and the Lawrence band that had decided to burst into an energetic marching song in front of the Emigrant Aid Office.

Jonah begged to be taken by his father and covered his ears when the celebratory gunshots competed with the blare of the band. Lisa's eyes sparkled with excitement as she clung to Cal's arm. Carver had never celebrated the Fourth of July at the orphanage and the two of them were ecstatic.

The crowd grew and shifted about, moving Lisa and her friends with the flow. Something was happening near the band and, with some effort, they were able to wend their way to where a woman was presenting a banner to the militia of Lawrence after which the crowd headed for a grove northwest of town. There, on the platform Lisa and Cal had helped erect the night before, was a large new flag flapping in the gusting prairie wind. The band played "Sweet Home" and a prayer was offered. Then the Declaration of Independence was read and Dr. Robinson got up to speak.

After the thunderous applause died down, a respectful silence fell on the crowd as they listened to Dr. Robinson describe once more the situation they were in under the bogus governance of the pro-slavery legislature. Cal slipped his arm around Lisa's waist and pulled her to his side as they took in Dr. Robinson's words. He urged the people to take care of their differences themselves and not call in Sheriff Jones, who had been appointed by the bogus Missouri legislature and was, in fact, nothing more than the postmaster of Westport. He stated that the people of Lawrence and other communities in the Kansas Territory should settle their differences among themselves.

The power in his words became more compelling as he declared that the election taken over by Missourians with guns was a fraud and an outrage on the rights of free men. He pounded the air with his fists as he told them to repudiate the illegal legislature and its rules. He said they should govern themselves as though that legislature did not exist. He shouted that they could not and would not submit to such an atrocity.

Thunderous applause followed and continued like a storm rolling across the prairie. It appeared that Dr. Robinson's words had been understood and the people knew what they had to do.

Managing to stay together in the surging crowd heading for the food tables, the friends chose to sit on the ground where Jonah could run and play. Everyone, including the out-of-towners, had brought food to share. Cal and Aaron worked their way to the tables and returned with enough for the five of them. They stayed through all the toasts, impromptu speeches and music. Jonah went sleepily from lap to lap until he finally went to sleep beside his father.

"Looks like it's time to get this little rascal home to bed," Aaron said. "Things are winding to a close anyway. It's been fun."

"Yeah, it's been a good day," Lisa said, holding back a yawn. "This is the most fun I've ever had in my whole life and the first day

I've ever been this relaxed, even with all these people around. Wonder how many came."

"My guess is over a thousand at the peak. A lot of people have already gone home," Cal said.

Lisa and Cal said good-bye to their friends and sat back down to watch until everything had been picked up and the last few people had wandered off.

"You wanna go dancing at one of the parties?" Cal asked. "Everybody's invited."

"Dancing? You're teasin' me. Right?"

"We could go watch. Maybe we could learn how," Cal said and began to laugh. "Guess not. I just thought I'd ask."

"It's a nice evening. Let's take our time walkin' home."

"Our lives have sure changed since we left the orphanage. I'm afraid we're growin' up, Lisa," Cal said as they slowly walked arm in arm under a blanket of stars made brighter by a brilliant crescent moon.

"I think you're right. There will come a day when we'll need to take responsibility for ourselves and not depend so much on the Pynes."

"I think you're holding your own by working for John at the shop but me... well, I've done about as much for him as he needs me to do." Cal stopped walking and took Lisa into his arms and kissed her, then held her out at arms' length. "I've been wanting to do that all day."

Lisa pulled herself back into his arms and returned his kiss with a warm hug and then whispered in his ear. "Let me tell you what keeps me awake at night." She stepped back and looked him in the eye. "Thinkin' about you maybe joining the cavalry."

Taken by surprise, Cal stammered as he tried to answer. "Lisa, I don't wanna leave you, but what am I gonna do here in this town? Besides, I en't said I was going."

"It sounds to me like this town needs its men to help defend it. Have you thought about joining the Stubbs militia? They're right here in town."

"I checked into that but it costs to join and I'd have to pay for my uniform. I en't got the money."

"Do me a favor, Cal, and go talk to Robinson or one of the other men that talked to you the first day we were here. Maybe they know of somebody that needs a worker. You learned to build a house and there are still people that'll be building in this town. With so many more people movin' here, maybe the general store or the drug store could use some help. Let everybody know you're lookin'. Maybe Aaron could help you."

Cal wrapped her in his arms again and stood quietly holding her. "Okay, okay," he whispered, stroking her hair. "Then, if I can make some money," he continued breathlessly, "we can get married. I've gotta *need* to be with you."

Lisa weakened in his arms as a familiar sensation traveled through her heart and down to her toes. "Me too," she whispered. "I guess lots of people get married when they're our age, but you're right," she said, moving away. "We gotta know we can take care of ourselves before we do that."

Before they went into the house, Cal kissed her again, running his fingers into her hair under the ribbon. "I'll come wake you up in the mornin'."

CHAPTER 32

THE NEXT MORNING came in on roiling black clouds and claps of thunder. Lightening flashed from cloud to cloud, flooding the darkness below with intermittent splashes of eerie brilliance. Lisa leaped from her bed to the window and pressed her nose against the glass. This doesn't look good, she thought just as a powerful wind-driven rain smashed against the window. Startled by the onslaught, she fell back on her bed, fully awake and shuddering. It took a few minutes to recover her composure

Not knowing what the day would bring, she dressed in her pants and shirt. The storm could blow over quickly and they would be able to work at the forge after all. She opened her door and found Cal with his knuckles poised to knock.

"Surprised you, didn't I?" Cal chuckled. "John sent me up. He thinks we oughta all be together in the kitchen to see what this storm's gonna do. He's watching for signs of a tornado."

Dashing down the stairs to the kitchen, they found John peering out the window, leaning an elbow against the frame, the lines between his eyes drawn tight. The wind was howling angrily around the corners of the house and whipping rain against its sides.

"De wind is fierce enough right now to cause a lot of damage. This will be a good test for our house to see how well we built it," he mused. "I think de people in tents are in trouble." Staring out the window into the turbulence, his frown deepened.

Rebecca, who had been nervously fussing around the kitchen, went to John's side. "I've poured water on the fire in the stove. We don't need another house reduced to ashes." Staring out the window, she suggested apprehensively, "Maybe we should wait this out in the storm cellar."

"That is very good idea. Then I don't have to worry about you *and* de storm. I will watch for a little while longer and then come to join you."

"I'll stay up here with you," Cal said.

"No, no you won't. You go with them. I'll be there soon. Now, go along. All of you." He waved his large hands at them, shooing them on their way.

Rebecca wrapped several candles and a box of matches in her apron and followed Cal and Lisa into the deluge. Cal lifted the heavy wooden panel that opened into the underground storage area and followed Rebecca and Lisa down the dark narrow stairway. Wet, chilled and shaking, it took Rebecca several attempts to light a candle after the panel fell into place above them. Huddled together in the center of the hole in the ground, with water running from their drenched clothing into their shoes and onto the dirt floor, they assessed their dark, damp refuge.

The hole was braced by rough-cut timber on all four sides with a solidly built wooden ceiling. Shelves lined the walls that would some day hold the canned food Rebecca would prepare from her garden.

"The walls are sturdy, so we're safe down here," Cal assured them.

"I guess we can sit down while we wait this thing out," Lisa said, picking out a spot against the wall. "This could take a while."

Nothing in the darkness gave them a reference to determine the passage of time, and the wait for John's appearance became interminable. The imagined weight of the door began to press on their nerves. There was not a reassuring sound from above to relieve the heaviness bearing down on them. Rebecca lit the last candle and sat down beside Lisa. Cal soon joined them.

With Cal in the middle, they drew closer together, listening to the roar of the wind, the brush of unknown things scudding across the top of the cellar, a sudden crash of an object directly above them. Cal wrapped an arm around each of them, hunching over as dirt sifted down on their heads.

Lisa's heart was pumping so hard she wondered if it might break her ribs. Jumping up from under Cal's arm, she ran up the steps with Cal at her heels. Together, they put their shoulders to the panel and pushed up. It would not budge no matter how hard they tried.

"Somethin' heavy has fallen across it," Lisa said, studying the underside as though she might see through it.

"Something terrible must have happened. Oh, I hope my John is all right," Rebecca worried aloud. "We're trapped." She glanced anxiously around the small enclosure.

"Let's think the best. We need to think he's okay," Lisa said, trying to console Rebecca and herself. Lisa wiped the dirt from her eyes with her shirttail and stared at the panel, willing it to open, but she knew the truth. They were trapped and something had happened to John. She wished she had her crucifix but knew she didn't need to have it with her to pray. Closing her eyes, she asked for protection for them and safety for John. Her heart began to calm down.

"We're gonna be okay," she said. "We need to believe that."

Time passed slowly and several times, Lisa caught herself dozing off.

Rebecca, on the other hand, was showing signs of claustro-phobia as her last candle slowly burned away. She paced from one wall to the other and her breathing became rapid. At the last flicker of light from the candle, she slid to the floor beside Lisa and Cal.

"Rebecca," Lisa said calmly and quietly. "Sit up very straight and take slow even breaths. Slowly. In… let it out… in… let it out… in… out…."

"I can't."

"Yes you can," Lisa said firmly. "In... out... in... out...," Lisa continued until Rebecca's breathing slowed down. "Now, lean your head back against the wall and close your eyes. Relax your hands in your lap and keep breathing slowly." Lisa began counting in a whisper until Rebecca appeared to be asleep.

Left in the darkness, they sat side by side against the wall and tried to stay calm. In the pitch-blackness, they clung to each other's hands as the walls moved in on them, compressing them into the space in which they sat.

"The roof is strong and it's not gonna cave in on us. I helped put in the supports along the walls and I *know* they'll hold. So, we'll just sit right here and wait. Somebody will come find us, eventually."

Rebecca continued to sleep while Lisa slept fitfully in the crook of Cal's arm. In spite of his assurances, Cal worried about Lisa and Rebecca and the condition of things above. His nerves were as tight as a freshly wound clock spring. Hours passed by, but he was sure they would be found. At last, unable to keep his eyes open longer, he fell asleep until they were awakened by loud voices and the scraping sound of a heavy object being pulled across the panel.

"Hello," someone shouted as the panel began to open. "Mrs. Pyne? We've come to get you out."

Cal unfolded his cramped legs and pushed himself up, offering his hands to Lisa and Rebecca. "They've come."

Lisa whispered, "Thank God."

When the panel was raised, they squinted into a bright midday sun. Stiff, cold and somewhat disoriented, they fumbled their way to the stairs. Cal helped Rebecca up the first few steps until someone from above took her hand. Soon they were all standing in the warm sunshine looking at three unfamiliar faces and a lot of damage. The roof had been torn from the house and much of it had landed on top of the cellar. The hand-hewn shakes were scattered about the yard and they dared not think of the rain soaked interior.

"Where is my husband?" Rebecca pleaded.

"We just took him to Doc Brewer's office," one of the men said. "We found him buried under here. Looked like he was heading for the cellar when the roof came down on him. He was very groggy so Doc Brewer wanted to watch him for an hour or so to make sure he's okay. Your husband told us you were in the cellar so we came back to get you."

"How in the world did you happen to find him?" Rebecca asked.

"There's a group of us going street to street checking out the damage and looking for any injured people. It appears to have been a small tornado. Looks like it came down right on your house. In town, some tents crumpled from the wind and the thatched roofs got a good soaking but no one's been injured."

Rebecca pulled herself together and held out her hand to the men. "I thank you very much for coming to our rescue and seeing to my husband." Looking through the kitchen window, she said, "Sorry I can't offer you something to eat or drink. It looks like we have much work to do."

"And it looks like you'll be needed here for a while," Lisa whispered to Cal.

"Yeah," he sighed. "But at such a toll."

CHAPTER 33

"YOU HAD A close call, John," Doc Brewer said as he daubed iodine on John's head wound. John winced at the burning sting of the medication. The cut traveled from the middle of his forehead into his hairline.

"Looks to me like you're lucky to come out of this alive. I want you to stay here in my office for a couple of hours so I can make sure you're steady on your feet before you go back home. You've had a bit of a concussion."

"Rebecca will be worried."

"Someone has already gone to your house to let her know you're all right."

"Thank you. I would like to lie down on de cot now."

"You'll need to take care of that wound."

"Oh, you can bet Rebecca will take good care of me" he said, looking up at the doctor. "I sure do know I survived a tornado this time, absolutely, but next time, you can bet I will go into de cellar with my family."

After Doc Brewer released him with firm instructions to take it easy, John and Lisa tromped through the mud to check out the forge. Debris from the house littered the area but, to their relief, they found the shop and tools soaked but undamaged.

John picked up a shingle and turned it over. "This hasn't been too much damaged," he said, placing it back on the ground and reaching for another. His eyes began to glow with relief. "There are many that can be used again."

He began to stack the pieces and Lisa pitched in to help. "Looks like we can be back to work as soon as we clean up this mess, but I think first, we fix up de house. That will give de shop time to dry out."

"Doc Brewer said you needed to take it easy so you probably oughta get back to the house and find a place to sit down for a while."

From the front stoop, John surveyed the ground around the house searching for a place to raise their tent but he saw that the grassy areas were filled with slush and the rest was simply bare mud. Returning to the parlor, he looked around at the soaked furniture and then up at the open sky. He scratched his chin as he mumbled to himself. Lisa's second floor bedroom had taken the brunt of the storm and saved the ceiling in the kitchen but the other rooms were open to the heavens. The walls appeared to have survived and looked stable.

"Cal, it looks like we'll be sleeping under de stars right here in de house until de ground dries enough to set up de tent."

"I was just thinkin' about that myself. But if it should rain, we could probably attach the tent to those beams over the parlor here and have a roof, or we can just all sleep in the kitchen."

John grinned. "That sounds better to me but maybe we won't have to do either one of those things. Look at the steam floating up from de grass and de mud. That prairie sun is good and warm today. It shouldn't take more than a couple of days for de ground to dry enough to put up de tent outside." He shook his head in disbelief. "It was all so good but it will be good again. You bet."

Will it? Lisa asked herself as she climbed the stairs to her bedroom. Her life was finally settling down and she was not looking for Carver or the deputies around every corner or behind every tree. *I know they can still find us but we're among friendly people now, people who think like we do. There's gotta be some protection in that.* Her nerves were on edge and she had become uneasy again. Being trapped in the cellar had affected her more than she wanted to admit.

She reached the top of the stairs and blinked at the brightness of the sun's rays pouring on her soaked belongings. Fresh air poured into what was left of her bedroom but the odor of wet wood was overwhelming. It wasn't disgusting. It was just strong and would be a reminder to her for a long time of what had taken place early that morning.

Her two dresses had been blown off the hooks and lay soaked and crumpled against the wall. She had been so careful to keep them clean and fresh looking and now they were flattened as though someone had stomped on them; sort of the way she felt as she looked about her room — flattened and stomped on.

Sadly, she could see that the bedding and her new cotton mattress were soaked through. She began tugging on the quilt but it was so water-soaked that it clung tightly to the mattress. Finally, she was able to pull it off the bed to the floor where it lay in a large wet lump. With hands on her hips, she surveyed her situation. She would need help to wring out the quilt but at least, with it off the bed, the sun pouring down on the roofless room should get a good start on drying out the mattress.

"Oh, my! My crucifix," she gasped, whipping around to see it shimmering back at her from its special place on the wall. With shaking hands she reached up and removed it from its hook and dried it with her shirttail. Carefully she swung it open and removed the letter and the portrait finding them dry and intact. "Thank you," she whispered and the lump that had begun to develop in her throat went away.

In the kitchen, Rebecca searched for food that might have made it through the storm. The room was mostly intact since it had been protected by Lisa's bedroom above but the wind had swept the rain inside through the door to the parlor. Pulling a loaf of bread from its bag, she found the outside of it damp but perfectly fine for eating. The ham and cheese were dry and the bean soup in the kettle was undisturbed. "How fortunate we are," she observed aloud.

"I feel the same way," Lisa said, breathing a sigh of relief as she came in from the parlor. "All my things are there. Soaked through and a mess but they are there. Looks like the tornado picked things up and dropped them right back down. How are things in here?"

"We have food for a few days," Rebecca said, drying off a chair and sitting down. "We will get through this, Lisa. It all looks so discouraging but if we take it one step at a time, we'll get back to where we were. Right now, I'm thinking of making butter and ham sandwiches for supper tonight. John and Cal have set up cots for us. We will sleep and then get up with the sun and begin cleaning."

With the stars shining down on them and the silence of the prairie comforting them, they fell asleep.

They were awakened by the sound of voices and loud knocking on the window above John's head. Thankful they had dropped on their cots in their clothes, he jumped up and opened the front door where a half dozen people waited with rags, buckets and tools.

Stunned, he asked, "What is going on? Rebecca, come."

"Oh, I see we woke you up. Sorry about that." The man speaking had a hammer in one hand and a piece of wood in the other. "I'm Dr. Lum and these are volunteers from my church; here to help you put your house back together. I've had a look around and the damage doesn't look too serious. The tornado seems to have come down only as far as your roof, lifted the whole thing up and dropped it. Some pieces are broken or splintered, but most of it is reusable. The shakes are scattered but we'll pick them up and see how many new ones we have to make."

John and Rebecca were stunned. "We don't know what to say. You are all strangers to us and you come to help?"

"We won't be strangers for long," Dr. Lum said and went back to work.

Slowly, John and Rebecca awakened to what was going on and John headed for the shop to pick up his tools. Rebecca began wondering how she would feed all these people and decided to send Lisa and Cal into town for a supply of food from the general store.

When they returned, Cal joined the men in gathering the strewn shakes and helping to sort the good pieces of lumber from the bad. Several men worked on the roof and in only four days, the repaired roof covered the house.

Women helped Lisa pull the soaked mattresses and bedding from the house onto the tent the men had spread out on the ground. The women dried down the walls and furniture with rags of all kinds brought from their own homes. Rebecca started a fire in the kitchen stove and began cooking for the people. It was a wonderful time of recovery and Rebecca and John worked with grateful hearts for their new friends.

Watching and listening to their conversations as the women worked, Lisa wondered what they thought of her. Not that it mattered. Or did it? Did they wonder why she continued to work as a blacksmith? She was pleased that they tried to include her in their conversations, even though she had very little to contribute; but she did notice their astonishment and their inability to relate to the bits and pieces of her past life that she chose to tell them. Lisa could see that they were happy being wives, mothers and cooks even as they struggled under the worst of circumstances in their new prairie homes. They appeared to take courage from each other and she found that courage remarkable and inspiring. She found that she wanted to be their friend.

But I'm happy, too. I really like workin' at the shop. I like being able to craft a knife or a tool or mend a wagon wheel or shoe a horse. Why do I have to give that up to be a woman? She vigorously sopped up the water around the fireplace and wrung out her rag in the bucket, no longer hearing the conversations around her. *My work contributes to the family and to society. I didn't ask to be raised a boy or be trained as a blacksmith, but I was.* Her swiping at the side of the fireplace became more intense as her thoughts became more determined. *I wanna be a woman who can work as a blacksmith and take care of a house, too. Doesn't seem impossible to me.* She sopped and wrung out her rag again. *Course, these women don't wear men's breeches and shirts, but I can't do what I do in a dress. But maybe I should have worn a dress today.* Self-consciously, she looked down at her pants and shirt and realized she couldn't have changed to a dress anyway as the only two she had were unwearable for the time being. She was glad that Rebecca picked that time to call them to lunch.

At the end of the fourth day, the crew of volunteers inspected their work and called it good.

"The roof is on and everything inside the house is dry and back in place," observed Maria, the woman who seemed to be in charge of the volunteers. "I think we're finished and you can go back to living like normal people again."

Rebecca, unable to hold back her tears, stood on the porch and faced them as they prepared to leave. "Thank you. Thank you so much." Twisting the edge of her apron through her fingers, she stammered, "I... we don't know how to thank you or how to repay you for all you've done. What really wonderful people you are."

"Oh, you don't need to repay us," a small woman named Tina replied emphatically. "We've already been repaid, just knowing things are back to normal for you."

"Please, all of you, know that we are here to help you if you ever need us," Rebecca said. She didn't know what else to say.

Maria spoke up again. "I think I say this for all of us. We may have come to this perilous prairie from many different places but we're here to become a town—a state—a people—the people of Kansas. To us, Kansas will be more than a place; it will be a way of life, guided by our shared beliefs. What we did here this week is a beginning. It's what families do for each other and we thank you for letting us help you. We all got to know each other better and that's good. Events like this make up the warp and the woof of the life fabric we're weaving here." She hesitated, realizing the people were nodding their heads, encouraging her. Embarrassed, she continued speaking. "Well, we all know that there are bad things about to happen here and they are right at our doorstep so we need to stick together." Maria was surprised to hear the people clapping. "Oh, dear," she added. "I really didn't mean to make a speech."

"Well said," responded Dr. Lum who had joined her on the porch. "We have your words to help us keep going. I, for one, certainly agree with them." Turning back to Rebecca and John, he said, "Now, it's time we leave you people to yourselves. May God bless you as you continue to make a life here, as we all are doing. Thank you for feeding us."

Together, John, Rebecca, Lisa and Cal watched until they were out of sight.

"I think we have a very good future here," John said.

After Lisa and John left for the blacksmith shop the next morning, Cal headed for town to look for work. Lisa was adamant that he search for work in Lawrence before considering the cavalry. He started with the Emigrant Aid Office, knowing that it was a place where people came to solve their problems. With luck, someone might check there when looking to hire a helper. James Donovan lifted a hand in a friendly greeting and set his paperwork aside, pointing to the chair across his desk. He had a tired looking face with heavy eyebrows weighing down upon heavy eyelids, but his smile was warm and friendly and his handshake was firm.

"I hear the Pyne's house is fully repaired and things are back to normal, at least as normal as things can be these days."

"Yeah, that's true," Cal said, sitting on the edge of his chair. "I'm at loose ends now that the work's all done there. I'd like to leave word with you that I'm available to anybody to do about anything. I never knew how to build a house before but I learned. I've dug a cellar and learned how to support it well. As you know, it held up through that storm."

"I heard about that. Must have been frightening being trapped like that for so many hours."

"It was, but we kept telling ourselves we'd be rescued. The worst part was when our last candle burned out. It was black as pitch and we were trapped. That's a fearful feelin'."

Donovan shook his head. "The whole event is a story this town won't soon forget." He leaned back in his chair. "So, now you need something to do."

"That's right. I need paying work. I can't live off the Pynes forever and, well, Lisa and I wanna get married and be on our own. She's got her job at the blacksmith shop but I need to find something. I'm willin' to put my hand to anything. I was hoping, since you're sort of a central place people go to, you might help me get the word out. I'm thinkin' somebody might come in here looking for help."

"You can count on it, Cal. We, here in this office, will do our best. You and your girlfriend and the Pynes are a good addition to this town. We need your kind of spirit and courage."

Feeling encouraged, Cal stopped by the businesses along Massachusetts Street and found that many of the merchants would like to help him but couldn't. He was sent from one place to another by well-meaning people. By the end of the afternoon, there wasn't a person in town who wasn't on the lookout for a job for Cal. If there was any work to be had, he would get it. He would always be thought of as the person who saved Jonah Pierce's life.

It took only two days for someone to rap on the Pyne's door and ask for Cal. A tall thin woman with large brown eyes that rested on high cheekbones and shallow cheeks stood there expectantly. She appeared to be in her fifties with a smattering of gray dusting her dark brown hair. He was immediately taken by her soft gentle but confident voice.

"The man in the Emigrant Aid Office says you are looking for work."

"Yes, I am. Won't you come in?"

She came into the house, nodding at the others while remaining near the doorway. "My name is Maggie Sheldon. I own twenty acres a mile west of town. I have a cow, two horses and a whole bunch of noisy chickens. No children and no husband. He died two weeks ago and I just can't keep up with it all." Tears lingered on her eyelashes but she managed to control them. Cal thought she looked very brave.

It was late afternoon and Rebecca brought her a cup of tea, inviting her to take a seat by a small table in the parlor. "I insist that you stay and join us in our evening meal. It's not quite ready so you and Cal can sit here and discuss what you have to offer."

Cal pulled a chair to the other side of the table and listened to her questions. Can you milk a cow? No. Have you ever harvested crops? No. Mended a fence? No. Can you learn? Yes.

He laid out the things he had done, the same as he had done for James Donovan. "Mr. Pyne over there can tell you if I did a good job or not," Cal said, pointing to John who was sitting near the window reading.

John looked up and nodded. "You couldn't get better," he said and went back to his book.

"Then, I'm offering you the job. I can pay you eight dollars a month and give you room and board if you want it. If not, I can pay you twelve and you can come out early each morning and stay until chores are done," she said and leaned back in her chair to await his answer.

Cal looked across the room at Lisa who had been listening intently. "Sounds good to me," she said, causing Mrs. Sheldon to raise her eyebrows.

"Is she your wife?" she asked.

"Not yet but will be soon as we can manage on our own."

"Then you have a reason to work," Mrs. Sheldon observed. "That's good."

"You bet I do," Cal said, grinning widely at Lisa.

"Supper's ready," called Rebecca from the kitchen doorway.

When they sat down to eat, Cal had not yet given her a positive answer. For the most part, he was pleased with the offer but he had to answer a few questions. Eight dollars a month could be saved since he wouldn't have to pay for room and board. But would he want to stay out there? Away from Lisa for days at a time? If he went into the cavalry, he'd be gone for months or years. He could stay out there and come see Lisa at least once a week. It began to sound better the more he thought about it.

Lisa watched him from across the table, knowing he was thinking it over and making a decision. It was his decision to make but she was sure their thoughts were paralleling each other. For now, it would be best if he stayed on the farm; but how would she handle that? *I've seen him every day since I was five years old.* She tried to make eye contact but he wouldn't look at her.

"Mrs. Sheldon. I'll give it a try and I'll stay out there with you if that's what you prefer."

"Oh, my," Lisa gasped.

"Is that going to be a problem? Do you two want to talk this over privately?" Mrs. Sheldon asked, looking at Lisa.

"Oh, no. I mean, yes. It's gonna be okay," Lisa muttered, embarrassed at her impetuousness.

"Then, I thank you, Mr. Hale. I don't need a bodyguard because I can shoot a gun and shoot it straight. My husband taught me. But, there is a lot to do on the farm and it's too much for me to do alone. I hear you're acquainted with hardship."

"That's right and so is Lisa."

"Lisa, is it really true that you grew up as a boy in a boy's orphanage?"

"It's true. And these people are helping me to become a girl." She swept her hand around the room. "I think they're succeeding but I en't gonna give up my blacksmith work. It's something I really love to do, like it's lodged in my bones." Lisa pushed her chair from the table. "Is it okay if Cal and I have a little time alone outside before he leaves?"

"Of course," she agreed and continued to sip her tea with Rebecca and John as Lisa pulled Cal outside.

"Drats. Do you realize this'll be the first time we'll be away from each other for so long?"

"Yeah. But remember, we're growin' up so things like this are gonna happen. We can handle it. Besides, I'll be coming to see you and I'm sure she won't care if you ride out to see me sometime. You could surprise me."

"I could, couldn't I," she said, mischievously.

"Come here, you," Cal said, pulling her into his arms.

CHAPTER 34

"THAT WAS A member of de Lawrence Safety Committee. As you know, I have been going to their meetings. They are good men," John explained to Lisa just after the man rode away from the shop. "While you were shoeing his horse, he told me some very disturbing news."

"He was talkin' awfully quiet over there so I thought it was private."

"Well, you know how we have had to watch out what we say because we don't want to make that Missouri legislature mad. Right?"

Lisa nodded disgustedly.

John picked up a long piece of iron with his tongs and held it toward the fire.

"Can you tell me what he said?" A December wind sent billows of icy air into the blacksmith shop pushing her closer to the fire.

"I should tell you, I think. It will make you anxious but I feel sure you should know." He laid the iron and tongs down and cast a concerned look at her. "Men from Missouri have been gathering around Franklin and along de Wakarusa River for several days now."

"Why?" Lisa asked, holding her palms against the heat.

"Remember when a man by de name of Dow was murdered in a fight over a claim? Then a man from here in Lawrence—I think his name was Branson—an abolitionist, said something against de murder in public and a Missouri man heard him and said he felt threatened by what that man said. That man from Missouri had our man arrested by that fake Westport postmaster sheriff. He and his posse went to Mr. Branson's home and dragged him away in front of his wife and children, all because he made a statement about how he felt about de murder."

"That's terrible. What were they gonna do with him?"

"I don't know what they planned to do but some of our men went after de sheriff and his posse and rescued our man without a fight and that is why all those men from Missouri have come here." John had to stop and take a breath before he could continue. "Now de fake sheriff says that those men broke de law by rescuing de arrested man. Of course, our men thought it was not a fair thing for de man to be arrested in de first place."

"How many men from Missouri are out there?" A lump moved into her throat. "Are they near Cal and Maggie?"

"I don't know. This man thinks there are about three thousand men. Even though de people of Lawrence had nothing to do with de whole matter, those men are ready to attack our town. They have been stealing food from de farmers."

The pressure on her throat made it hard to breathe. "Oh, my! I wonder if Cal and Maggie know about this," she gasped.

"I am sure they do, Lisa."

"It's been six months since Cal went out to help Maggie. He's been comin' home every week and things have been all right on the farm. Come to think about it, he oughta be here tomorrow."

December had moved in on Lawrence bringing steadily dropping temperatures with each day. The sun fought to keep it warm but lost its battle as warm coats, scarves and mittens were brought out of chests and drawers.

Lisa worked with a special determination the rest of the day, struggling to keep a clear head. She had heard many stories from travelers who had stopped by the shop. Stories were told of whole families being killed by pro-slavery guerillas in their isolated homes on the prairie. Often, it was only the men. She had dismissed these stories as unbelievable rumors only. How could they be true? Her work that afternoon was as precise as ever but it was done with muscles as tight as the traces on a horse pulling a heavy load up a hill.

John studied her face as she worked and at the end of the day, as they hung up their tools, he said, "I know it's been very hard on you today. I am worried, too. Why don't we go into town and see what we can find out? I will go to de Emigrant Aid office and you can visit your good friends, Martha and Aaron."

Stopping by the house to tell Rebecca to hold their supper, they quickly walked the fifteen-minute stretch into town. Reaching the north end of Massachusetts Street, they were stunned to see deep trenches surrounded by mounds of dirt in the middle of the street. Hundreds of armed troops were encamped alongside them. John and Lisa soon learned that these men would defend the town at these points, should it be attacked. The largest trench at the crossing of Massachusetts Street and Pinckney was reinforced with cut timber. If an assault came, this would be a refuge for women and children.

The anxiety in the air engulfed Lisa and John like a thick gray fog and added to their already deep concern. They parted and Lisa ran to Martha's home, her pulse racing with her footsteps. Martha and Aaron had discarded their tent and built a frame house before the winter set in. They had just sat down to a meal of beef stew, which Lisa declined but accepted a hot cup of tea instead. Lisa warmed her hands over the fire in the kitchen stove before taking a seat.

"Things have sure been happenin' here in town that we didn't know about out where we live," Lisa said. She told them what she had learned just today at the shop about the agitated Missouri men camping southeast of town and wondered why they hadn't heard about it sooner.

"It's only been a few days since it all began. It's a disorderly bunch of men; some are troops and some are just men looking for a fight. One of the newspaper reporters went out there and found a lot of drinking going on and saw that some of the men were just there itching for a fight but others didn't seem to know why they were there. It was like they were looking for something exciting to do."

"Is it true they're stealin' from the farmers around here?"

"Oh, yes. Some of the farmers have come into town for protection, especially those who have had their cows and chickens stolen and their gardens cleaned out."

Lisa leaned back in her chair and cracked her knuckles; worry straining her eyes.

"You're worried about Cal, aren't you?" Martha asked, placing a hand on Lisa's arm.

"Yes, I am. Travelers comin' by the shop have told us lots of stories about people being killed in their homes but I didn't wanna believe they were true. I thought it just couldn't be happening."

"Oh, it's happening all right," Aaron said. "We're under siege. There's no doubt about it. But we outfoxed them in one way. We sneaked in several hundred Sharpe's rifles right under their noses in boxes marked 'Books' and our troops out there are armed with them right now. Those rifles are fearful weapons and the best made. I hear the Missourians are scared to death of them."

Jonah finished his stew and waved his spoon toward Lisa, making clucking sounds with his tongue.

"That's something he's picked up recently and he loves the sound of it, to the point of being a...," Martha stopped. "No, I won't say that," she said as she ran her fingertips along Jonah's cheek. "It's a precious sound and, with the uncertainty surrounding us, he can make all the noisy sounds he wants and I will be happy."

Jonah giggled and put out his arms to Lisa. She swept him up and held him close. "You just keep on clucking, little one. You're my little buddy, right?"

She received a wet kiss as a reward. Lisa had made their home her second home since Cal had been away. Martha had been teaching her how to sew quilt patches together and soon they would be setting up a bed size quilt on a frame and she would learn how to do the tiny quilting stitches. It was an effort that was contradictory to her work as a blacksmith and, at times, her strong muscles rebelled at the minute detail they were subjected to. Lisa was determined that she could be a good—no—a great wife as well as a great blacksmith.

"I'd best go meet John and get back to Rebecca. I guess no one knows how long this siege is gonna last or what those men out there will do. I'm guessing John's gonna come back into town and help."

Handing Jonah to Martha, she hugged them all and went out into the bitter cold to look for John.

The next day arrived, colder and with an added crispness brought on by higher humidity. This was the fourth day of the siege and the day Cal should come home. John ate a quick supper and went into town to see what he could do. He had begun to keep his Sharpe's rifle close by and carried it wherever he went. Today, he would get two firearms for Rebecca and Lisa if there were any left at the general store. Lisa remained at the house to wait for Cal, her nerves tighter than whipcord.

John returned well past the middle of the night and found Lisa asleep on the sofa, rolled into a tight ball for warmth. The socks she was knitting for Cal lay on the floor where they had dropped from her hands. Only embers remained in the fireplace. He climbed the stairs to her room to retrieve her quilt. As he pulled it from her bed, the portrait of her father slipped from under the pillow. Studying it in the flickering light of his candle, he saw the resemblance and knew that she had memorized his face, longing to see him some day. John admired her steadfastness and believed she would, one day, see him face to face.

Laying the quilt over her, he felt the restlessness of her sleep. She had become a daughter to him and Rebecca and they would always take care of her. They would also help her find her father if an opportunity presented itself. He promised her that, as he watched her sleep. He would wait until morning to tell her what he had found out that night.

CHAPTER 35

CAL TURNED UP his collar and snugged his cap down around his ears as he hurried to the barn. Maggie had generously given him her husband's winter clothing, for which he was grateful. She and Tom had only worked on their claim for two summer months when his heart unexpectedly gave out. They had made all the preparations to survive the Kansas winter while they waited for spring to arrive so they could plant their acreage in corn and increase the size of their vegetable garden. Tom's clothing was neatly folded inside a large wooden box that she moved into Cal's room upon his arrival.

"Most of these clothes are new and they aren't doing any good lying here in this box. Tom was a bit taller than you but not much heavier. You can roll up the sleeves and the pant legs. You'll need the warm things soon enough come winter," she told him.

He had felt strange wearing the clothing at first, but soon found that his own was inadequate. As the wintery air began moving in, he willingly dug into the box for a heavy coat, pants, cap and gloves.

The below freezing temperature during the previous night had left a coating of ice crystals on the snow, made blindingly beautiful by the morning sun. He was energized by the crisp air as he mucked out the barn and provided clean hay for the horses. He had easily taken to farm work, mostly because it kept him outdoors. Maggie had taught him much in the past several months.

Stepping up to Mary Belle's stall, he folded his arms across the gate and looked into her eyes while he rubbed her head. "We had quite a time getting to know each other, didn't we?" Mary Belle blinked her somber eyes, swaying her head under his touch. "You remember, too, don't you?"

Milking Mary Belle was one of the first things Maggie taught him. He chuckled aloud as he recalled that day. "You didn't like me much, old girl, and I didn't much like you either. I didn't know what to do with you."

He hadn't thought of her by name then. He couldn't think of a cow having a name; after all, it was a cow. Cows didn't have personalities like horses. Cows stood all day, chewed their cud and gave milk. "How wrong I was, eh, Mary Belle?"

"Moo."

The day after Cal moved to the farm, Maggie had given him a demonstration that looked easy enough to do.

"Talk quietly to her and call her by name. She doesn't know you so sit on the edge of the stool ready to jump back if she gets ornery. I've secured her head in a stanchion and given her some oats to keep her busy. She needs to know you're her friend."

How could he warm up to a cow standing there eating and flipping its long tail all over the place? After all, he and Maggie had barely begun to get acquainted. He knew he had to give it a try. With Maggie watching, he squatted down on the low three-legged stool and grabbed a teat in the circle made by the thumb and forefinger of each hand. The cow jumped and whipped its tail in Cal's face sending him flying off the stool. He looked up at Maggie with a half-grin.

"Gently, Cal. *Talk* to her," she reminded him.

"Okay, cow. Let's you and me be friends," he said, placing a palm on the cow's flank while taking his seat again.

"Her name is Mary Belle, Cal," she had said. "*Mary Belle.*"

Cal had begun to get the message and sat down to try again. Mary Belle sensed what was happening and began a little dance with her hind feet.

"Don't let her get the best of you. Act like you know what you're doing," Maggie said, repressing a grin.

Cal took a deep breath, took hold again, only more gently, and cooed, "Mary Belle, old girl. Give me a chance. Now, here goes." With a positive squeeze of the thumb and forefinger, then rolling his other fingers gently down the teat, he managed to get a good squirt into the bucket. He took a deep sigh of relief and tried the other hand. Back and forth, one hand then the other until he had filled half the bucket. He looked at Maggie who was smiling at him. Feeling full of confidence, he squeezed again with more gusto than needed. Mary Belle's hind foot came up and caught Cal in the shin, sending him sprawling on the floor into a pool of spilled milk. Mary Belle looked at him and let out a triumphant "moo" that echoed to the next farmhouse.

Maggie checked his leg and told him he was lucky it wasn't broken. He limped for several weeks while the leg turned a deep purple and was painful to touch. Maggie hadn't let him give up on the milking and had him try again the next day. It took a week for Cal to conquer Mary Belle's aversion to him and his to her. When Mary Belle realized things weren't going to change, she began to accept Cal, which made Cal more at ease and gave him confidence. For a long time, they tolerated each other until they actually began to like each other.

"We had quite a beginning, Mary Belle," he said warmly as he rubbed her head one more time. Cal tossed some feed in her trough and whistled quietly as the bucket filled. "Good girl," he said, heading for the kitchen where he poured the milk into two large jars and went outside to rinse the bucket at the pump.

The sound of hooves cracked crisply against the frozen ground and he looked up to see their neighbor, Platt Solomon, cautiously urging his horse along on the dangerous surface. Cal dropped his bucket at the back door and hurried out to meet the man.

Platt pulled up on the reins. "I don't have much time. Let's get inside and talk to Maggie."

Cal held the door for Platt as they pounded the snow off their boots. Maggie was waiting for them with the coffee pot in her hand and three cups set out on the table.

"What's going on Platt? You look troubled," Maggie said.

"I am. You know about all those men from Missouri camping to the south of Lawrence?"

Maggie nodded and poured her strong thick coffee into the cups.

"Ash Tilson came by our place not an hour ago and said some of those men, most of them drunk, had come and cleaned them out. Took their cow and chickens and the food from the kitchen and the cellar. His two horses were out in the pasture so the men missed them. Oh, and they took their hog. They scared his little boy to death. The men had guns and actually pointed them at that little four-year-old."

Platt sat back to get his breath. He removed his gloves, wrapped his cold palms around the hot coffee cup and brought it to his lips.

"Good coffee, Maggie. Lots of strength. Thanks."

"Welcome. So what's Ash going to do?"

"He told his wife to bundle up all the clothes, blankets and such and dig out the old tent from the loft. He went out for the horses and rode as fast as he could to let me know. He's loading up his wagon and heading for his brother's place south and little west of Lecompton."

Cal listened intently, wondering what he would be expected to do. This was the day he was to go see Lisa and that's what he planned to do. She would worry herself sick if he didn't show up.

"What do you plan to do, Platt?" Maggie asked, the lines around her eyes deepening as she studied his face.

"I told my boys to pack everything they can. I told them to just start throwing things into bags and boxes and we'll load the wagon when I get back."

Maggie stood up and paced the floor, her hands clenched behind her back. "Why are you running, Platt? You've got a gun. A couple of them, just like I do. Seems like we could stave them off."

"There are too many rumors about homesteaders being killed by renegades from Missouri. I'm just leaving long enough for these men to go home. I have two young sons to protect. We'll be coming by here in about an hour if you want to join us. We're going just far enough to find a temporary safe haven. We're coming back."

He set his empty cup on the table and thanked her. "Ash and I both think it's best if you leave. Rumors are they just kill the men in the family." He glanced at Cal and nodded, then turned to Maggie. "I'd like to see you safe from here as well."

Maggie walked him to the door. "Thanks for taking the time to come, Platt. I really mean that. You're very kind."

After the door closed behind her, Maggie dropped into a chair like a deflating balloon.

"What should we do, Cal?"

Her question and the use of "we" pulled him firmly into the situation, taking away any chance of heading for the Pyne's. Maggie was his employer and one look at her anguished face drew him further into her problem. He knew he couldn't desert her.

Seating himself across the table from her, he gathered her hands into his. "We'll pack the wagon, hitch Range and Star to it and tie Mary Belle to the back. We'll leave the chickens for the men who come and maybe a few jars of your canned fruits and vegetables in the cellar. That way, they'll get somethin' and won't be mad and burn down your house."

By making this decision, he had taken over and Maggie appeared to be relieved. Under normal circumstances, he knew she would be fine but after losing her husband, he was sure she feared losing him, as well.

Determination replaced the fear and indecision in her face and she said, "Let's get busy."

By the time Platt and the boys came by, Cal and Maggie were waiting for them. Mary Belle was complaining noisily, her sad eyes more pathetic than usual. Cal had removed the bell from around her neck.

"You'll get used to it, old girl. We can't be attractin' attention," he told her.

CHAPTER 36

LISA STRETCHED HER cramped muscles and opened her eyes. Someone had laid a blanket over her where she had fallen asleep while waiting for Cal to arrive. The house was quiet with the faint light of morning sweeping away the night. Lisa sat up and rubbed her eyes, wondering if John ever returned home. She had stayed awake worrying about Cal and then added John to her concerns when he didn't return from Lawrence. Eventually, Rebecca went to her bedroom but Lisa stayed by the fire to greet the men when they arrived.

She stepped to the window and saw streaks of a new day appearing in the east. *Where are you, Cal? What's happened to you?* She leaned her head against the icy windowpane and quickly pulled away. The frost had made delicate lace patterns on the window, something that usually delighted her, but not this day. The design only reminded her of the intense cold outside.

In the kitchen, she built a fire in the stove and put on a kettle of water for tea. There was no way she could eat a breakfast but a hot cup of tea would warm her inside and out.

"Thought I heard you moving around in here," John said, coming up behind her. "How about making another cup for me?"

Lisa set out two cups and filled them both. "I sure was worried about you and Cal last night. I'm glad to see at least one of you got here."

They pulled their chairs closer to the warmth of the stove and wrapped their cold fingers around the hot cups.

"I need to tell you what I did last night," John said. Choosing his next words thoughtfully, he continued. "Fred Williams, Jed Mason and I took a little trip out to some of de farms west of town, including Maggie's. Fred was worried about a friend of his who took a claim out dat direction and I wanted to check on Maggie and Cal since he hadn't yet come to us. Rev. Jed just wanted to come along. He is worried about dis whole mess going on around here."

Lisa sat poised on the edge of her chair, her tea quivering inside the cup as she tried to steady her hands. Her eyes remained focused on John's face, waiting for him to continue. She knew he was stressed by the way he was letting his German slip into his speech.

"We had to sneak around to de north to avoid those men from Missouri. We passed several abandoned farms. De barns, de homes and de cellars were empty."

Lisa found a voice that didn't sound like her own. "What did you find at Maggie's?"

"Nobody there. Horses, de wagon and de cow were gone. We hope that means Cal and Maggie got away before those men came. There were chicken heads all over de yard so those men must have taken them back to de gang and made themselves a feast. De house and de barn were in good condition. De door to de house was open so we closed it tight up."

Tense muscles pressed against her throat but she was able to whisper, "What do you think happened to Cal and Maggie?"

Recognizing her desperation, John put a consoling hand on her arm. "I think they took what they could and headed toward safety, probably west and north. There was no sign of violence, so I'm sure they got away."

"He could've sneaked here like you did," Lisa murmured.

"Yes, he could have but I think he couldn't leave de widow on her own. She is his employer and she has been good to him. Maybe they thought they would attract too much attention coming this way with all of her things. Maybe they went together with some neighbors for safety. I don't know, Lisa. Let's do some of dat positive thinking you always talk about."

Lisa nodded her head and took a deep breath. At least John hadn't found the worst. She shuddered to think what that might have been. She refilled John's cup and returned to her own with steadier hands.

"I suppose you would like some breakfast now," Rebecca said in an attempt at being cheerful upon entering the room. She cracked some eggs in one pan and tossed some bacon in another and soon the room was filled with the mouthwatering smell of bacon cooking. Lisa's empty stomach was responding, giving the day a more hopeful outlook.

"Thank you, John, for checking on Cal and Maggie. You put yourself into danger for them and for me. You've pulled me through so many tough times, I'll never be able to repay you."

"We don't expect repayment and don't you even think that way. You and Cal have become our family. You have brought so much happiness into our lives."

"Cal and I have talked about this, too. You've taken the place of our parents. We were two strays and you took us in. You don't know how much that means to us." Lisa's eyes took on a wistful look as her thoughts took her away from the room.

John recognized her sudden distance and said, "We know that you want to find your father. I don't want to take his place. I couldn't, but I will be a substitute until you find him."

"Even if I find him, you will still be what you are to me right now. You and Rebecca have a place right here, always." She placed her hand on her heart.

By the time they had finished eating, the sun had cleared the horizon and Lisa ran up the stairs to her room. Before she reached the top, she heard John calling to her.

"I think you should go to Martha's house today and work on that quilt you two are making."

"Thanks, but I couldn't do that today. I need to do some pounding to get rid of this tension."

"I guess you want to be near de house, too. Right?"

Lisa nodded and continued to her room, closing the door behind her. Picking up her crucifix, she went down on her knees and prayed with the same fervor as when she was running from Jonas Carver. *Here I am again with my problems. You know where Cal is and I don't, so please take care of him and bring him back safe and sound. Thanks. Amen.*

Reaching for her father's portrait, she added, *and if you could help me find him or bring him to me, I'd sure be grateful. Thanks and amen, again.*

Grabbing her coat and cap, she rushed out to the shop feeling that things were going to be all right. In spite of the fact that no one came by, she found many things to keep her busy. John took off for downtown to find out what, if anything, was happening. The town leaders had taken him into their trust and he and Rebecca were doing all they could to help the town feed the free-state militia troops that had come to help. There was a story going around that Governor Shannon was coming to Lawrence to talk to the Safety Committee and to the agitated and impatient men on the outskirts of town. John had purchased guns for Rebecca and Lisa and had taught Lisa to shoot. He felt the times warranted that they be armed should they be threatened, especially during his absence.

"They are to be used and not just for show," he had told them. "But sometimes, if they can see you are armed, they will leave you alone."

Lisa wore hers in a holster attached to her belt when she was working in the shop. When she went into town, she carried it in her pocket. She had yet to be threatened but in the present climate, anything could happen. The thought of using it on someone was appalling. She knew she couldn't kill anyone, but she was sure she could shoot him in the foot, arm or leg without hesitation.

The temperature continued to fall and she hoped Cal and Maggie were safely situated in a warm house with a generous family. During supper, John did his best to get Lisa's mind off Cal by reporting on the happenings in town.

"You know that cannon that's sitting on Massachusetts Street? That was ordered some time back and when it arrived in Kansas City, three men from Lawrence went to get it with their teams of horses. It was in several boxes and de warehouse man wouldn't let them take it until he knew what was inside. Well, he took an axe and broke one of de boxes open and saw de cannon's wheels and thought it was a carriage. So he let them take it."

He stopped to swallow some food and then continued. "De really funny part is when they got to a hill this side of de river, de horses couldn't get that cannon up that hill no matter how hard they tried. You can't guess who came to help them. It was a bunch of those Missouri ruffians. They thought our men were going to Leavenworth —that's a pro-slavery town as you know—so those ruffians helped push that cannon right up that hill. When our men got close to Lawrence, one of them went ahead to get help and some of de soldiers escorted them and that cannon right through that drunken mob outside of our town."

By now, John was laughing hard and Lisa and Rebecca were in tears. "Everybody is laughing about it, even de men who delivered de cannon. They said they didn't think it was funny until they got into town. They said they were nervous and scared de whole time."

"I got another story but I need to eat some of this good food Rebecca made. Lisa, you tell me how it went at de shop after I left."

Since Lisa had nothing much to report, things grew quiet at the table for a time except for the ordinary sounds of eating. John cleaned his plate, pushed it aside and accepted a cup of coffee from Rebecca. "I see we still have some of this good stuff left. Lisa, take a cup. It will do you good. I know you want to leave it all for me but I want you to have some. It would make me happy."

"Thanks." Lisa smiled and accepted the hot cup from Rebecca. "I need to spend some time with you in the kitchen some day, Rebecca. I really oughta know how to cook before Cal and I get married." As she mentioned his name, her voice broke and she took a deep breath, stretching her arms and cracking her knuckles under the table.

"I think it is time for me to tell de other story. It is shorter and maybe not as funny but it is a good one, too."

He took a swallow of coffee before continuing. "You make good coffee, Rebecca. Doesn't she, Lisa?"

Lisa nodded and raised her cup to her lips.

"Yesterday, de troops reported that they didn't have enough ammunition for their Sharpe's rifles. Well, all de extra ammunition was kept at a man's house somewhere on de other side of that mob. No one could figure out how to get it when two ladies offered to go for it in their buggy. De men didn't want to let them but de ladies insisted. Those two brave ladies went right past all those men, picked up that ammunition and hid it under some clothing they took with them. Then they bravely rode right back through that dangerous crowd. For some reason, de ruffians didn't bother those ladies at all. Maybe they were too drunk to notice but de ladies said they were sure scared. Isn't it amazing what people will do?"

He leaned back in his chair. "That's de end of my stories for de day. Some stories, huh? All true. It sure seems like desperate situations can bring out the courage hidden inside some people."

Pushing himself away from the table, he went into the parlor while Rebecca and Lisa tidied up the kitchen. When they joined John, he rose and put his large hands on Lisa's shoulders. "You see? Good things do happen even in hard times. Everything is going to be all right."

Lisa gave him a wan smile and picked up her knitting. Another day was ending without word from Cal.

CHAPTER 37

BY SATURDAY MORNING, December 8, Lisa's nerves were shredded like the frayed edge of a weather-beaten flag. She was ready to go out looking for Cal but the situation in and around Lawrence had heated up to a fever pitch. John reported that Governor Shannon had worked out a treaty which was accepted by the Safety Committee of Lawrence but was rejected by Sheriff Jones and his deputies representing the three thousand men who wanted action and were tired of waiting. Governor Shannon's plea for assistance from federal troops at Fort Leavenworth was denied.

John said the people of Lawrence were ready to fight to defend the town and he was going to join them. Lisa wanted to follow him but he asked her to stay with Rebecca. From the parlor window, they watched him walk away with determined steps, his Sharpe's rifle in his hand. When he was out of sight, Rebecca went to the kitchen and busied herself with cleaning up the remains of breakfast and wiping her eyes with her apron, revealing the bulge of her pistol in her pocket.

Lisa had slipped into a dress that morning, knowing she would not be going to the forge. Now, she was glad she had because her small pistol fit well inside one of the pockets. She dropped the crucifix into the other. Strange bedfellows, she thought, but these were strange times.

At midmorning, the cold wind shifted to the north and the temperature plummeted thirty degrees. Sleet began to spit against the windows and by late afternoon, the sleet had changed to heavy wet snowflakes making it difficult to distinguish the pathway beyond the porch. The blazing fire in the fireplace was fighting a losing battle, unable to send its warmth more than a few feet into the cold room. John had recently had a cord of wood delivered from Kansas City but now Rebecca wondered if it would last until spring as she put another log on the fire.

By midafternoon, there was only silence from the direction of the town, which was nearly as unnerving as the sound of battle would have been. It was impossible to know what was going on, not only because of the distance but because the cold combined with the heavy snowfall muffled any sound beyond their front door. Not a shot could be heard. No cannon fire, no rifle fire, no shouting, none of the sounds that they could associate with an attack by so many men. Neither Lisa nor Rebecca thought to eat, their senses so intent on the dangerous possibilities surrounding them. Would they hear the footsteps of an enemy or the beat of a horse's hooves? If they couldn't see out through the heavily frosted windows, could an enemy see inside? Would their eerie cocoon keep them safe or expose them to unseen danger?

Sunset was obliterated by the dark clouds and afternoon moved into evening. Rebecca and Lisa sat by the fire, each listening intently for any unusual sounds. Lisa found it useless to work on Cal's stockings, finding it impossible to keep track of the knits and purls. The clock on the mantel chimed nine o'clock when Rebecca opened the parlor door once more, hoping to see or hear something.

"Oh," she gasped and squinted against the snow blowing into the room. "Someone is coming." She placed her hand around her gun for only an instant. "Oh, Lisa, it's John. He's coming home. Go put the coffee pot on," she cried, running out into the storm to greet her husband. Her tears froze on her eyelashes as she threw herself into his snow-covered arms.

"All is well," he told her as he picked her up and carried her inside. "I am very hungry."

Over plates of warm ham, beans and bread, he passed on the events of the day. When the temperature dropped suddenly to ten degrees below zero and the sleet came with such enormous force, the enemy gave up and moved out. It took them most of the day to dismantle their tents and load up their arms and munitions under the extreme blizzard conditions.

"They left and we cheered. There is celebrating in Lawrence tonight and a banquet tomorrow. We won de battle this time. We think they will be back but we can relax for now."

"Now all we need is for Cal to come home," Lisa said wistfully. She had been waiting six days.

After the celebrations ended, the days were spent setting things back to normal along Massachusetts Street. Within three days, the free-state militia groups returned to their home territories and businesses opened their doors again. The sun appeared and people sloshed through melting snow, happy that the siege was over.

Lisa and John returned to work waiting for word from Cal and Maggie. For the next week, Lisa ended her days sitting on the porch anxiously watching for Cal to appear, foregoing her weekly visits to Martha. Surely, Cal would know how worried she was. *Seems like if he's not okay, he could send somebody to let me know. I would go to him, wherever he is.*

On Saturday evening, she made a decision and discussed it with John. "It's been almost two weeks since Cal should have been home. I wanna go out to the farm tomorrow and see if Cal and Maggie have come back. It's safe enough and I need to know something," she said fretfully. "It's been way too long. Would you let me ride Rainbow out there?"

"Of course. I've been wondering when you would ask. I was going to suggest it tomorrow. I will go with you if you don't mind."

"I'd appreciate it if you would."

With a bright sun warming their backs, the temperature hovering in the mid-thirties and dry ground underfoot, Lisa and John headed for the other side of Lawrence. Rebecca had hung a bag of bread and cheese over John's saddle horn at the last minute and wished them a safe trip. Rainbow took off at a brisk trot, bobbing her head excitedly in the clear cold air.

"She's been cooped up too long," John said from his mount, an older version of Rainbow who was accustomed to pulling wagons instead of carrying a rider.

Skirting the town to the north along the river road, they were in sight of Maggie's house within thirty minutes. Two wagons sat at the side of the barn and Lisa could see four horses in the pasture. There was nothing abnormal about the scene as far as she could tell; although, she thought Maggie only had two horses and one wagon. She pulled up on the reins and rested her hands on the saddle horn.

"What do you make of it, John? Looks to me like everything's fine. Maybe Cal didn't wanna come home."

"I don't believe that for a minute and neither do you. Let's go on to de house," he encouraged. "You'll see there is a reason why he hasn't been home."

No one answered her knock so Lisa gently pushed the door open several inches and peeked inside. A pale and thin Maggie was asleep on her bed, which had been moved into the kitchen apparently for warmth since there was no fireplace in her little house. Lisa and John quickly moved inside and shut the door behind them. Maggie heard them and opened her eyes, waving a sign of recognition. Removing their wet coats, they moved further into the kitchen and warmed themselves at the stove before approaching Maggie.

"It appears you have been ill, Maggie," John said. "What can we do here to help you?"

"Where's Cal?" Lisa asked. "Is he all right?"

Maggie shifted to a sitting position. "Cal is fine. He's out milking Mary Belle. She's angry as a hornet because her bag was full when we got back here a little while ago and Cal has just now had a chance to relieve her."

In spite of the drawn look of illness on her face, a mischievous glint flashed in her eyes. "He's been very worried about you, Lisa, but a lot has happened to us since the day we left here. For one, we had to go a long way before we found a family that would take us in for a few days. They were very generous and even took Platt and the boys. It was a man and his wife and their house was small so we were pretty crowded. I made things worse by coming down with pneumonia and we had to wait to come home."

Maggie leaned back against her pillow and asked for a drink of water. Then, she looked into Lisa's eyes and continued.

"That man of yours, Lisa, has a heart as big as the world. As much as he missed you, he wouldn't leave me. He stayed until I was well enough to travel. Then he made me a bed of hay in the wagon and tucked me in nice and warm under my coat and the two quilts and brought me home. He's been so concerned about you and planned to get over to see you today after he fixed my supper and tucked me in for the night. You are a fortunate young lady."

A wan smile spread across her face at the sound of footsteps approaching the back door. "He has quite a surprise for you."

Lisa's heart took a turn as she watched him set the full bucket of milk on the table and remove his cap. "Cal?" she cried and rushed across the room throwing her arms around his neck. "I've been so worried." She stepped back and looked into his eyes when his arms didn't fully wrap around her. She saw happiness but not the excitement he would have shown the last time she saw him.

"What's the matter, Cal? What's happened?" She moved back toward John and saw that he shared her confusion.

Maggie could see the welling heartbreak in Lisa's eyes and said, "That's enough now. Open the door."

Stunned, Lisa watched as the exact likeness of Cal came through the door. She glanced from one to the other and then at Maggie whose face was full of apologies. "I didn't know they were going to try to fool you until just one of them came in the door. I'm sorry, Lisa."

The two men standing in the kitchen were the perfect images of each other but she knew which one was Cal. She'd known him too long to mistake him when compared directly with the newcomer. She ran across the room and began pounding on Cal's chest and arms. "That was the meanest trick you've ever pulled on me," she cried. "I've been so blasted worried 'bout you."

Cal grabbed her arms to calm her down. She slumped into his chest and stammered on the verge of hysteria, "I... I... thought you'd changed, you big d... olt. Thought you d... didn't love me anymore."

"I'm sorry. It was mean. It seemed like a good joke but not anymore." He wrapped her in his arms and held her, burying his face in her hair and ignoring everyone in the room. Whispering in her ear, he said, "You just did the most exquisite girl thing you've done so far. I love you and don't you ever forget it." He began rocking her as her arms relaxed and she began to shiver.

"You're freezin' me to death. Take that blasted coat off and get warmed up, then tell me what's goin' on."

Maggie invited Lisa to sit beside her on the bed while the others found chairs and a stool to sit on. Lisa's anger had subsided some but the shock had not worn down.

Cal was the first to speak. "Lisa and John, I want you to meet my twin brother, Conrad. He goes by Con. At least, we must be twins 'cause we look to be identical and his name is Conrad Edwin Hale. I know you're shocked just like Con and I were when we first saw each other and we still feel kinda funny when we look at each other. For some reason, our parents must have separated us when we were babies. En't no question we're twins, is there?"

Lisa and John shook their heads.

"But how did you happen to get together?" Lisa asked.

Con spoke up this time, his voice having the same quality as Cal's but speaking with greater clarity. "I work for a man named Bank at Westport Landing and he sends me out on errands. Yesterday, I made a delivery to the farmer that had taken Cal and Maggie in and I nearly

316

passed out when Cal answered the door. I thought I'd lost my mind and Cal just stood there staring at me letting all the cold air into that man's house."

"You can't have any idea what it felt like to open that door and see myself starin' back at me," Cal said. "That family and Maggie were all in a dither when they realized we didn't know each other."

"These boys have not stopped talking since yesterday morning," Maggie interjected. "This is most unusual—most unusual."

"Then, that's why the boy with the red suspenders at Westport thought Cal was you," Lisa said to Con.

"It looks that way. When I got back from that errand, he told me about seeing Cal. He was frustrated because you were gone and he didn't know where to find you."

"Now that you've discovered each other, what are you gonna do?" Lisa asked.

"For now, I have to get back to Mr. Bank with the wagon and the money from that farmer. I'm a day late but I can make an excuse for that." A broad grin crossed his face as he looked at Lisa. "Cal's told me all about you. Now, that's a captivating story if I ever heard one. I can see why he loves you so much. Looks to me like you're quite a girl and just as pretty as he said you were."

"Yeah, and she's all mine," Cal said.

Heat rushed to Lisa's face and there was no way to stop the sight of it. She had found that blushing was part of being a girl and she had done enough of it to seal her fate.

"I hate to break up dis wonderful party but I have a pretty girl at home expecting us for supper."

"When will you be able to come home, Cal?" she asked, and then looking at Maggie she added, "I know you need him here to take care of things until you're better. I was just wonderin'."

"I'm really better than I look. The only thing I need help with is milking Mary Belle. Tomorrow, I'll ask Cal to go see if Platt would take care of her for a few days. I'm sure he would. Cal can stack some wood in here for the stove and I can feed myself. We brought enough food back from those good people we stayed with that I can take care of myself for several days. If all this works out, Cal will be there to see you tomorrow."

"Con, can you come see us from time to time? John has a blacksmith shop northeast of Lawrence. I work for him."

"I think I can manage that sometime. That is, if you don't mind having a man from Springfield, Missouri, in your house."

"That won't make any difference as long as you're not there to kill us like those other men from Missouri."

"I should tell you that my stepbrothers are riding with one of the Missouri gangs and they wanted me to go with them. I'd heard some of the stories of their escapades into Kansas Territory and I didn't want any part of it. I guess it's a hereditary thing I share with Cal. They weren't happy with me so I left home and came to work for Mr. Bank."

"Thank you for telling us that. We would like to have you as our guest anytime you can come. I can't wait to tell Rebecca what has happened here today."

"You'll come for our wedding, I hope," Lisa said with a grin. "We decided to get married when I turn seventeen in May."

"Of course, I'll come."

"Well, now, Lisa. You haven't told Rebecca and me that bit of news yet so now I have more to tell my Rebecca when we get home."

CHAPTER 38

THE WINTER OF 1855 proved to be a harsh and bitter antagonist. The Pyne's house turned out to be well chinked, keeping the wind and snow from finding their way inside. Many of their friends were not so fortunate, waking up to piles of snow on their floors after a nighttime blizzard. Often the businesses were closed down and people went to their beds to keep warm. Lisa and the Pynes spent much of their time bundled up in front of the fireplace.

The winter months brought a feeling of safety to the people of Lawrence but they knew the volatile temperament of the men who had dragged themselves away in December would bring them back when the warm weather returned.

Cal's visits were rare during those harsh months. Lisa understood the reason as travel on horseback was difficult on the snow and ice and walking that distance was out of the question. Thinking of him outside chopping wood for that little wood stove, mucking out the barn and milking the cow in weather that delighted in staying below zero most of the time, gave her much to be concerned about. She prayed for spring so that his work would be easier and she could get back to the forge on a daily basis.

She tried to make the best use of the days she was confined to the house because of the weather. The example set by Rebecca and her friend Martha, along with the things they were teaching her, were drawing Lisa into the realm of womanhood and maturity. Her knitting was improving and she had learned to make bread. She hoped Cal would be happy that she had learned to use a stove and put a meal together by the time of their wedding.

She had a lot of time to think as she knitted quietly during the long evenings. There were lonely times thinking of her mother, Charlotte, and the years they had together. Her dedication to Lisa's upbringing and the love she poured into it gave Lisa a solid strength to hold on to. Life had been a struggle and continued to be in many ways, but Lisa had been and would continue to be able to survive. She felt as though she had matured ten years since she had escaped from the orphanage and from Boston. She liked emulating Martha who she considered a strong woman and definitely feminine, but not frilly. Lisa knew her arm muscles would always be strong while working in the shop and her hands and nails would always look rough. She could accept that if Cal could. She was getting better at not cracking her knuckles every time she got bored or nervous. It was a longtime habit that was hard to break.

The first week of March blew in on a strong warm prairie wind and Cal came in with it. It was midafternoon and Lisa and John were busy at the shop helping customers catch up on all their needs that had been postponed during the winter. It was a good time and Lisa pounded away with all her stored-up energy, loving every minute of it.

"You better watch out or the head of that hammer's gonna fly right off and hurt somebody."

"Cal," she screeched. "Stay right there until I finish this blade." Lisa was a perfectionist in her work and even in her excitement, she expertly shaped the blade and slipped it into the water with perfect timing.

John was busy attaching a metal strip to a wagon wheel and nodded at Cal. "It's good to see you, Cal. You'll be spending the night, won't you?"

Cal nodded. "I'm gonna be here three days if that's okay with you."

Lisa laid out her blade on a tray and threw her arms around Cal, planting a big kiss on his mouth. She jumped back as a stranger entered the shop.

"Uh-oh!" she murmured. "That musta looked strange." Then she remembered that, even though she was in her shirt and pants, she was wearing a big girlish bow around her hair at the nape of her neck.

The stranger wore a wide-brimmed hat with a rounded crown that he wore well down on his forehead so that his eyes and the upper part of his face were obscured. He was well dressed in a leather jacket and brown wool pants that appeared to have withstood some stressful weather.

"Mind if I water my horse out here in your trough?"

"Of course not. Please do," John replied, stepping outside to take a better look at the animal. "This is a beautiful horse. I haven't seen a cream-colored Morgan before."

"We've been traveling since before sunrise so we're both pretty tired." He led the horse to the trough and threw the reins over the rail.

Returning inside the shop, he nervously took in his surroundings. "I've heard there's a good hotel in town. I wonder if they have a place to shelter a horse."

Before answering, John laid down his tools and told Lisa and Cal to get out. "Your work is done for de day, Lisa. You two go back to de house. Now scoot," he said, shooing them away with his hands.

After they were gone, he turned to the man and inquired, "How can I help you?"

"I had a letter from a friend saying that you had a girl blacksmith. I am curious about her."

"Were you sent here by that Jonas Carver in Malden, Massachusetts? If so, you can just get out of here right now, quick."

Taken aback, the man stepped away holding out the palm of his hand as though to ward off a blow. "No, no. I don't even know the man. I was just coming through Lawrence and thought I'd like to see some of her work."

"Well, she is de best blacksmith around. She's been working for me since she was nine years old. She is de girl I just sent home."

"She looks like she is sixteen. Am I right?"

His question was friendly and held no animosity or threat so John thought it would do no harm to tell him.

"She will be seventeen on May thirteen. Now, no more answers until you tell me who you are and why you ask these questions."

"I think I might be her father, but I don't want to say anything to her until I am sure."

John gasped and glanced out the door to make sure Lisa and Cal were out of sight. His forehead folded into a concerned frown as his eyes surveyed the man more closely. "Lisa has carried de idea of her father in her heart for all her life. She never knew who he was until a year ago. What makes you think you are that man?"

"My name is Pierre Bellamont. Does that mean anything to you?"

John drew a deep breath. "It sure does. That's her father's name."

The man grabbed the doorframe to steady himself. "I can't believe it's true. I had no way of knowing," he murmured. Mr. Bellamont shook his head as he clung to the doorframe for support. "So many years," he said. "So many years ago and no one told me. I had no way of knowing."

"Will you be all right?" John asked as he watched the color drain from Mr. Bellamont's face.

"Yes, yes. I'll be all right. Discovering I have a sixteen-year-old daughter is quite a surprise. I thought my former lifetime was lost to me forever. It seems, however, that it has followed me in the form of lovely young girl." He looked at John and asked, "What do I do now?"

"Well, I think you can't just go up to her and tell her who you are. That would be too much of a shock."

"I know that. Will you help me figure out a way to reveal myself to her?"

"Of course, I will. Lisa has become a daughter to us over these years and she has a special place in our hearts. We love that girl very much."

"I can see that you do and I don't want to take that away from you but you must understand that I didn't even know she existed until I got that letter. Once she knows I'm her father, there is more to tell her."

"I will tell you that she and Cal are getting married on her seventeenth birthday. She has much to tell you about that. We have a long evening ahead of us."

Upon being chased out of the forge so abruptly, Lisa and Cal headed hand in hand down the path toward the river through a grove of trees. The south wind had dried all of the winter's moisture and the leaves crackled under their feet. Her feet had taken wings and her heart was uncontrollable. When they were out of sight of the shop, she threw herself into his arms and he lifted her off the ground.

"I've missed you, buddy," Cal said.

"Buddy?"

"Some habits are hard to break."

"Yeah. Like me cracking my knuckles, but I'm workin' on it."

He tried again. "I've missed you, sweetheart. How's that?"

"That's better," Lisa giggled. "I've missed you, too."

He released her and dropped onto a small clearing under a tree, pulling her down beside him. "I have a lot to tell you," he said.

"So do I but you start," Lisa said, lying in the curve of his arm across his chest.

"Platt and Maggie are going to get married. Maggie said 'no' at first but Platt said it would be a marriage of convenience because he needed a wife to take care of his house and she needed a husband to take care of her farm. They may not know it but I can tell they like each other. That kinda put me out to the wind but Platt said she would move into his bigger house and I could live in her little house and help take care of both farms."

"That's a wonderful arrangement for Maggie," Lisa said, a pout forming on her lips. "But where does that leave us? You'll still be out there and I'll still be here."

"Which is exactly the way it would be if she didn't marry Platt." He took his thumb and forefinger and forced a smile onto her lips.

"That's right. We still en't figured out where we're gonna live when we get married."

"That's still a problem we've gotta solve. We'll have a place at Maggie's but that'll be quite a way from the blacksmith shop. We've gotta be together, Lisa. And soon, I hope," he said, lifting her face to his.

"Me, too," she said when she was able to catch a breath.

"Now, what's your news?"

"Well, nothing like yours but…," she began to giggle. "I've learned to bake bread and it's good, too. There were a lot of winter days when we couldn't go to the forge so Rebecca taught me to cook bean soup and put a whole meal together. And I even knitted you a surprise."

"Well, I'll be a…."

"No you won't." She jumped up and pulled him to his feet. "Let's get to the house and tell Rebecca you're here. Besides, I want to put on a dress. I'm gonna show you what a real lady I am."

"Wow. I can hardly wait," he said with his most mischievous grin.

Rebecca jumped with surprise when they flew in the door together.

"You go in the kitchen with Rebecca while I dash upstairs and get cleaned up." She looked at her hands. "I don't think I'll ever get these to look clean even when I scrub them hard, and my fingernails are past repairin'."

"Doesn't matter," Cal said, rubbing the ends of his fingers on her cheeks. "See, mine are rough from all the outdoor work I did this winter. They were dry and chapped and the cracks are still healin'."

Watching Rebecca from the kitchen doorway, Cal asked, "How can I help you? I did a fairly good job of following orders in the kitchen when Maggie was sick."

"Just sit and tell me about your winter and how you managed out there. There has been a lot of worry going on in this house about you so talk to me while I'm working."

He told her about Maggie and the arrangement they had made. "Lisa's not too happy that I'll be out there living in Maggie's house but I've gotta make a living somehow," he said. "I know she doesn't wanna give up her work with John. It's gonna be a real problem come May when we get married."

Rebecca stopped working, her chopping knife poised in midair. "You give her time, Cal. You would be surprised at how much she has changed this winter. She has become quite a pretty young woman and a very good cook."

"Are you two talkin' about me?" Lisa stood in the doorway, her light brown hair combed and hanging in ribbons of waves that brushed her shoulders. A narrow band of white lace traced the edge of the modestly lowered neckline as well as the ends of the three-quarter length sleeves of the rose-colored dress. Her hands were carefully hidden behind her back, her eyes filled with anticipation.

Rebecca broke into a broad grin at the sight of Lisa riveted to the floor waiting for Cal to say something.

Cal was too stunned to respond to what he saw as a vision of beauty. When words finally came to him, all he could say was, "Wow! Golly… you're beautiful." Turning to Rebecca, he asked, "Is that really my girl Lisa?"

"That's one and the same," Rebecca replied.

"And to think you used to crawl around on the ground beating me at marbles."

"Still could," Lisa teased, waiting for him to say more.

"You look… well, you look incredible, I mean…." He jumped up and took her hand and pulled her into the kitchen. "I thought you knitted me something but this… this is hardly knitted."

"I did knit you something. Rebecca made most of this dress but I'm learning. We didn't know when you'd be back but we tried to have it ready when you would and we did, have it ready, I mean." She looked at Rebecca. "Looks like we did good."

"We did," Rebecca said, her eyes bright with satisfaction.

Lisa scooted out of the room and returned in seconds holding out a pair of wool socks to Cal. "These are what I knitted. They were my first efforts so they've got some flaws, but I think you can wear them next winter."

Cal studied them and tried to overlook what seemed to be dropped stitches and the fact that they were not quite the same size. "Thanks, Lisa. They look like you put a lot of work into them. They're—uh—nice."

Lisa cuffed him on his shoulder and chuckled. "Come on, Cal. They're awful. I don't expect you to wear them. I tried all winter to learn to knit but the small muscles in my fingers have trouble working together. I'm used to poundin' and lifting big stuff. But I'll keep trying. Rebecca says I'll catch on some day. I've got another pair started but you can't see them yet."

"Now let's get the supper on the table. John should be here any minute," Rebecca said.

CHAPTER 39

LISA WAS THE first to hear voices coming up the path to the front door. "It sounds like we're gettin' company," she said.

Rebecca looked at her pot of stew and said, "I've been making extra in case Cal would come home. Now we have another person but I think there will be enough. We'll make it do."

John opened the door and stepped in with the stranger from the blacksmith shop. The man laid his large saddlebags by the door and placed his hat on top.

"This man came by de shop a while ago looking for a place to board his horse for de night so I invited him to join us for supper. We put his horse in de stable with ours. He's ridden a long way today."

Lisa glanced at him and continued pouring tea, then adding a cup and bowl to the table. Cal collected a chair and brought it to the kitchen.

Rebecca shook the man's hand and said, "My name is Rebecca." She motioned for Lisa and Cal to join her. "This is Lisa and this is Cal. We are very happy to have you with us this evening. The stew is hot and the bread is fresh from the oven so let's sit down and eat."

Rebecca recognized the growing bewilderment on Lisa's face and said to the visitor, "I'm sorry. I didn't hear your name."

John spoke up quickly. "That's my fault. This is Mr. Louis Bell."

"You've got an interesting accent, Mr. Bell," Lisa said as she ladled stew into her bowl, glancing up as she dipped. "Where you from?"

"You are a very astute young lady," he said. "I am originally from France but that was a long time ago." He focused on her eyes until she turned away. "You are not from here either. Where do you come from?"

"I was born in Boston but I grew up in Malden, Massachusetts."

"You are a very pretty young woman in that dress. I wouldn't have recognized you as the same person I saw at the blacksmith shop." His voice was soft and kind and sincere. "You look like... I mean, you must look like your mother."

"I wouldn't know. Both my birth mother and my real mother are dead."

John recognized the pain that crossed the man's face filling his eyes and knew it was time to change the subject if Rebecca's meal were to be enjoyed. "Louis is a traveling salesman. Can you believe it? He sells furniture like beds and desks to hotels and businesses. Over there in his case, he has some miniature working samples of desks that make into beds. He showed them to me before we came to de house. You should take a look at them when we finish eating."

"Did you run into any bad weather on the way?" Rebecca asked. She was watching the exchange of looks between Mr. Bell and Lisa and an electrifying thought began niggling at her mind.

"Yes, indeed. Weather on the prairie can give you a surprise from one hour to the next."

Rebecca served the pudding and refilled the tea. "Have you ever been to Boston, Mr. Bell?"

Hesitantly, he answered, "Yes, many years ago."

Lisa's eyes glazed over as moisture began to collect under her eyelids. "Would you excuse me a minute?"

"You en't finished your pudding, Lisa," Cal said. "You okay?" He had not had the advantage of seeing the exchange between Lisa and Mr. Bell from where he sat.

"I don't know, Cal. I'll be right back."

She rushed upstairs where she pulled the portrait from under her pillow. She had that face memorized. Was it possible? The man downstairs was named Louis Bell. Bell... Bellamont. He had the same nose but the hair had streaks of gray. Lisa's heart was pounding so hard against her ribs and lungs that she found herself gasping for breath. She knew it was possible but how had it happened that he would come to her? *She* had planned to go hunting for *him*. Yet she was sure that man downstairs was her father and he knew it—and John knew it too. *Why didn't they tell me when they came into the house? Why this game?* The portrait slipped from her shaking fingers. *Did they think it'd be better to let me discover it gradually rather than have him walk in the door and say, "Hi, Lisa. I'm your da?" Did they think it'd be less of a shock?*

An angry wave surged against her nerves and then disappeared as she thought of the times she had longed for this moment. *Yeah, I guess I'd have been more shocked if he'd done that. This way, I could come up here and think it over and be sure. I am sure, but I'm so shaky that I'm not sure I can make it down those steps. He was shakin' too. He must feel like I do.*

"Cal," she called down the stairs. "Come up here, would you?"

Cal took the stairs two at a time. "What's up? That guy down there is so shaken up he can hardly carry on a conversation."

"Cal. Look" She handed him the portrait. "What do you think? Is he the man downstairs? Is he my da?"

"Golly, Lisa. I don't know. I haven't had a chance to really look him in the face since I'm sitting beside him." He stared hard at the face in the portrait. "It sure could be. Yeah. I think it is. Look at the nose."

"I'm sure it's him," she said in a trembling voice. "What do I do now?"

"You go right down those stairs and ask him."

"I'm shaking so hard I don't think I can make it down the stairs."

"Come on, buddy. You stood up to Carver and the marshals and those boys on the street. You can do this, too. You've waited for this for a long time. You just take some of those deep breaths you always talk about and hang onto my arm. We'll go down together."

Lisa put the crucifix in her pocket along with the portrait and went with Cal. Stepping into the parlor where John, Rebecca and Louis Bell were waiting, Lisa cleared her throat and bravely stepped up to Louis Bell and asked, "Da?" Cal kept a hand under her elbow as she waited.

"Lisa," Mr. Bell said, jumping up to greet her. In a trembling voice, he said, "My full name is Pierre Louis Bellamont and I believe I am your father. I have no way to prove it; however, I certainly hope I am. You are beautiful, just like your mother, Adrian Kennicot." His eyes glistened with unshed tears and hopefulness.

"I can prove it," Lisa said and pulled the crucifix out of her pocket.

"My God. I never knew if Adrian got that or not."

"She did but she never got to read your note. There's a letter to me from my mother, Charlotte, who raised me. She explained it all. I found the notes and your portrait by accident."

"Charlotte? That name sounds familiar."

"It should. She was Adrian's personal maid, the one who helped her sneak out to see you."

"There is much I need to know," Pierre said.

"And a lot I need to know, too," Lisa added.

For the moment, they stared at each other. "I guess we could go sit at the kitchen table and I'll lay out these letters for you to read."

Rebecca hurried ahead of them. "And I'll make you some coffee from John's special tin. This is certainly a special time." She looked at John and added, "I'll make enough for you and Cal, too, but you two stay in here and let them talk."

Pierre read the letter he had written to Adrian as tears flowed freely down his cheeks. "She never saw this, you say?"

"No, she didn't. The next letter explains that." Impulsively, she placed her hand over his. "Adrian died of a broken heart, I think. Her father allowed her to nurse me and then had me taken right away each time. I wish I could've seen her."

"All you have to do is look in the mirror. It's uncanny how much you look like her. I knew you were her daughter even as you stood at the forge in those terrible baggy breeches and shirt you were wearing."

Lisa chuckled, embarrassed by his words. "I never thought of 'em as terrible. I've worn pants for so many years that I had to learn how to wear a dress. Did John tell you about my upbringing?"

"Very little. He said you would tell me."

For the next two hours, the muffled sound of their voices could be heard in the kitchen as Pierre read Charlotte's letter and they told each other of their pasts.

"So, Charlotte loved me, too, enough to take my name and give it to you. Adrian was very sensitive and I'm not surprised she was unable to survive under her father's firm unforgiving hand. He couldn't tolerate me as a Frenchman or as a Catholic so I'm sure Adrian's pregnancy, with my child, was more than he could bear. I didn't know Charlotte was Catholic. I'm very pleased she raised you in that faith."

"We didn't ever make it to Mass because old man Carver kept her working so much, but she had this crucifix on the wall in our room and she prayed every day. She taught me herself."

"I owe her much."

"Well, if you ever get back to Boston, she's buried in Malden. The priest at Immaculate Conception can tell you where. It makes me so sad to think about her all alone and with no one to tend her grave. She was my mother in every way."

Now Pierre extended his arm and placed his hand on hers. "You have turned out very well and, at this moment, I cannot see a sign of the boy in you."

"I'm not sure I wanna totally lose that boy Lee. He'll always be a part of me just like my ma Charlotte. You would have been impressed with the way she worked to keep us off the streets, even to the day she died."

Lisa quietly told Pierre about Charlotte's death, reliving the trauma of her dying moments. She had already told him of her anger at Carver and the slash she gave him followed by her flight from the orphanage. She thought it best not to mention the Pyne's involvement in the Underground Railroad since one never knew the sympathies of another, even her newly found father.

"Now, you have one more question to answer. How did you know I was here? You didn't come here by accident."

"You're right. I got a letter from a lady named Ramona in Westport. You should remember her and her daughter, Chrissy."

"Yeah, I do. Ramona was really nice. She let us take clothes from her back room. I showed her this little portrait of you and asked her if she'd ever seen you. She seemed to know you. I told her you were my da."

"Lisa," he said looking in her eyes. "Ramona is my wife and Chrissy is my daughter."

"Oh, my gosh! No wonder she kept starin' at me after I showed her your portrait. She never let on you were her husband. Wonder what she's been thinkin' this whole time since we were there." Lisa stared at her father in awe. "You mean I've got a ready-made family right near by?"

"Ramona is your stepmother and Chrissy is your half-sister. I don't know how this is all going to play out, Lisa. I never told Ramona about Adrian because I found no reason for her to know. I didn't know anything about you so, you see, I have some explaining to do when I get to Westport. I truly want it to be a good thing. You've been through so much. Will you bear with me while I work on putting this family together?"

"You bet I will," Lisa said, her eyes sparkling with hope. "Just do it before my birthday next month. I want you to bring them to our wedding."

"I'll do my best." He stood and reached for Lisa. "I would like to give my daughter a hug. Is that permissible?"

"You betcha," she said.

"Ah hah! I think there is still some of that boy in you. It is part of your charm." Pierre smiled as he gathered her in his arms.

They found Cal asleep on the couch. It was long after midnight and too late for Pierre to walk to the hotel so he settled into the rocking chair and put his feet up on the round needlepoint footstool. "Goodnight, daughter."

"Goodnight, Da." She climbed the stairs to her room, her head filled with visions of her new family and Cal's brother and the wedding. It would be difficult to go to sleep.

CHAPTER 40

"I DON'T KNOW one thing about what happens at a wedding," Lisa said. "I've never in my life been to one." She, Rebecca and Martha were seated at the table in the Pyne's kitchen ready to begin planning for Lisa and Cal's marriage. Martha had brought her special oatmeal cookies that filled the room with the aroma of walnuts, raisins and cinnamon. Freshly brewed tea steamed on the table in front of each of them. The mid-morning sun added its brightness to their spirits.

Martha wrapped her hands around her cup and sipped the hot liquid as she looked across the table at Lisa. "Lisa, we're here to help you so don't you worry one little bit," Martha said.

"I en't really worried. I just don't know where to begin. It might help if you would tell me about yours."

"There wasn't much to planning our wedding," Rebecca said. "There were just the two of us, my sister and her husband in their parlor, and the preacher, of course. John had no family in this country and my parents were against my marrying that big shy German who could barely speak English, so they wouldn't come."

"That's really sad," Martha said.

"It was, but it was a good thing for us because we've been happy together for over twenty years. Not a regret in my body."

"I hope we can make it that long. Aaron and I were married in the church in front of fifty people," Martha said. "My mother insisted on a big wedding and she did all the planning and the work. She made my white dress and filled the church with flowers. Aaron and I felt like it was ostentatious and that we were on display. We knew we were coming out here to start our new life in a tent and leave all that behind but my mother wanted to show us off. So we let her. It seemed important to her."

"I can't see myself in any fancy white dress." Lisa swept her hands down her body and made a face.

"A very pretty dress like the rose-colored one we made for you would be perfect. Cal thought you were beautiful in that," Rebecca said, laying out some butter and jam sandwiches she had made earlier.

"Nothing says you have to wear white. In fact, wearing a fancy white dress isn't very practical because you can't ever wear it again. I think your rose dress would be perfectly beautiful," Martha said. "I'll make you a lovely head piece with a veil that covers your face." Martha's eyes sparkled with her mounting excitement. "Flowers are beginning to bloom so you could have a nice bouquet to carry down the aisle of the church."

Lisa had been listening closely. "There's one thing for sure. Cal and I don't belong in a fancy setting. We're just us. Two people who've played together, climbed trees, raced each other and pounded on each other. We just wanna get married and be able to live together in the same house without raising people's eyebrows." She draped a leg over the arm of the chair and leaned back, a pose she had taken many times as a boy. "Maybe I'll just get married in my pants and shirt."

Rebecca gasped. "You're teasing, aren't you?"

"Yeah, I am." She pulled her legs together again and straightened her skirt. "I want a pretty wedding but it's gotta be simple. Simple doesn't mean it can't be nice. Cal really did like that rose dress, didn't he? That's what I'll wear. And I want Rev. Jed to marry us right here in this house." She studied their faces for a reaction.

Rebecca began to smile warily. "I think that would be nice but you have many friends that will want to come. Remember your friends from the train and those you have made since we have been here. I know you're hoping that your father and Ramona and Chrissy will come. Oh, and there's Conrad and Maggie and Platt." She stopped to count the people on her fingers. "That's close to twenty-five people. How would we ever get them in this little house?"

Lisa got up and paced the length of the parlor and then the width, nibbling at her sandwich as she deliberated. Returning to the table, she swallowed the last bite and said, "The parlor would hold 'em if we put all the furniture in your bedroom. They'd have to stand during the ceremony but after that part's over, we could bring the furniture back in and people could sit and eat in the parlor and in the kitchen, on the porch and, even outside, like a picnic. We could spread some blankets."

"I can see you've made up your mind," Martha said. "It actually sounds wonderful to me. Do you think that would work, Rebecca?"

Stunned, Rebecca couldn't answer immediately. "I thought this was going to be difficult and here you have it all worked out. How long have you been working on this, Lisa?"

"Just now. I think it's what Cal and I'd want. Nothin' fancy. Just our friends to back us up and some good food to eat." Lisa began to grin. "I think I've become about as much of a woman as I'm gonna."

"We'll see about that," Martha said looking at Jonah who was curled up in the corner, sound asleep.

"I can't think about kids yet," Lisa said, surprised at the thought.

"Right. Let's get you married and settled in your home first." Furrows deepened on Martha's forehead. "Did I understand that you are going to move out to the farm with Cal?"

"That's right, but only until we can get enough money together to pay for a claim. John offered to lend Rainbow to me to get back and forth to the shop. For now, we decided I'd work three days a week."

"What will you do when you own some property?" Martha asked.

"That's gonna be a long while before we do, but we want it on this side of Lawrence so I can get to the forge easier. Cal wants to farm and have a boarding stable for people like my da who need a place to keep their horses overnight while they're at the hotel. He's hoping to build up a local horse business eventually. That's our goal and, in the meantime, we'll stay in Maggie's house."

"Have you told John of your plan?" Rebecca asked.

"Yeah. He's pleased. Thinks it's a good one."

The days went by quickly. She and Cal had already been together so long and they knew each other so well that marriage was simply the seal on an already loving and committed relationship; but she discovered an excitement building up inside of her as the time drew near, much like the breathless feeling she had when they were alone. She was becoming restless.

John heard rumblings of unrest involving the contingent from Missouri, and the men of Lawrence were making preparations for more problems. Nothing was confirmed so John kept the information to himself. Life had to go on and these two children had waited patiently and faithfully for the day they could marry; however, he decided to suggest changing the date of their wedding to Sunday, the eleventh. Sunday would be a more convenient day for most people and, if something were brewing outside the bounds of Lawrence, it would be better to have the wedding sooner than later.

"I don't know why I didn't think of Sunday," Lisa said, agreeing to the change of date. "Rev. Jed and the church goin' people will still be all dressed up to come in the afternoon. Good idea, John."

She pitched in and helped Rebecca with the house cleaning and the food preparation. As the day of the wedding drew near, Lisa began to watch for her father and his family. She was sure he would come but would his wife and daughter? Lisa was willing to accept them as family but would they be willing to accept her? Would they accept his explanation as to why he hadn't told them he had a daughter? It didn't seem all that difficult to Lisa. It was a plain fact that he had loved another woman eighteen years ago and he didn't know she had his child. That was a long time ago and now, he loved them, Ramona and Chrissy.

Lisa answered a knock at the door the afternoon before the day of the wedding and found her father standing there alone. She searched the area behind him. "Where are Ramona and Chrissy? Didn't they come?"

"Yes, they did. They are settled in at the Free State Hotel. Things are going to be all right. It took some talking on my part but we worked it out. She liked you and Cal when she saw you in Westport before you showed her my portrait and that helped. She's all right with it now."

"Boy, am I glad. I'm glad, too, that you got my message about the wedding being on Sunday."

"I need to get back to them and see that they get fed tonight. I wanted to let you know that all three of us will be here tomorrow afternoon."

"Please come early so Chrissy and Ramona and I can talk some before the wedding."

"We'll do that." He reached down and kissed her cheek and disappeared down the path.

Lisa was feeling especially good. Several things had come together for her: her father had come with a reconciled family; Conrad had shown up at the farm a week ago; and she had been able to convince Eli Holt to play his harmonica at the wedding. She had been surprised at the reception her invitations had received. Everyone planned to come and, if the sun would shine, the day would be perfect.

Sleep eluded her that night. In preparation for the next day, John had filled the washtub with warm water heated on the stove and he and Rebecca slipped away into their bedroom while she leisurely bathed and washed her hair in the kitchen. She relaxed and let the water sooth her muscles and her soul. Her mind drifted to the past: the two of them at five, getting acquainted; at ten, playing marbles and throwing dirt at each other; at twelve, racing to their private place under the pine tree; at fifteen, realizing they were more than buddies and Cal discovering her true identity. She chuckled as she remembered his reaction—and her's too. And look at them now. Tomorrow, they would be man and wife and be able to fulfill the desire they had carried within themselves so faithfully these many months.

Her heart made quick rhythmic ripples in the water as it reacted to her excitement, or was that her imagination. *What is Cal doing now? Is he thinking about tomorrow, too? Bet he is.*

Moonlight illuminated her bedroom assuring her that the coming day would be clear and beautiful. Lying on her back, she breathed deeply, controlling her excitement. Her dress hung on a hook by the door and her veiled hairpiece lay on her windowsill. She tried to picture herself standing in front of the preacher next to Cal but she had no idea what Cal was going to wear and he had refused to tell her. He and Conrad had been hibernating for the past week and who knew what they would come up with. It didn't matter. She would marry Cal in overalls if that was what he wore.

At long last, the moonlight changed to sunlight and she found that she had slept after all. She jumped up and peered out the window where a brilliant blue cloudless sky greeted her. Her heart jumped into her throat and tears of joy filled her eyes. *Thank you, God. It's finally come—what Cal and I've been waitin' for. Help me hold back my excitement so nobody will laugh at me trying to be a woman. I am a woman. That's what you made me in the first place. Mostly, I wanna be who I am inside and that's Lisa Bellamont, soon to be Lisa Hale. One more thing, please don't let bein' married change anything for me and Cal. I got a lot a confidence in your help, just like my mother did. Thanks.*

There was work to be done so she dressed quickly and hurried down the stairs. Cal was not to arrive until just before the vows were to be made because Martha said it was bad luck for the groom to see the bride before she came down the aisle. There wouldn't be an aisle.

She would just come down the stairs and he would be there to watch her. According to Rev. Jed's instruction, they would join hands and step up together to be married. Her heart began thumping again. She felt like she would be absolutely no good to anyone this morning.

Breakfast was laid out for her on one corner of the kitchen table. It appeared she had slept late and Rebecca and Martha had begun setting out dishes and utensils for the guests. Jonah was busy being underfoot in the parlor where John and Aaron were moving furniture into the Pyne's bedroom.

"Looks like I slept kinda late," Lisa said as she picked at her cold bacon and scrambled eggs. "I'm here to help now, though."

"There's nothing for you to do today. People will start coming at one o'clock and that's only three hours away. Eat your breakfast and have a cup of coffee. If you need something to do after that, work on your knitting. Everything is under control." Rebecca smiled, but her tone was firm. Lisa was to stay out of their way.

"If you're inclined to, you can entertain Jonah. Take him outside and let him run around out there. He needs to get rid of some of that stored-up energy," Martha suggested after noting the disappointment on Lisa's face. "We want you to be relaxed. At twelve-thirty, we'll scoot you up to your room to get in your wedding dress and if you want help, Rebecca or I will come up."

Playing with Jonah helped make the time go more quickly until her da brought Ramona and Chrissy. Although they had met briefly at Westport Landing, this meeting carried a deeper significance. Ramona and Chrissy could either accept her and they could be a family or they could reject her and never want to see her again. She so hoped they would want to be a family as much as she did; maybe not as much but at least enough to give it a try. By the time Martha called her inside, the tension had relaxed and conversation had become easier. Lisa felt hopeful.

"Do you want me to come up and help you?" Rebecca asked as Lisa began to climb the stairs.

Lisa shook her head. "No. I wanna get dressed by myself. You just give me a holler when it's time for me to come down."

Lisa hesitated on her way up to her room and glanced below. The parlor was devoid of furniture and the floor was scrubbed clean all the way into the corners. A tall vase of yellow, purple and blue flowers sat on each side of the fireplace. The windows sparkled and the kitchen table held bowls and baskets of the food prepared during the previous week.

"Get going, Lisa," Rebecca urged. "You only have half an hour to get ready." Impulsively, she threw her arms around Lisa and pulled her close. "I'm so happy for you and Cal but I will truly miss you," she said, pulling a handkerchief from inside her sleeve. "Now go."

From her upstairs window, Lisa could see buggies and wagons approaching. She had pulled on her dress and began combing her hair when she heard Rev. Jed's voice below. It would soon be time. Her small round mirror helped her place the veiled crown exactly where Martha had shown her. Rebecca had given her a pair of white slippers for her birthday that were to be worn this day for her wedding.

"Lisa," John called. "Everyone is here and we're waiting for de bride."

Taking a deep breath, she opened the door. At the foot of the stairs stood Eli playing *Home, Sweet Home*, the only song he knew that was slow enough for her entrance. Beyond him were the faces of her friends and beside Rev. Jed stood Cal. She studied his face, especially his eyes, as he looked up at her. She had to be sure it was Cal and not Con. His smile told her it was Cal and she smiled back. She took the steps slowly, just as Rebecca and Martha had rehearsed her.

Soon she was standing beside Cal who was dressed in a new pair of brown cotton pants and white shirt, his hair washed, combed and freshly cut. He handed her a small bouquet of pink prairie phlox from behind his back. Conrad moved beside him and Martha stepped up beside Lisa as planned.

"Whenever you two are ready to get married, please let me know," Rev. Jed whispered, smiling warmly.

"I guess now's a good time," Lisa said, turning to invite John to come stand behind her. It was expected that the father would give the bride away but Pierre had insisted that John do that.

"He has been more of a father to you than I have. I have been in your life for such a short time and John has been your mentor and teacher and, yes, father to you for many years. Please give him that privilege."

Lisa and Cal shared a warm loving glance before repeating their vows. Lisa wasn't sure what she had expected in this moment of pledging her life to Cal but, as the words were spoken, she felt a surge of happiness and fulfillment.

"I, Lisa Bellamont, take thee, Calvin Hale, for my lawful husband, to have and to hold from this day forward, for better, for worse, for richer, for poorer, in sickness and health, until death do us part."

"I, Calvin Hale, take thee, Lisa Bellamont, for my lawful wife, to have and to hold from this day forward, for better, for worse, for richer, for poorer, in sickness and health, until death do us part."

"I pronounce you husband and wife. Calvin, you may kiss your bride."

He did. Then he winked at Lisa and whispered, "We did it. You are absolutely beautiful, Lisa. Wouldn't old man Carver be surprised?"

"Oh, don't mention him and spoil the day."

Rev. Jed tapped Cal on the shoulder suggesting he release Lisa and turn around. "I introduce to you, Mr. and Mrs. Calvin Hale."

The room filled with cheers and applause. There were some wet eyes including Pierre's, John's and Rebecca's. When the furniture was returned to the parlor, in came a table full of unexpected gifts. There was the completed quilt she and Martha had worked on, some pots and pans, various dishes, an embroidered apron and a Fannie Farmer's cookbook from Rebecca, a Bible from Rev. Jed and Abigail, a promise of a new bed to be delivered later from Pierre, Ramona and Chrissy and a set of newly crafted kitchen knives from John. Maggie and Platt gave them two piglets that were waiting for them on the farm. They were all practical gifts for which Lisa and Cal were thankful. Their farmhouse was small and plain and they were starting out with very little. They sat on the floor among their gifts holding hands and showing their gratitude to their friends when John handed them an envelope. There was an air of expectancy as Cal opened the envelope and read it.

Cal gasped, "Oh, golly." He shook his head in disbelief as Lisa read it in stunned silence.

"How... what...?" Lisa could find no words to reply to the impact of the note and the contents of the envelope.

John came to her rescue. "Because Cal saved Jonah's life and stood by Maggie at some sacrifice to himself, and to you Lisa, some of de people in town wanted to give you something, even though they were not invited to de wedding. As you can see, their names are listed on de note. Everyone in this room has contributed something and Pierre and I rounded it out so dat you can pay for a claim on de land you want. Hope that doesn't complicate things for you."

Unfamiliar tears ran down Lisa's cheeks and Cal's eyes grew damp as he stared at the bank notes. "I don't know what to say. I'm dumbfounded. There's no way I can thank these people, and you, enough. There's just not...."

Lisa ran the back of her hand over her eyes, and found her voice. "You're all so kind. You've stood by us, some as far back as Boston, and now you do this. We'll be thankin' you, and the other people on this list, for the rest of our lives."

"We'll go to the claim office tomorrow morning," Cal said.

"I think they have held onto a piece of land you will like. You can still work and live at Maggie's but you can work your own land, too, until you can build a house. When de weather is good, you can use our tent if you want to stay out there sometimes."

Lisa jumped up and hugged John and Pierre, then turned to Ramona. "Thank you for comin'. I'm happy you turned out to be family."

Cal nodded as Lisa spoke and pulled her toward the kitchen. "Rebecca says it's time to eat."

As the sun headed for the western horizon, Lisa and Cal prepared to leave. Pierre, John and Conrad loaded the gifts onto the wagon insisting that Lisa and Cal stay inside and say good-bye to their guests. Cal shook Con's hand and then gave him a hug. "Thanks for comin'. Come out and see us like we planned. Okay?"

Con nodded and slapped Cal on the shoulder.

Pierre hugged Lisa and shook Cal's hand, promising to be back to see them after his next trip west. He reminded them that the bed would be delivered as soon as it arrived in Westport.

"I'm sorry I missed the first part of your life but we have many years ahead of us. I want to be around when you make me a grandda."

Lisa and Cal both gasped. "We gotta take one step at a time. Haven't thought about that yet," Lisa said.

A slight breeze filled with the fragrance of prairie wildflowers, grass and the ever-present dust greeted them as they stepped outside. Guests gathered around Lisa and Cal to watch them get their first sight of the wagon. There across the back hung a banner proclaiming "JUST MARRIED" with streamers hanging from the sides. Scrambling aboard, Cal picked up the reins, clicked his tongue and Range and Star moved out as good-byes wafted over their heads and around their ears. If the horses knew something was different, they didn't let on.

"Do you feel married, Cal? The back of this wagon says we are."

"Yeah, I do. I can't say I *feel* married but I know I am and that puts a *whole* new perspective on our relationship." He reached over and pulled her closer to him. "We've changed, and I feel that. The Lee and Cal of the orphanage en't around anymore. We're grown up, Lisa, and we're on our own. Looks like we're gonna grow old together."

"I don't *feel* married either but I know we are, too. I wanna be a good wife to you, Cal. Lee still wants to pop up now and then but I know how to get rid of him now. We've got so much to look forward to." She put her hand under his arm and said, "I love you, Cal." She was sure he could feel the beat of her heart thrumming through her wrist as she laid it next to his.

"I love you, too." He laid the reins across his lap and took her in his arms, knowing that Range and Star would take them home without his help.

In the distance, they could see their home standing quietly waiting for them in the waning sunlight. They would soon light a lamp and, with it, bring their own light of happiness into the house. Morning would break into a new and glorious future filled with promise.

END

ABOUT THE AUTHOR

Pearl Gladwyn Burk is an author of short stories, a screen play, articles and poems., three of which received awards. This is her second novel, which takes place during the settlement of Kansas in the mid-1850s. She is retired from a career in business during which time she raised five sons, earned a Bachelor's Degree and wrote her first novel, *Crossing Sand Creek*. She is a member of the Society of Southwestern Authors and has served on its board. She and her husband live in Arizona.

2 ∞

Made in the USA
Lexington, KY
19 September 2016